MaryLu Tyndall

Grace,
Thank-you so much
for all your help!
You are such a
joy

She Walks in Majesty

Protectors of the Spear

MaryLu
Tyndall

She Walks in Majesty

Protectors of the Spear 3

by MaryLu Tyndall

© 2020 by MaryLu Tyndall

All Scripture quotations are taken from the King James Version of the Bible.

All rights reserved. No part of this publication may be reproduced, stored in a retrieval system, or transmitted in any form or by any means without the written permission of the author, MaryLu Tyndall.

Library of Congress Cataloging-in-Publication Data is on file at the Library of Congress, Washington, DC.

ISBN-13: 978-1-7344420-2-1
E-Version ISBN: 978-1-7344420-1-4

This book is a work of fiction. Names, characters, places, incidents, and dialogues are either products of the author's imagination or used fictitiously. Any similarity to actual people, organizations, and/or events is purely coincidental

Cover Design by Ravv at raven.com
Editor: Louise M. Gouge

Dedication
To those who are lowly and humble in heart

Thou art worthy to take the book, and to open the seals thereof: for thou wast slain, and hast redeemed us to God by thy blood out of every kindred, and tongue, and people, and nation; And hast made us unto our God kings and priests: and we shall reign on the earth.
Revelation 5:9-11

Author's Note

Dear Reader, I labeled this novel a Medieval Fantasy Romance. However, don't be confused by the fantasy title. This is not a fantasy as most people would classify that genre. This is a Medieval Romance that is not set in an historic real place. In other words, I took license with places, names, and also with some language. Hence, do not read with the intent of learning Medieval history! However, the fantasy label in no way can be attributed to the powerful acts of God described in the story. Those are quite plausible for those who follow Him.

If you wish to see character pictures and scenes from the book while you're reading, visit my Pinterest page at

https://www.pinterest.com/mltyndall/protectors-of-the-spear/she-walks-in-majesty/

CHAPTER ONE

Pray, what angel is this who hath descended from heaven to grace our path?" The tall man chuckled and sauntered toward Seraphina de Mowbray, slowly, methodically, his eyes sweeping over her, no doubt seeking hints of a weapon hidden amongst the folds of her cloak. Upon finding none, he rubbed the stubble on his dirt-streaked face and glanced at his two friends behind him.

"Come now, Borin, leave 'er be," the man who remained upon his horse said with a sigh. "There's trollops aplenty in town. She's but a maiden."

The other man, who was shorter than the first, dismounted and headed toward her, licking his lips as one would when viewing a foam-capped mug of ale on a hot day. "Aye, and 'tis the maidens which be the sweetest."

The first man nodded, an unsettling leer in his eyes as he reached for her.

Before she could retreat, he grabbed a lock of hair that had escaped her hood and fingered it between his grimy fingers.

And at that moment Seraphina knew two things for certain. One, she was surely the most foolish woman ever to have lived, and two, she would now never complete her mission. Even worse, she would disappoint her friends, friends who had been more like family to her—her *only* family.

"'Tis as soft as it looks, the feel of white silk." The man all but drooled as he continued fondling her hair.

Seraphina's stomach flipped. Swallowing down a burst of terror, she slapped her hair from his hand and recoiled. She'd been traveling for nigh two days, keeping off the main roads, ducking into the shelter of trees whene'er anyone came along, keeping her cloak about her, her hood up to cover her face—all things she had learned to do when she and Lady Cristiana had been on the run.

How she had missed seeing these three loathsome men traveling by the wayside, she could not fathom. More importantly, how had she not known they were there? For she'd always had a gift of knowing things ere they happened, of seeing things others could not. A gift from God, Friar Josef had said, though now she wondered, for these villains had pounced upon her before she could dash behind the brush. Hence, her foolishness in thinking she could travel without benefit of escort or protection, that she could make the journey to Regalis unscathed with the Spear, the document, and her maidenhead intact.

The latter in serious jeopardy at the moment.

"Come hence, mistress, we'll do you no harm if you cooperate." The tall man gestured with his fingers for her to draw near. A fly buzzed about his unwashed hair.

Seraphina would attempt to flee into the woods if the man and his friends weren't strapped with more weapons than knights of the kingdom. *Knights.* The thought brought back memories of Sir Damien and a sudden wish he were by her side.

"Ask 'er if she has any coin, Borin," the shorter man said, running his sleeve beneath his nose.

The tall man cocked his head. "I suppose we could leave you be for the right price."

Seraphina's legs wobbled beneath the strain of maintaining a brave front when all she longed to do was scream as loud as she could and bolt away.

"I have no money, sir. I beg you, if there is any honor to be found in your heart, prithee allow me to pass without harm." She lifted her chin and hated the tremble that coursed through it, surely detectable by these men. "I am on a mission of great importance."

The man on the horse snorted. "Honor. You'll find none o' that in Borin d'Allemach."

The tall man sent his friend a scathing glance but then faced her and snorted. "A mission?" He dropped his gaze to the hem of her common tunic peeking out beneath her cloak.

"You? You're but a plebeian. What could you be about that has any import?"

Seraphina bit her lip and gathered her cloak tighter about her. She couldn't very well tell the vermin that she was in possession of the Spear of Destiny—the tip of the Roman spear that had stabbed Christ. In truth, the powerful artifact was strapped to her thigh, as she'd seen Lady Cristiana do so oft when *she* was the protector, hidden safely in a place where no eye dared roam. Nor could she tell him how she'd witnessed its power over and over and how it was sought after by kings and power-hungry men throughout the kingdom. She also couldn't tell him that she had a signed confession tucked in the pocket of her surcote, one that could possibly set her friends free from the charges of treason and witchcraft.

Hence, she remained silent, feeling akin to a rabbit cornered by three ravenous dogs.

Damien LaRage, Knight of the Eternal Realm and former King's Guard, gripped the pommel of his sword and focused on the royal carriage careening down the road in the distance. *Couldn't be.* Surely Bishop Montruse remained at Luxley Castle. Yet Damien knew *that* carriage, recognized the bishop's personal crest on the door—a shield surrounding a likeness of the man himself wearing his heraldic vestments. Damien and his fellow King's Guards had been assigned to protect the bishop in his travels from Regalis to Luxley over a year ago. Sunlight glinted off the silver crest even now as the carriage ambled down the king's highway, and memories of that journey rose to haunt Damien. Had it only been eighteen months ago? It seemed a lifetime. The bishop had been assigned by the king to find the Spear of Destiny and not return without it. Hence, there could only be one reason he now left Luxley.

He had found what he sought.

Which meant he had found Mistress Seraphina. *Foolish lady*! Roaming about the dangerous countryside without benefit of armed escort. Why? But he knew why. To protect *him.* To protect them all.

His destrier, Revenge, pawed the ground beneath him and snorted, anxious to be on his way. Damien couldn't blame him. He'd spent two days traveling the back roads searching for Seraphina, scouring both street and forest for her tracks, hunting through every passing village, asking every peasant he met whether they had seen her.

Either she had learned how to be invisible or the bishop had indeed captured her.

Plucking a slingshot from his belt, Damien reached into his pouch and found a good-sized rock. Then carefully positioning it, he pulled back the sling, closed one eye, and found his mark.

The driver of the carriage fell from his perch. The horses slowed. The guards began shouting and cursing.

Damien drew his sword, the sound eliciting a snort and ripple of muscles down Revenge's back. Holding the reins tight, Damien counted the guards surrounding the carriage. Three. Only three. Fools! From the looks of them, 'twould be mere sport to dispatch them quickly. And quickly he must, for if Seraphina was in the carriage with the bishop, he must not allow him time to do her harm.

Flexing his jaw, Damien narrowed his eyes, tightened his grip on the pommel of his blade, and uttered the command that sent Revenge into a full gallop toward their prey. "To battle!"

The poor soldiers barely had time to pull out their swords ere Damien was upon them.

Hefting his blade high, he met the first man's sword with a mighty clank, sending him teetering on his horse. Before he could recover, Damien slammed his boot into the man's stomach and shoved him from his mount. He toppled to the ground with a groan.

The next guard charged Damien, the tip of his sword pointed straight at his heart, whilst the third man came at him from behind. Uttering a guttural growl, Damien struck the first man's sword so hard, it flew from his hand. Quickly, he plucked a knife from his belt and flung it at the second man. It plunged into his side. A look of shock consumed the poor man's face ere he gripped his side and fell from his horse.

A screech, followed by a "Get up, you imbecile!" blared from within the carriage.

Leaping to his feet again, the first guard joined the second, who had dismounted to retrieve his sword, and together they approached Damien.

Sliding off Revenge, Damien exhaled a sigh of frustration as he twirled his blade through the air before them. "Not had your fill?"

Recognition, followed by terror, crossed one of the soldier's eyes. "'Tis Sir Damien, the King's Guard."

"Kill him!" The bishop's face popped through the carriage window like a turtle from its shell. "He's wanted for treason!"

In the brief moment the curtains were parted, Damien searched for a sign of Seraphina, but, like a cowardly turtle, the bishop withdrew into his shell as quickly as he had come out.

Fear tightened the men's expressions as they advanced upon him. He wished them no harm, but how to be rid of them without ending their lives?

He met the first man's blade, shoved him back, then struck the second man's so hard it flew once again from his hand. Before he could retrieve it, Damien slammed the hilt of his sword on the man's head. He folded to the ground.

The first man charged yet again.

"You are persistent, sir. I give you that." Damien met the thrust of the man's blade with one of his own.

The ring of metal on metal chimed through the air as the sun beat down on them from above. Beneath his leather doublet, sweat slid down Damien's back. He drove the guard backward, swinging this way and that until the poor man could hardly breathe and his sword hung limp from his hand.

Damien kicked the weapon away and leveled the tip of his blade at the man's throat. "Leave and I'll let you live."

Nodding, the man mounted his horse and galloped off, his horse's hooves kicking up dust as he went.

Damien sheathed his sword and ensured the other guards were unable to move. Then approaching the carriage, he yanked the door off its hinges, tossed it to the ground, and leapt inside. The floor slanted beneath his weight, along with his heart when he did not find Seraphina within. Growling, he plopped down on the leather seat opposite the bishop—a man he had come to loathe this past year.

Streaks of gray lined the fiend's dark, short-cropped hair that matched his trimmed beard and mustache. A pointy nose and brown eyes completed a face that failed to hide the dark intent lingering behind it. A jewel-embedded cross hung over his black robe, and the knife in his hand trembled as he pointed it toward Damien.

"How dare you attack my guards and enter my carriage without my permission!" A flood of obscenities spilled from his mouth. "I am the king's bishop, and he will have your head, fallen knight." He lunged toward Damien.

Easily grabbing the knife from his hand, Damien shoved him back and held it to his throat.

Red exploded on his insolent cheeks. "So, are you to kill me now? You rebel, traitor to the crown and sorcerer."

Damien's hand shook beneath his own fury. What he wouldn't give to end this miserable vermin's life. But he needed information first. Hence, he withdrew and leaned back on the cushion. "Judas! You speak of yourself, Your *Eminence*. For you know all too well I am none of those things."

Bishop Montruse swallowed and rubbed his throat, smearing a drop of blood over his pale skin. Sweeping aside the velvet curtains, he glanced outside. "Why have you stopped me? Killed my guards and driver?"

"They will recover. Where is Seraphina?"

The bishop's brows rose. "Who?"

Damien took no time in forcing the bishop back with the knife to his throat once again. The man blubbered like the swine he was.

"Mistress Seraphina de Mowbray," Damien ground out.

The bishop squirmed. "Alack, I have no idea of whom you speak."

"Lady Cristiana's lady's maid. The one with hair as light as the sun."

Recognition sparked in the bishop's eyes. "The lady's maid? Why would I know of her?" He studied Damien with suspicion.

Damien sat back with a huff. The man was telling the truth, of that he was certain. "Why are you returning to court?"

"What business is that of yours?" His tone was indignant once again.

Damien could make it his business with a flick of his blade. Instead he studied the man, who, along with Sir Walter LeGode of Luxley, had made fugitives of him and his friends, had hunted them down like animals, and had nearly burned Alexia at the stake. "Do you have the Spear?"

The bishop's mouth twisted at the unexpected question as his gaze shifted over the inside of the carriage. Wind whisked past the windows, stirring the curtains and allowing fresh air to enter. Still it did naught to sweep away the stench of this man, his sweat, his arrogance and fear.

Damien pointed the knife at him again. "Do you have the Spear?"

"Nay," he shot back.

"Then why return to a king who will surely have your head without it?"

The bishop brushed off his robe as if he could as easily brush away Damien. "I am told it is no longer at Luxley but on its way to the Regalis."

Damien fingered his beard. How would he know such a thing if he hadn't captured Seraphina? "Who gave you this lie?"

"Sir Walter LeGode."

Damien chuckled. "Sir Walter is too bird-witted to know much of anything."

The bishop snorted. "Finally we agree on something."

The horses whinnied and the carriage jerked forward slightly. Damien glanced out the window, but the two guards and driver were still lying on the ground.

"Then, pray, how would he know such a thing?" Damien's patience was nearing its end.

"He has…access to someone with knowledge." The bishop grabbed his cross.

"His warlock." Damien rubbed the back of his neck.

The bishop looked surprised.

"Aye, we know about him." But now, what was Damien to do with this monster, this false prophet? He obviously had no knowledge of Seraphina, but to leave him alive to inflict his malevolence on others would be a crime.

The bishop pursed his thin lips. "If you are quite done threatening me, I have a proposal for you, Sir Damien."

"I want naught from the likes of you." Grabbing the edges of the doorway, Damien hoisted himself up, intending to leave.

"Ah, but I believe you will when you hear what I have to say."

Damien glanced back. "Be quick about it."

The bishop smiled. "I believe you search for the man who defiled your mother twenty years ago?"

Damien's stomach tightened into a ball as a plethora of emotions swarmed him—hatred, anger, fear. "What do know you of him?"

"Much. His name and where he lives."

Damien settled back on the seat, fingering the knife still in his hand. "Tell me or die!"

The man merely smiled and lifted his chin. "Kill me and you'll never know."

"What do you want?"

"I want the Spear, of course."

"I don't have it."

"Aye, but I think you know who does. Mayhap this Mistress Seraphina?" His grin dripped poison. "Bring me the Spear, and I'll give you his name."

A groan rose from outside, and Damien glanced through the window. The two soldiers he had knocked unconscious were stirring. He had no desire to battle them again.

"Do we have a deal, Sir Damien?"

Damien cursed under his breath. The last thing he wanted was make a deal with the devil. But he needed that name. He'd been searching for the man who ruined his life for the past ten years, and he'd do anything to find him. Even betray his friends and give up the Spear. Alack, 'twas just an old rusty relic! Damien was not convinced of its power, nor was he convinced there was a God behind any of the strange events he'd witnessed.

Mayhap he'd be doing his friends a favor by getting rid of the thing.

Hence, against everything within him, Damien said, "In addition, convince the king to drop all charges against my friends and the D'Clere sisters, and we have a deal."

The bishop's eyes grew cold and malevolent ere a slight smile tainted his lips. "Done."

CHAPTER TWO

Seraphina did the only thing she could think to do. She prayed. In truth, that should have been the first thing she did, but she wasn't sure God would bother listening. After all, who was she—naught but a common maid—that the Almighty would take note? Still, as the two lecherous men advanced upon her and the third remained on his horse looking bored, she lifted up a plea for help, for rescue from a violent defilement that would scar her forever.

Prithee, Lord, if you can spare a moment to come to my aid!

Though she tried to keep it at bay, terror must have appeared on her face, for both men smiled in delight at the sight.

"As I said, mistress, if you cooperate, 'twill go much easier." The first man, whose words and tone bore the benefit of an education, drew a knife from his belt and halted before her.

The other shorter man ran his sleeve beneath his nose and grinned. "If not, there's nothin' like a good struggle to stir my blood."

Seraphina took a step back. *God? Where are you?* Why wasn't He answering her prayer? She glanced toward the main road just beyond the trees, seeking a carriage, traveler, rescuer, anyone she could call to for help. But naught moved save for a whirlwind of dust on the path and dark clouds rising on the horizon…like the clouds of doom hovering over her now.

Something warmed her right thigh. *Odd. Wait.*

The first man grabbed her arm.

The Spear! It grew warm on her thigh where she'd strapped it.

Hope pierced her panic. But what was she supposed to do now? Lady Cristiana had only used the Spear to heal.

The shorter man grabbed her other arm, and together they pulled her toward them. The first man tore her cloak from her and tossed it to the ground.

"Nay, please! I beg you!" She twisted and turned, punched and kicked, but to no avail. The men only laughed and forced her to the ground.

The Spear grew hot.

Fury burned, chasing away her fear. "In the mighty name of Christ, leave me be this instant!" she shouted, not believing for a second the men would listen to her.

Thunder rumbled in the distance as a breeze tore through the forest, stirring leaves on the ground. A large bird—a falcon?—screeched above.

The men released her as if she were a hot coal. Confusion and fear contorted their expressions as they backed away.

"Faith! You two lost your nerve?" The man on the horse chuckled. "I can hardly credit it."

Yet his smile faded as his friends continued their retreat, staring at her with an expression akin to…horror? Nay. Reverence? Finally, they mounted their horses, nudged them forward through the trees, and sped off with nary a glance back.

The Spear grew cold again.

Seraphina curled into a ball, her breath coming fast, her heart pounding against her ribs. She waited until the world came into focus again, grabbed her cloak and bag, and hugged them tightly against her chest, seeking any comfort she could find. Why had those men left when there had been naught to stop their nefarious plans?

The Spear. It protected her. It kept evil at bay! *Thank you, Lord.* She hadn't been sure it would work in the hands of a common maid. Wiping her tears away, she rubbed the sign of the Spear on her wrist, still shocked the Almighty had chosen her as its protector. She had assumed 'twas but a temporary assignment, one in which she would deliver it safely to its new protector once she arrived at Regalis. Mayhap the king himself.

In truth, she ne'er considered she could make use of its power. But what else could have sent those men away in such haste?

It took several more minutes before enough strength returned to Seraphina's legs to enable her to stand. By that time, dark clouds had suffocated the sun and cast a gray shroud over the landscape. She opened her bag, waded through her belongings, and pulled out her swaddling cloth, lifting it to her lips. 'Twas the only thing left from her parents, the cloth in which she had been swaddled when she arrived at Luxley Castle. Why she kept it, she could not know. But for some reason, it brought her comfort, strength even. She fingered the strange emblem embroidered into the torn and faded fabric, a sword encircled by a wreath of flowers. Though she had asked everyone she met whether they'd seen it before, she had not discovered its origin or meaning and had long since given up her quest.

What did it matter, anyway?

Stuffing the cloth back into her bag, she swung her cloak about her and proceeded down the road, keeping to the trees and brush that grew along the side should she encounter another traveler. She was but a day's journey from Regalis, and if she pressed through the night, she could arrive in the morning, for the sooner she got off the dangerous highway, the better.

It began to rain. Not a mere mist, but heavy, pelting drops, accompanied by lightning and thunder that caused her to jump with each blast. Hours passed. Darkness transformed the green rolling hills into giant sea serpents. Patches of trees became spindly ghouls. Lightning flashed an eerie silver over the scene.

Tugging her hood further down against the driving torrent, Seraphina shivered and trudged along. Her cloak had long since soaked through to her tunic, water dripped from the tips of her hair, and her shoes were so caked in mud 'twas like lifting anvils each time she took a step.

Flickering light brought her gaze up to see what must be a coach inn up ahead. Oh, how she longed for a dry bed and some warm pottage, but a woman traveling alone would be frowned upon. Not only frowned upon but taken advantage of by wicked sorts. In addition, she only had five pence in her possession, and she had no idea if that would pay for a room at all.

Horses whinnied from the stable to the side of the main building from which light tumbled out, streaking the mud in gold.

Gathering her strength, she uttered a quick prayer, took the steps to the door and pushed it open. The wind whisked wet leaves inside and fluttered lanterns atop tables, and she quickly closed the door. Gathering the hood of her cloak tighter about her face, she swallowed as six pairs of eyes latched upon her like misers to gold.

Men sat around tables eating and drinking, whilst an older woman wove through them, hoisting a tray of steaming bowls and foaming mugs on her shoulder. She was the only other woman in the room, which did naught to ease Seraphina's nerves. Thankfully, the men quickly went back to their meals, though as she proceeded, she felt like a prized horse at auction.

An older gentleman looked up from behind a long table at the end of the room and eyed her curiously. The owner, no doubt.

Heart pounding, Seraphina made her way to him and attempted a smile. "I would like lodging for the night, kind sir, and a bowl of your lady's stew."

"Ah, you would, would ye? And are ye travelin' alone, mistress?" He glanced behind her.

"My husband is delayed, but I expect he shall be arriving anon." She cringed at the lie, but it could not be helped.

He wiped down the table, set two mugs atop it and poured ale into them from a pitcher. "There's a common room in the back, but a bed will cost ye three pence."

Common room? "How many others will be sharing it?"

"The six travelers you see 'ere." He gestured with his chin behind her.

Once again Seraphina felt eyes poke her back like arrows on a timid dear. "Prithee, do you have private lodging?"

"I got one room I keep for nobles and gentlefolk." His gaze scanned her wet clothes and muddy shoes ere it rose to meet her eyes again.

"Is it occupied, sir?"

"Nay."

"How much?"

"'Tis sixpence, mistress, but seems I've not made myself clear. Should I rent it to ye, I'll 'ave to toss ye out if a nobleman arrives. An' I'll keep my money."

Sixpence. She only had five. And no money for stew. "Will you rent it to me for five pence? And if a nobleman comes, I'll happily leave."

Her stomach growled, announcing to everyone in the room her desperation. "Pray, sir, I beg for mercy. I have traveled all day, my feet are sore, my stomach empty, my clothes cold and sodden. Can you not make an exception for a lady?"

"A lady, is it?" He snorted. "Ye can 'ave a bed in the back for that coin." He thumbed toward the far end of the room. "An' an old piece of bread but no stew."

Lord, help me. Seraphina bit her lip. She would not be safe in the common area, nor would she get any sleep. 'Twas hard enough for her to sleep in a safe place.

Her thigh warmed beneath the Spear.

"What'll it be, mistress?"

"I beg you, sir, allow me to lodge in your room. Upon my honor, I'll take no food or drink, and I will leave should a nobleman arrive."

The woman approached the bar, perspiration gleaming on her thin face. She swiped graying hair from her face, and after a quick glance at Seraphina, began loading the mugs full of ale onto her tray. "I need two more o' these," she said. "An' the man in the corner said his mutton is cold."

"Mayhap ye should move faster, woman," the owner spat out ere he turned to grab two empty mugs.

"Mayhap ye should stop chattering with this doxy." The woman gestured toward Seraphina.

Heat swamped Seraphina. "I am not—"

"Be gone with you," the man interrupted, pouring ale into the mugs. "We don't take beggars 'ere. Either sleep in the common room or sit down an' spend your money on food. Henry!" he shouted for a lad mopping the floor in the corner. "Otherwise, I'll 'ave my son toss you out in the storm."

The Spear grew even hotter, but why wasn't it working?

She needed to eat. She needed a good night's sleep. If not, she'd arrive at the king's palace looking like the pauper she was. His majesty would ne'er grant her an audience, and her mission would fail before it began.

Grabbing the mugs, the woman sneered at her and left.

Feeling faint, Seraphina leaned on the top of the counter. She could not go back out in that rain, for surely if she did, she'd never make it to see the king. "Give me the room, sir." She meant to add a gentle plea. She meant for her tone to emerge much kinder, but it sounded more like an order from someone in authority.

The man shook his head as if overcome with sudden dizziness. Blinking, he rubbed his eyes and then stared at her in awe as if she were made of gold. His lanky son arrived. "Escort the lady to the room upstairs at once and stoke the fire." He faced her. "I'll 'ave my Maggie draw you a 'ot bath."

Seraphina could only stare in wonder at the sudden change in both the man's demeanor and disposition. Mayhap she'd fainted from hunger and weariness and was only dreaming. Nay. The lad tugged on her cloak and gestured for her to follow him, and she decided 'twas best to do so ere the owner changed his mind.

"And bring 'er some of your mother's stew as well," he called after them as they mounted the stairs.

Ducking out of the rain, Damien entered the coach inn and slammed the door behind him. Water dripped from his mantle onto the wooden floor as his eyes grew accustomed to the many lanterns flickering about the room. To his right, two men sat at a table, their slurred voices raised in an argument as an elderly woman brought them another round of ale. To his left, three other men played a game of dice in the corner whilst a lone man stood in the far shadows, staring out a window. None of them a threat.

Heat from a fire in the hearth in the back wafted over Damien, and he shrugged out of his sodden coat, relishing in the blast of warm air. The scent of boiled meat, ale, and sweat swirled beneath his nose as all eyes drifted to assess the newcomer, each widening when they saw the myriad weapons hanging from his belt, and each quickly shifting their gazes away. Wise choice.

No sign of Mistress Seraphina.

Alas, 'twould do no harm to ask if they'd seen the lady and also fill his stomach with food. *And* a mug or two of ale.

Licking his lips, Damien advanced toward an older man in the back of the room who sat on a stool by four large kegs, arms folded over his portly belly and chin dipped on a chest that rose and fell beneath loud snores.

"Pardon." Damien nudged the man, but he didn't move. He nudged him again, this time harder, and the man started to fall off the stool, but caught himself and stood. Fury inflamed his face as he opened his mouth no doubt to curse Damien, but then his gaze rose to Damien's full height and lowered to assess the weapons. He took a step back.

"What can I do for ye, sir?"

"I'm looking for a woman. About this tall." Damien lifted his hand up to his neck. "Hair the color of the snow, comely, and—"

"Ah, yer wife, sir! She came in an 'our ago. I gave 'er my best lodging, sir. Aye, that I did. She said ye'd be along."

She did? Damien maintained a level stare at the man.

"Henry!" The man nervously shifted his eyes away as a skinny lad darted toward them. "My son will show you to the room, sir."

Damien grunted and turned to follow the boy, more excited than he'd been in a long while. Seraphina was here! Alack, unless there was another flaxen-haired beauty wandering the countryside alone.

"Um, sir?" The man's cowering voice turned Damien around. "The lady said ye'd pay for the room when ye got 'ere."

Damien narrowed his eyes. Unlikely since Seraphina would not have known he was coming.

"Eight pence, sir." He tentatively held out his hand.

Damien grimaced. "'Tis robbery, and you know it."

The hand remained, though the man's gaze lowered.

A hand Damien could slice off ere the man knew what was happening. But he was more anxious to see Seraphina than he was to deal with this greedy snake. Hence, reaching inside a pouch at his belt, Damien counted out the coins and tossed them onto the counter to the right of the man. "Bring up two bowls of pottage, some bread, and a pint of ale."

The man greedily gathered the coins and nodded.

Damien followed the lad up the creaking stairs, then down a long corridor to a door at the end. Dipping his head, the boy skittered away without saying a word.

Damien stood there for a moment, finding himself slightly nervous—a condition most unfamiliar. But then again, this was Seraphina, and he'd not yet put a name to the whirlwind of emotions she stirred within him.

Should he knock? Nay. Once she discovered 'twas him, she may escape out the window. And he could not lose her again.

Gripping the door latch, he opened it and burst inside.

CHAPTER THREE

The room was small, containing only a bed, a table, two chairs, and hooks lining the wall used for hanging clothes. No rug graced the wooden floor, though rich damask curtains covered the single window. None of those things caught his eye for long, for perched before the crackling fire in the hearth was a copper tub filled with steaming water. A river of pearly hair flowed over one edge down to the floor, whilst two bare knees poked through the water like islands in the sea.

The lady screamed and twirled around, sloshing water over the sides. Frightened blue eyes latched upon him as the rest of her sank beneath the waves.

Damien spun and shut the door. "My apologies, mistress," was all he could think to say, ashamed when the blurred vision of her shapely body filled his mind.

"Fire and ashes! Sir Damien!" she shouted hysterically.

Water sloshed. The pad of wet feet slapped the floor. "How dare you!"

"I…I…a thousand pardons…I had no idea."

"Lecherous swine! Ill-bred ruffian!" The flutter of cloth sounded.

"Aye, I admit to being both." And much worse, if he were honest.

"Did you ne'er learn 'tis improper to barge in on a lady's chamber unannounced?"

"I learned many things, mistress. Very few of which have aided me in life."

Silence reigned, save for the drip-drop of water and crackle of flames.

"Why are you still here?" she finally said. "Acquit me at once!"

"Nay."

"Nay?" Her tone was indignant.

"It has taken me two days to find you. I shan't lose you again. May I?" He raised hands at his sides in a gesture of surrender. He didn't wait for her reply, but slowly turned to face her. She had donned her chemise and tunic, which normally would have hung loosely about her small frame but instead clung to her wet skin. Saturated strands of ivory hair rippled about her waist, whilst eyes the color of sapphires shot icicles his way.

An angel sent from heaven.

He couldn't help but smile.

Crossing arms over her chest, she approached the fire. The maroon blossoming on her cheeks pricked his guilt, and he shifted his stance.

"I'll not gainsay that you have a right to be angry. 'Twas not my intent to intrude upon your bath."

She cast him a fiery look. "Then I recommend you cease grinning at me, sir, for it gives you away."

"It only gives away how pleased I am to see you."

She looked back at the fire, and Damien took the opportunity to glance around the room for the Spear. Surely if she kept it on her, she would have removed it to bathe. 'Twould be a simple task to slip it into his pocket, though it would pain the lady greatly to lose it. He sighed. What was he even thinking? How could he betray such a lovely creature? Especially when she trusted him. Especially when his main concern was to keep her safe on her journey.

A rap on the door brought Damien around, knife plucked from its sheath and at the ready. But 'twas only the lad again with a tray of food and drink. Taking it, he thanked him, shut the door, and set it down on the table, daring to glance at Seraphina again, fearing her anger remained.

Her eyes were on the food.

"Can you forgive me?" He gestured toward one of the chairs. Could she not at least tell him she was happy to see him as well? Oh, how his foolish heart ached to hear those words.

"Why are you here?" she asked curtly, taking the seat.

He crossed arms over his chest. 'Twas not the reunion he had envisioned. "You left with neither word nor escort. 'Tis unsafe for you to be traveling alone."

"If I had wanted a guard, I would have asked you to accompany me."

Damien grimaced, remembering how fondly she had gazed at him back at Luxley, how many walks through Emerald Forest they had enjoyed together. "I beg you, what have I done to lose your good grace, mistress?"

She released a heavy sigh. "Naught. But this was *my* journey to make." She lifted pleading eyes to his. "Should you set one foot within Regalis, you will be arrested and tossed in the dungeon."

So she *did* care about him. The thought flooded him in warmth. "Forsooth! Allow me to worry about that. I can well take care of myself."

She shook her head. "Stubborn lout."

Damien approached and knelt before her. "Enchanting nymph."

Finally, a smile graced her lips. And in that smile, Damien saw a world of hope and happiness.

She took his hand in hers, affection sparkling once again in her eyes. "'Tis truly wonderful to see you, Sir Damien."

He lifted her hand to his lips for a kiss, relishing in the sweet scent of lilacs that always lingered around her. "'Twas not my intention to frighten you, nor to violate your privacy."

Red appeared once again on her cheeks, and she glanced down.

"I saw naught, mistress. You have my troth." He squeezed her hand.

Tugging it from his grip, she glanced at the tray of food. "Shall we eat? I know you must be as hungry as I." She arched a playful brow. "We shall discuss your future on this journey when our bellies are full."

Rising, Damien removed his sword and a few of his longer knives and set them down on a table, then slid beside her on the couch and handed her a bowl of stew. The scent of boiled rabbit, onions, and cabbage lured a growl from his stomach, and they both laughed. Not much was said as they hungrily consumed the pottage and bread. Not the best pottage he'd eaten, but it filled his belly nicely.

Setting her empty bowl down, Seraphina took a few sips of ale, but then handed her mug back to him. Aye, he remembered she cared not for the bitter drink. He, on the other hand, welcomed it whole-heartedly as more of a necessity than even water. The ale went down smooth and refreshing, and within minutes, he relished its calming effect. Rising, he added another log to the fire, then sat back down to find her staring at him.

She had pulled her damp hair over her shoulder and was combing her fingers through the strands, and he licked his lips, longing to do the same.

"What are your plans, strong knight?" She eyed him coyly, but then, forsaking her hair, began adjusting the ties of his doublet.

He shrugged as he stayed her hand. "To escort you to see the king."

"Surely, you know I cannot allow you to do that." She pursed her lips, defiance in her eyes.

"Surely you know you cannot prevent me."

Groaning, she gazed back at the fire.

He leaned forward, hands on his knees, happy for her concern, but frustrated that she thought him so incompetent. "What say you to this? I will escort you safely to Regalis and then disguise myself and stay far behind you. Will that suffice?"

She frowned and released a heavy sigh. "I suppose it will have to, for 'twould seem you will not be put off."

"At last we are in agreement." Yet suspicion rose. He rarely won a fight with this lady so easily.

"Then 'tis settled." She glanced around the room. "However, upon my honor, you cannot stay the night in here with me."

"Alack, you tease me, *wife,* for that is what you told the proprietor downstairs." He inched closer to her on the couch.

She smiled. "How else was I to ward off the wolves?"

"Wise lady." He grabbed a lock of her hair, still damp but as soft as it looked. She allowed it, which surprised him.

"I have but half a day's journey left," she said, "and I don't wish any harm to befall you."

"Nor I you. Which is why I am here."

Relinquishing her hair, Damien took another sip of ale and reached for her hand. Flipping it over, he found the mark, the outline of a spearhead on her wrist. "So 'tis true. You are the new protector."

She rubbed it. "I can hardly believe it."

"What power does it give you?"

She shook her head. "None that I can tell, though it grows warm when I encounter trouble." She paused, her thoughts seemingly far away. "Did not Friar Josef say it harbored no power at all? That the power comes from Christ Himself living within us?"

"Aye." Damien rubbed the back of his neck. "Yet how can that be? Though I admit to witnessing things I cannot explain."

"We shall make a believer of you yet, Sir Damien."

He chuckled. Unlikely. Too much had been taken from him. Too much tragedy had befallen him to e'er believe a loving God existed. "And where is this holy relic?"

One delicate brow rose. "Where no man dare find it."

He returned her smile, his mind spinning with the information. The Spear must be on her person, in a private place he dared not even think of. Which made it all the more difficult to get.

Mayhap he'd have opportunities as they traveled together. Or mayhap he should merely explain his situation and ask for it once they got to Regalis. Surely she had no need of its power with him by her side.

"What is your plan, mistress? To march right up to the king's castle and gain an audience?"

"In truth, aye. Surely the king speaks to any subject who requests. Mayhap not right away, but in time."

Damien shook his head. *Naive woman.* "If so, he'd be far too busy for naught else."

"Then I shall tell him I have the Spear. Surely that will grant me favor."

Damien felt like screaming. Instead, he kept his tone steady. "I would not do that, dear lady. There are many who would gladly kill you for such a prize."

"That prize you speak of kept both Alexia and Cristiana safe, healed and delivered many people. Why would it not do the same for me?"

Even as she said the words, she doubted them. Even after the Spear had seemingly helped her thus far, for why would the Spear grant power to someone like her? Skepticism rang from her tone, luring Damien's curious stare.

Ah, but 'twas good to see him! She could hardly believe he was sitting beside her. So close she could smell his unique Damien scent, all spice and earthiness. Dark brown hair surrounded a face as strong and sturdy as the rest of him. A trimmed beard lined his firm jaw whilst dark green eyes hid a world of wonder within their depths—sorrow, anger, aye, yet also…overwhelming possibility. Shoulders as broad as an ox yoke led down to a massive chest and thighs as sturdy as tree trunks. He harbored a strength that all the leather and armor covering him did naught to hide.

Aside from the shock of having a man barge in on her bath, and aside from the fact she didn't want Damien to accompany her, Seraphina was overjoyed. His mere presence brought her such comfort, and for the first time in days, she felt safe again. Not to mention how she loved the way he looked at her—as if she were more precious than all the gold in the kingdom.

Though it had only been a few days, she had missed him, this massive, impetuous warrior who always ran straight to danger instead of away from it. *Foolish woman*! There was no time to form attachments to strong, honorable knights. No time to give her heart to someone who deserved much better than she. He was a King's Guard and she but a servant. Marrying her would do him no service in this world.

He must have sensed her admiration, for he took her hand in his once again. "Even should the king see you, what do you hope to accomplish?"

The gentle way he caressed her fingers sent her senses reeling. So gentle for such a strong warrior. She snagged her hand away ere she gave in to the look in his eyes, a look that beckoned her to lean on him, to allow his arms to encompass her with their strength.

Rising, she inched closer to the fire. "Show him the document signed by Sir Walter."

"The faded and smeared document?" He chuckled. "And when he doesn't accept it as valid? When he doesn't believe Sir Walter's forced confession of our innocence nor send men to investigate as you hope?"

She lifted her chin. "I will speak the truth. If he is the good king everyone proclaims he is, he will believe me."

Damien rubbed his eyes. "You have obviously not been to court."

"Nay, I have not. I am but a servant. But *this* servant intends to save my friends. And you, as well, Sir Damien. Allow me to at least try."

"And what benefit to you?"

"Does there have to be one?"

He only stared at her in wonder.

"They…you are my only family. I am an orphan, abandoned by my parents at birth. If the only value I have in this place is to be able to save my friends, then so be it."

Sir Damien stood and approached her. "I am sorry. I never knew you were an orphan."

She turned ere he saw the moisture in her eyes. "Aye, 'twas Alexia and Cristiana's parents who took me in, though they never told me why. They raised me as maid and companion for their daughters."

"I see now why you consider them family. And they you. Alexia and Cristiana love you like a sister."

She swiped a wayward tear. "Aye, and it has meant the world to me."

"Yet you wish to know who your parents are?"

'Twas a question she was unsure how to answer. "Nay. Why would I wish to know people who tossed me aside like so much refuse?" Though there were times, if she admitted it, that she longed to know why.

Drawing a deep breath, she waited for her tears to dry, then faced Sir Damien. "And what is it you search for, strong knight? The revenge you have oft made mention of?" She searched his eyes as a haze of sorrow covered them. "It has not escaped me the many times you longed to return to court."

Shifting his gaze away, he stared at the fire. "'Tis a long and dreadful story, which would do neither of us good to relay. But, aye, I seek revenge for the murder of my parents."

Murdered? She had no idea his past bore so much suffering. "And you believe you will find the answers you seek at court?"

"Perchance. I have reason to believe 'twas someone there who did the deed. But pray, know that is not the reason I sought to escort you." He eased his hand beneath her chin and caressed her jaw with his thumb, his gaze wandering over her face in admiration and finally landing on her lips.

She bit them to keep herself from succumbing to his charms and allowing his kiss, a liberty she had ne'er granted any man. And a liberty she knew if she granted *this* man, 'twould forever seal the fate of her heart.

Spinning away from him, she took the pitcher, poured the remainder of the ale into his mug, and handed it to him. She hated to play on the man's propensity for drink, but she needed him to sleep deeply this night.

He took it with a smile and gulped it down whilst she went to gather a coverlet from the bed. Returning, she laid it before the hearth. “Your bed, strong knight.”

“I’ve had worse,” he said, setting down his mug. The slight glaze of alcohol covering his eyes did naught to hide his desire for her. Yet, as quickly as it had appeared, he shook it away, swung his baldric over his head, unbuckled his belts, and began unfastening his leather doublet

Feeling her face heat again at the cavalier way he undressed before her, Seraphina retreated to the bed, unable to keep her eyes off him withal.

He stripped down to linen shirt and breeches—neither of which hid his rounded muscles beneath—and then cast his clothing aside.

“Do you always toss your things onto the floor?” Shaking her head, Seraphina went to pick them up, folded them, and placed them on the couch.

He stared at her curiously. “Where else would I toss them?”

She couldn’t help but laugh, for despite the man’s status as an elite King’s Guard, he was by far the most disheveled man she’d met, in both appearance and, apparently, habits as well.

“I am going to sleep now, Sir Damien.” She made her way back to her bed. “And you are going to stay on your side of the chamber.”

He winked. “You have my troth, mistress.”

And, despite the wink, she believed him. Which endeared him to her even more.

Seraphina lay down on the bed, waiting for the sound of Damien’s deep slumber. She didn’t have to wait long, for the man’s heavy breathing filled the air within minutes. Of course he fell asleep fast and slept soundly. Naught seemed to cause the man any alarm. Even should war break out and an army surround them, he would no doubt sleep like a babe.

She, on the other hand, rarely slept through the night. Whether ’twas her high-strung nerves or her constant feeling of being adrift on endless clouds, she couldn’t say. Alack, she’d grown accustomed to it over the years. This night, 'twas to her benefit.

After allowing her body a few hours rest and Damien to enter the deepest sleep possible, she rose, donned the rest of her clothing, grabbed her pack, and headed for the door. She stopped to glance at him lying on his back before the fire, the fading flames outlining his strong features, his massive chest rising and falling with each breath. She hated to leave him, hated to betray him. But she could never allow him to risk his life on her account.

Even before she reached the door, the sensation of being alone in the world…the emptiness, the fear…struck her yet again. Yet God was with her, wasn't He?

She had to believe that.

"Goodbye, strong knight," she whispered and then slipped out the door.

CHAPTER FOUR

The capital city of Regalis was not at all what Seraphina expected. She'd only visited a few of the towns and villages of the kingdom of Enclasen, and though she knew Regalis would be much larger, she did not expect such grandeur. As she approached the regal city, the pointed lead roof, flying buttresses, and colossal towers of the main cathedral could be seen high above the stone walls, along with several other tall buildings of prominence. Two round towers, at least fifty feet high, stood on either side of the gate, connected by an archway that bore the imperial crest of the king and an etched likeness of His Majesty in gold.

Travelers, wayfarers, merchants, wagons, and an assortment of livestock crowded through the entrance, bumping and jostling each other as they went. Ducking her head further beneath her hood, Seraphina gripped her bag and flowed along with them. The stench of human sweat, animal waste, and rotted fruit pinched her nose as the crowd fanned into the main street like prisoners freed from their cells.

Young boys with dirt-stained faces and worn leather shoes swarmed her. "Mistress, do you want a room? A bed for the night? Food?" They tugged on her cloak and attempted to drag her off.

"Nay. I thank you." She swatted them away gently, and they left her as quickly as they had come, pouncing onto the next traveler who appeared to have more money than she.

Seraphina hastened down the main street where dirt gave way to stones and the peace of the countryside to the shouts of laborers, ringing of church bells, and a hundred voices of travelers and town criers. Narrow dirt roads angled off from the main avenue like legs of a spider, each one filled with people hustling here and there. Chickens scattered before a rattling dray, whilst a squealing pig darted in her path.

She was amazed at the fine homes and inns lining the road. The gabled ends of their steeply angled roofs loomed over her head, providing shade from the afternoon sun. Packhorses and wagons ambled past her, laden with grain, no doubt heading toward the market square. Farmers drove their sheep and cattle into market, whilst others pushed carts filled with eggs, milk, and cheese. Seraphina drew a hand to her nose as the fetor of animal droppings alerted her to beware where her feet trod. A priest robed in black with a silver crucifix hanging from his girdle strode calmly in the midst of them.

Just before the market square, Seraphina passed the Church of the Holy Trinity. Sunlight angled off the most splendid stained glass she'd ever seen, causing her to blink at its brightness. Tradesmen and merchants lined the streets, displaying their wares before tiny shops and crying out to her as she passed.

"A new cloak for you, mistress! Candles! Paintings! Jewels for the lovely lady!"

Farther ahead, flies swarmed over deer carcasses hung in front of butcher shops as the sharp tang of recently carved meat joined the plethora of other unpleasant odors. A band of troubadours, dressed in brightly colored garments, sang and danced in the middle of the square.

Avoiding eye contact, she passed by them all, her one goal, her *only* goal, to reach the king's palace. Even now, she saw its towers, strong and white, perched on a plateau at the end of the street. Making her way there, she ascended the hill and halted before the massive wooden gates, both banded in thick iron braids, feeling like an ant begging entrance to heaven. Alack, the guards standing there barely afforded her a glance.

A trickle of sweat slid down her back. Blood raced through her veins, and she feared she'd faint on the spot if she didn't do something soon. Lifting her chin, she approached one of the guards, a man nigh as large as Sir Damien, but with sour features, tiny eyes, and no chin. Why could she not get thoughts of the strong knight out of her mind, for she'd thought of little else on the journey? How angry he must have been with her when he'd woken to find her gone. But it could not be helped.

"Away with you, woman," the guard said with a snort.

"Sir, I must see the king at once. I have—"

His laughter interrupted her. "The king does not see peasants."

"I am no pea—" She slammed her mouth shut, seeking any knowledge God would grant her, but no wisdom flooded her mind, no prophetic insight of things to come. Instead, the Spear warmed. Or mayhap 'twas merely the heat of the day. *God?*

"I have important information for the king. He will see me," she said with an authority she did not feel.

The other guard approached, his expression a bit kinder than the first. "What information? We will gladly inform him."

"I must deliver it myself. 'Tis of the utmost importance, information on a nefarious insurrection against His Majesty." Mayhap she'd exaggerated a bit, but 'twas mostly true.

"Humph." The first guard scowled.

The second studied her. "What is your name?"

"Seraphina de Mowbray from Luxley Castle in Emerald Forest."

The Spear grew hot.

"Mowbray?" The first guard laughed. "I've not heard of you, nor this Luxley Castle of which you speak."

Anger churned in Seraphina's belly. She'd come too far to be put off by ignorant guards. "Do you speak for the king, sir? Do you know all the castles in the land?"

He narrowed his eyes. A fly buzzed about his ear.

Sunlight glinted off the armor on his arm. She squinted against the brightness. "In the name of Christ Jesus, I demand you allow me entrance," she said with a commanding authority that hailed from within. But instead of prompting the guards to mock and dismiss her, the kinder one frowned. "Very well, I shall give the king your message. Wait here."

And wait she did. Minutes slogged by as her heart pounded so fast, it drowned out the sounds of the city. *Think, think.* The speech she'd practiced over and over on her way here paraded through her mind like a caravan of sickly animals, each one, each point, weak and dying. And none worthy enough news to disturb a king. She was but a servant in possession of a stained document and an outlandish tale.

You will make a fool of yourself! The words came from without, but stung her nonetheless.

'Twas true. She clutched her bag to her chest and glanced over her shoulder, longing to turn and flee. Who was she that the king would heed anything she said?

Mind made up, she turned to leave when oddly, a shout to open the gates sounded, and the two massive doors creaked and groaned as they were pushed apart. The guard emerged and gestured for her to enter. "The king grants you an audience."

Seraphina gulped. Numbness crept up her legs.

The gates opened to a world that seemed as far away from the city behind her as heaven was from earth. Tall, manicured hedges in the shapes of horses and angels spread over a landscape decorated with flowering bushes in every color imaginable. Stone fountains gushed and bubbled with water that glistened in the setting sun as lords and ladies in fine attire strolled about the gardens like butterflies flitting from flower to flower. A stone pathway wove through the lush greenery to a white castle in the distance. Round towers rose from each corner, crowned with spires that seemed to touch the blue sky. A massive wall surrounded the palace, topped with battlements through which knights defended the king.

Seraphina glanced down at her threadbare attire and winced.

"Mistress?" the guard said.

Forcing a smile, she stumbled forward, praying for her strength to return, praying for God to be with her.

By the time Damien entered Regalis, his anger had abated. *Almost.* He still had trouble believing that sweet Seraphina could be so deceitful, even though he knew she was only trying to protect him.

Protect *him*? Judas, he needed no protection, not from her. Not from anyone. He shoved his way through the throng of tradesmen, travelers, and farmers, wove around cows, sheep, and pigs, and ignored the hawkers trying to sell him all manner of goods.

Most people happily stepped out of his way, especially after seeing his King's Guard uniform and the weapons decorating his chest and hips. Others stared, whilst some whispered amongst themselves. Damien didn't care. Nor did he care that he could be arrested at any moment. They'd have to kill him to stop him from finding Seraphina.

He hadn't been in Regalis in over a year, not since he'd left with his friends Ronar and Jarin. The three of them had been assigned to escort Bishop Montruse to Luxley Castle to find the Spear of Destiny. After all that had happened—much of which he still could not explain—it felt odd to be back. As if he'd entered a new life since leaving, a new reality filled with love and hope and purpose, a place in a different world where the impossible became possible.

Strange that he had once loved being a member of the elite King's Guard and the prestige and power that came with it. And when it had been stripped from him and he'd been falsely labeled a traitor, he'd become depressed and angry. Yet now as he made his way to the king's castle, marching through this city he'd marched through a thousand times before, he felt naught. Naught but fear for Seraphina and his ever-present need for revenge.

Passing through the marketplace, he glanced up at the sun slowly descending to the mountains of Gladdick in the west and rubbed the sweat from the back of his neck. Had Seraphina even made it this far on such a hot day? But of course she had. This was a woman who had traveled nigh three days by herself, cold and hungry, to get help for Cristiana. Indeed, the lady may appear silky and feathery on the outside, but inside she was made of iron.

Which was one of the reasons he found her so enchanting.

The familiar smells of the city—human and animal waste, butchered meat, fire smoke, herbs, and flowers—assailed him as he approached the castle and turned left down a narrow street. 'Twould do him no good to attempt to get in through the front gate, though he recognized the guards who stood there. He was still wanted for treason. Nay, he knew a secret entrance used only by the King's Guard, and one that would grant him access to the throne room itself.

"Mistress Seraphina de Mowbray," the herald announced after she'd whispered her name to him in response to his question. *After* he'd scanned her from head to toe with unabashed disdain.

Seraphina stood frozen at the tall open doors, mesmerized by the opulence of the throne room. Mesmerized *and* terrified. Huge bronze pillars stood on either side of a raised marble dais with steps leading up to two golden thrones embedded with jewels. To the right of the king's throne and on one step beneath it, stood a man in a regal purple tunic, whilst three ladies in silk attire and golden belts flanked the queen. Large flaming fire pits dotted the room, crackling and spitting, silk-woven rugs clothed the floor, and lush plants in big pots fluttered in the breeze. Four ivory statues of angels were perched against the walls on either side of the throne. Behind the raised dais, huge windows allowed in streams of sunlight that cascaded over the thrones, making it hard to see the faces of the royalty who sat thereon.

Several guards stood at attention before the king, whilst a throng of people stood to either side, chatting amongst themselves, both men and women, all of them in noble attire. All of them looked up to assess the newcomer and all of them quickly returned to their discussions. Even the king himself was talking to the man who stood beside him.

The herald seemed about to announce her again when a woman hastened into the room from a hallway to the right. She wore a simple brown tunic strapped at the waist by a leather belt and a bright red wimple on her head. 'Twas hard to tell her age, for her back was to Seraphina, but whoever she was, she drew the rapid attention of all within the room, including the king.

"Panora," he said. "You have a word?"

"Aye, Your Majesty." She dipped a brief curtsy ere rushing to the bottom of the dais and gazing up at the king. "'Twill be a flood, my king. A fierce storm is coming. Rain will fall for three days and the lake will rise."

"Indeed?" The king rubbed his chin. A few noblemen gasped. Others drew hands to their mouths.

"Aye, Your Majesty. I would warn your people to move food and valuables to the top floors of their houses and shops."

Seraphina stared at the woman whose voice held more authority than it should before a king. A prophetess? Mayhap. And a good one from the attention and respect she garnered. Yet as Seraphina searched within her spirit for any word from the Lord about a flood, she found none. No warning, no vision of rain or flood waters rising. Strange.

"Thank you, Panora. That will be all." The king waved her away, then turned to address the man beside him.

Seraphina could not recall a time when she had been more terrified. Nor a time when she doubted she could even speak, let alone walk.

God, prithee, grant me thy strength and your words.

The herald announced her again, so loudly this time, both she and her heart leapt nearly to the high ceiling.

King Peter II finally looked up.

Seraphina could not feel her legs.

The herald touched her elbow and pushed her inside.

Drawing a breath, she started walking. All eyes were upon her, women whispered behind raised hands, whilst men assessed her as if she were the evening's repast. The king tapped his fingers on the arm of his throne.

What was she doing here? But 'twas too late to run. Her gaze was drawn to her left where Panora stood gaping at her as if Seraphina were a bug to be crushed beneath a boot. Odd. Why such hatred? Alack, not only hatred, but something heavy stirred within her at the woman's presence.

Shaking it off, she halted several steps before the throne, unsure of the protocol for speaking to the king, and lowered her gaze.

"Come hither, mistress. We do not bite," the king said, eliciting laughter from all around.

Seraphina took two more steps.

"You have permission to speak," he said with neither kindness nor anger. "Look up. Let us see your face."

Seraphina slowly raised her gaze and blinked at the light coming through the back windows, unable to see much of anything. Yet as her eyes grew accustomed to the brightness, she could make out the features of the man on the throne. A crown sat upon dark hair streaked in gray with a short beard and mustache to match. A golden robe trimmed in white fur was flung over one shoulder, covering a red silk doublet embroidered with emblems of gold and blue. He sat straight, his eyes on her, and while his features were high and noble, his face was kind.

She dared to breathe.

"I…I hail from Luxley Castle in Emerald Forest, Your Majesty," she managed to squeak out.

The man beside him leaned to whisper in his ear.

"Luxley, you say?"

"Aye, Your Majesty."

"Closer. Remove your hood. I wish to see your face."

Seraphina's legs trembled, but she took another step nonetheless as she slid the hood from her head and lifted her chin.

One of the ladies standing beside the queen gasped. Merely a slight sound, but loud enough for the queen to turn to her. No doubt 'twas the color of Seraphina's hair, a most unusual shade of ivory. The king must have found it equally remarkable, for he leaned forward on his throne and stared at her quizzically. Nay, *more* than quizzically, for shock appeared in his eyes.

"De Mowbray," he said, his tone oddly one of despair. "That name is not familiar to me. Who are your parents?"

Seraphina lowered her chin. "I know not, Your Majesty. I am an orphan."

Snorts of disdain rose from the crowd behind her.

The king quieted them with a wave of his hand as he sat back, clearly uneasy. The queen stretched forth her hand to him, but he waved her away.

"State your business, mistress."

"I have a document, Your Majesty." Hands shaking, Seraphina reached inside her cloak and brought forth the parchment. "A signed confession from the steward at Luxley."

The king gestured for one of the guards to bring it to him, but ere the man could snatch it from her hand, a shout, a familiar shout echoed across the arched ceiling.

"Traitor! Spy!"

All eyes glanced toward the right where a man dashed toward them, robes flinging about him like black flags in the wind and a gold crucifix bouncing over his chest. Dark, piercing eyes latched upon her ere sweeping to the king as he took the first step toward the throne and halted.

Seraphina's heart turned to wax. What was *he* doing here?

CHAPTER FIVE

"What is the meaning of this interruption, Bishop Montruse?" The king's shout brought all to attention in the room.

Terror buzzed across Seraphina's skin, numbing everything it touched. Including her mind. But not before her worst nightmare rose to torture her. Not being tossed from the throne room in disgrace, as she had expected, but to be imprisoned and hanged for treason.

"This woman,"—the bishop shot her a seething glance—"is naught but a servant at Luxley, a maid and companion for Lady Cristiana, the same lady who is wanted for witchcraft, along with her sister, Alexia D'Clere!"

Mumbling swept through the crowd.

The bishop opened his mouth to continue, but the king raised a hand to silence him.

"Is this true, mistress? Are you associated with Lady Alexia D'Clere of Luxley and her sister?"

Seraphina gulped. "I am, Your Majesty, but I beg you, hear me out. Things are not as they seem, which this confession will prove." She held up the parchment, and the king nodded for the guard to take it.

Once in his hand, he examined the seal, broke it, and glanced over the contents. His expression soured. "What is this? Forsooth, I cannot determine much of the contents nor even the full signature."

"Forgive me, Your Majesty, but unfortunately the document got wet." In a deluge of demonic water through the tunnels of Luxley, a flood that nearly killed them all, if she were bold enough to say.

"Humph." King Peter continued reading ere he glanced up again. "If 'twas so important, could you not have handled it more carefully? How am I to believe a confession cared for with so little concern?"

The man beside the king once again leaned to whisper in his ear.

The bishop huffed. "You are not to believe it, Your Majesty."

The king lifted the document in his hand. "Perchance, is that because it says that you and LeGode conspired to falsely condemn the D'Clere sisters and my knights? Begad, is this true?"

The bishop began puffing like a dragon. "Do you call God's appointed a liar?"

Murmuring rumbled behind Seraphina.

The king stared at him with all the authority of his station. "I made no such insinuation, and you'll remember your place, bishop!"

The bishop neither bowed nor tore his gaze from the king, though, to his credit, he kept silent.

King Peter faced Seraphina again, and she wondered how she remained standing, for the room began to spin.

"Are you familiar with these knights?"

"I am, Your Majesty, good and loyal men all. Sir Ronar LePeine, Sir Jarin the Just, and Sir—"

"Damien LaRage!"

She would ne'er forget the sound of that voice, its deep, authoritative tenor with a slight scratch that made it all the more masculine.

Silence descended on the room as all eyes shifted to the large knight marching toward the king.

It took but a few minutes for Damien to assess the situation from his spot by one of the huge pillars at the back of the throne room. And in those few minutes, he determined Seraphina was in dire straits and in need of assistance. He'd not been surprised at the sudden appearance of the bishop, for he knew the unholy fiend would arrive at the palace long before he did. That he should have warned Seraphina about the man only occurred to him now. But then again, he could not have known she'd arrive here without him.

His eyes swept over her as he approached, offering her a small smile of comfort. But only shock and fear appeared on her comely features. Turning, he bowed before the king, sweeping out his hat before him.

"At your service, Your Majesty!"

The bishop's sharp eyes speared him, yet he said not a word.

King Peter II rose, took two steps down toward Damien, and halted. "Sir Damien, how dare you enter unannounced." Though his tone was harsh, a brief hint of admiration filled his eyes, withal. And that gave Damien hope that his prior acquaintance with this man would count for something.

"Would you have received me otherwise, my king?"

Now that he stepped into the light, Damien noted the pallor of the king's skin and the bluish shadows beneath his eyes. Had he grown worse since Damien had left?

The brief hint of a smile appeared on the king's lips ere his jaw grew stiff again.

"Permission to speak," Damien said as his gaze took in Sir William standing beside the throne. Did his longtime friend and mentor also believe him capable of treason? But nay, William smiled and nodded his head ever so slightly toward Damien.

"Speak, though I dare grant a traitor thus." The king waved a jeweled hand before him, then swung his fur-trimmed mantle higher on his shoulder. Yet as he did so, he swayed slightly. The queen stood. One of the guards moved to assist him, but King Peter sent him back with a snap of his fingers.

"The confession this lady holds is valid," Sir Damien said. "The D'Clere sisters are no more witch than I. And I and your fellow King's Guards have always been loyal to you."

Minutes passed whilst the setting sun leeched its light from the room, leaving it in shadows. King Peter stared at Damien, studying him as if he could find the truth within his eyes. He wavered, caught his balance, then perused the document again. Finally, he turned and with difficulty mounted the steps to his throne.

Dropping into his chair, he released a heavy sigh as Queen Eleanor resumed her seat as well. Damien could feel the bishop's eyes bore into him, but he refused to look his way. He could also sense Seraphina's terror swirling in a storm around her. He longed to take her hand in his, if only to give it a squeeze for comfort.

King Peter closed his eyes for a moment, leaned his head back against his throne, and drew a deep breath. "Arrest this man at once and toss him in the dungeon!"

Seraphina grabbed Sir Damien's hand. She no longer cared what gossip the affectionate gesture stirred among those in the throne room. She could not lose this man.

"Nay!" Her shout caused a hush over the room. "I beseech you, this man is innocent. He speaks the truth!"

Two guards approached Damien, both sizing him up with wary looks. No doubt they knew the knight and were well aware of his strength.

"Halt at once!" Seraphina said with all the authority she could garner. "In the name of Christ!"

Yet the guards continued.

Why wasn't the Spear warming? Why wasn't it helping her?

"Blasphemy!" The bishop pointed a crooked finger her way.

"Silence!" The king's command seemed to take the last of his strength as he leaned forward on the arm of his throne. "Beware, young maiden,"—his eyes latched onto her—"or I will toss you in with him."

Damien squeezed her hand. "'Twill be all right. Do not—" Ere he could finish, the guards grabbed his arms, one on each side, and dragged him off, pulling his fingers from hers and leaving her cold and frightened. For him. For her. For her friends.

"I will, however," the king continued ere Damien left the room, "consider your words and this document."

"Your Maj—" the bishop began but was instantly silenced by a look from the king.

Damien cast one last glance at Seraphina over his shoulder as the soldiers escorted him away.

Gasps and murmurs bounced in the air.

She couldn't tear her gaze from him. Was this the last time she'd see the strong knight? 'Twas all her fault! If she hadn't ventured to see the king with Sir Walter's confession, Sir Damien would not have followed to protect her. And they'd both be safely back in the friar's secret home beneath Emerald Forest.

The guards dragged Damien down a corridor to her left wherein he soon disappeared in the shadows.

Seraphina faced the king, awaiting her punishment.

"Until I decide what to do with you, you shall be locked up as well, Mistress Seraphina."

One of the fine ladies standing beside the queen leaned to whisper something in her ear, and ere the king could order the guards to take Seraphina away, Queen Eleanor turned to him. "Not in the prison, my lord. Surely this woman poses no threat. Mayhap one of the chambers here in the castle?"

Without glancing at his wife, the king nodded. "Very well. Take charge of it, my dear." The poor man seemed out of breath as he gestured to one of the guards.

The man faced the crowd. "Leave at once. The king is tired!" His command scattered the nobles like bugs before the sunlight, including the bishop, who cast a scathing glance at her ere he swept his robes about him and left.

The queen descended the stairs, spoke to one of the guards, and then approached Seraphina. Heart pounding, Seraphina lowered her eyes and curtsied. "Your Majesty."

The lady smelled of jasmine and heliotrope, and her embroidered silk gown swished as she walked. "This man will escort you to your chamber, mistress, where you will be locked within until the king is able to determine the truth. Never fear, your every need will be provided."

Seraphina dared to glance up and found a pair of beautiful fawn-brown eyes set in a comely face surrounded by auburn hair. The lady was at least ten years younger than the king, yet there was a sadness about her, an emptiness, despite the jewels adorning her ears and neck and flung about her waist on a silver belt.

Seraphina could not draw her gaze away, and as she stared at the lady, a vision blazed across her mind, a vision of the queen sitting on the grass in the moonlight beside a bench, sobbing, sobbing so violently, her body shook, and tears streamed down her cheeks.

Then as quickly as it had appeared, the vision dissipated.

Shaking it off, Seraphina bowed her head. "I am in the debt of your kindness, Your Majesty." She could think of naught else to say, yet it must have been acceptable, for the queen smiled as the guard started to lead Seraphina away.

Yet something deep within her prompted her to stop. Tugging on the man's grip, Seraphina faced the queen once again. "The flood will not happen as that woman predicted. Tell the king."

The lady's delicate brows folded as suspicion filled her eyes. "Who are you to say?"

"I am no one of import, I assure you. Merely a servant of the Lord. Yet, in His mercy, He sometimes reveals things to me." And ever since Seraphina had witnessed the hatred in Panora's eyes, she knew what the woman had said was false. How she knew, she couldn't say. But when the knowledge came, it had never failed her.

The queen nodded, then gestured for the guard to take her away.

Down a long corridor, through the main hall, where servants prepared the evening repast, and up two flights of stairs, the guard escorted Seraphina with a tight grip on her arm. Her stomach growled as the scent of roasted pheasant and boiled onions filled her nose, yet the guard kept a rapid pace, his boots echoing over the stone walls.

Finally he halted before a door at the end of a long hallway, opened it, shoved her inside and slammed it behind her. The jangle of a lock clicked on the other side.

Seraphina hugged herself. Save for a sliver of moonlight floating through the narrow window, the chamber was dark. Shadows rose from every corner like hungry demons ready to pounce. The odor of mold and dust told her the room had not been used in quite some time.

Lord, where are you? She touched the Spear on her thigh, the Spear that had been cold throughout her exchange with the king. Why? Why had it not granted her the favor it normally did when she uttered a command in the name of Christ? For Alexia, the Spear had granted her the power to fight, to see into the spirit realm. For Cristiana, it had granted the power to heal and to love the unlovable. But Seraphina? Thus far, it had sent attackers running and granted her favor with the innkeeper and entrance into the king's palace. Alack, it had not warmed when she needed it the most.

Confusion joined the fear in her heart.

She fell to her knees and clutched her bag to her chest. "What am I to do now, Lord?"

CHAPTER SIX

Luxley Village, Northland Goodryke

Ronar LePeine, former member of the elite King's Guard, hoisted the deer, with the help of Jarin the Just, over the wall of Luxley village. Only two more to go and they could join their ladies inside the small town to help distribute the meat, along with the fruits and nuts they'd brought. He smiled at Jarin as they both grabbed the second carcass.

"Never thought we'd be hauling meat to hungry villagers as a profession."

Jarin shrugged and lifted the heavy deer as together they shoved it over the wall to the waiting hands of the town's butcher, Wimarc. "In truth I'd rather be fighting evil men and protecting the innocent but feeding them is the next best thing."

"Indeed. And knowing this will infuriate Sir Walter helps a great deal." Ronar winked.

They both grabbed the last deer.

"'Tis the least we can do for these people who have been forbidden to hunt and have had most of their crops confiscated by Sir Walter. All because they will not betray us."

"Aye. Their loyalty deserves much more than a few scraps of food, but 'tis all we can do for now." Ronar groaned as he pushed the carcass over the uneven stones. "Alack, I do miss wandering about the castle's tunnels causing mayhem." He wiped his hands on his breeches.

"We could still do it merely for the enjoyment." Jarin chuckled.

Ronar slapped him on the back. "I like the way you think, my friend."

Lifting hoods over their heads, they grabbed their sacks full of nuts and berries foraged from Emerald Forest and mingled in with a group of travelers entering through the main gate of the village. Perched on the towers on either side, two soldiers scoured the peasants below, no doubt on the lookout for the Knights of the Eternal Realm.

Nimwits. If Ronar were in charge, he'd be on the ground examining every face as they passed. But mayhap 'twas far too demeaning to spend the day down among the stink of peasants and farm animals. Now, should Sir Walter offer a hefty reward? But, nay, the man was too miserly.

Once inside, Ronar and Jarin wove amongst the crowd, searching out Alexia and Cristiana. Cristiana was easy to find, *far* too easy.

Jarin growled as he approached the crowd that formed around her. Ronar followed him, quick to tug him back ere he gave them away. Yet, there the lady sat before the spicemonger's, laying hands on a sick infant in her mother's arms.

"Begone illness in the name of Christ Jesus!" Lady Cristiana spoke with such authority and love, it always surprised Ronar.

Jarin gently grabbed her arm as she handed the babe back to its mother. "I beseech you, no more! What did I tell you about healing people in the public square?"

"'Twas not in the square but near the spicemonger's, dear knight." She offered him a sweet smile as he led her away and the crowd parted. "How can I allow these people to suffer when God has given me such a marvelous gift?"

"You cannot heal if you are dead."

"Such wisdom from so lowly a knight." She gave him a teasing smile.

Jarin ran a thumb down her jaw and kissed her forehead.

Ronar's heart warmed at the sight. These two were well suited, and he was as happy for them as he was for himself and Alexia.

Speaking of the Falcon of Emerald Forest, they found the expert archer in front of the village chapel, handing her bags of fruit and nuts to the priest for distribution.

Ronar and Jarin added theirs to the bunch.

"May God richly reward ye," Father Francis said, his eyes twinkling with youth despite his old age. "The people of Luxley would starve if 'twere not for yer kindness."

Cristiana took the old man's hands. "'Tis our pleasure, Father."

A worried look overcame the priest as he glanced up and down the dusty street. "But alack, I fear they are aware of your charity, for soldiers were here yesterday inquiring where the villagers got their food. I denied it, told them we had no food, God forgive my lie. But they didn't believe me. They'll be looking for you, to be sure."

As Ronar feared. Sir Walter was vile, but no imbecile. It had taken two weeks, but the steward had finally noticed the villagers weren't starving as he had hoped. Ronar and his friends would have to enter the village through the hole beneath the wall on the east side from now on, and never together.

"Thank you, good Father," Jarin said as they moved away from the chapel.

Together they crossed the busy market square where hawkers displayed their wares on pushcarts and people crowded around to see a juggler entertain them with a ball and trained monkey. Shops surrounded the square, selling all manner of items—rushlight holders, ironware, scissors, cloaks. The distant clang of the blacksmith's hammer could barely be heard over the chatter of the people and the grunt and squeal of the few remaining farm animals. A few of the villagers recognized them even beneath their hoods and offered smiles and nods but said naught.

The thump of soldiers' boots sounded in the distance—a sound Ronar knew all too well.

Without saying a word, the Knights of the Eternal Realm separated, mingling with a crowd of peasants who swiftly moved in front of them, hiding them with their bodies. The soldiers entered the square, halted, and studied the throng. Ronar peered at them from the edge of his hood as he stopped and pretended to examine an etched copper bowl for sale.

"Disperse at once!" the captain of the guard shouted, and the people slowly made their way down the street.

Ronar and his friends did the same, slipping one by one down the tiny path between the butcher and leather worker. The butcher appeared out the back door. "Hurry. You must leave at once. I will stall them should they come this way." He led them behind a row of shops to the back of a small wooden home with a thatched roof.

"Thank you, good sir." Ronar gripped his shoulder as his friends disappeared behind a row of drying laundry and through a patch of blackberry bushes.

The skinny man nodded, then headed back toward his shop.

Ronar joined his friends at the wall, happy to see that Jarin had already shoved aside the large rock that hid the hole. Dropping to his knees, Ronar assisted him in digging the loose dirt from the opening.

"Jarin and I were thinking a trip into the castle is in order." Ronar glanced up at Alexia.

"For what purpose, Sir Knight? We no longer need anything from Sir Walter."

"For the fun of it," Jarin added.

"To cause trouble for the man." Ronar continued digging. "In truth, I grow bored hunting and foraging."

She knelt beside him and smiled. "Poor little knight with no one to fight, no one to kill."

He smiled and kissed her on the nose. "Come now, love, you of all people must agree with me. Your bow and arrows have sat languid for weeks now."

"They have caught deer to eat. 'Tis enough." She stood and glanced at her sister. "Besides, we await news of Sir Damien and Seraphina."

"'Tis only been a fortnight," Jarin said, sitting back on his haunches.

"And whilst we wait, why not have some fun?" Ronar grinned.

Alexia cocked her head at him. “I begin to think you love danger more than you love me, Sir Knight.”

“How could I? The two are inseparable.”

Lady Cristiana laughed. “I see Ronar has become well acquainted with your ways, sister. Why, you should have seen her as a young girl sneaking out—”

“That’s quite enough, dearest.” Alexia silenced her with a smile. “Ronar has no interest in my youthful antics.”’

“Quite the contrary.” He winked at Cristiana, and she returned a mischievous nod. “We shall talk later.”

Alexia glanced at the castle, easily spotted on the hill above the village. “I suppose we could venture inside to see if Anabelle has further information to disclose.”

“And to make sure she is well,” Cristiana added.

“Then ’tis settled.” Ronar stood and followed Alexia’s gaze to the castle, noting her expression had changed from levity to one of concern. “What is it?”

“Darkness,” she mumbled. “A thick black cloud grows over the castle. Can you not see it?”

Ronar saw naught but blue sky, white clouds, and a sun that was descending in the west. He closed his eyes and sought the Spirit within as the friar and Alexia had taught him. When he opened them, the castle’s turrets were cloaked in a black mist. “I see it.”

Jarin rose, brushed dirt from his hands, and stared at the castle. “See what?” He exchanged a confused glance with Cristiana.

Alexia frowned. “Darkness grows at Luxley. Thick and heavy.”

“All the more reason to see if Anabelle is all right,” Cristiana said.

Sir Jarin took her hand. “At the moment we should leave this place. I sense danger.”

“I do as well.” Alexia nodded. “And not from the soldiers. Come.” Dropping to her knees, she shoved her legs into the hole and squeezed through. Cristiana followed, then Jarin, and lastly Ronar.

Once on the other side, they separated and made their way across fields of wheat, intermingling with the peasants who harvested the ripe grain. 'Twas infuriating to know they'd have to forfeit most of it to Sir Walter.

Ronar kept a keen eye on his friends, on the soldiers at the gate, and on anyone who might be following them. No one out of the ordinary, as far as he could see.

Once they regathered within Emerald Forest, he would feel much better. Once he saw his fiancée's beautiful face and her sweet smile, his insides would relax.

But her beautiful face bore no smile. Instead, she halted just inside the first line of trees and glanced back toward Luxley as if a storm was coming.

Oddly, Jarin did the same, tugging on Cristiana's arm to halt her.

Ronar followed their gazes to see a black ribbon advancing toward them over the wheat fields.

Together they drew their blades, even Cristiana, who drew the knife Jarin insisted she carry at all times.

Soon the thu-ump of pounding paws, the snarls and heavy breaths of beasts on the hunt pricked their ears.

Ronar tightened the grip on his sword, instinctively nudging Alexia behind him. But she reappeared by his side, arrow strung taut in her bow, eyes locked on the advancing horde.

The ribbon transformed into wolves, at least thirty of them, eyes full of hatred, mouths open, fangs sharp, paws eating up the ground and spitting dirt into the air.

Not wolves. *Demons*. Ronar allowed himself to relax slightly. They'd defeated them before. Yet…there was something different about these beasts, something more malevolent, more powerful.

"In the name of Jesus Christ, I command you to halt!" Ronar shouted.

The wolves halted as if they'd struck a wall. Their whimpers and howls filled the air. Then…they charged forward again.

Fear like he'd never known in battle pierced Ronar's every nerve.

"Cease and depart in the name of Jesus!" Alexia shouted.

Once again, the wolves reeled as if something struck them. They licked their legs, whimpered, and paced, staring at Ronar and his friends.

Before they charged again.

Cristiana stepped from behind Jarin, the knife trembling in her hand. "We must say it together." She dropped the knife and reached out her hands, one for Jarin and one for Alexia.

Lowering her bow, Alexia gripped her sister's hand and reached for Ronar.

The wolves were nearly upon them, so close Ronar could smell the stench of their rotted flesh. He gripped Alexia's hand and gave her a nod. She smiled. Either God would intervene or they'd both soon be in heaven. Neither was a bad outcome.

Cristiana began to speak, and the others joined in. "In the name of Jesus, we command you to stop and return from whence you came!"

One of the wolves leapt for Ronar. Its yellow fangs dripped saliva just inches from his neck. Hot, putrid breath blasted over him until he could barely breathe.

Then the creature was gone. Disappeared in a puff of dark mist.

A chilled breeze stirred black dust into eddies where each wolf had been. The tiny cyclones joined together into a massive cloud that twisted and gyrated before rising higher and higher into the sky.

Hands still gripping each other, all they could do was stare as the massive vortex formed into the shape of a giant creature with wings and horns. It spread its wings wide and snarled as if it were about to pounce on them.

Ronar felt Alexia tremble beside him. Still, she shouted above the wind. "Stand your ground, knights!"

Cristiana added. "Greater is He who is in us than you who are in the world!"

The demonic creature opened its jaws wide as if to devour them with one bite.

Instead, it uttered a blood-curling growl and disintegrated, leaving naught but blue sky above them.

CHAPTER SEVEN

Damien had thrown many a man into this very dungeon, locked them in irons, and slammed the grated door in their faces. He had done so on the orders of his king. But never in his imagination would he have believed he'd be on the other end of a guard's lance and shoved into this dark pit. Particularly by a guard who once had served Damien, who had been obliged to obey his every command.

How far he had fallen.

Judas! What a fool he had been to believe he could march into the throne room and count on the friendships of both William and the king to keep him from being arrested. But it had been over a year, and many a tale of treason had no doubt stained their ears. Lies all! But what could he do to convince them otherwise if he was locked in this pit?

And pit it was.

Cold, moist stone made up the floor and walls of the tiny cell, at least what he could see of it. A flaming torch outside the iron bars provided the only light. No bed. No chair. No window. With only bugs and rats for companions, Damien had spent the past two days alternating between drowning in a pool of self-pity and praying for Seraphina. Aye, *praying*. Something he hadn't done in years. But what else could he do to help her? Mayhap the Almighty would listen to a prayer for such a saint as she.

He had not seen her escorted past his cell. Hence, he had to believe she was in a better place. He prayed she was being treated well. *Stubborn woman*! Hadn't he warned her this would happen? Told her to quit her foolish quest? But she would not relent. And now they would both die as traitors to the crown.

Rising, Damien took up a pace across his cell, thankful they had not locked him in irons. At least he could stretch and move about, let out his anger by punching and kicking the hard wall. Which is more than he could say for his companions in this place. Their screams of agony and moans of despair echoed off the walls day and night, joining the tap-tap of rain outside and occasional thunder. A storm had risen shortly after he'd been locked below, one that seemed unwilling to relinquish its angry deluge on Regalis. Mayhap God was angry at the injustice done to Damien and Seraphina. But that couldn't be right.

Grabbing the bars, he shook them with all his might, as he had done so oft these past few days. And like all those times, they barely moved, and all he received for his trouble were cuts on his hands and dust on his head. Backing away, he drew a deep breath, instantly regretting it as the foul stench of human excrement, death, and decay swamped his lungs, attempting to penetrate into his soul to steal his remaining speck of hope.

How could he ever get his revenge now? When he'd been so close! How could he help clear his friends' names? All he needed was that blasted Spear! No doubt the relic was already in the impious bishop's hands, for surely they would have searched Seraphina ere imprisoning her.

Dear sweet Seraphina. Damien leaned his forehead on the cold bars. How he missed her. How he feared for her. Alas, he'd never really had the chance to express his deep affection.

A door in the distance squealed open, and footsteps padded over the stone floors, growing louder and louder. Most likely their noon meal of water and moldy bread. Forget the bread. What Damien wouldn't give for a pint of ale.

But it wasn't the steward of the dungeon with tray in hand. Instead the man who rounded the corner with two guards by his side gave Damien the first sliver of hope he'd had in days.

William Huntley, Earl of Haleford approached Damien's cell, hand to his nose and a smile on his face.

A rat crossed the path before him, but he paid it no mind as he stopped and reached through the bars toward Damien.

Hesitating, Damien studied his old friend and mentor, unsure of his intentions. Unsure of everything these days. Yet the light from the torch in one of the guards' hands revealed naught but kindness on William's face.

Damien grabbed his arm and squeezed.

"I beg your forgiveness, my friend," William said. "I tried to see you long before this, but I needed permission from the king, and he has been ill."

"Still?"

"Aye, it worsens." William frowned.

"I am sorry to hear that." Damien meant it, his own circumstances, withal. The king was a good man, a just leader, and the kingdom of Enclasen would suffer without him. Though with no heir, 'twas the man who stood before Damien now who would assume the throne.

"'Tis so good to see you, Damien." William finally released Damien's arm. The man was twice Damien's age, yet his grip was firm and his eyes clear. Brown hair graying slightly at the tips crowned a strong face with but a few lines around his eyes to indicate his age. His tunic was a rich vermilion, trimmed in gold filigree and studded with jewels, but his expression bore a humility which had always drawn Damien to him. That and the fact that William had been like a father to him after his own had been killed. Egad, he'd even gotten Damien his post as an elite King's Guard.

How disappointed the man must be in him now. Yet naught but affection appeared in his eyes.

"'Tis good to see you, as well," Damien finally admitted.

"You should know that I did not believe the lies I heard of you and your friends."

'Twas like a weight lifted off Damien's soul to have this man he so admired believe in him. "I am overcome. Thank you."

"And I intend to get you out of here. Tomorrow, I hope. Turns out the bishop has good things to say of you as well. The king is feeling better and has granted both the bishop and myself an audience in the morning."

Hope dared pulsate through Damien's veins once again. "'Tis good news." Even better, it meant the bishop did not yet have the Spear. Which boded well for Seraphina's wellbeing.

"There may be"—William flattened his lips and hesitated—"conditions you must agree to."

"Such as?"

"We shall see."

"What of Mistress Seraphina? How fares she?"

William's lips quirked in a sly grin. "Ah, I should have known you had affections for the woman. A true beauty, if a married man may admit such." He winked at Damien ere continuing. "She is well, I believe. Locked in one of the chambers with her every need met."

Damien could not help the wave of relief that swept over him. He nodded. "Then I shall await to hear good news on the morrow, my lord."

William gripped his hand again. "Indeed."

Then as quickly as he had come, the man turned and left, taking his torch, his hope, and his scent of bergamot perfume with him.

Leaving Damien once again with the stench of feces and vomit and a darkness that could penetrate a man's soul and drain all life from him if he allowed it.

Damien would not.

Seraphina dreamt of Emerald Forest, its lush greenery, ripe berries, and happy creatures skittering about—squirrels, deer, beavers, and a host of colorful birds singing and flitting among the treetops. Alexia D'Clere stood high upon the branch of a tall tree, arrow drawn taut in her bow toward their enemy, whilst below, her sister Cristiana fed a hungry deer from her hand. Was Seraphina home again? Was all well?

But then a thick darkness rolled in like a giant wave of pitch. Everything in its path shriveled and turned to ash. Woodland creatures darted away. Trees crumpled to the ground. Even the dirt transformed to an inky ooze before the black horde.

"Run, Alexia! Run, Cristiana!" Seraphina screamed. But they couldn't hear her. Instead Alexia leapt to the ground, flung her bow over her shoulder, and laughed with her sister about the way the deer was licking Cristiana's hand.

The darkness was nigh upon them. In seconds it would devour them!

Seraphina jerked to sit up, her breath coming hard, fear tingling her skin.

She blinked to clear her eyes. *Only a dream*. She blew out a sigh. *Only a dream*.

A chamber formed around her. Small but well-appointed with a bed, table, two chairs, and a wardrobe. An iron brazier gaped dark and cold in the corner, whilst sunlight angled in from the narrow windows, creating spears of sparkling dust.

Sunlight! The first she'd seen in two days, for naught but rain had poured from the sky, cloaking everything in gray. Just as Panora had said. Yet still, Seraphina knew 'twould not end in a flood.

She shivered and hugged herself, seeking a blanket. But as she had determined the past two days, there was none to be found. In truth, there were few comforts to be found in the chamber at all, naught but dust and mold and neglect.

As she eased her legs over the side of the mattress, her stomach growled, and she wondered how Damien fared. Much worse than she, no doubt. The thought threatened to crush her, force her to lie back down, curl in a ball, and surrender all hope.

Fire and ashes! She hadn't counted on Bishop Montruse being present—the man who, along with Sir Walter, had nearly burned Alexia at the stake, drugged Cristiana into a stupor, and proclaimed their knight friends as traitors to the crown. How was she to convince the king of their innocence when a man as powerful as the bishop was here in person to accuse them?

But, no matter what happened, she couldn't give up now. Sir Damien needed her. Forsooth, she had the Spear! Surely it would provide a way to gain her and Damien's freedom. Wouldn't it?

Rising, she made her way to the window and glanced out at the most glorious scene. A massive lake extended from the palace as far as the eye could see, sparkling like colorful jewels in the morning sun. Beyond it, the green hills of Gladdick rose like emerald towers, protecting the royal city. Beneath her on a long porch, lords and ladies strolled about in fine attire, enjoying the first sunshine in days.

Seraphina drew a deep breath, hoping 'twould scatter the nightmare of Alexia and Cristiana. Were they in trouble? Seraphina oft had foreknowledge of events, but she prayed this time 'twas just a bad dream.

"Oh, Lord, please protect them. Help me to save Sir Damien and my friends."

You? Save? Ha. You can't save anyone, not even yourself.

A chill slithered down Seraphina's back. *That* voice. That voice that hailed from someplace dark, mayhap her own soul. That voice that always stole her hope. For how could she argue with the truth?

Clanking rang through the chamber, followed by the screech of a hinge and the creak of wood, and Seraphina spun to find the door opening. Three servants entered, followed by a lady in fine attire. One of the servants held a pail of coals and a shovel, another's arms were full of linens, and the third bore a tray of food.

Seraphina's stomach lurched at the sight of cheese, bread, and a cluster of grapes spread across the tray. She'd not been served so fine a fare these past days, but rather cold pottage and stale water.

The lady began spouting orders to the servants to ignite the brazier and clean the room, her gaze taking in the poor conditions, and her nostrils flaring at the sight. Finally, her eyes latched onto Seraphina still standing at the window.

"You poor dear. My apologies for not tending to your needs these past two days, but I was unable to convince the steward to provide you with basic necessities."

Seraphina recognized her as one of the ladies who had stood beside the queen in the throne room.

She studied Seraphina with an odd expression on her face, ere she glanced at the sunlit window. "'Twould seem your prediction of no flood has caught the interest of the queen, mistress. In truth, she hardly remembered until the sun rose this morn and the waters of the lake remain within their boundaries."

Seraphina allowed herself a smile.

"Besides," the lady continued, "your only crime thus far has been by association. Hence, there is no need for you to be kept a prisoner."

"I thank you, my lady, for your kindness. And prithee thank the queen for me as well. I give my troth that my only wish is to prove the innocence of my friends."

The lady smiled again, then turned to instruct the maids further.

Confusion spun in Seraphina's mind as she studied her. Hair the color of gold was braided and pinned at the nape of her neck. A tunic of red taffeta fringed in silk netting clung to her thin frame, whilst from a leather belt about her waist hung a purse and various tools and keys. A few lines on her face and loose skin at her jaw aged her slightly, but the youthful sparkle in her eyes made her look much younger.

"Indeed, mistress." The lady faced her again. "You may give your thanks to the king and queen in person, for they have requested your presence in their study."

Surely Seraphina was still dreaming. "They wish to see *me*?" She glanced down at her stained tunic, even as the smell of her body rose to pinch her nose. "I fear I am in no condition to see their majesties."

"A bath and gown will be provided, my dear."

Seraphina could only stare at the lady, dumbfounded. Mayhap the Spear had not stopped granting her favor, after all.

"I am Jane Winsome, Lady Rochford."

Seraphina curtsied. "A pleasure to meet you, my lady, and may God bless you for your kindness."

Lady Rochford turned to leave.

"Prithee, my lady." Seraphina clasped her hands together. "What of Sir Damien?"

"I know naught of your knight, mistress," she replied ere she gathered her skirts and left.

Oh, Lord, keep him safe. She swallowed the nervous lump in her throat. Oh, how she wished Sir Damien was by her side when she spoke to the king and queen. He had been at court for years and knew how to converse with royalty. Not to mention, his presence always made her feel safe.

Who was she to be granted a private audience with the king and queen? Merely a servant. Anxiety threatened to steal her breath, but she had no choice. The king and queen had summoned her. Mayhap she could further plead her cause, even procure Damien's release.

Now she *was* dreaming.

Not ten minutes after Lady Rochford left, the servants had the coals searing in the brazier, fresh linen and blankets on the bed, and the room dusted and swept.

Seraphina couldn't move fast enough to the tray of food. Thanking God for it, she prayed Damien had also been given something to eat.

After she filled her belly, she sat by the brazier and allowed the warmth to wrap around her and chase away the chill of the night.

"Lord, I don't know what I'm doing here, nor why your Spear grants me such favor, but I thank Thee. Help me to trust You in all things."

In truth, trusting the Almighty Creator was easy.

Trusting herself was quite another thing.

CHAPTER EIGHT

"Come closer, child." Queen Eleanor ushered Seraphina further into the room, a large chamber, perhaps a study or library due to all the scrolls lying about on several desks and various tomes lining the shelves. Colorful tapestries decorated the walls and a warm woolen rug covered most of the stone floor. The light from several flickering lanterns added to the sunlight streaming in through two narrow windows.

Seraphina gulped down a knot of fear and took a few more steps, noting the king sat in a high back chair behind one of the desks, and the man who had oft conversed with him in the throne room now stood at his side. Unfortunately, Bishop Montruse was also present, though he slunk about the shadows in the far corner.

She nervously pressed down the folds of her emerald green overgown that opened at the sides to reveal an undertunic of white silk. A thick velvet belt hung about her waist, its ends veiled in silver netting. She'd never worn such rich attire in her life.

And she'd never felt more out of place.

The king began coughing, softly at first but then more violently as Seraphina waited uncomfortably. If only Cristiana were here, she could heal the man of whate'er ailed him. Finally, gripping a pewter mug on the desk, he took a few sips, then settled back in the chair, gazing at her as if she were a fairy who'd flown in through the window.

His ardent stare offered Seraphina little encouragement, though the queen smiled her way.

"How did you know there would be no flood?" King Peter asked, his voice scratchy. "Panora has never been wrong."

Seraphina bit her lip, wondering how to explain her gift. "The Lord oft tells me things, Your Majesty."

The man beside the king snorted.

The king's brows rose. "God speaks to you?"

"Blasphemy! What further proof do you need?" the bishop shouted from the corner, pointing a ringed finger her way.

"Silence!" The king's shout appeared to tax what was left of his strength, for he slumped in his chair, attempting to catch his breath. When he recovered, he lifted stern eyes to the bishop. "You are on thin ice, Montruse. You were not to return empty-handed, and yet here you stand."

The bishop shot Seraphina a searing glance. "What you seek is either with this woman or with her friends. They use witchcraft to elude us, Your Majesty."

"And yet here she stands before me, eluding no one," the king retorted with sarcasm.

"'Tis pure trickery, Your Majesty. I—"

"Hold your tongue!" the king interrupted. "Surely you realize Sir Walter's confession accuses you of being a traitor to the crown, of intending to give the Spear to the Holy Prime instead of your king. 'Tis a wonder I even tolerate your presence."

The bishop's face hardened into a red sheen. "I…I…" The bishop wrung his hands. "All lies. The confession is naught but lies! I have—"

A lift of the king's hand silenced him. He faced Seraphina. "Do you know of this Spear of Destiny?"

To lie or not to lie? *Lord, what do I do?* "Aye, Your Majesty. I know of it."

"And do you know where it is?" he asked pointedly.

"The Spear is not an object which man can possess, Your Majesty. It goes to whom it chooses."

A sound akin to a pig snort emanated from the bishop.

The queen fingered the amethyst brooch at the neck of her satin gown. "Does it possess great power, as we have been told?"

Seraphina blinked. "Aye."

The bishop emerged from the shadows. "This woman must be stripped and searched at once! Forsooth, she may have the holy relic on her person."

The queen whirled to face the man. "How dare you say such a thing? She's but a poor maiden. Would she have allowed us to imprison her if she had the Spear? Would she even now be standing here shivering with fear before us? I marvel that a man of God would suggest such a depraved act."

Ere the bishop could offer a retort, the king spoke. "Acquit us, bishop. I grow weary of your presence."

"I have a plan to acquire the Spear, Your Majesty." The bishop bowed his head toward the king, his tone slightly quavering. "If you but grant me some time."

"Time? Why do you think your head is still attached to your body?"

Bishop Montruse clutched his neck, as if the action could prevent such an atrocious fate.

Seraphina couldn't help a tiny smile. The queen took note and added her own, ere she turned to the king to say something. But he waved her to silence.

Odd. Seraphina felt sorrow for the lady who was clearly pained by the king's affront. She folded her hands before her, sensing the Spear warming slightly on her thigh. Ah, what sweet comfort that brought her!

With a huff of indignation, Bishop Montruse stormed from the room.

The king swept his gaze to her. "Where are your friends, Mistress Seraphina? The D'Clere sisters and my knights?"

Seraphina's heart thumped so loudly in her chest, she feared they would hear it. "Your Majesty, surely you know I cannot betray them. Besides, I have no knowledge of where they are at the moment."

The king's jaw tightened, and his eyes narrowed ere he closed them for a minute.

The man beside him stepped forward. "The king wishes only to receive them here at court, hear their tales, and discover the truth."

"'Tis my wish as well, my lord."

"Mistress Seraphina, may I present William Huntley, Earl of Haleford." King Peter gestured toward the man.

"Lord Haleford." She dipped a curtsy. "I wish justice as well. I have come to plead the cause of my friends and to show you Sir Walter's confession."

Lord Haleford gave her a haughty look. "The bishop informs us 'twas signed under duress."

She could not deny it. "Its contents are true nonetheless."

The king drew a deep breath and straightened his shoulders. "I want two things, Mistress Seraphina. The Spear and justice in this Luxley case."

Seraphina lowered her gaze. "I can aid you in neither, Your Majesty, save in answering what questions I can with honesty."

The king assessed her for several long, unbearable minutes, minutes in which the clang of sword, laughter, and the sweet sound of a flute drifted atop a breeze through the window, minutes in which Seraphina kept her eyes lowered. She had been impertinent to the king. No doubt, he would order her back to her prison chamber, or worse, toss her in the dungeon.

Instead King Peter II rose and approached her, a strange look akin to admiration in his eyes. But that couldn't be.

"I find myself astonished, mistress. You are not only beautiful but brave and loyal. Even at the risk of your own life, you refuse to betray your friends."

Her? Brave? She had never been called such. She dared to raise her gaze to his and found eyes full of kindness and wisdom…and something else she couldn't place. Oddly, this king, who had the power of life and death over her, did not cause her fear to rise but, rather, instilled within her a sense of peace.

"I find this highly commendable," he added before turning back to his chair.

"Your Majesty," Lord Haleford began. "Nonetheless, she betrays you by not divulging the location of the Spear and that of her friends."

Ignoring him, the king resumed his seat. "In truth I am not convinced she knows either. I will allow it for now."

"What of Sir Walter's confession?" Seraphina asked, knowing she was pressing her good fortune, but the warm Spear prompted her onward.

"Inconclusive at best, mistress." He slumped back into his chair, and the queen drew near to assist him. But once again, he waved her away.

Lord Haleford spoke up. "The king has sent a magistrate and a contingent of troops to investigate."

"I thank you, Your Majesty. 'Tis all I ask for." And precisely what Alexia had said he would do.

"In the meantime," the king said, "until I hear from them, you are confined to the palace. You may not leave its walls, but you are free to wander about as you please. I do this because I see something good in you, Mistress Seraphina, and because you were right about the flood."

Relief settled her thrashing heart. Dare she inquire after Damien? Would one more question spill the king's annoyance over the edge and send her back to her chamber?

"If I may, if you please, Your Majesty, what of Sir Damien LaRage?"

CHAPTER NINE

"Where is the Spear?"

'Twas not his friend, William, who stood on the other side of the iron bars this time, but that insolent clod, Bishop Montruse.

In truth, he had jarred Damien from a rather pleasant dream—if one could have such a thing in the midst of such squalor—of flower-laden fields and glistening waterfalls and Seraphina's silvery hair flowing around her comely face as she smiled at him.

"I don't have it." Damien pushed against the cold stone and rose, ignoring the aches in his muscles and emptiness in his gut.

The bishop huffed and drew a handkerchief to his nose. "Then I suppose my only recourse is to inform the king that I, myself, witnessed your traitorous activity and that of your friends." A bug the size of Damien's hand skittered up the wall beside the bishop. He leapt away from it with a shriek.

Damien snorted. "Have you not already done so by calling Mistress Seraphina a traitor and the D'Clere sisters witches?"

The bishop wiped dust from the wide sleeves of his tunic. "I merely commented on her association with them, naught more."

"Alack, you called her a traitor!" Damien rubbed his eyes. "How will you retract such an accusation without looking the fool?"

He shrugged. "I will admit to being wrong, to believing Sir LeGode, to not having witnessed any traitorous or devilish behavior myself."

"And why would the king believe your change of heart?"

"I will simply tell him I accused rashly, that I was distraught at his anger and distrust toward me when I returned without the Spear." He glanced upward and smiled. "That I prayed, and God revealed the truth to me." He huffed as if the idea were ludicrous, then narrowed his eyes at Damien. "'Tis your doing the king has lost confidence in me. If you'd given me the Spear, none of us would be in this difficult position. Now he awaits news from the magistrate he sent to Luxley." He gripped the cross hanging about his neck. "However, I *do* still have his ear and could offer my opinion of the happenings at Luxley any time I choose—good or bad. Your choice, knight."

But Damien's mind was still focused on the word, magistrate. 'Twas good news, for surely the man would discover the truth.

"Ahh." The bishop must have seen Damien's smile. "You believe this magistrate to be your saving grace, eh? I assure you, he will not. Sir Walter will see to that! And I will regain the king's trust, mark my words." He cocked his head, studying Damien. "If you do not get me the Spear, per our agreement, then, well…" He shook his head, feigning a sorrow he surely did not feel. "'Tis a shame you and your friends' lives will be cut off so short."

Anger burned raw and hot within Damien's gut. He took in the single guard the man had brought with him and knew he could dispatch him in seconds. Then, with fingers wrapped around the bishop's throat, he could finally rid the world of this vermin.

If not for the iron bars between them.

A rat scampered across the path. A visible shiver coursed through Bishop Montruse ere he continued. "And what will happen to your lady fair, Mistress Seraphina?" He grinned. "As lovely as she is, I'm sure I can find some use for her other than execution."

Iron bars or not, Damien charged the man, thrusting the full weight of his body against the cage. To his surprise the bars loosened, raining pebbles and dust upon them.

The bishop leapt back, terror streaking across his features. The guard drew his sword.

"When I am set free and no iron protects you, nothing will stop me from plunging my blade into that black heart of yours."

A flicker of fear appeared in the bishop's eyes ere he smirked and dabbed the cloth over his brow. "Alas, if I am dead, I cannot absolve you and your friends, or"—he dared lean closer to Damien, nearly within reach—"tell you who ravished your mother."

Those words alone made every muscle within Damien tighten, especially his heart where a palpable and *familiar* pain throbbed. "For all I know, 'tis you who did the deed. You were at court during that time, weren't you?"

"Forsooth!" The bishop laughed. "Do you think me so vile?"

Did he truly expect Damien to answer that? Instead, he studied the holy man, his suspicions rising.

The man pursed his lips. "Upon my own, I am not an animal that I must satisfy my desires in so violent a way. Nay, there *is* a name I will give you." He shrugged. "Hence, all your problems will be solved once you give me the Spear."

Damien snorted. "And when I do and you inform the king that I and my friends are innocent, why would he believe you when you waited so long to exonerate us?"

The bishop gave a sideways smirk. "I will simply tell him I did not think he would believe me, that I feared I'd lost his trust and thought it best to wait for the magistrate to return and confirm my tale. In truth, giving him the Spear will reestablish my position of favor."

Damien sighed, studying the beast before him. He was right about one thing. The chances of the magistrate returning were not good. Sir Walter and his warlock would see to that.

"Hence, we return to the object in question." The bishop huffed. "Since you are here at the palace, I must believe the Spear is also."

Damien retreated into his cell. "I came to protect Mistress Seraphina."

"Aye. But surely the best way to protect her would be to acquire the Spear and give it to me?" He chuckled. "Ergo, she must be in possession of the holy relic."

The man was smarter than he looked. "She is but a maid and in possession of nothing."

"Hmm. Do we still have a bargain, Sir Damien, or am I to look forward to your soon execution and that of your friends?"

"I will get the Spear." Curse the man for a demonic swine!

"Very well." The bishop fluttered his handkerchief around him as if he could sweep away the stench. "You are to be released soon. I trust you will hold up your end of the bargain? Or I fear it will not go well for you or your friends, including the lovely Seraphina."

Damien knew well the bishop's propensity for young maidens. Gripping the bars once again, he gave the fiend his fiercest look. "Touch her, and you will die."

Smirking, the man spun and started back down the tunnel, his black robe fluttering behind him.

He was free! Damien could hardly believe it. A lone soldier escorted him out of the dungeon and across one of the many baileys of the castle. He breathed in the fresh air until his lungs were near bursting. Sunlight warmed his skin, and if he believed God had anything to do with it, he'd get on his knees right then and there and thank Him. But Damien had never been sure the Almighty existed. He much preferred to believe in himself, his wits, power, strength, and cunning.

They entered another courtyard where soldiers and knights engaged in mock battle, honing their skills, for one never knew when an enemy would attack. He recognized a few of them, men he had commanded more than once in battle, men he had trained. The clank of sword and grunt of exertion was music to his ears. The elite King's Guards normally trained elsewhere, yet he could swear he saw one of them among the regular troops.

No matter. Damien was out of that beastly dungeon, and he had but three things on his mind, a bath, a meal, and finding Seraphina.

The soldier led him through a gate into another bailey where caretakers tended vegetable and herb gardens, pigs and chickens wandered about, and young milkmaids labored beneath pails of fresh creamy milk. Finally, they entered a courtyard Damien knew all too well, one that flooded him with happy memories. Across one side stood a two-story building that housed the commanders of the army and the elite King's Guard. Beside it, mighty destriers snorted and whinnied from the stables as young squires tended them. He started across the dusty yard, taking in the rows of weapons lining one wall and the few knights eating pottage at a table in the corner. How many days had he spent in this courtyard mock fighting with Ronar and Jarin? How many nights had they spent relaxing in that building with wine and song?

His fellow King's Guards must be out on a training exercise, for none were to be seen. But Damien could not help the leap of his heart. Was he to be reinstated? 'Twas too much to believe.

But nay. He was not brought to his private quarters but to another chamber in the building for lesser ranked knights. Still, 'twas a comfortable room with a cot, chair, brazier, and desk. All he needed.

The soldier left without a word, and three servant boys entered, carrying a wooden tub half full of water.

"Good day to you, sir," the shorter one said as they set the tub down. He laid soap, a towel, and a change of clothes onto the chair beside the tub.

Damien had no time to reply ere they left. In truth, he took little time to disrobe, grab the soap, and leap into the barrel. The cold water sent a shock through him, but ahh, it felt good to scrub the stink of the dungeon from his skin and the sweat from his body. No sooner had he finished and was getting dressed when another servant arrived with a tray of plums, cheese, slice of bread, and a flagon of wine.

Now suspicion began to dampen his good mood, for 'twas unclear why he was being treated so well. Nevertheless, he poured himself some wine and began popping plums in his mouth…when a shadow appeared in his door, and he glanced up to see William.

"Is this luxury your doing, my friend?" He should address him as lord, as was his station, but he and William had been friends far too long.

William smiled. "Aye, the food, bath, and lodging I arranged. The freedom was granted by the king, though I suspect my good word on your behalf aided his decision." He sauntered in, the silks and satins of his attire at odds with the common surroundings.

Damien gulped his wine, relishing in the sweet taste. "I thank you, William. I fear I would have died in that dungeon."

"I would not allow that to happen." He smiled.

"You've always…" Damien swallowed his mouthful and glanced at his friend. "You've always been my champion, William. You rescued me from my uncle's shop, made me a squire, had me trained as a knight, and convinced the king to enlist me as one of the elite King's Guards. And now this." He stopped, unable to speak for a moment. "I know not why."

"Forsooth! Of course you do. I have no son, no offspring. And I knew your father well." He rubbed his temples, pain appearing in his eyes.

Did the man still suffer from headaches? "Alas, none of those things make me your responsibility."

William gripped Damien's shoulder and gave it a squeeze. "I think of you as my own son, Damien. You know that." The sincerity and affection in his eyes caused Damien to lower his gaze, overcome.

"Alack, I could not get you reinstated into the King's Guard," William added, moving away. "At least not yet. But I have spoken to the captain of the Guard, and he would be most pleased to have you assist in training the new knights."

"It would be my honor."

"Excellent." William nodded.

"If you please, what news of Mistress Seraphina?"

"She is well. She has intrigued the king, and for that he allows her freedom at the palace."

Damien laughed. He should have known. Seraphina intrigued all who met her.

"Where did you find such a woman?" William asked, an odd twinkle in his eye.

"She is lady's maid to one of the sisters at Luxley."

"Humph." William brushed a finger over the table, leaving a clean trail in the dust. "Do you know from whence she hails?"

"Only that she is an orphan and was brought to Luxley as a babe."

This seemed to upset William, for his expression crumpled, and he turned aside. But why? Why was he so curious about Seraphina?

Yet by the time he faced Damien, his smile had returned. "I should like to know more about her. I see how smitten you are with her, and I do not wish you to entangle yourself with the wrong woman."

Ah, so that was it. "Are my sentiments so obvious from the mere minutes you saw us together?" If so, Damien must work on that, for he'd always prided himself on hiding his emotions.

"You forget, I know you, Damien."

Damien offered William some wine, but he declined. "You have not yet told me the price of my freedom."

"You are not free. At least not yet. The king wishes to question you about the happenings at Luxley. I suggest you be truthful. Then when the magistrate returns with his report, he will decide your fate and that of Mistress Seraphina."

Damien nodded.

"For now, my dear friend"—William swept the hem of his purple robe over his shoulder and headed toward the door—"enjoy your limited freedom, and I shall do all to ensure you remain free."

"Again, I thank you, William."

He stopped at the door. "Come to the evening repast in the great hall. The king expects you. And Mistress Seraphina will be there." He winked, then disappeared outside.

Walking to the open door, Damien gripped the frame and watched his friend leave. A sudden cloud cast a shadow over the courtyard, along with Damien's freedom. What a tenuous road he and Seraphina traveled upon. There were too many unknowns, too many uncertainties upon which their lives hung. What if the magistrate never returned? Or worse, what if he returned with a bad report? Alack, Damien was not one to wait upon others to determine his fate.

The only way—the only *sure* way—to save Seraphina and their friends *and* ensure his revenge was to steal the Spear from Seraphina.

To betray the woman he loved.

CHAPTER TEN

The king did not respond to Seraphina's request for information on Damien. Hence, all she could assume was that he was either still imprisoned, or worse, the unthinkable. The rest of the day passed in a cloud of hopelessness as she wandered the corridors and arched pathways of the royal palace. 'Twas the most magnificent castle she'd ever seen, yet its beauty and grandeur did naught to lighten her mood. For if Sir Damien was gone, if she was not to see him again, she found her life suddenly devoid of all that made her smile.

Not that she didn't feel the presence of God. His love and joy filled her. If not for that, she'd surely crawl into her bed, cover her head with the quilt, and ne'er come out. 'Twas simply that she had not realized her true affections for the strong knight, her need of him, her admiration for his courage and kind heart. Not until he was taken from her. Yet wasn't that the way of humans?

Now, as the sun pulled the last vestiges of light from the palace halls, Seraphina made her way to the great hall for the evening repast with Lady Rochford by her side. Indeed, Lady Rochford had been by her side all day.

"You do not have to accompany me, my lady," Seraphina had said earlier as they strolled through the herb gardens. "Surely, being one of the queen's ladies-in-waiting, you have more important matters to attend."

"The queen requested I be your escort, mistress. 'Tis improper and unsafe for you to be wandering about on your own."

"You have my thanks then, my lady, for surely you find my wanderings quite tedious."

But the lady had denied such and quite emphatically insisted she was enjoying her time with Seraphina.

Voices, along with the clank of plates and mugs, brought Seraphina back to the present as they approached the hall, and once again her heart sped at the prospect of dining with royalty—at the king's palace!

"The queen seems quite pleasant," she said. "Prithee, thank her for the lovely attire and for your companionship." Seraphina swept hands down her violet gown kept in place at her waist by a silk corset embroidered in gold.

"She is a most generous and kind lady," Lady Rochford replied as a group of courtiers passed them and entered the hall.

"And the king?" They stopped at the arched doorway to see a host of people seated at white-clothed trestle tables set in succession of rank, various servants scurrying about, and the man in question seated at the high table on a raised dais. Bishop Montruse sat on one side and the queen on the other. Seraphina wrung her hands. More people attended this evening meal than attended grand affairs at Luxley.

The smell of smoke, expensive perfumes, roasted meat, and wine swirled beneath Seraphina's nose

Lady Rochford leaned toward her. "You will find the king a stern man, a just man, but also kind and good. Though he is much pained of late."

"What ails him, if I may ask?"

"The physicians do not know." The lady frowned as true sorrow shadowed her face. "He grows weaker every day."

Seraphina wondered who would succeed him since 'twas known throughout the kingdom that he had no heir. Attempting to steady her heart, she glanced over the room, seeking anyone she might know. But of course, she would not know anyone here. Nobles in their finery and frippery sat just beneath the king. After them, sat the knights, boisterous and deep in their cups, which offered a great contrast to the more peaceful and quiet clergymen who were seated next. Nobles of lesser rank, along with courtiers, filled the tables at the end.

Candlelit chandeliers hung from ceilings covered with paintings of cherubs, whilst lanterns hung on walls and candles on tables set the entire scene a-glitter. Against the far wall, flames danced in a massive hearth whilst troubadours set up their instruments in the corner. Above the mantle hung a painting of the king and above that, his coat of arms, two swords crossing a golden shield that bore a black cross and the likeness of a red eagle.

Ere they could step into the room, an icy chill slithered over Seraphina. Forsooth, even the flickering lanterns and candles around her seemed to dim. Confused, she hugged herself and sought the source. To her right, a woman moved toward them, oddly attired in a tunic made of layers of colorful gauze that fluttered around her like wings. A gold circlet sat upon her head from which flowed a red netting that crowned her head and spread over her shoulders.

Panora.

Her eyes met Seraphina's as she passed before her. Black and hard as obsidian, they stared at her as if she were a rodent to be exterminated. Then she was gone, fluttering about the guests all smiles and laughter.

Lady Rochford must have noticed Seraphina's reaction, for she said, "The king's mystic." But her tone harbored disdain.

"Why does she hate me so?"

"Alack, I have not seen her react so spitefully with any other. Mayhap 'twas because you proved her wrong about the flood."

"There is darkness around her," Seraphina mumbled to no one in particular.

"Indeed. But she has proven valuable to the king."

As Seraphina stared at the mystic, everything around them grew distant and blurred until only Panora remained. The scene transformed into an open, grassy field. Panora, dressed in black, hanging from a gallows, oscillating in the wind as ravens circled above her. Gasping, Seraphina threw a hand to her mouth. Then, as quickly as it had come, the vision was gone.

"Are you all right, mistress?" Lady Rochford took her arm. "Allow me to lead you to your table. Mayhap some food will grant you strength."

"Thank you." Indeed, the food smelled delicious, stuffed chicken and a loin of veal, from what she could see on the trenchers as the lady led Seraphina to one of the tables perched beneath the king's dais. Many eyes followed her as she crossed the room, assessing the newcomer ere they grew bored and went back to their first course.

She glanced up at the king and queen, desiring to nod her head in appreciation, but their attention was elsewhere. Instead, she gazed down the long high table and found Lord Haleford standing beside a lovely lady in the finest of tunics speaking to….

Seraphina blinked. Her heart leapt nigh into her throat. Sir Damien LaRage! Was she seeing things? Nay! There he stood, hale and strong, attired in his usual leather doublet over woolen tunic, brown breeches, and tall boots. Belts and baldrics were strapped across his thick body, though the absence of weapons stuffed within them made him appear somehow exposed. His dark hair had been cleaned, brushed, and pulled behind him. He laughed at something Lord Haleford said and took a sip from a mug in his hand.

Then, as if he sensed her presence, he turned her way. Their eyes met, and a slow smile stretched his lips.

"Seems your knight is well, mistress," Lady Rochford said with a grin. "I shall leave you in his charge."

"Thank you, my lady." Yet Seraphina could not remove her eyes from Damien, afraid he would disappear again. *He is alive and free*! Her knees weakened, and she nearly dropped into her chair as he instantly turned, made his way down the stairs of the dais, wove amongst the crowd, nearly pushing people aside in his effort to reach her. In truth, several ladies turned to watch him pass, their admiring smiles attempting to catch his eye. How could she blame them? Sir Damien LaRage carried a presence like none other—all man and strength and honor.

She lifted a hand to her chest to slow her heart's joyful beating. Ahh, but to run into this knight's arms, to feel him encase her in a fortress of muscle. But propriety raised a wall between them as he halted before her, his eyes alight with such love and excitement, she thought she would melt on the spot.

"I was told you would be here." He lifted a hand to touch her, but then dropped it. "If you had not appeared, I intended to find you." The sting of wine surrounded him.

"You are alive." She dared squeeze his arm and found rock-hard muscle.

"Alive and at your service, my lady." He dipped his head before her as a courtier would a noblewoman.

"Stand tall, Sir Damien. I am no lady." She glanced around, embarrassed, but he gripped her hand and placed a kiss upon it, still bowing.

The kiss sent a warm shiver through her arm and across her shoulders ere he rose and smiled at her again. "I am most pleased to see you, mistress. Even though you betrayed and abandoned me." One eyebrow arched.

"For your own good, strong knight. Alack, you did not heed my advice and were imprisoned, as I feared." She reached up to adjust the angle of his collar, which was slightly askew, then straightened the leather ties of his jerkin.

"Yet here I am." He spread his arms wide and glanced around. "Here we both are."

"By God's good grace, 'twould seem."

Sir Damien glanced over his shoulder at Lord Haleford, now seated at the high table. "Nay, 'tis William…I mean Lord Haleford's doing. He has been a father to me. Come, you must join us." He gently grabbed her arm and began to lead her away.

She jerked from him. "I could not. 'Tis not right. I am a mere servant."

He frowned, turned to request wine and food from a passing servant, then gestured toward the bench before them. "Then I shall sup here with you."

He would give up his place at the High Table to sit at a table of lesser ranked nobles…for *her*? Seraphina knew not what to say. Yet as they shared a trencher full of chicken in a fruity wine sauce, she couldn't have been more thrilled. A few of the people at their table greeted him with exuberance, but mostly they left them alone. Troubadours began playing music as jugglers and jesters wove through the boisterous crowd now well into their cups, eliciting laughter and song. 'Twas far too loud for conversation, but Seraphina was happy merely to be close to Sir Damien.

Three more courses were placed before them ere the final course of plums stewed in rose water, along with fruits and sweet pastries, was served. Sir Damien downed his fourth glass of wine. Not that she was counting, for she knew the knight imbibed far too much alcohol, but for some reason, this night it unnerved her. Despite her misgivings, he appeared fully competent, continually smiling at her, and more than once lifting her hand to his lips for a kiss. 'Twas like a romantic dream, a fairytale young peasant girls dreamt of during the long, cold winter nights, to be in the opulence of the royal palace with a man like Sir Damien, to sample the exquisite fare, gaze at the elegant nobles in fine attire, enjoy the music, sit amongst lords and ladies of the kingdom. And all while Sir Damien gazed at her as if he never wished to look anywhere else.

After the meal, he rose and extended his hand. Taking it, she followed him through the crowd toward the hearth. There, Lord Haleford stood alone, staring at the flames, and she assumed Damien wished to introduce them, though the king had already done so. But a woman slid beside him, and he flung his arm around her and drew her into an intimate embrace. Surely the young maiden must be his daughter. But the way he took her hand and led her from the hall….

Damien changed course and led Seraphina out a wide doorway toward the back of the room onto the long open porch that extended the length of the palace. A nearly full moon hung upon black velvet, casting streaks of glistening silver over the lake. Seraphina drew a deep breath in awe at the magnificent sight.

Damien placed her hand in the crook of his elbow and strolled along as if they hadn't a care in the world, as if they both weren't prisoners awaiting a trial that could end in their deaths. Indeed, the knight seemed deep in thought as the hum of chatter and music faded behind them.

She had so many questions to ask him, but she hated to disturb this precious moment of peace.

Other couples sauntered by, and finally Damien stopped at the railing to stare out upon the lake. "We are to meet Lord Haleford in his quarters later tonight." He smiled her way. "He wishes to become acquainted with you."

"Me? Whatever for?" She longed to ask about the young lady he had been so intimate with but kept her tongue. 'Twas not her place to question the man who had freed Sir Damien. When the knight didn't answer, she changed the topic. "Though we are free within the palace, I fear what will become of us should the magistrate return with bad news."

"So you know about the king's commission?"

"Aye, and we must pray for the man's safety and that he discovers the truth."

"I shall leave the praying up to you, but I quite agree." His jaw flexed.

"In the meantime, can we do anything to aid our cause and that of our friends?"

Damien didn't have the heart to tell Seraphina of the bishop's threat—that unless Damien gave him the Spear and unless the magistrate returned with irrefutable evidence of their innocence, the king would believe the bishop's lies over a simple knight like Damien.

"We can do our best to convince the king of our innocence," he replied, though his tone lacked the conviction he knew she sought.

"Yet surely your friend Lord Haleford speaks highly of you to the king?" She touched his arm, her blue eyes searching his.

"That he does." He offered her a confident smile. "And I am to speak to the king myself on the morrow. In the past, he and I have had many conversations, and I count on that acquaintance."

"Friends with the king? I had no idea you and Sir Ronar and Sir Jarin were men of such import." She withdrew slightly. "Forsooth, the king's chief adviser is like a father to you!" She glanced at the lake. "I find myself unworthy by comparison."

Unworthy? Though her tone bore a hint of humor, Damien knew she was serious. How could he tell her she was the worthiest woman he had ever known? Even now, as she stood staring over the silvery lake, she appeared more angel than human. Wise, kind, generous, humble. He could list a hundred things he loved about her, a thousand things that drew his heart and soul. When he'd first seen her in the great hall, standing there in her lovely violet gown, looking more princess than pauper, his entire body reacted in a way he'd ne'er reacted to any woman before. Not merely an attraction, but an intense desire to protect, cherish, to never leave her side.

Now as she stood here, her skin radiant in the moonlight, her hair a waterfall of ivory down her back, the silken threads of her long lashes fanning her cheeks, he longed to take her in his arms. And ne'er let go.

Instead he reached for her hand. "I am naught but an orphan like you. I was an apprentice in my uncle's shop when William…Lord Haleford rescued me and made me a squire. 'Twas he and *only* he who then advanced me up the ranks to my current position."

"Then you owe him a great deal."

"I owe him everything."

Pushing from the railing, he placed her hand in the crook of his elbow yet again and continued walking.

Despite her baseborn beginnings, she strolled the palatial porch in the moonlight as if she were created for such grandeur, a vision of grace and majesty, like that of a swam floating over the glassy sea.

A lovelier creature he had not seen in all his days.

Then he remembered his bargain with the bishop. *Judas!* How he hated to put anything between them this night, this magical night when for the briefest of moments, he felt what it would be like to court this precious lady. He sighed. Alack, if he did not obtain the Spear from her, neither of them would be courting anyone. "Do you still have the Spear?" he dared ask as nonchalantly as he could.

"Aye. I believe 'tis what has kept us safe and granted our freedom. God watches out for us."

"The king wishes it, you know." He glanced at her.

"I do. But 'tis not mine to give. If the Lord wishes him to have it, if He finds his heart and soul worthy of its power, then it shall go to him, as it came to me."

Rubbing his eyes, Damien groaned inwardly. How could he convince her to relinquish the relic? "The bishop desires it as well."

"That vile man?" She shook her head. "He's the last person who should possess such power."

Halting, Damien faced her. "What if giving it to him would free us and our friends and restore Luxley to Alexia and Cristiana?"

"Forsooth, you speak nonsense, strong knight. No doubt you've had too much wine."

Of that, she was right.

She tugged her hand from his arm, her mood suddenly souring. "I would rather die along with all my friends than place such power in the hands of such evil."

And Damien would rather die than not get his revenge on the man who murdered his parents.

CHAPTER ELEVEN

Seraphina did not wish to spend time with Lord Haleford and his wife. She wanted to stay on the moonlit porch with Damien, talking, strolling arm in arm, smiling and gazing at one another as if there were no one else in the world. The perfect ending to the perfect evening. All save for Damien's odd comments about giving the Spear away. Mayhap he merely wished to appease his courtly friends. Alack, he never truly believed in the Spear's power. In truth, neither did her friends or Friar Josef. But Seraphina had experienced the power herself. The Spear had granted her favor, opened doors, scattered would-be ravishers. There was no other explanation. And she would use it to convince the king to pardon her friends and release her and Damien.

A servant led them into the receiving hall of Lord Haleford's chambers on the west end of the palace. The room was well-appointed with elegant carved wood furniture, woven silk rugs, velvet curtains, paintings and tapestries as befitting of Lord Haleford's station.

Lady Haleford rose from a plush red velvet chair to greet them as the lord himself turned from the hearth and smiled.

"Damien." He approached, drink in hand, his satin tunic, trimmed in fur, shimmering in the candlelight. "Thank you for joining us." His blue eyes snapped to Seraphina, an odd glimmer within them. "Wonderful to see you again, Mistress Seraphina. May I present my wife? Marion Vanberg, Lady Haleford." He gestured to the lady in question, who approached, a tight smile on her lips.

Dressed in an elegant cote of rich vermilion velvet with a gold, jewel-embedded belt about her waist, the lady's ebony hair, aquiline nose, and high cheeks made her a true beauty. One could not tell her age, save for tiny lines about her mouth and eyes, eyes that carried no warmth save when they swerved to look at Sir Damien.

"Pleased to meet you." Seraphina dipped her head before the lady, who finally gave her a cursory glance.

"You are both welcome," she responded in a velvety voice.

"Come, sit." Lord William gestured toward a sofa by the fire and snapped his fingers. A servant emerged from the shadows to pour them a drink. Seraphina declined the cup offered to her, but Sir Damien took them both. Had he not had enough spirits for one night? She glanced his way, but his eyes were on Lady Marion. How could she blame him? She was the perfect picture of poise, manners, and good breeding, elegant in every way.

Lord Haleford leaned back in a chair across from them, drink in one hand, whilst his wife sat in another chair closer to Seraphina and Damien.

Damien had informed her that his lordship wished to become further acquainted with her due to the affection he saw growing between them. That he had noticed their closeness elated her. That he wished to inquire about her past terrified her, for she had naught to tell of her life that would do her much credit.

"Mistress Seraphina, do tell me from whence you hail."

Seraphina lowered her gaze. "I do not know, my lord. I am an orphan who was brought to Luxley as a babe."

He shook his head and moaned. "How difficult for you. Did the lady who brought you leave no note, no indication of who sired you?"

"Nay. She was but a servant herself, they tell me."

Lord Haleford rubbed his well-trimmed beard. "And why did Lord and Lady Luxley take you in?"

"Out of kindness, my lord. They raised me with their two girls, Alexia and Cristiana."

Lady Marion smiled her way. "Very generous of them."

Yet Lord Haleford shifted his gaze to the flames flickering in the fireplace as if the thought disturbed him.

Damien sipped his wine. "I told you these things already, William."

"Indeed, I merely wished to hear them from the woman herself."

Seraphina swallowed. "I fear, my lord, I have naught to recommend me. I am but a companion and maid to Lady Cristiana and Lady Alexia D'Clere of Luxley. I have lived there my entire life."

He cocked his head and studied her. "May I ask your age?"

Seraphina could not imagine his purpose in knowing her age. Mayhap he attempted to find something to dissuade Sir Damien from pursuing her. Mayhap he thought her too young, too common for the knight he thought of as a son. Yet surely the Spear would grant her favor with this man. Still, it pricked her ire, and she found herself not wishing to disclose anything further. "I do not know."

Lady Marion fingered a gold bracelet on her arm. "Oh, leave the girl alone, William. She clearly has naught else to tell you." She turned toward Seraphina, the first glimpse of kindness passing over her face. "You must forgive my husband. He—"

"Make no apologies for me, Marion!" Lord Haleford's shout ricocheted off the stone walls. "As the king's chief adviser, I must know what sort of people he has given permission to roam about the palace."

Damien tossed the remainder of one cup of wine to the back of his throat and groaned. "William, I have more than vouched for the lady's character."

Lady Marion pressed her lips together, folded her hands in her lap, and stared into the fire with a look that bespoke of both rage *and* fear.

"Forgive me." Lord Haleford waved a hand through the air. "I fear my wife is correct. I oft am overzealous in my efforts to protect the king."

"To be commended." Damien picked up the second glass of wine.

"Yet, I should trust you, Damien. And I do." Lord Haleford leaned forward and smiled at Seraphina. "Prithee, forgive my inquisition."

She smiled in return, sensing a genuineness in his words. After all, Damien would not ally himself with a dishonorable man.

Anxious to change the topic to anything but her, she asked, "Did I see you with your daughter earlier?"

"Daughter?" Lord Haleford flinched, stared at her, gulped his drink, and slammed down the cup.

"The young maiden you were with in the—"

"William, may I have a private word with you?" Damien interrupted and jumped to his feet, and it seemed Lord Haleford was all too happy to join him by the window some distance away.

Rising, Lady Marion moved closer to the hearth where Seraphina sat and once again stared into the flames. "We have no children."

Mortified, Seraphina lowered her gaze, feeling her face redden. "I beg your forgiveness, my lady." Now she could well understand why the lady so oft frowned. How painful it must be to have such betrayals flaunted before her day and night. She could not imagine.

"No need." Lady Marion slid fingers over her ruby necklace. "'Lord Haleford is a man of great power, and being his wife, I enjoy many benefits of his station."

Alack, it seemed the woman had practiced her speech, for it emerged rote and without emotion.

Seraphina would have to mention this to Damien. His friend may have been kind to him, been a father to him, but he certainly showed no compassion for his wife.

And that did him no credit in her eyes.

"He will be king one day, you know," Lady Marion added, as if that somehow covered all his sins.

Seraphina glanced at the man talking with Damien by the window, his confident, regal stance, the exquisite embroidery on his sleeves and collar. "Nay, I did not know."

"The king has no heirs, and the queen is barren."

"But isn't it required that someone of royal blood take the throne?"

"He *has* royal blood." She swept sharp eyes to Seraphina. "He and the king are half-brothers."

Seraphina's gaze snapped to the man again, shocked.

"He is the illegitimate son of King Peter I through a concubine."

"Forgive me. I had no idea."

"Hence, you see why I tolerate his dalliances. I am to be queen one day." She lifted her chin as if practicing for the role.

Indeed, it explained much. Why William and the king were so close, why he held such great power at court. And why he'd been able to help an orphan rise from a mere apprentice to become one of the king's elite guards.

Yet, as she studied the lovely lady before her, she couldn't help but wonder whether being queen would ever fill the emptiness and pain of a loveless marriage. She stood to join her, mayhap console her as the woman stared at her husband.

But she wasn't staring at her husband. Her eyes were all over Sir Damien.

Against her will, a plethora of emotions surged through Seraphina. Anger, fear—and most of all, jealousy. She cast them away. Ridiculous. What woman wouldn't admire a man like Damien, especially when her husband offered her no affection?

Taking a step back, Seraphina shifted her gaze between Lady Marion and her husband. Mayhap God would grant her knowledge about these two. Were they good, evil, to be trusted or not? But all she saw was darkness, swirling black darkness, and a stone wall between them.

A servant appeared in the doorway. "Lord Haleford!"

The man turned to face him. "Aye. What is it?"

"'Tis the king! He is ill."

Clutching Seraphina's hand, Damien followed William and Lady Marion through the halls of the royal palace, up several sets of stairs, and into the private quarters of the king and queen. When the guard standing at the door leveled his lance in front of Damien to forbid him entrance, William spun about.

"They are with me."

That particular favor was granted only because Seraphina had insisted she could help the king. And though William had at first denied her request—for very few were permitted entrance into the king's chambers—the lady had been quite convincing. Now Damien could only hope she could do what she claimed.

The lance withdrew, and Damien led Seraphina through the receiving parlor and into the royal bedchamber at the back. Damien had only been in the king's quarters once before and never in his bedchamber, but there was no time to admire the elegant furnishings and exquisite art, for his eyes were immediately drawn to the king lying on the massive four-poster bed. Devoid of his crown and rich attire and with face pale and gaunt, he seemed so small, so powerless beneath the coverlet.

Queen Eleanor sat on one side holding his hand, whilst Bishop Montruse stood on the other, chanting in Latin from an open book. A man Damien assumed was a physician held the king's right forearm over a bowl where blood dripped from an open wound. The woman, Panora, paced before the foot of the bed.

Leading Seraphina inside, Damien stopped just past the threshold. He heard her gasp, and he squeezed her hand tighter, suddenly wishing he hadn't imbibed so much wine. He needed his wits about him, especially with Panora and the bishop present.

William slowed his approach and halted beside the queen, who stared up at him, her eyes red and face streaked with tears.

"He was well at dinner, enjoyed his food, laughed, and even sang. Then…" She glanced down at her husband. "When we came to our chambers, he fell to the ground unconscious. The servants placed him here."

William gazed at his half-brother and expelled a deep sigh. "Has he awoken?"

"Aye." The king's scratchy voice filled the room as he pried one eye open a slit. "I'm not dead yet." He smiled, withdrew his hand from his wife, and reached for William. "I asked you to come. Should I get worse, I have important matters to discuss."

"Of course, Your Majesty, but you mustn't talk like that."

Damien could tell from the catch in William's voice that the man truly cared for his brother.

The king glanced at his arm and shook his head. "Forsooth, if this doctor and the bishop have their way, I'll die ere morning comes."

Bishop Montruse's lips twisted as he looked up from his reading. "You would not wish to leave this world without receiving your last rites, Your Majesty, as is my duty."

Ignoring him, the king jerked his arm from the bowl. Blood dripped over the coverlet ere he could grip the wound with his opposite hand. "Cease this madness! I will not be quartered and drained like a deer!"

The physician huffed, his expression indignant at first. But fear took over as he bandaged up the wound as best he could.

"My lord." The queen brushed hair from her husband's face. "The physician wishes to help you, to heal you. Please allow him his ministrations."

"He has drained me of more blood this past year than could fill Lake Gladdick," he retorted with a growl. "And yet I am still ill."

The bishop began reciting Latin again, but with one look from the king, he closed his book, drew it to his chest, and said naught.

"What say you, Panora?" King Peter addressed the woman pacing at the foot of his bed. Halting, she glanced up, uttered a string of sentences in a strange tongue Damien had never heard, then clasped her hands together and lowered her head. "I see naught but sickness, pain, and death in the future, Your Majesty. I am sorry."

Queen Eleanor began to sob, dropping her head onto the bed.

The bishop opened his book again.

The physician nodded his agreement ere he took his instruments and retreated to a side table.

William remained motionless.

"Nay!"

The feminine shout came from beside Damien, and before he realized it was Seraphina, the lady had moved to the foot of the bed beside Panora. Without glancing at the prophetess and with a noticeable quaver in her voice, Seraphina uttered, "I beg your pardon, Your Majesty, but I see naught but good health, victory, and happiness in your future."

All eyes snapped to her, the bishop's and Panora's narrowing, the queen's and William's widening, and the doctor uttering a snort of disbelief.

"You dare enter my bedchamber!?" The king's face reddened, and he began to cough.

William cleared his throat. "Forgive me, Your Majesty. 'Twas I who brought Sir Damien and the lady. They were with me when news came of your illness."

"Lies! Lies!" Panora hissed in her direction.

Damien moved to stand between the two women.

The king drew a breath that seemed to pain him. "Are you a prophet, Mistress Seraphina?"

"Nay. As I have told you, the Lord tells me things, things I could not possibly know."

"And you have seen my future?"

"I believe so. As I stood in the corner, I asked the Lord to reveal to me where this sickness will lead."

"And?"

"I saw you sitting on a cushioned bench before a small pool, the queen by your side. You were both older than you are now. A babe sat upon your lap, and I knew 'twas a grandchild."

Panora gave a sinister laugh and shook her head. "Your Majesty, clearly the woman lies. You have no children."

Without looking at the woman and maintaining a calm Damien knew Seraphina felt not, she responded, "I can only tell you what I saw."

"Describe this pool and bench," the king said.

"'Twas a long wooden bench, cushioned in purple velvet. The pool was only large enough for one person to sit in, but 'twas surrounded by marble statues of angels."

Once again, all eyes shot to her. Including Damien's.

"She has been there!" Panora circled the bed to stand beside the bishop.

The queen rose. "She has not. No one in this room has been to the king's private bath, save the king and I."

Damien stared at Seraphina in wonder. Only *he* would notice the slight tremble in her bottom lip, for she had spoken with courage and authority.

The king studied her for several seconds ere he glanced at Panora. "And what of my sickness this night?"

She flattened her lips. "I fear you will worsen, Your Majesty."

He shifted eyes to Seraphina, who shook her head. "Nay. You will recover, but the illness will remain for a time. May I pray for you?"

"Blasphemy!" the bishop shouted, casting a narrowed glance at Damien that bespoke of him keeping the lady in line.

But Damien had learned long ago 'twas not possible with this lady.

"Cannot ordinary people pray?" Seraphina added.

"Indeed, but not for kings and queens!"

Seraphina shrugged but remained silent.

Seemingly weary of the exchange, the king faced the bishop. "Leave us."

If the man's eyes were daggers, the king would be dead on the spot. As it was, he stomped toward the door, searing Damien with a look that said he'd better get him the Spear. *And* soon.

When Damien turned back around, Seraphina had circled the bed and stood beside the queen.

Judas! What was she thinking? This was not some trifling peasant who had the ague. This was the king of Enclasen! One false move would cost her head.

Kneeling beside the bed, she laid her hand upon the king's. "In the name of our Lord Jesus Christ, I command your strength and health to return."

For several moments, silence reigned, for no one dared speak. But finally the king closed his eyes as if he could no longer keep them open. "Now off with you all. I wish to rest."

Panora shot a fiery gaze toward Seraphina ere she stormed out, her gauzy tunic flowing behind her.

William nodded. "Recover, my king. I shall see you on the morrow." Then spinning about, he gestured for Damien and Seraphina to follow him.

"You as well, Eleanor, leave me be." Damien heard the king address his wife as they left the chamber.

After bidding good eve to William, Damien escorted Seraphina back to her chamber in silence. He longed to tell her how brave he thought her, how beautiful, kind, and generous she was. But she seemed lost in her own thoughts. Now, at her door, he took both her hands in his and lifted them for a kiss, longing to do the same with her lips.

"Will your prayer work?" he finally asked. "Will the king indeed recover?"

Seraphina knew not how to answer the strong knight. Thus, she merely stood before him, adjusted his baldric, and sighed.

Reaching up, he stilled her hand ere she fussed more with his attire. "Was it the Spear? Do you think it healed him?"

"In truth, I have no idea," she finally said, attempting to make out his features in the shadows. She had not felt the Spear heat. What, then, had prompted her to dare touch the king? To pray for him with such authority? What if her prayer didn't work? Surely Sir Damien intended to chastise her foolish boldness. Instead, he ran a finger down her jaw.

"You are a brave lady, Seraphina."

The sensual way he spoke her name, his gentle touch, sent warmth spiraling through her, and she never wanted the night to end. But end it must, for she sensed by the way he was staring at her lips that he intended to kiss her.

And in her present need for him, her fear and loneliness, she knew she'd not be able to resist.

"I bid you good eve, strong knight." She smiled. "And I thank you for a wonderful evening."

"Should I stay and guard your door?"

She laughed. "'Twill do no good for my reputation should anyone see you lingering about my chamber."

"Very well." He returned her smile and kissed her hand once again. "Sleep well, my lady."

She wanted to correct him once again as to her lack of a title, but instead she remained at her door, admiring his strong gait as he walked away until the darkness absorbed him.

Then turning, she reached for the door latch.

A hand gripped her arm as the tip of a dagger pierced her neck. Seraphina barely had time to see who attacked her when the woman spoke.

"Stay away from the king and away from me or you shall regret it, witch!"

Panora. The intense hatred in her voice and spite in her dark eyes caused Seraphina's throat to close. Hence, she uttered not a word ere she jerked from the woman, opened her door, dashed inside, and slammed it on the woman's face.

Bishop Montruse glanced up from his desk as a servant entered his quarters. "Mistress Panora to see you, Your Eminence."

"Show her in." Rising Montruse set down the Holy Writ and adjusted his robes. How he loathed hailing the evil woman, hated being in her presence. But it couldn't be helped. He needed her.

Panora swept into the room, her gauzy tunic floating around her, and halted before him. No bow of respect, no reverential greeting, not even a look of obeisance on her face. He'd have her flogged if he didn't fear her so.

"You wished to see me," she said, glancing around the room.

"Why is King Peter still among us?" The bishop stiffened his jaw. "I brought you to court, gave you position and power, so you could curse him with an incurable illness, did I not?"

"And I have," Panora returned, meeting his gaze with equal intensity. "Curses take time. Especially on those who are walking in the light, those with pure hearts. He is ill and nearly dead, as I promised you." She flung out her fingers as if flicking away some unseen entity.

A sudden chill struck the bishop, and he moved to the hearth, holding out his hands to the fire. Indeed, the king had been very ill of late. As soon as he met his untimely death, Lord Haleford would be king. And the bishop had William in the palm of his hand. Even if that plan did not work, Montruse may soon have the Spear, and with it, more power than he ever dreamed of. He would not only rule Enclasen but all of Christendom once he presented the relic to the Holy Prime!

All his plans, all his hopes revolved around getting that Spear!

"Alas, I fear the curse will not run its course." Panora's voice spun him around to see the lady's features pinch as if she smelled something foul.

"'Tis this Mistress Seraphina," she continued as her eyes narrowed to dark holes devoid of light. "Her prayers, her very presence, dwindles the effect of the curse. You must speak to Lord Haleford. Have him execute her for witchcraft or at least toss her in the dungeon."

Aye, 'twas true. The woman was proving to be a nuisance. The bishop gripped the cross around his neck. "I must tread cautiously there. William has great affection for Sir Damien, and Damien has great affection for this woman."

Panora took a step toward him. "Coward! She opposes everything I say, makes me look the fool to the king and queen! I will not have it!" She glared at him. "You assured me I would have the king's favor, that he would listen only to me!"

Anger battled against fear within Montruse. How dare the woman speak to him thus? Were it anyone else, he'd have them led away in chains. Not this woman. She had powers, dark powers, that terrified him. How oft had he wished he'd never summoned her to court? He attempted a smile. "And the king *has* favored you. Per my demands, Lord Haleford shouts your praises to the king, encourages him to heed your every word."

She gave him an evil half-smile. "Pray tell, why do you have such power over the king's adviser?"

The bishop chuckled. She was a fool to think he'd disclose such a thing.

Panora marched to the single window and stared out with a huff. "There's a power around her. Strong power. Stronger than anything I've encountered."

"'Tis the Spear of Destiny, my little witch."

She spun to face him. "With the blood of Christ on it?" A visible shudder coursed through her.

"Aye. And I have tasked her knight to retrieve it for me."

"And why should he do that? 'Tis obvious he loves the wench."

Montruse smiled. "Because I have information he is desperate to know." He moved from the hearth, grabbed a decanter, and poured himself a drink. "However, should he fail me, mayhap you could get the relic?"

"Tell me where it is and I will! Then her power will come to naught!"

The bishop faced her. "I believe she keeps it on her person. And of course I, being both a man and a *holy* man, have no access to such private areas. But you…"

Panora approached him, a wicked smirk lighting up her face. "Aye, and I know just the person to aid my cause."

CHAPTER TWELVE

Luxley Castle, Northland Goodryke

Sir Walter LeGode, steward and soon to be lord of Luxley, descended the spiral stairs leading to Drago's vile lair. How he hated visiting the warlock's repulsive quarters, but 'twas the only way to get an update on the whereabouts of the Knights of the Eternal Realm, along with any news of his son, Cedric. He had long since regretted the bargain he'd made with Drago—Cedric as the warlock's apprentice in exchange for the warlock's powers to make Sir Walter Lord of Luxley—but there was naught to be done for it now. Besides, under Drago's tutelage, Cedric had transformed from a sniveling ninny to a man of great power, albeit *dark* power. Yet surely he would be happier wielding authority, commanding what he wanted from life, than living in cowardice at the whims of others.

As Sir Walter took each step downward, a putrid stench grew until he was forced to hold a handkerchief to his nose. Yet with each descending step, his hope oddly rose. The bishop was finally gone! How Sir Walter loathed that man! He'd been forced to endure his pompous company for far too long. Of course, Sir Walter had been unable to give him the Spear, but thank God for Drago, who had told them both that the holy relic no longer resided at Luxley but was well on its way to Regalis. Whether that was true or not, Sir Walter could care less. As long as it sent Bishop Montruse on his way!

Now he had one last encumbrance to overcome, one last problem to rid himself of before he could take his place as Lord of Luxley—the Knights of the Eternal Realm. His chuckle echoed over the stone walls. Bah! Ridiculous name, suggesting a power they did not wield in any realm. Regardless, they were on the run, the knights wanted for treason and the ladies for witchcraft. And with his soldiers searching for them along with the kings' men, not to mention Drago's dark powers, 'twas only a matter of time ere they were caught and executed.

Devil's blood! Why did Sir Walter give a care? With the bishop's word that he would entreat the king to make Sir Walter the new master of Luxley, why concern himself with these renegades? Yet he had to admit 'twould be difficult to enjoy his new power and position with them still running about free. Nay, they remained a festering sore in his otherwise healthy outlook, for as long as the D'Clere sisters lived, there was always a chance they could clear their names.

Taking the final step, Sir Walter drew a deep breath for courage—and instantly regretted it—then shoved open the door and stepped into a room cloaked in black fog.

He batted it away, wishing he could as easily bat away the foul odor. Coughing, he continued forward, peering through the haze toward a single flickering light on the other side of the room.

"Drago?"

The warlock appeared out of the dark mist, his white robe a contrast to both his surroundings and his blackened soul. "Why have you disturbed me? Can you not see I'm busy!"

"All I see is fog." Sir Walter hid his fear of this man behind a stoic tone.

"Look again."

Confused, Sir Walter glanced at the mist, but this time, a thousand pairs of eyes opened and glared at him from within it.

Shrieking, he leapt back, slamming against the closed door.

Drago's wicked chuckle sent ice through Sir Walter's veins.

The warlock swept a hand through the air, and the fog disappeared, leaving Drago's normal chamber, which was no less frightening, but at least familiar.

Sir Walter found his voice and took a step forward. "I came to get information on Cedric and those infernal knights we seek."

"I have both," Drago said as a bat released its hold above them and flew up into the tower. Ignoring it, he swept back his long gray hair, which always reminded Sir Walter of burnt straw, and stirred the ever-present bubbling brew sitting atop a brazier of red-hot coals. "But I wonder why I should grant you any further favors."

"Because we still have a bargain, do we not? Cedric and this dungeon in exchange for my becoming Lord of Luxley."

"Yet our bargain transforms more than a shape-shifting demon!" Drago hissed, the movement shaking the many hideous trinkets hooked to his robe—bird claws, amulets, rodent tails, and various talismans. "The deal was Cedric as my apprentice in exchange for his marriage to Lady Cristiana. Then, it morphed into the retrieval of that heinous Spear and *your* marriage to the lady. And now, it has mutated into you being lord."

Sir Walter repressed a groan. "The end result was always for me to become lord, which has not yet occurred." Which meant, if the bishop did as he promised, he would have no further need of this warlock's help. In truth, once the Knights of the Eternal Realm were dead, why keep him here?

Yet deep down, he wondered how he could ever rid himself of the man. Perhaps with Cedric gaining power, he wouldn't have to.

"What of Cedric? Have you seen where he is on your table?" Sir Walter glanced at the iron slab where, after scattering a few coals, the warlock oft saw objects and happenings in other places.

"Nay. But I sense him. He is heading home."

Sir Walter clapped his hands. "Good news."

"Yet something is wrong. A wound grows on my side, a pain." The warlock gripped his right hip as if the injury were real.

"Surely not from Cedric? Last you informed me, he had grown powerful."

Drago snorted, flaring his nostrils. "Aye, but I no longer see darkness around him."

"Mayhap he has grown too powerful for even *you* to see."

Drago's eyes became sharp blades. A cockroach skittered across the table, and he crushed it with his fist. "Mine is the power that grows, you brainless toad. I see these knights now. I sense their movements."

Sir Walter shrugged. "Surely they are cowering somewhere in hiding, the pigeon-livered loons."

"Who do you think feeds your villagers?" Drago shouted, stirring another bat, which took flight.

For a moment, Sir Walter could only stare at the warlock. "Devils blood! I have soldiers in every part of the village day and night. They would not be so bold as to show their faces." He fingered his pointed beard. "Surely one of the villagers would turn them in for the reward."

"If you think so, you are more rag-headed than I thought." Grabbing a dusty tome from the shelf, Drago set it on the table and began flipping through pages.

Sir Walter ignored the insult, storing it in a chest of a thousand reasons to rid himself of this menace. "One thing I have learned over the years, Drago, is that money speaks louder than loyalty."

"Not if your belly is being filled each day," Drago said without looking up, his long black fingernail sliding down a page of the book.

Sir Walter sighed, his hope of moments ago dissipating like the eyeball fog. "Well, at least they haven't dared come into the castle. Do tell, where are they hiding?"

"I cannot see the place. My enemy covers it in light. But soon…very soon…" His finger stopped, and Drago spun to retrieve a bottle off the shelf.

"And then we send your wolves."

"Nay, they know how to defeat them." Turning, Drago held the bottle up to the light, smiling, and Sir Walter could swear he saw toes floating in the elixir. "I must conjure up something far more powerful next time."

Sir Walter didn't want to know what could be more powerful than a band of ravenous, demonic wolves. He rubbed his chin. Mayhap it wouldn't be a bad idea to keep this warlock around even after he became Lord of Luxley.

Lord... He couldn't help but smile. No doubt he would soon receive word from the king with documents granting him the estate. So occupied with pleasant thoughts of his future, he failed to see the warlock's face twist in agony. "They are here!"

"Who?"

"Those holy knights and their ladies! Who else, you bloated whoreson?"

"In the village?"

"Nay, inside the castle!"

Alexia D'Clere, dressed as a common servant, moved aside the chest and crawled through the tunnel hole into one of the many corridors of Luxley Castle. Ronar, Sir Jarin, and Cristiana followed, and soon they were all once again within the walls of the home she had known in her youth. A home that once had been full of love and laughter, joy and music, but also a home where death had taken hold and deprived Alexia and her sister of both parents. A home where an evil man then plotted to kill them both. And for what? Wealth, position, land. What did it matter in the end?

She brushed dirt from her cloak. How foolish people were to believe that this life was all there was, that there was nothing beyond this one, rather than believe in a far more real world, a place so wonderful one could not even imagine it. She had seen glimpses of eternity, as had Sir Jarin, and in seeing those visions Alexia had been ruined for anything in this present world. If only others could see as well. But of course they could if they truly wished to, if they read the Holy Scriptures and sought the One who could reveal all things.

She turned to the others. "Remember we are here only to seek out Anabelle, not to cause trouble."

"Of course not." Jarin winked and took Cristiana's hand in his, whilst Ronar only smiled at Alexia. She had wanted to leave them all safe in their underground haven with the friar, but Ronar insisted he come along to protect her, and Jarin and Cristiana would not be left behind.

A chill unlike any other iced through her. She hugged herself and looked around. Save for two rushlights flickering in their holders, the hallway was empty. Nay. Not empty.

A mist as dark as night curled around a far corner and slunk toward them. The others glanced toward it. Cristiana eased against Jarin, and he wrapped an arm around her, whilst Ronar took Alexia's elbow and ushered them forward.

"The sooner we be about our business and leave this place, the better," he said.

"What is that?" Cristiana asked, fear biting her tone.

"I know not." Alexia hurried along, casting occasional glances behind her. They turned a corner and ascended a flight of servant stairs. Still the mist followed, growing thicker and thicker, like a sea serpent rising from the depths.

Alexia stopped at the top of the stairs and waited for Cristiana and Jarin to pass. "I've ne'er seen anything like it," she said to Ronar as he took her arm and tugged her forward.

Together, they darted down another hallway, but despite their rapid pace, the mist caught up with them. It hit Ronar first, snaking around his boots and up his legs. Alexia pulled on his arm to tug him away from it, but he shook his head. "I cannot move." The mist continued upward, spiraling around his torso. "Go!" he said. "Before it reaches you."

"Nay, I will not leave you." Alexia stood defiantly by his side, watching with terror as the mist circled her feet and ascended up her body. Its touch was icy cold, paralyzing, squeezing air from lungs and blood from veins.

Jarin and Cristiana glanced back and retreated to help before Alexia could warn them, and soon, they too, were covered in the black mist.

What to do, Lord? Alexia glanced at Ronar as the fog reached spindly fingers for his neck. What would happen should it surround their heads? Would they be able to talk? To think?

"In the name of Christ, I command you to cease!" Ronar shouted.

The mist halted but did not leave. It remained, gyrating around them like living chains, keeping them frozen in place.

Shouting, followed by the mighty thump of boots, bounced off the stone walls.

The soldiers knew they were here.

Cristiana began mumbling a prayer. Jarin shut his eyes. Alexia sought the Spirit.

One word blared through her mind.

Praise.

"Praise God. Sing! Praise His name!"

Though the others looked at her as if she'd lost her mind, they all began shouting the praises of the Almighty. Jarin sang a song. Cristiana lifted her face to heaven in worship. Ronar began reciting the glorious attributes of God, whilst Alexia bowed her head and spoke words the Spirit gave her.

She knew the minute the mist left, for she could breathe again, and her legs were freed.

"Come, make haste. They search for us." Ronar grabbed her hand and headed toward the servant quarters near the kitchen.

Sir Walter left Drago's lair and charged up the stairway as fast as his legs could carry him, wishing more than anything he was young again, for he had to stop twice to catch his breath. Mayhap Drago had some potion to restore his youth. Certainly that would be a good enough reason to keep the repulsive warlock around.

But those knights! Brazen fools! How dare they enter Luxley again? This time they would not escape.

Growling beneath his breath, he dashed into the great hall, found the first available soldier, and ordered him to gather any men who were not in the village to search every inch of the castle for intruders.

The man sped off, and within minutes, Sir Walter heard the shouts of soldiers and stomp of boots echoing off the high ceilings.

Why would they risk entering the castle after all this time? Surely they didn't intend to force him to sign another invalid document! Not after their last several attempts had ended in disaster. He smiled as he made his way through the great hall and up the circular stairs.

Devil's blood! He could not figure out how they'd escaped Drago's last attack—a mad rush of water through the tunnels where the knights had been hiding. That the renegades had been in the tunnels when the water hit, of that Sir Walter was sure. They should have all drowned, yet they emerged unscathed to torture him another day. Drago had cursed and shouted that they had the Almighty on their side. Bah!

Almighty or not, if Drago's power had increased, as he said, then anything he sent their way now would surely result in their demise.

Turning a corner, he made his way up to the second-floor chambers. He could search there as well as any other. A flash of red hair caught his eye.

Halting, he ducked behind a corner, waited for a moment, then peered around. No one was there. But he was sure he'd seen that witch Alexia. Her hair the color of a flaming ruby was unmistakable.

He inched forward, listening. Drawing his sword, he passed the first chamber reserved for important guests. No one was inside. Whispers came from Lady Cristiana's old chamber around the corner.

"We must make haste!" a soft voice urged.

Sir Walter moved along the stone wall, careful to not make a sound. Halting at the open door, he peered inside.

A woman in a cloak and hood stood talking to Anabelle. He could not see the woman's face, but a wisp of scarlet hair peeked at him from the side. Alexia! Three more hooded figures stood by the hearth.

Drago was right. Four of them were here. Sir Walter was good with a sword, but he was no match for the elite King's Guard. Glancing down the hall, he searched for any soldiers, but of course none were in sight.

Voices brought his gaze back inside the room. Why was Alexia talking with Anabelle? And why was the maid smiling?

He leaned his ear closer to hear but couldn't make out their words. The shrew! He trusted Anabelle. She'd been his personal servant ever since he'd come to Luxley. Traitor! He'd have her head for this.

After he had Alexia's.

Creeping away from the door, he dashed down the hallway, found a group of soldiers, and commanded them to draw their swords and follow him.

With the open door in sight, he shouted. "This way. They are in the lady's chambers!"

He had them now. There'd be no way to escape,

Rounding the corner in front of his men, Sir Walter charged into the room, brandishing his blade before him.

Anabelle turned from the window, shock and fear twisting her fair features. Ignoring her, he scanned the room.

No one else was there.

Lifting his face to the ceiling, he growled as loud as he could, then rushed toward Anabelle and gripped her throat. "Where are they?"

Coughing and gasping, she clawed at his fingers, her eyes wide with fear.

"Who?" she managed to shriek out.

Sir Walter released her with a shove that sent her reeling backward. She struck the wall and gripped her throat, gasping.

Sir Walter faced his soldiers. "What are you standing here for? Search everywhere. They must still be here!"

Yet, after a thorough sweep of the chamber, no one was found.

So be it. Sir Walter studied the young maiden and smiled. He knew exactly how to trap them now. Grabbing Anabelle's arm, he dragged her from the room.

CHAPTER THIRTEEN

Seraphina couldn't sleep. A cauldron of conflicting emotions brewed within her, stirring and churning and bubbling until she flung off her quilt and moved to the single narrow window overlooking the lake. There, sitting on the ledge, she hugged herself and thought about the strange events of the night—the wonderful meal with Damien, the romantic stroll in the moonlight, the disturbing meeting with Lord Haleford and his wife, and finally her prayer for the king.

When Damien had questioned her about it, she had not known how to respond, for she was unsure of it all herself. The Spear had not heated. She had merely seen a good future for the king and thus believed she must pray for his health.

But she had made an enemy. She gripped her throat where Panora's blade had pricked. A formidable enemy, for she now knew that the woman received her foreknowledge from dark forces. Why her predictions were not coming true now, when apparently they had for years, baffled Seraphina, but it must have something to do with the Spear's presence in this place. Indeed, she patted the relic strapped to her thigh. Surely the power of God resting on the Spear would protect both her and Damien.

Her gaze drifted down to the empty porch below, then beyond to the lake, shimmering like black diamonds in the moonlight. She'd had such a lovely time with Damien on their stroll after the evening meal. If only the night had ended there, 'twould have been the perfect evening, the makings of every lady's romantic dream.

But Damien had wanted her to meet Lord Haleford, wanted his approval of her, she supposed. In truth, aside from his infidelities, William seemed a wise and honorable man, a man fit to be king. Though 'twas a shock to learn of his parentage, Seraphina saw no desire within him for the king to die, but rather a genuine concern for the health of his half-brother. That alone did much to assuage her initial dislike of him. That and the fact he was the one responsible for Damien being free. And, with the ear of the king, he would be the one to aid them the most in pardoning their friends.

She only hoped she had made a good impression on him.

"Oh, Lord." She bowed her head. "Please help us gain our freedom and that of our friends. Please protect them back at Luxley. I am naught but your humble servant."

She lifted her wrist to look at the Mark of the Spear, still shocked she'd been chosen to protect it. "I don't want to let them down. I don't want to let You down, Lord."

Movement below caught her eye. A flash of green and brush of auburn hair. The queen? Nay, couldn't be. But the attire was not that of a servant, and the color of her hair was distinct. Mayhap she was in some sort of trouble. Quickly donning her tunic and cloak, Seraphina left her chamber and made her way to the porch, feeling slightly guilty for disobeying Lady Rochford's orders never to go about without escort.

No one was around at this hour, save a few guards at their posts. Though they gave her a cursory glance, they did not stop her, for which she was glad. At the end of the porch, stairs led down to a garden where cultivated shrubs shadowed the landscape like hunched-over monsters. Water trickled from fountains as a brisk wind stirred the leaves of a nearby elm tree. The chill of autumn was in the air, and Seraphina adjusted her cloak tighter about her neck. What was she doing out here? Whirling about, she began mounting the steps again when a woman's sobbing reached her ears. She started toward the sound, creeping between rustling shrubs and crunching over gravel pathways past a marble fountain depicting a statue of a horse rearing its front hooves in the air. Finally she entered a small enclosed garden surrounded by mulberry bushes.

The queen lay on the soft grass—her arms across a bench and her head lying atop her arms—crying. Softly crying, barely audible.

Seraphina didn't know what to do. Alack, she shouldn't intrude on this private moment, especially since this was the queen! Turning, she started to leave when the queen's voice stopped her. "Who goes there?"

"'Tis only I, Your Majesty, Seraphina." She faced her. "I beg your forgiveness. I heard crying and thought someone was in need of help."

Sniffing, the lady rose and eased onto the bench, saying naught for several seconds.

Should Seraphina wait to be dismissed?

"I do need help," the queen finally said. "But there's naught to be done for it."

Taking that as encouragement, Seraphina stepped closer. "Mayhap 'twould help to tell someone."

"You are but a…"

"Servant, aye. Hence, I have acquired a good ear for listening as well as the ability to keep a secret."

The queen smiled and brushed a wayward strand of hair from her face ere she glanced over the shadowy garden and drew a deep breath.

"'Tis the king," she finally said.

Seraphina took another step forward. "How fares he? Is he ill again?" She did not possess Cristiana's gift, but she had hoped to have at least cast aside his recent bout of weakness.

"Nay, he is resting quite comfortably since you left. I thank you for your kindness."

Seraphina smiled, still wondering at the source of this woman's pain. Did she have the same empty marriage as Lady Marion?

"He does not love me." She gave a sad smile, then patted the spot beside her on the bench. "Not truly."

Sitting down, Seraphina knew not what to say, for she hardly knew either of them and she'd never been one to offer empty platitudes.

"Ours was a marriage of convenience. Arranged by William."

"Lord Haleford?" Seraphina noted the queen's puffy red eyes in the moonlight and wished she'd brought a handkerchief to give her.

"Aye. Poor Peter. He was so lonely after his first wife died in childbirth."

"How horrible. I didn't realize."

"Aye. Ascilia, countess of Naville, was his first and greatest love, you see."

"And the babe must have died as well." Seraphina bit her lip.

The queen nodded.

So much sorrow. Seraphina's heart grew heavy. A brisk wind fluttered leaves around them and sent a chill over her, but the queen seemed unaffected.

"Years passed, and the king refused to take another wife. William was concerned for him. His mood increasingly grew dour and his health declined. Or so they told me."

"How did you come to meet the king? Were you one of the noblewomen at court?"

"Nay, not an ounce of noble blood flows in my veins. I am but the daughter of a gentleman who owns a sizable plot of land." She lowered her chin as if embarrassed by that fact. "So you see, I am not much different from you."

"You are quite different from me, Your Majesty. No matter your beginnings, you are now queen of Enclasen, and you hold yourself with the poise, authority, and elegance of your position."

She gave a gentle smile. "You are kind. I see why Sir Damien is fond of you." After several seconds of silence, she said, "William, who was a dear friend of my father's, arranged the marriage. You see, I was well known for my beauty, intellect, and grace, and many sought my hand. Hence, 'twas William who brought me to court. I suppose the king showed interest at first, and William encouraged him to wed again, promising him it would ease his wounded heart. The arrangements were made, my father was given a title and brought to court, and after a few signatures and a small ceremony, I became queen." She laughed as if the entire tale was somehow ludicrous.

"An incredible story, Your Majesty, from landed gentry to queen! 'Tis the stuff of romantic tales."

"Aye, 'twould be, indeed, if it had a happy ending."

Seraphina remembered how easily and often the king dismissed his wife.

"Alack, I have been able to neither please the king nor heal his broken heart."

"I am sorry." Seraphina touched her hand. "I pray he isn't cruel to you."

"Nay. He is a good man. He merely ignores me or dismisses me. 'Tis not the marriage I envisioned for myself." A tear slid down the queen's cheek, but she swiped it away. "I feel guilty for complaining. I am queen. Any woman would die to be in my position. Who am I but the daughter of a gentleman farmer?"

Seraphina could relate. She'd never felt worthy in any regard. Not even worthy enough for her parents to keep, 'twould seem.

"If only I could give him a child, mayhap I could win his love."

Risking the queen's ire, Seraphina gripped her hand. "Then I shall pray for your womb to bear many children, Your Majesty."

Snagging back her hand, she began to sob. "'Twill do no good, mistress, for I have made a pact with the devil."

Damien left the king's chamber feeling no better than when he had entered. He'd been summoned first thing in the morning to answer the king's questions, which he had done with all honesty, all save giving the exact location of his friends. However, that didn't seem to anger the man.

"Your answers are the same as Mistress Seraphina. Hence I must believe either you are both speaking the truth, or you have both conspired to lie."

Damien had dipped his head. "I assure you, we speak the truth, Your Majesty."

The king appeared much better this morn than when Damien had last seen him. Color had returned to his face, and he sat upright in the chair in the receiving room of his chambers, sipping his tea. Thank God the bishop had not been there to refute everything Damien said, or would he? For he still needed Damien to acquire the Spear.

The king's eyes met his, and for the briefest of moments, a sparkle of the camaraderie they had once shared appeared. "I would not have thought it of you, this traitorous activity, Sir Damien."

"Because neither I, nor my friends, would ever betray you. We are and always will be your loyal servants."

"Humph." The king frowned. "I would like to think so, but I have discovered that men who hold positions of power as myself can trust no one."

"I hope you will discover otherwise, Your Majesty."

"Very well. We shall see when my magistrate returns."

If your magistrate returns, Damien wanted to say, but didn't.

"Until then, because we were once friends, I will allow you your freedom at the palace. Should you dare defy me and leave, I will have you hunted down like a dog and executed on the spot."

Damien cringed. So much for friendship. "As I would expect."

The king dismissed Damien, and he now trudged through hallways of the royal castle in a foul mood. With all the strange happenings at Luxley, not to mention the warlock who was aiding Sir Walter, the chances of the king's man returning with good news looked rather bleak.

Alas, he had no choice but to steal the Spear from Seraphina and give it to the bishop.

But how? Would he have to seduce her to reach it beneath her gown? The thought disgusted him, for he could never dishonor her in such a way.

He needed a drink.

With these thoughts consuming his mind, Damien marched through the gate that led to the courtyard of the elite King's Guard and his temporary lodgings, happy to find the Guard had returned from whate'er mission they'd been on. Some ate stew from trenchers atop tables, others practiced sword fighting, whilst others stood talking. All of them looked his way.

He'd been labeled a traitor, and from the looks in their eyes, some believed that to be true. A few spat on the ground, but others started his way—Sir Bellamy, Sir Rogers, Sir Chaucee, all friends who greeted him warmly.

"We ne'er believed the tales they told of you and Ronar and Jarin," Bellamy said, crossing arms over his chest.

"Thank you." Sir Damien nodded and gripped Sir Roger's extended arm. "Alack, I hope to convince the king of that as well. How has the Guard fared these days?"

The men proceeded to tell Damien of their recent exploits, guarding the frontier from the kingdom of Erialla and escorting the king and high nobles to the Council of Nanes, making Damien long for the days when he, Ronar, and Jarin fought side by side with these men on behalf of their king.

"We all spoke up for you," Sir Chaucee said.

"As did I." The powerful voice preceded the appearance of the captain of the King's Guard, Sir Tybalt LeReed. Around forty years of age, with skin as rough and wrinkled as leather, and hair that had long since gone gray hanging to his shoulders, the man could fight like one half his age.

Damien stood at attention before him.

"No need. You are no longer King's Guard."

Something Damien hoped to rectify.

"Sir Damien! Damien LaRage!" The shout came from behind Damien, and he spun to see a man, brandishing a sword enter through the open gate. At first he didn't recognize him devoid of his King's Guard uniform. In its place he wore the simple linen shirt, cote, and breeches of the common army.

"Adred?" Damien took a step toward his one-time friend—his one-time *good* friend.

Alack, there was no kindness on the man's hard-lined face.

"Aye 'tis me." He inched forward, his eyes shifting over the regiment of King's Guard who watched with interest. "I have no quarrel with any of you."

"I have no quarrel with you, my friend." Damien spread open his arms.

Adred gave an evil chuckle ere he halted before Damien, the tip of his sword but inches from Damien's chest. The man looked older, sadder, his beard overgrown, his hair filthy and disheveled.

"By the code of the Knights of the Royal Guard, fight me. One of us dies this day."

Damien studied his friend, seeking a reason for this madness. "Are you drunk?"

"Nay, quite sober ever since I heard you returned."

Captain LeReed stepped between them, nudging Adred's sword away. "Stand down, Sir Adred." Then turning slightly to Damien, he said. "This scoundrel was kicked off the King's Guard for cheating at dice and for insubordination."

"I have my right to challenge!" Adred spat back, his face a red mass of fury and hatred.

Damien could make no sense of it. Rubbing his eyes, he sought an answer to this madness as the sound of men talking, horses snorting, and the eerie screech of blades being sharpened spun in his ears.

"Fight him, Damien!" one of the knights shouted, followed by others.

"Teach the little weasel a lesson!"

Damien huffed and glanced over at the men who had shunned him when he'd first entered. *Now* they were on his side?

Captain LeReed stepped aside and rubbed the back of his neck. "He has the right, Sir Damien. Do you accept his challenge?"

Damien stared at Adred. He had no wish to fight his friend, but neither could he turn down a challenge to his honor. If he did, he'd never be reinstated as a King's Guard.

Sunlight poured down upon him as his fellow knights urged him on. "Fight! A fight to the death!"

"I don't wish to kill you," Damien said, hoping this last attempt would dissuade the man from his foolish quest.

Adred grinned and circled his sword through the air, *whoosh, whoosh*. "There's no fear of that, my friend. I have been practicing since you betrayed me."

Betrayed? Damien scratched his beard.

"Damien," one of his friends hailed him from behind, and a sword flew through the air. He caught it, spun it around to loosen his muscles, then assumed his warrior stance.

Adred lunged first. Damien caught his blade with a mighty clank. The other knights backed away from the fight, forming a circle around them as cheers and jeers pummeled the air.

"Friends don't rat on friends," Adred ground out ere he spun and attempted to slice Damien's legs.

Damien leapt out of the way, caught the man's blade as Adred swung it up, and attempted to fling it from Adred's grip, but to no avail.

The man had, indeed, been practicing.

"You told him!" Adred tilted his sword downward against Damien's attack, then swung it back up. "You were the only one who knew."

"About your cheating at dice?" Damien backed away, sweat streaming down his back, and stared at his opponent. Ah, it made sense now. "Ask Captain LeReed. He came to me, asked me a direct question."

Adred thrust his blade at Damien, missing by an inch. "And you told him the truth."

"I did. I will not break my code of honor for you or anyone." Damien rushed him, their swords clanging together this way and that, the mighty hiss of steel ringing through the air. So that was it. Adred wanted revenge. Something Damien could well understand. But oh, how ugly a monster it was when one met it face to face.

Growling, Adred charged, met Damien's blade yet again, then spun, dipped, and came in on Damien's right side, slicing across his doublet.

Somewhere above him, a woman shrieked, but he had no time to look.

Pain etched across his side but not enough to warrant a glance. He'd been injured far worse.

Adred chuckled. "Lost your touch, Damien? No longer the best swordsman in the Guard, eh?" He glanced up and a sinister smirk twisted his lips. "Your whore is here to watch you die."

Damien didn't have to glance up to know that Seraphina was standing there. Nor did he care. The insult to her character enraged every part of him.

Glancing to his left, he grabbed a cloak lying on a table, then rushed Adred. He flung the garment through the air and circled it around the man's blade. With a flick of his wrist, he snapped the sword from Adred's hands, then dropped the cloak and pointed the tip of his blade at his throat.

For the first time, real fear screamed from his friend's eyes.

CHAPTER FOURTEEN

Lady Rochford had awoken Seraphina from a deep sleep. Little did the woman know she'd only lain down on the bed a mere two hours before. After her encounter with the queen, she'd returned to her chamber and spent some time in prayer for the lady. So much sorrow filled this palace, it surprised Seraphina. These people had every luxury at their fingertips, yet none of it mattered when one's heart was broken, when one did not have love or a sense of value.

"Rise, rise, mistress, the day is afoot and we've much to do." Lady Rochford burst into the room in a storm of cheerfulness and excitement, two maids behind her.

"Much to do?" Seraphina sat up in bed and rubbed her eyes.

The lady halted and snapped her fingers at the maids, one of whom opened the wooden slats that covered the window, letting in a stream of light and blast of chilled air.

"Well, mayhap not much to do, but laziness is not befitting any woman. Besides, I wish to give you a tour of the gardens. I am so rarely able to leave the queen's side."

Flinging her legs over the edge of the bed, Seraphina couldn't help but smile at the woman's exuberance.

Lady Rochford tucked a strand of loose hair into her braid and picked up Seraphina's pack. "What is this?" She began to open it. "Shall I have the contents washed?"

"Nay, nay." Seraphina leapt to her feet and took it from the lady. "Merely personal belongings. Naught of import." Underthings, soap, a few coins, a parchment bearing portions of written Scripture the friar had given her, *and* her swaddling cloth. It must never be washed, for 'twas so old, it might fall apart. She hugged the pack to her chest. Why had she kept it? Mayhap she should have thrown it out long ago just as her parents had done to her.

Lady Rochford eyed her curiously ere smiling. "After you are dressed, we shall break your fast and then venture to the gardens. They are most beautiful in the morning sun."

The meal was taken in a much smaller room than the great hall. Only a few of the lesser nobles were eating there, along with some of the knights. Still, the fare of fresh bread, cheese, and an assortment of blueberries, cherries, and grapes was better than Seraphina was accustomed to.

Lady Rochford was pleasant company. Funny, witty, and always cheerful, she shared such stories of intrigue at the castle, albeit none too damaging to anyone's character. Seraphina wondered if she knew about Sir William's indiscretions and how unhappy the queen was. But of course she would know such things. Especially the latter, for her normal duties involved being in the queen's presence at all times.

Oddly the woman was also quite inquisitive about Seraphina's past. Mayhap she was merely being polite, for why would a noblewoman care to know anything about a mere servant? Especially odd things such as her favorite color or food or what type of music she preferred.

Hence, by the time they started out for the gardens, Seraphina doubted there was anything the lady didn't know about her.

Shouts and the clang of steel on steel filled the air as they emerged from one of the arched doorways onto a porch that ran along the group of inner baileys.

"The knights are practicing, no doubt," the lady said as they moved along,

Yet it sounded more like a real battle than practice to Seraphina. In truth, the closer they came, the angrier the mob sounded. Curses filled the air, along with grunts and groans and even laughter. Odd. They passed one of the baileys but found it empty, save for a stable boy brushing down a horse.

Finally a throng of knights appeared below in the next courtyard. Seraphina recognized the uniform and crest of the King's Guard on the group of nigh thirty men as they shouted and cursed and swarmed around two knights doing battle. Her gaze searched for Damien among the mob, but upon not finding him, she shifted her eyes to the battling men, intending to pass by as quickly as possible, for she hated to see anyone injured.

Drawing a hand to her mouth, she gasped. Sir Damien fought sword-to-sword with a man in common soldier's garb.

Lady Rochford remained by her side. "No doubt a challenge of some sort. An insult to honor."

The soldier swiped at Damien's side, slicing his doublet.

Seraphina let out a shriek, and the man attacking Damien glanced up at her, said something to Damien, and continued his attack. Whate'er he said caused Damien to react with full force, as if up to that point he'd not been giving it his all.

Her fear for him quickly transformed into admiration.

She could only watch in amazement as Sir Damien fought. She knew he had been one of the elite King's Guard. She knew he'd been trained to protect the king at all costs. But she had no idea how strong, how fierce, nor how skilled he was. Granted, the man he fought was good as well, but no match for Damien.

"I wonder at the anger hailing from Sir Damien's opponent," Seraphina said. "If 'tis mere practice."

"'Tis not." The male voice rang above the clamor as Lord Haleford slipped beside Seraphina.

But Seraphina could not take her eyes off Damien. The knight quickly snagged the sword from his opponent, tossed it to the side, and held the tip of his blade to the man's throat.

The mob of knights began chanting. "Kill him, kill him, kill him!"

Gripping her throat, Seraphina could only stare in horror. "Surely, he won't kill the man."

"'Tis the way of the challenge, mistress," Lord Haleford said, his tone nigh one of anticipation.

The throng continued their morbid shouts. Lord Haleford adjusted the lace at his sleeve. Lady Rochford touched Seraphina's elbow and attempted to pull her from the scene.

Instead, Seraphina whispered a prayer, refusing to be moved.

Sir Damien withdrew his sword and stepped back.

The man scrambled to his feet, his eyes scanning the crowd with terror, ere he turned and bolted away.

Lord Haleford let out a disappointed huff.

"You are not pleased to see mercy instead of death this day, my lord?" Seraphina dared ask with a hint of sarcasm as she allowed herself to breathe.

He gave a tight smile. "I excuse your ignorance of the ways of knights, but 'tis cowardly to not follow through with a challenge."

On the contrary, whether 'twas ignorance or not, Seraphina's esteem for the strong knight only grew.

Lord Haleford extended his arm. "A stroll in the gardens, Mistress Seraphina?"

It sounded more like a command than request. Hence, she took his arm and allowed him to escort her to the lavish grounds. Thankfully, Lady Rochford followed close behind as propriety dictated, for the man made her feel uncomfortable, though she couldn't say why. Mayhap 'twas merely his position and power at court that caused her ill ease.

"Lord Haleford," she said as they passed by one of the largest fountains, guarded by a marble statue of a massive angel brandishing a sword, "I must thank you for your kindness over the years to Sir Damien. He informs me 'twas you who rescued him from a life in the metalworking trade and aided him in being accepted into the King's Guard."

He smiled. "Damien is a man of keen intellect and strong principals. I saw his potential early on."

"I beg your indulgence, my lord, but how could you see his potential from here at court? How did you come to be acquainted with him?"

His mouth twisted slightly as he pressed fingers to his temples. "His father was the Constable of the King's Calvary ere he died. I knew him well, along with his mother, a beautiful and gracious lady. Hence, after their deaths, I kept my eye on Damien as he grew."

A group of courtiers passed, dipping their heads in respect toward Lord Haleford as the scent of lavender overwhelmed Seraphina from a large bush streaked with purple flowers up ahead. She drew in a deep breath and tried to relax the tension strung tight across her shoulders.

"How did his father die, if I may be so bold?"

"He hasn't told you? Hmm." Blinking, he once again rubbed his forehead. "A tragic story, that. I can imagine why Damien would wish to forget. Sir Hewe LaRage was a great warrior who had won many battles for the king. So sad that he was struck down by a stray arrow during training."

Confusion tromped through Seraphina's mind. Hadn't Damien said his father had been murdered? "I am sorry to hear it. And his mother?"

"Another tragic tale, I'm afraid, mistress." A strange sorrow on his face, he halted and stared up at the sun, now hanging in a blue sky directly over the gardens. Once again, pain pinched his features and he closed his eyes.

"Are you unwell, my lord?" Seraphina withdrew her hand from his arm and stepped back.

He blinked and glanced down at her. "Headaches. I've had them for years, my dear. Naught to concern you."

"Mayhap I could pray for you as I did the king?"

"Ah, no need. 'Tis but a trifling annoyance and not worthy of disturbing the Almighty."

Turning to the left, they proceeded down a winding stone pathway, lined with flowers of every shape and color—heather, poppies, and yarrow. Seraphina breathed in the sweet fragrances as she glanced over the magnificent scene, so at odds with the grim tale Lord Haleford told.

"Sir Damien tells me his parents were murdered." She knew she was being far too brazen for her station, but she was desperate to know, desperate to understand the man she loved.

His brows shot up. "Indeed. Mayhap indirectly." He took her hand and placed it in the crook of his elbow once again, caressing it with his fingers.

A sour taste rose in Seraphina's throat.

"His mother was ravished."

The words, spoken so dispassionately, caused Seraphina to halt. She closed her eyes, wading through a flood of emotions rising within her. Lord Haleford must have taken this as a sign to further caress her hand. Tugging from him, she stepped away and turned her back. "I can't imagine."

"She was a very pious woman. Some say she died from shame."

Oddly the man's tone bore a hint of emotion. Seraphina faced him. "You must have cared for her."

He shrugged. "I was but eighteen at the time. But aye, I cared for both of Damien's parents. His father, being ten years my senior, taught me many things."

Seraphina nodded. That surely explained his interest in Damien. Mayhap this man did possess a kind heart, after all.

"Alas, let us not talk of such dreary things. I wish to know more about you, mistress." He approached and once again placed her hand on his arm, brushing up against her.

Not wanting to offend him, Seraphina cast a quick glance behind her to ensure Lady Rochford still followed, yet the look the lady gave her was not one of comfort, but rather caution.

William proceeded to inquire into Seraphina's past and preferences in much the same way as Lady Rochford had done. However, with each of her responses came compliments, starting out as vague flatteries about her character, but ending up with rather personal ones about her appearance.

Flushed and heated with embarrassment, Seraphina finally pulled from him and slid onto a stone bench. Surely the man was merely being kind and had no intentions of luring her into his bed? Especially not if he cared so much for Damien? She was being silly.

She was *not* being silly, for he turned and dismissed Lady Rochford with a command that bespoke of no defiance. After casting Seraphina a look of alarm, the lady turned and walked away.

Seraphina attempted to rise and follow her, but Lord Haleford grabbed her arm and kept her in place. His stark blue eyes assessed her as if searching for something. But what? He lifted a finger and stroked her cheek. "You are truly a beauty, Mistress Seraphina."

Heart thumping, Seraphina turned her face away. "My lord, you assume too much." Tugging from him, she rose and lifted her chin.

He stood beside her, gripping her arm once again. "I assure you, men of my position and power *never* assume."

Seraphina attempted to free her arm, but his grip was too tight. "You're hurting me, my lord."

A smile curved one side of his lips as he leaned toward her, his scent of bergamot suffocating. "I have the power to grant your every desire, mistress."

She turned her face away yet again to avoid his kiss, wondering if she should scream. Or would such defiance get her tossed in the dungeon. This man was heir to the throne!

But he didn't kiss her, nor attempt to do so. Instead he dove his head into her neck and buried his nose in her hair.

Alack, Damien's eyes betrayed him. 'Twas the only explanation for the vision before him, William forcing a kiss upon Seraphina. Indeed, the lady appeared alarmed at the man's grip on her arm, struggling to free herself, turning her face away. Yet, just moments before as Damien approached, were the two not smiling at one another?

Damien burst between two shrubs that granted the couple privacy just as William withdrew his face from Seraphina's neck and turned to face the intruder.

"Ah, there you are, Damien." William smiled and released Seraphina, who promptly stepped away and rubbed her arm.

Damien shifted his glance between them. "Judas, do you make a mockery of me, William?"

His smile tightened, his look pointed, and it seemed he would castigate Damien for his lack of respect. But then his countenance changed. "Your lovely lady and I were merely becoming acquainted, Damien." William glanced her way. "She intrigues me. I find her quite charming and intelligent."

"As do I." Damien's eyes met hers and finally a smile graced her lips, a grateful smile.

William lifted his hands and gestured for them both to come close. "You have my approval to court this young lady. She has passed my final test."

Was that it then? Damien released a breath. William was merely testing Seraphina, to see if she would succumb to his flirtations and the promise of wealth and power that came with a man who would be king. From what Damien had seen, she'd rejected his advances.

He smiled. Of course she had. Damien had never met a lady of such integrity, honor, and decency,

"I am pleased to hear it." Damien extended his hand toward Seraphina, glad when she accepted it.

Unfortunately, hers was still trembling, Hence, he gave it a squeeze.

The look in her eyes, one of affection, fear, and hope all jumbled together, made him long to take her in his arms. Made him nearly forget the reason he'd come looking for her.

"I extend to you my sincere apologies, Mistress Seraphina." William smiled her way. "I meant no insult or harm to you, but I can see I frightened you. For that, I hope you'll forgive me."

Though the lady made no response, she nodded her head.

"The king summons us," Damien said. "'Tis why I came looking for you." 'Twas also why he had hurried after a worried-looking Lady Rochford who had gestured to where she'd last seen them.

"Then let us not keep him waiting." William slapped Damien on the shoulder.

"But you are hurt." Seraphina's gaze dropped to where Adred had sliced through Damien's doublet.

"A scratch, mistress. I'll have it attended later."

She frowned.

"Come, come, make haste." William took the lead and gestured for them to follow.

Back in the great throne room, Damien approached King Peter with William on one side and Seraphina on the other.

A hush fell on the room from the various nobles loitering about, soldiers protecting the king, and the peasants who had come to petition his majesty on one matter or another.

Halting, Damien bowed. Seraphina did the same as William mounted the stairs to stand beside the throne.

"You summoned us, Your Majesty," Sir Damien said.

Panora, the king's mystic, slithered from between two guards and stood at the foot of the dais, eyeing Damien and Seraphina with malice.

"Aye," King Peter began. "Panora has given me a most dire prophecy, and I wish to ask Mistress Seraphina what, if anything, she sees on the topic. Ergo, we shall finally determine which one of you hears from God and which one hears from the devil."

CHAPTER FIFTEEN

Once again, Seraphina found herself standing before the king terrified for her life. To make matters worse, the way Panora was looking at her now, she wouldn't be surprised if the woman weren't casting a curse on her. In truth, the bishop wore the same expression from his spot on the first step of the throne dais.

Damien stiffened beside her but made not a move.

"Panora has just informed me," the king began in a loud voice that echoed across the high stone ceilings, "that the Marundes beyond the eastern sea plan to attack our kingdom, that they even now board mighty ships filled with warriors to cross the waters, land on our shores, lay waste to our towns, and murder our people."

The crowd remained quiet. Naught could be heard save the scuffling of feet, the whistle of wind, and a cough. Seraphina dared glance at the queen and found her eyes upon her, sympathy making an appearance within them. Lady Rochford smiled at her from behind the queen.

Regardless, what did Seraphina know of such things, of distant enemy lands and battle plans? Her blood turned to ice.

"What say you, Mistress Seraphina?" The king cocked his head, his expression stern, and she wondered if he remembered that 'twas through her prayer that God had healed him. "Should I assemble my armies to meet these invaders, or are they coming at all?"

Lord, help me. Seraphina closed her eyes, attempting to settle her nerves and her spirit, for she needed to hear from the Almighty. She needed a word, a vision, now more than ever.

She heard Damien shift beside her. Someone snorted in derision. Another cough. Laughter tumbled in from outside.

Then it appeared. A vision, an image of mighty ships at sea tossed to and fro in a violent storm ere sinking beneath the waves. 'Twas but a glimpse, a glimmer, a flash, and then it was gone. *Grant me more, Lord*? she silently pleaded, wanting more proof of what she'd seen. But the heavens were silent. The Spear, however, warmed, and she knew favor would be granted her.

Thus, with her head held high and her eyes open, she addressed the king. "Your Majesty, Panora speaks the truth. The Marundes have indeed filled ships with their best warriors and are this very minute journeying over the sea to invade our land."

Gasps of fear and moans of anger rang from all around them.

Panora smiled.

"However!" Seraphina shouted above the din. "The ships will never reach our shores. They will all sink in a storm, every man aboard perishing in the deep."

The groans transformed into whispering chatter.

Bishop Montruse crossed himself. "Forsooth, the woman speaks only things meant to tickle the king's ears."

More chattering erupted, along with shrieks and groans, growing so loud that the king finally shouted, "Silence!"

Damien cast a look her way, his eyes full of unusual fear for the brave knight.

Panora glared at her but remained where she was.

The queen leaned to say something to the king, but he brushed her away, opting instead to listen to Lord Haleford.

After nodding toward his adviser, King Peter sat back on his throne. "We shall prepare our army nonetheless, and we will send scouts to our shores to determine which one of you speaks the truth."

Seraphina bowed her head, hoping beyond hope that the vision she saw was from God.

Bishop Montruse cornered Damien ere he could leave the throne room with Seraphina. With a look that brooked no argument, he gestured for Damien to follow him to a small enclosure to their left. Damien had not missed the intense look

Panora gave the bishop as she left the room, nor had he missed their many glances during the king's inquisition. Odd.

After ensuring Lady Rochford approached to escort Seraphina, Damien smiled her way. "I shall meet up with you anon."

"But you are wounded." Her glance took in his side where blood stained his doublet.

"I'll have it tended. You have my troth." He gave her a nod of assurance, which did naught to wipe the concern from her sweet face.

"Do you have it?" The bishop spat a string of vile curses when they were away from spying ears, whilst his eyes, sharp as daggers, stabbed Damien.

"Nay." Damien fisted hands at his sides. 'Twas all he could do to stop himself from strangling the man. "As I have told you, I know not whether she has it at all."

The bishop tugged on his pointy beard. "You know as well as I that she does. You also know as well as I that one word from me to the king would either have you and your mistress hanged or set you and all your friends free."

Damien stared at the fiend, wondering if it wouldn't be prudent to simply do away with him here and now. Alack, if Damien weren't already going to hell, certainly murdering a bishop would seal his fate. Besides, how would he dispose of the body? Particularly when he was forbidden to leave the castle grounds. Still the thought must have placed an unbidden smile on his lips for the bishop grew incensed.

"You find this amusing, knight!" He pointed a quavering finger in Damien's face. "My patience grows thin. You have two days to get me the Spear, or I go to the king."

Damien narrowed his eyes. "Mayhap the king's magistrate will return with the truth by then, leaving your threats impotent."

He gave a sordid laugh. "You think me impotent? The magistrate and his soldiers are as good as dead."

Damien ground his teeth. "What dealings do you have with Panora?"

The bishop blinked, then snorted. "With that witch? Naught!" Yet he would not meet Damien's gaze.

"Hmm." Damien studied the man.

"Do you still wish to know who murdered your father? Ravished your mother?" The bishop's lips curved in a maniacal grin, and once again, Damien wondered if it weren't the man himself who had done the deed. He was certainly evil enough to have committed both crimes.

Blazing heat inflamed Damien's gut. "Tell the king your lies, and you will never get your precious relic, *Your Eminence*."

"After your lady hangs, I'll rip it from her dead body."

Damien gripped the man's neck and squeezed. And for the first time, real terror crossed his dark eyes. He coughed and gasped as Damien tightened his hold, fury empowering him to do what every ounce of him longed to do. But he was no murderer, and Seraphina wouldn't approve.

He released the monster.

The man backed away, gripping his throat and gasping for air. "I'll see you hang for that." He called out, and two of his personal guards appeared from around the corner and darted to his side.

"Not if you wish the Spear." Damien spun and marched away, knowing he held the upper hand. At least for now.

"Mistress, 'tis improper for us to be here," Lady Rochford said as Seraphina pushed open the gate leading to the King's Guards' courtyard.

"Never fear. We shan't stay long, my lady. I only wish to see how Sir Damien fares." In truth, she longed to be by his side again, for it seemed only in his presence did she truly feel safe. In the midst of this palace full of intrigue, dark secrets, and smiling people who, she sensed, would stab her in the back unawares, Damien was the only person she trusted. She also *knew* the strong knight, knew he'd most likely not tend his wound as he should.

Those of the King's Guards who were in the bailey stopped to stare at the ladies as they made their way to the building that housed the knights. Some were eating, others playing cards, and still others tossing knives onto a target.

Halting, Seraphina shielded her eyes from the sun and asked one of them if he'd seen Sir Damien.

He gestured toward an open door in the building.

Thanking him, she proceeded through it, blinked as her eyes adjusted to the dim light, and then stood frozen at the sight before her.

Damien, shirtless, sat on a stool whilst another man tended a deep gash on his side.

Muscles as round and hard as boulders billowed over his arms, whilst thick ripples lined his firm stomach.

Heat flooded her, no doubt turning her face into the color of a ripe apple. She averted her gaze. "Ah…oh… oh, forgive me."

Lady Rochford turned and stepped just outside the door.

"For what, mistress?" His voice held amusement.

She faced him again, doing her best to avoid looking at his chest. "For intruding when you are…when you are…."

"Undressed?" he finished with a smile that told her he knew exactly the effect he had on her.

Fire and ashes! Why was she such a dolt? Determined not to play his game, she sauntered into the room, pretending to examine with disinterest its contents, which consisted of a cot, chamber pot, table, lantern, and hooks on the wall. "I am glad to see you are having your wound tended."

"Were those not your orders?" he asked playfully.

"Aye." She gave him a coy smile. "But when have you ever done as I requested?"

He smiled.

The physician finished his ministrations and began packing up his things. "That should heal nicely, Sir Damien." Grabbing his sack, he dipped his head toward Seraphina and left.

Pressing a hand over his side, Damien rose, and Seraphina suddenly felt rather small next to this knight, who stood a foot above her and was as strong as a battering ram. Yet she knew he would never do her harm. Quite the opposite. He'd always be there to protect her. She'd never had a father, never had a brother or relative to stand up for her. 'Twas an odd feeling to be cherished and protected by such a man.

He took a step toward her, his eyes brimming with an intimacy born of spending hours in each other's company, enduring hardships, and facing danger together.

He raised a hand to caress her cheek, the feel of his rough skin so tender on hers. His scent of sweat and spice so unique to him rose to tantalize her senses—that familiar scent that never failed to make her pulse race.

Only this time it seemed devoid of the sting of spirits that usually hovered around him.

She looked up at him, her gaze taking in the strong features of his face, longing for a kiss, longing to be held by those massive arms.

Lady Rochford coughed from the doorway.

Damien stepped back, glanced her way, and slipped on his linen shirt.

It took Seraphina a moment to regain her senses, and she was suddenly grateful for Lady Rochford's interruption.

"Did you speak truth to the king?" Damien asked, putting on his doublet and belts. "Did you see something?"

"I did. I believe it to be from God. Besides, the Spear grants me favor."

He nodded. "I hope you are correct, mistress."

Seraphina approached to adjust the man's baldric, which always seemed to be askew, along with the carelessly fastened ties of his linen shirt.

He laughed. "Should I call you every morn to aid me in dressing?"

Heat swamped her as she realized what she was doing, and she backed away. "Forgive me. I overstep. Alas"—she cocked her head and smiled—"you *could* use some assistance." For someone of the knight's rank, the man oft presented a slovenly appearance.

She changed the subject. "What are you about today, Sir Damien?"

"I have been summoned to William…Lord Haleford's quarters." He glanced out the door and then back to her. "Would you do me the honor of meeting me at sunset by the lake just beneath the clock tower?"

Seraphina couldn't help but smile. "Of course. But why?"

"A surprise. You shall see."

And with that, he slipped on his hat, winked at Lady Rochford, and left.

CHAPTER SIXTEEN

Still furious from his meeting with the bishop and still reeling with desire from his time with Seraphina, Damien attempted to calm the whirlwind of emotions storming through him. He'd never been good at controlling his passions, good or bad. Oh, how he'd wanted to end the bishop's miserable life and oh, how he'd longed to kiss Seraphina! Alas, he'd done neither, and that wasn't like him.

He needed a drink. Several of them, in fact.

Hence, as he made his way to William's chambers, he licked his lips in anticipation, for his patron always encouraged Damien to have his fill of wine.

And indeed that was the case this day.

"'Tis a fine day for hunting," William had said, after they'd had a small repast and several mugs of wine. "I'll gather my dogs and two crossbows, and we'll venture into the forests surrounding Regalis.

Damien, however, was quite enjoying the cushioned chair in William's chamber, along with the endless fountain of wine. "I am not permitted to leave. You know that."

"I have already obtained permission from the king. Come." William rose, and Damien saw there was no arguing with the man. Besides, he could use some time on the hunt. It had been far too long, and there was naught he could do about the bishop or the Spear at the moment.

Not with Lady Rochford constantly at Seraphina's side.

Mayhap the fresh air would clear his mind.

Lady Marion rose from her seat beside them, seemingly unhappy they were leaving her. Yet she said naught, merely smiled, and stepped out of the way, her eyes scouring Damien as he passed, as they'd been doing all morning. The oddest look filled them, but he couldn't place it. Sorrow? Longing? Fear? No matter.

The remainder of the day passed in pleasant activity and good company. The crisp fall weather was the perfect complement to the hot sun above, and it did good for Damien to get out from the confines of the palace.

He and William hunted, laughed, and even stopped to eat berries and nuts, enjoying each other's company and reminiscing about humorous moments they'd shared in the past. They even spoke of Seraphina, and Damien was most pleased to hear William approved of her wholeheartedly, that he'd been testing her loyalty earlier in the garden, as Damien had suspected.

Damien had missed William, and 'twas good to see and hear that he fared well at court, that should the king not have an heir, he took his responsibility to rule with great seriousness and humility. He would make a good king. He had been a good friend, and Damien's hopes were renewed that, if all went well, William could get Damien and his friends reinstated as King's Guards.

After, of course, Damien had his revenge on the man who murdered his parents.

By the time they entered the palace again, the sun was low in the sky. They handed the two pheasants and five rabbits they'd caught to a servant to take to the cook ere they entered William's chamber for a drink.

Lady Marion had changed into a lovely green satin overgown, laced at the sides, with a gold-chained belt and a matching necklace that sparkled over her low neckline. Attempting to keep his gaze from her chest, Damien sat, drank more wine, and, together with William, shared their adventures of the day with the lady. However, when the last vestiges of sunlight slipped out the window, he rose.

"I fear I have an engagement, William. Lady Marion." He dipped his head toward her as he set down his empty cup.

"Very well." William slapped him on the back. "We shall see you at this evening's repast."

Feeling more hopeful than he had in a long while, Damien made his way through the halls of the castle, down two flights of stairs, past servants quarters and storage rooms and out onto the long portico that overlooked the lake.

Footsteps alerted him and, reaching for his sword that was no longer there, he swung around.

Lady Marion darted up to him, out of breath, and gazing at him with pleading eyes that were slightly moist, as if she'd been crying.

"My lady." Damien drew close and took her hands in his. "What has you so distraught? Why did you follow me?"

"Oh, Damien." The woman collapsed against him, her sweet rose scent filling his nose.

Not knowing what to do, Damien gently nudged her back. "Has someone done you harm? If so, let us at once to William and tell him."

She glanced down. "'Twould do no good since 'tis he who has done me harm."

Damien shook his head. "What foolery is this?"

"Damien." She looked up at him. "He does not love me. He has many mistresses. You know this."

'Twas the one thing he disapproved of about his friend, but Damien also knew 'twas the way of powerful men. "Aye, I have heard the rumors, my lady, but surely, if true, these women mean naught to him, for 'tis you he loves."

"Nay. I live a loveless life. He is not the man you know, not the man you think."

"Judas! What devilment is this? William has been naught but kind to me, generous. He saved me. He saved my life."

Lady Marion fell against him again, her soft curves molding against his doublet. "Oh, Damien. I long to be loved." She glanced up at him, lifted her hand to stroke his face. "Love me, Damien. No one has to know."

Shock buzzed through him, followed by disgust. Grabbing her hand, he lowered it and took a step back. "I cannot. You are my good friend's wife."

"In name only, Damien."

"Nay. I could never betray him." He pushed her back, keeping her at arm's length, for he was not immune to her allure. “You are a rare beauty, Lady Marion, but I love another.”

“Humph.” Her countenance changed from one of seductress to snake. “Then go be with your servant girl.”

He needed no further invitation. Spinning around, he started down the long porch.

Her angry voice slapped him on the back. “You will regret this affront, Damien. I will have my way.”

Ignoring her, Damien made his way down a flight of stairs to the beach below, confusion and sorrow attempting to destroy his excitement at seeing Seraphina.

But there she was standing on the shore. Nay, not standing. She took one look at him, whirled about, and marched in the other direction. Movement in the shadows beneath the portico caught his eye, and he glanced that way, only to see the back of a man darting away.

A man in a soldier's uniform.

Seraphina heard Damien call her name, heard his boots clomping in the sand toward her. But she didn’t care. Appointment with Lord Haleford, indeed. More like an assignation with Lady Haleford. For what other conclusion could she reach after what she’d seen up on the portico—warm embraces, gentle caresses, whispered words of affection.

She was a fool. After their near kiss in the King’s Guard quarters, she’d thought he had asked her here for a romantic walk along the shore, mayhap even to request a formal courtship. When in truth, he only wished to add her to his long list of mistresses, for it had not escaped her notice how many noblewomen gazed at him with familiar affection.

Indeed. She was a fool.

“Mistress Seraphina!” He caught up to her, gripped her arm, and turned her around.

Shock rode high on his brow at what must surely be anger on her face.

“Where are you going? Were we not to meet?”

Jerking her arm back, she placed both hands on her hips. "I wouldn't want to interrupt your time with Lady Haleford."

He stared at her for a moment ere his expression began to crumple, and laughter spilled from his lips. "You think I and…" He continued laughing. "You think Lady Haleford and I are lovers?"

Seraphina glared at him, finding no amusement in the situation, but also finding her anger abating a bit. "If not, then surely she is your sister or your mother for all the embraces and kisses I witnessed."

His brows arched above eyes filled with mirth. "Kisses? Embraces, I'll grant you, but kisses? Your eyes deceived you." He grabbed her hands still planted on her hips and drew them close. "The embraces were not my doing. I had no part in it, nor did I encourage them."

Wind coming off the lake whipped around them, stirring his dark hair about his neck, along with the sand at their feet, as the final rays from a setting sun glimmered in his eyes.

Alack, only now did she remember how oft Lady Marion had looked at Damien, though from what she witnessed, he ne'er returned her interest.

The sweet smell of wine wafted around her. "You're drunk."

"Mayhap." He smiled and eased a lock of her hair from her face. "But not enough to receive anyone's advances save yours."

"You flatter yourself! I intend to make no advances, strong knight."

He placed a hand over his chest. "Forsooth, my heart cannot bear it."

"You are pleased to mock me, sir."

"Nay, I am pleased to see you jealous."

"Jealous?" She blew out a sigh and backed from him. "I merely thought you more honorable than to steal your mentor's wi—"

Damien's lips were on hers before she knew it. Warm lips that instantly devoured hers with a passion so overwhelming she could not deny it hailed from more than mere desire. His taste was wine and spice. Her senses reeled as his strong arms encircled her and pressed her close, surrounding her with a safety and warmth she'd never known. All of her anger, all of her jealousy fled as the strong knight ran fingers through her hair and kissed her so deeply, she never wanted him to stop. Heat swept through her, stirring sensations she'd never felt, longings she'd only dreamt of.

The shame! She returned his kiss as if she were no maiden, as if she'd kissed a dozen men before. Yet she could not stop.

He withdrew, brushed fingers over her cheek and planted kisses over her lips and down her neck.

Nay! *Reason, I demand your return!* Seraphina backed away, her chest rising and falling with the same passion as his. He took her hand and raised it to his lips. "Forgive me, I could resist you no longer." His smile was so charming, she thought he must be Sir Jarin and not the serious and sullen Sir Damien.

"Is that proof enough that I have affections for none but you?"

She laughed. "Was that the only purpose of such an impassioned kiss, *rogue*?"

Damien rubbed his eyes. Prove his love? Could the lady not tell how much he cared for her? How deeply his interest and passion ran? "Nay, the kiss was merely something I have longed to do. Alack, I heard no complaints."

A tiny smile appeared on her lips, and he knew he'd been forgiven. He glanced around. "Where is Lady Rochford? Surely were she here, she would not have allowed me such liberties."

"The queen summoned her, and since you were soon to be by my side, I told her I was safe enough until you arrived."

"Then I shall thank the queen for calling her away."

She smiled. "Rogue."

"Without a doubt." His gaze dropped to her lips again, longing for another kiss. But he'd not overstep his bounds, not with this precious lady. Though he could not deny that the intensity of her passion had surprised him, delighted him. Taking her hand, he placed it in the crook of his elbow and started walking.

"What are you going to do about Lady Marion?" she asked.

The sun disappeared behind the mountains of Gladdick, painting the sky with splotches of red and gold that reflected in the wavelets crossing the lake. Such beauty among such wickedness.

"Nothing. She is lonely and unhappy with William, but 'tis not my place to interfere in their marriage. She will most likely find a lover elsewhere."

"Such a shame, so empty a life…and *immoral*."

"I agree, though 'tis often the way at court. Alas, I cannot imagine why she thought I would agree to betray my friend." Or why she impugned her husband's character. Damien had never known the man to be anything but honest. A libertine, aye, but honorable in every other respect.

"I believe, strong knight, that she thought you a worthy prize and therefore worth the risk."

"A worthy prize?" he asked, half joking, wishing he hadn't imbibed so much wine, for he was having trouble gathering his thoughts.

But instead of smiling, she grew serous. "Far too worthy to court a mere servant."

"Forsooth! I am a mere knight, mistress, untitled and devoid of land or wealth."

"You are a member of the elite King's Guard and no mere knight. Besides, your mere knight friends are now espoused to Alexia and Cristiana, baronesses." Withdrawing her hand from his arm, she continued walking. "Lady Marion is exceptionally beautiful, as well as wealthy and of noble blood. Surely there are other eligible ladies of equal station who would suit you. Do you not wish to improve your position?"

Damien halted and stared down at her. Hair the color of virgin snow waved about her in the wind as sapphire eyes searched his. "I do not. Position and power mean naught to me. You should know that by now."

From the way her lips pressed together and the look in her eyes when she glanced toward the lake, he assumed not. But he would prove it to her. Alack, the Spear! Why did he always forget it when in the lady's presence? How he wished the old relic did not stand between them.

"So what was your surprise, Sir Damien? Was it the kiss, or is there another far better gift?"

"Better?" He laughed, enjoying this playful side of her. "I doubt I could improve on your enjoyment with anything else."

She gave him an impish grin and slapped his arm. "You assume too much, Sir Rogue."

Laughing, he turned and gestured to the boat hoisted upon the sand. "I intended a romantic boat ride on the lake. 'Tis so peaceful as the sun sets, but alas, it grows too dark now." He glanced up at the stars poking through the darkening veil.

She looked disappointed. "Another time, mayhap?"

"Indeed." He patted her hand and drew closer to her as they both stared out over the water. Laughter, idle chatter, and the clank of bowls and mugs rode on the wind coming from the great hall where the evening repast was being set. He'd rather skip the meal and spend more time alone with this lady, precious time alone they rarely had.

But as the last sun pulled its last threads of orange, yellow and red over the choppy water, a glorious idea occurred to him.

He knew exactly how he would get the Spear.

CHAPTER SEVENTEEN

Emerald Forest, Northland Goodryke

Cristiana was not one given to discouragement, but Seraphina and Damien had been gone a month now. Without word, it was hard to keep up hope they were still alive. To make matters worse, the darkness had grown so thick over the castle that Alexia said she could no longer see the structure itself. Though Cristiana did not possess her sister's gift of seer, if she concentrated and prayed, she, too, could see the black cloud. Ronar felt it more than saw it, and Jarin agreed. Sir Walter's warlock was growing in power, and that did not bode well for them at all.

Of course they knew God's power would always prevail, but they also knew that their own human weakness—doubts, fears, discouragements—could make it of meager effect. Cristiana had learned that important truth from the many hours sitting at the friar's feet as he taught them from the Holy Scriptures. Ahh, the sweet Word of God, like honey to one's soul! How it had opened her eyes to the Almighty's plan for mankind, to his love and desire to save everyone from the clutches of their enemy. She especially loved the stories of warfare, of the great patriarchs and saints who had prevailed against Satan and his demons. But those same glorious tales also made her wonder whether she was capable of doing the same.

She picked an apple from the tree and added it to her basket. Through the leaves she spotted Alexia doing the same. Ronar and Jarin were nearby harvesting nuts. They'd had to move farther from their underground hideout to find enough food to feed the village since they'd foraged most of the fruit and nut trees nearby. Still, she wondered if they weren't wasting their time.

They'd been unable to enter the village in over a week, ever since Sir Walter had posted soldiers all along the outside wall. Hence, they'd had to leave two deer carcasses, ten rabbits, and a basket full of fruit at the edge of the forest, hoping one of the villagers who ventured forth to tend the fields would find it.

Alack, other animals and birds ate it before they did.

Cristiana sank onto a fallen log and brushed hair from her face. What good were they doing?

A squirrel scrambled across the clearing, nut in his mouth. Halting, it rose on its hind feet and stared at her as if she were some oddity. Above her, birds chattered and chirped as they leapt from branch to branch without a care in the world, whilst farther above them, branches of pine and oak gripped arms, forming a lattice of wood and leaves that shielded them from the sun. She drew a deep breath of the sweet scent of life and earth and herbs, which always helped settle her nerves.

A slight moan rode on the wind. Cristiana looked around, listening. There it was again. Rising, she started in the direction it had come, but halted. She wasn't supposed to go any closer to the king's highway for fear she'd be spotted. Putting fingers to her lips, she gave the whistle Alexia had taught her to use when she needed help. Within minutes, her sister appeared, dressed in her leather breeches and vest, with her bow and arrows flung over her back and her red hair dancing about her. Truly Cristiana would never tire of seeing her warrior sister.

Knife drawn, Alexia looked around ere finally facing Cristiana. "What is it?"

"I hear a moan, but 'tis near the highway. Shall we go check it out together?"

"A moan?"

No sooner had she asked than it sounded again, this time louder. With a nod, her sister took the lead and started for the sound.

The closer they came, the louder and more pathetic the groan became until finally, brushing aside a hedge of tall grass, they came upon a man—or what was left of a man—lying on a mat of blood-soaked dirt and leaves.

What remained of a beautiful silk tunic and gold-embroidered vest revealed torn flesh, raw and festering, and swarming with flies. Cristiana gasped and held a hand to her mouth lest she lose the food in her stomach. Alexia knelt before him. Removing the pouch from her side, she held up his head and attempted to give the poor man a drink.

The water seemed to revive him a bit, and his eyes fluttered open. "Thank ye, kind woman."

Cristiana knelt on his other side, examining his wounds for the best place to start cleaning and bandaging, but there were so many…

"I am Wilfred Cummings, the king's chief magistrate," the man managed to mumble out.

From the elegant attire and the king's emblem on his shoulder, she believed him.

"What happened to you?"

"Wolves." He struggled to breathe. "A pack the likes of which I've ne'er seen before."

"Surely there were soldiers with you to fight them off." Alexia glanced around. "Where are they?"

He shook his head. A tear spilled from the corner of one eye.

Cristiana took his hand in hers. "I will pray for you, sir," she said, but as she glanced over the man's wounds, she realized the Lord would have to raise him from the dead for him to live. "Be healed in the name of our Christ Jesus. I command your wounds to heal."

The man shifted weak eyes her way and smiled. "Bless you, child."

But the wounds remained.

Footsteps brought Alexia to her feet, knife in hand, as she turned in the direction of the sounds.

Ronar and Jarin appeared out of the greenery, both their gazes taking in the situation and then scanning their surroundings.

"The warlock's wolves," was all Alexia said ere she knelt again.

"Who is he?" Jarin asked.

"The king's magistrate, he says."

Ronar stooped beside Alexia. "Will he—" But her frown and a quick shake of her head gave him his answer.

An answer Cristiana had come to herself. The man had mere minutes to live, mayhap less.

Jarin glanced at her, a questioning look in his eyes.

"I already prayed," she said, then looked back at the poor man. Why wouldn't God heal him?

The man's eyes fluttered open again, and he seemed to be trying to focus on his surroundings.

"Dear sir," Ronar said. "What do you know of a knight who calls himself Sir Damien and a maid with hair the color of ivory?"

The man nodded. "They…are kept under guard…at the palace until I return…" he rasped out, trying to catch his breath. "With information the king seeks."

"What information?"

But the man's eyes had closed again.

Cristiana leaned over him. "Do you know the Savior, sir? Do you trust Him for the salvation of your soul?"

"Aye, my lady, I do," he whispered.

She smiled. Thanks be to God.

"What information?" Jarin asked, but the man's breath grew more labored until finally he expelled one last burst of air and was gone.

"Go with God." Cristiana placed his hand down by his side. She did not know why she was so stricken with sorrow over a man she didn't know, but she could not stop the tears from streaming down her cheeks.

After Jarin and Ronar gave the man a proper burial and said a few words over him, Jarin encased Cristiana in his strong arms and allowed her to cry on his shoulder until her tears were spent. He never once questioned the foolishness of those tears, nor did anyone utter a word on the way back to their underground home.

"This warlock's power is too great." Ronar tossed his weapons onto the table with a growl. "Every magistrate the king sends will be killed by his wolves."

"We must have hope, Sir Knight." Alexia hung her bow on a hook on the wall. "That the king sends men to investigate what is happening at Luxley means he seeks the truth of what Damien and Seraphina have told him."

Ronar shook his head. "Aye, but if the warlock keeps killing them, he will never discover that truth."

Jarin helped Cristiana to sit before the fire whilst Friar Josef entered the room from the back chambers. "Cease your loud grumblings. The babe sleeps."

"Thank you for watching her, friar," Cristiana said. Her one bright light in all this madness—Thebe.

"She was no trouble. Now, what has you all in so foul a mood? Unheard of from Knights of the Eternal Realm!" The friar cast an accusing glance over them.

Ronar huffed and rubbed the back of his neck. "The king sent a magistrate to investigate the happenings at Luxley, no doubt upon Sir Damien's request, but we found him dead, most likely devoured by the warlock's wolves."

"Ere he died," Jarin added, "he informed us that both Damien and Seraphina are under arrest."

Alexia warmed her hands by the fire. "We should go to Regalis."

Cristiana looked up at her. "We will be arrested. We can't even go into the village to help the poor. What use are we?"

"And in the meantime"—Ronar moved to stand beside Alexia—"Sir Walter lavishly sits in his—nay, *your* castle," he glanced at Alexia, "enjoying his power whilst his warlock grows stronger."

Friar Josef shook his head. "Did you not defeat the band of wolves that recently attacked you?"

"Aye, but it took all of us together." Jarin sat beside Cristiana.

"And the strange mist in the castle. Did you not defeat it with praise? What of all the times God has protected you?"

Alexia nodded. "Yet each time it takes more and more of God's power flowing within us."

The friar shrugged. "Is God's arm too short that it cannot save? Does His power have an end?"

"Of course not."

"Then why do you doubt? Why do you complain?" The friar gave them a look that said he thought them fools.

Cristiana dropped her head in her hands. "Nothing is going our way. All we ever hear are bad tidings."

"The friar is right," Jarin said, gripping Cristiana's hand. "We must not doubt, no matter how dire things appear. We must believe God will work things out in the end."

"Indeed, my good knight." Friar Josef moved to his desk and picked up the Holy Scriptures. "God has told us how to defeat our enemy. The more powerful the evil, the more we need to fast, pray, and praise in unity. You forget we are warriors in this unseen battle. There can be no doubts, no discouragement, no complaining for a true warrior of Christ."

Alexia uttered an amen, along with Jarin, as Thebe darted into the room and flew into Cristiana's arms. She squeezed the little girl tightly, never wanting to let go. Indeed, they were involved in a fierce battle. Against powerful forces they couldn't even see or touch. Sudden fear coursed through her. How was she going to protect this precious child?

Sir Walter disdained being summoned like a common servant by this depraved monster before him. Yet he supposed 'twas better than having that *depraved monster* ascend into the castle to frighten the maids and servants to their deaths! Not to mention disclose the fact that the rumors were true. That there was indeed a warlock in the castle.

Still, as he entered Drago's lair and saw the supercilious look on the warlock's face, it bristled him to no end. Until the fiend spoke and good news spilled from his lips. For once.

"They weaken!" Drago smiled, if the contorted expression on his face could be described as such.

Sir Walter could only think of one "they" he could be referring to, but he had to make sure. "Who?"

"Those accursed Knights of the Eternal Realm, you bloated buffwart. Who else?"

Sir Walter bit back a retort. "Weaken how?"

Grabbing a handful of simmering coals from the fire, Drago cast them over an iron table. Gray smoke sizzled upward, forming odd shapes as the warlock studied the coals. "Their power. The power that comes from our enemy. It weakens in them."

'Twas good news indeed.

Drago spun and scanned a row of books on a shelf with his long black fingernail, then grabbing a cloth to cover his hand, he pulled down one of the tomes and opened it.

Even from where he stood, Sir Walter could see 'twas a Holy Bible. Odd that Drago would have such a thing—the words of his mortal enemy.

"Doubt! Aha. Doubt!" He faced Sir Walter, his eyes darker than usual. "And complaining. Oh, how our enemy hates that!"

Sir Walter nodded. "They are discouraged. This is good."

"It weakens them, lessens the power of the enemy."

Mayhap this news was worth the trip into this cesspool, after all.

Covering his hand with the cloth, Drago returned the book to the shelf. "'Twould be a good time to go forward with your plan to trap them." One dark brow raised.

Sir Walter was about to agree when the row of bats hanging above them began to move, flapping wings and teetering back and forth. Whatever foul mixture brewed in the iron pot atop the fire began to bubble and emit a stench that only added to the rancid odor of the place.

Drago's widened eyes shot to the door behind Sir Walter.

It opened, and in walked Cedric.

For the briefest of moments, Sir Walter's heart leapt in his chest at the sight of his son. Though they'd never had a good rapport, he'd always loved him in a way, always wanted the best for him. Which was why he'd given him to Drago as his apprentice.

Without even glancing his way, Cedric entered and bowed before Drago.

The last time Sir Walter had seen him, he'd looked pale, haggard, his skin and hair had become dull and lifeless, his eyes empty, devoid of light or the mere hint of kindness. Even his voice had become deep and dark. Drago had said the lad's power was growing and that one day he'd be a mighty warlock.

At the time, Sir Walter had begun to wonder if he'd made the right choice.

Yet now, Cedric looked far better. His skin bore the blush of the sun, his hair had turned light again, and from what Sir Walter could see beneath his black cloak, his slight frame had filled out with muscles.

"Where have you been?" Drago circled the table and stood before Cedric, scanning him as one would a condemned prisoner.

"I did not wish to return to you empty, my master," Cedric responded in a voice much deeper, but which bore hints that reminded Sir Walter of the boy he'd raised. "I continued my search for the Spear."

"You had Lady Cristiana and the Spear in your grasp! I saw it!"

"She and the relic proved to be more powerful." Cedric shrugged, not an ounce of fear on his face.

"Dragon scales!" Drago clutched Cedric's cloak and shook the boy. "I trained you better than that. Another disappointment!" He released him, and Cedric stumbled backward.

Sir Walter reached out to settle him, but he caught his balance and stood, meeting Drago's stare with equal intensity.

Black ink swam in Drago's eyes. "There is something different about you. Tell me what it is."

"I am the same, if only weaker than when I left." Cedric glanced around the putrid dungeon. "I have returned to continue my apprenticeship and gain back my power."

"Humph! We shall see!" Drago spun about, growling. "I should rid myself of you both!"

"And have some God-fearing noble take over the estate?" Did Sir Walter need to remind the beast of that every time? "Continue your work with my son as our bargain states." Sir Walter faced Cedric. "I am glad you are returned to us."

Cedric, however, gave no indication that he heard *or* cared.

"Very well." Drago frowned, then waved a hand at Sir Walter, dismissing him. "Carry on with your plan, Sir Walter. And if you do not fail, we will finally rid ourselves of these Knights of the Eternal Realm!"

CHAPTER EIGHTEEN

"Why does the king wish to see me?" Seraphina inquired of Lady Rochford, who walked beside her as they hurried down the hallway.

"I believe the troops he sent to the coast have returned, mistress."

"Please call me Seraphina, my lady. You are the only person aside from Damien who knows me here. I feel we are friends." Halting, she pressed a hand to her chest as her heart squeezed so tightly she feared it would stop beating.

"Are you ill?" Lady Rochford led her aside as others passed them by.

"Nay, merely nervous." She swallowed and glanced toward the throne room. "What if I was wrong and Panora was correct? Will I be hailed as a witch as the bishop desires and burned at the stake?"

"Now, now, dear." Lady Rochford squeezed her hands. "Look at me."

Seraphina did, and thankfully the lady's soft brown eyes were full of a peace Seraphina rarely felt.

"The king will not pronounce you a witch for one mistake. He is a good king, a just king."

Seraphina allowed herself to breathe. "Of course. You are right."

Turning, they started on their way again. She'd not seen Damien in two days. Odd after their kiss and his declaration of affection. But mayhap he was reconsidering their courtship after she reminded him of her lowly station. Regardless, she had so hoped to spend time with him, for she grew bored passing the hours and days in this place where she didn't belong, where she felt as out of place and vulnerable as a rabbit in a fox's den.

If his interests no longer lay with her, she would be heartbroken, and 'twould take long to recover. But recover she would. She had much to offer a man, a *worthy* man, even if she bore no title or fortune.

Yet *that kiss*. That wonderful, passionate kiss…a kiss she doubted she would ever forget, nor one that could ever be matched. A delight which would have ne'er occurred with the lady beside her present.

"If I may be so bold, why did the queen wish to see you two nights past when I was to meet Sir Damien at the lake?" she asked Lady Rochford merely to pass the time and get her thoughts off her coming audience with the king.

The lady's brow furrowed. "Oddly, 'twoud seem she did not summon me at all, for she knew naught about it. I suppose the servant made a mistake."

Servants rarely made mistakes, especially servants to the queen. However, all such thoughts abandoned Seraphina as she entered the great throne room for the third time, more times than she thought she ever would in a lifetime. And as usual, the mob of nobles and courtiers who always loitered near the king ceased all conversation and watched her as she halted before the throne and bowed.

Lady Rochford moved to stand with the other nobles, and Seraphina's quick glance in that direction revealed Damien stood there as well. He smiled her way and gave her a nod of assurance, which at the moment did naught to steady the mad rush of blood through her veins.

Panora emerged from the crowd to stand beside her, her look one of brewing disdain.

From the dais, the bishop licked his lips, no doubt in anticipation of pronouncing her a witch, whilst the queen smiled her way. The king, however, at Lord Haleford's touch, finally opened his eyes, as if he'd been resting them a moment. His pallor, along with the bluish shadows beneath his eyes, told her his illness had returned. Or mayhap it had truly never left.

Sudden sorrow overcame her fear as he leaned forward and examined her. "I have summoned you both here because my captain has returned with news from the coast."

Seraphina did her best to remain still with her chin high, though she sensed Panora shifting nervously beside her.

"The scouting ship he sent out returned with tales of a mighty armada that sank in a vicious and unusual squall that rose upon the sea."

Terror released its grip on Seraphina's heart, and she breathed out a sigh of relief. Beside her, a low growl emerged from Panora. The bishop's gaze lowered, his jaw tight. The crowd began chattering.

"Hence," the king continued, silencing all, "'twould seem you both were right in a way, though I'll grant Mistress Seraphina the victory." His gaze shifted to Panora. "Whate'er ails you of late, I suggest you get well, or I will be forced to banish you from Regalis. I cannot tolerate false information or lies that could damage this kingdom and its people." He sat back, clearly taxed from the exchange. "However, I am not without mercy, and since you have served me well up to this point, I shall grant you one more chance. You are dismissed."

Panora dipped her head before the king, but the glance she gave Seraphina held naught but fiery daggers. Grabbing her skirts, she spun and stomped away.

Damien smiled at Seraphina and gave her a quick nod

"Mistress Seraphina." The king addressed her once again, drawing her gaze forward. "You have me quite baffled at your ability to see the future, to best Panora, when none other could."

"'Tis from Almighty God. He is the one who tells me these things."

"Blasphemy!" the bishop shouted. "God does not speak to mere servants, but only to holy men of the clergy."

The king silenced him with a lift of his finger. "We shall see from whence you acquire this knowledge when my magistrate returns, mistress, whether from the devil as the bishop declares or from God. If he returns with tales of Lady Alexia and her sister involved with witchcraft, then I will assume you are also a witch. If not…well, we shall see."

Seraphina lowered her gaze, waiting to be dismissed. Thankfully, the king did so immediately, just as the bell rang for the noon meal. Lady Rochford dashed toward her and squeezed her arm. "I told you 'twould be all right."

"Aye, you did, my lady." Seraphina finally allowed herself to smile as Damien approached. "Though now I must pray for a good and *honest* report from the magistrate."

"I will join you in that prayer," Lady Rochford said.

In minutes, nearly all the people had left court, including the king and queen and that horrid man, Bishop Montruse.

Damien extended his arm. "Let us not concern ourselves with it now, for there is naught you can do but pray. May I escort you to the meal?"

Lady Rochford excused herself. "I will join you later, mi—Seraphina. I have an errand for the queen to attend."

"Thank you, my lady." Seraphina watched her leave, then looped her arm through Damien's, delighted to see him. "So, will you join me in prayer as well, strong knight?"

Chuckling, he rubbed the back of his neck. "I shall leave that in your capable hands. Yet surely if God grants you such valuable information to win the favor of the king, He will allow only favorable news to return from Luxley."

"Mayhap, as long as I have the Spear."

"So you still carry it with you where'er you go?"

"How could I not? 'Tis what has kept us alive thus far, what grants us favor with the king."

"Hmm. Mayhap. Though I grant you, I can find no other reason."

"Then you do believe God exists." She teased him as he led her down the hallway.

"How can I not when I see how He works through an angel like you?" His eyes assessed her with affection.

She blushed. "I see you have learned the art of flattery from Sir Jarin."

"That rake?" He chuckled. "Nay. I speak from my heart, Seraphina."

Her name spoken so affectionately on his lips did odd things to her insides as they entered the great hall, already a'bustle with a host of guests moving to find their seats at various tables set in order of rank and title. Servants carrying jugs of wine and ale wove through the crowd, whilst others held stacks of trenchers filled with steaming food.

In the front corner, troubadours began tuning their instruments beside a huge fire crackling in the hearth. Ah, what she wouldn't give for a quiet meal with Sir Damien, but that was not to be, as Lord Haleford stood and gestured for them to join him. Oddly, Lady Marion was not present.

There was something about that man that set her insides churning, something she couldn't understand or name. Hence, as they made their way to him, Seraphina lifted up a prayer for the Lord to show her the man's true nature.

That nature seemed one of kindness and humility when she realized he had abdicated his position at the high table to sit at a table of lesser nobles and knights merely for her sake. Or so he said.

Feeling guilty for her ill thoughts of him, she attempted to enjoy her meal—rabbit pie with eggs and saffron, stewed pheasant, and a minced loin of veal—along with the company surrounding her. The food was delicious, the company dull and annoying, for the people at their table either continually prodded her with questions about how she knew the future, or they spoke of themselves, bragging of their holdings, positions, and wealth. A few of the men brazenly flirted with her, making inappropriate suggestions. She longed to slap them across the cheek, but instead, merely did her best to ignore them. Alternatively, the women, at least most of them, only had eyes for Damien.

Damien saw none of this. He was so deep into his wine she'd thought he'd sink beneath the ruby waves. Alack, she was being selfish. The man was enjoying the company of old friends, not only that of Lord Haleford, but three king's guards, Sir Conrad, Sir Bennett, and Sir Luther, along with a lesser noble and his wife, three young ladies, and two court officials.

Hence, Seraphina took the opportunity to study Lord Haleford, finding him a conundrum she could not solve. Good or evil, he continued to make her insides squirm. Yet he'd done so much for Damien and with no expectation of benefit to himself.

Yet, as she gazed at him and the clamor of the crowd grew distant, a black circle appeared on his silk cote, right atop his heart. The circle grew larger and larger until it encompassed his entire chest. Then, as quickly as it had come, it disappeared, and his silk cote reappeared in all its shimmering vibrancy.

Seraphina checked her mug, but found she'd hardly consumed any wine, even as she wondered why she kept seeing darkness around this man.

The king suddenly stood from his chair at the high table and left the room, waving away people who attempted to assist him, including the queen. From his slow and tentative gait, Damien assumed he was not feeling well. A hush fell over the crowd as everyone stood in respect until he had left. Alack, the king's departure seemed to drain away the joyful festivities of the meal. Even the minstrels halted their song.

Within minutes, people began to leave, including Damien and Seraphina. He led her out of the hall and down one of the long porches overlooking the stables. Blinking, he attempted to clear his vision and his thoughts from the haze of wine. 'Twas so good to see her! He'd purposely avoided her the past two days whilst he kept busy training young knights for Sir Tybalt, captain of the guard. The kiss they'd shared had sealed his heart to hers more than he'd expected…or *wanted*, for he still needed to get the Spear. Hence, he'd spent the time away from her, both to protect his heart and to plan how to best acquire the relic.

Yet now as she walked so close by his side, he found his heart longing even more for her. Halting, he leaned on the railing and glanced down at several young boys brushing down the royal horses whilst others carried pails of oats and hay.

"Would that we could go for a ride, and I could show you the lush landscape surrounding Regalis. The countryside is stunning this time of year."

She smiled. "I would love that, were we not both prisoners here."

Damien gazed up at the blue sky. "If our good fortune continues, I hope that will change soon. Then I can court you properly."

"Court?" Her surprised tone snapped his gaze to hers. "I don't recall that you asked my permission."

The sparkle in her eyes told him she taunted him. "Did you not grant me such two nights ago by the lake?" How lovely she was. The skin on her face and neck glistened in the sun, her braid of alabaster hair waved about her waist, and her eyes were the lightest and most beautiful shade of blue he'd ever seen. She wore a simple turquoise gown with a lace décolletage that matched the fringe on the golden sash about her waist. Her ever-present lilac scent rose to tempt him. He leaned closer.

Her cheeks pinking, she turned her face away. "Speaking of the lake, I believe you still owe me a boat ride, Sir Damien."

"And I shall keep my promise." He squeezed her hand and brought it to his lips for a kiss.

She pulled it away, though an impish smile sparkled from within her eyes. "Mayhap you should do so soon, for I fear we will both be locked up should the magistrate either return with bad news or not return at all."

"There may be another way to gain the king's favor."

"I don't understand."

"We could give him the Spear." There. He'd said it, though he avoided her eyes.

She opened her mouth to protest, but he held up his hand. "Hear me out. He's been searching for it for decades. Surely giving him such a prize would win us our freedom and the freedom of our friends."

"As I have told you, the holy relic, stained with the blood of Christ Himself, is not mine nor ours to give. I could ne'er do such a blasphemous thing."

Judas! Stubborn woman. Her belief in this invisible God would be the death of him. Literally.

The coquettish joy in her eyes dissipated, replaced by fear and suspicion, and he regretted saying anything at all. "Did Lord Haleford put you up to this?"

"Nay. What does he have to do with it?"

She shook her head and stared down at the horses and squires attending them. "I saw something at our noon meal, a darkness. His heart was black, Damien. Blacker than the night."

"You saw?" He chuckled. "Are you saying you have Alexia's gift now?"

"Nay. I don't know. I'm merely telling you what I saw."

"I know you are jealous, but you should not blame him for his wife's actions."

"I am…I do not!" She stamped her foot, icicles firing from her blue eyes.

He was upsetting her, and that's the last thing he wanted. "Forgive me. You must understand the man is a father to me. I can do naught but defend him when he is falsely accused."

"Then I shall take my leave, Sir Damien." And with that, she turned and walked away.

He should run after her. He should beg her forgiveness. But he knew he had no choice now but to break her heart.

CHAPTER NINETEEN

Distraught over her argument with Damien, Seraphina skipped the evening repast and remained in her chambers. Lady Rochford kept her company for a time, and the lady's cheerful chatter and kindness nearly caused Seraphina to disclose what had happened with Damien. Oh, how she longed for a mother during these moments, or even a friend who was familiar with the ways of men. Someone to explain the confusing way their minds worked and instruct Seraphina on how best to approach them, or at least how to approach this particular stubborn knight.

Yet she could disclose neither the Spear nor that she'd seen darkness in Lord Haleford's heart. Hence, she kept these things to herself and merely smiled when Lady Rochford teased her about Sir Damien's affections.

After the lady left and night had fallen, Seraphina's mind refused to quiet and allow her rest. 'Twas not only her argument with Damien, but all the strange happenings at court—the king's returned illness, the immoral philandering of the noblemen, evil Panora, and the fact that her and Damien's fate hung on the word of a magistrate who might never return.

Hence, she rose from her bed, got dressed, and headed out into the night. She had seen a chapel perched beside the outer wall in one of the baileys and hoped to find some privacy there to pray, a holy place to clear her mind of the troubles of this world.

Lifting the hood of her cloak about her head, she kept to the shadows, hoping no one was about at this late hour, though she knew she should not wander out alone. She padded down a flight of stairs to emerge on the ground floor of a long corridor she oft traveled with Lady Rochford. During the day, sunlight streamed through wide windows, shimmered over marble floors, and rose to bring out the vibrant colors of tapestries and paintings lining the walls. Nobles and their ladies dressed in finery strolled up and down, chatting amongst themselves. Now, however, the passageway resembled the tongue of a serpent emerging from a cave to devour her. Silver moonlight slithered in from the windows, creating shifting shadows in dark corners.

Gathering her cloak about her, Seraphina proceeded, the tap of her shoes echoing off the tall ceilings. Mayhap she should return to her chambers. Halting, she turned to look behind her. Ridiculous. She was no child afraid of the dark.

She faced forward. A shadow leapt out before her.

Seraphina screamed. Turning, she started to run when a hand gripped her arm so tightly, her fingers grew numb.

"Not so fast, *mistress*."

That voice. A voice that chilled the very air around them.

Panora.

Facing the witch—for what else could she be?—Seraphina tugged back her arm and rubbed her fingers.

"What do you want?"

The woman huffed and began circling Seraphina, the swish of her long tunic slicing like a whip through the darkness. "I want you gone from the palace."

"No more than I." Seraphina glanced over her shoulder as the woman slunk behind her.

"*Whatever* you are." She came back around to face Seraphina. "Whatever powers you possess, they are naught compared to mine."

Moonlight coated the woman in bluish-silver, transforming her eyes into dark arrows devoid of light

"Then why am I the one who speaks the truth?" Seraphina knew better than to verbally joust with a witch, but the Spear began to heat on her thigh, which must surely mean it would protect her.

The lady cocked her head, studying Seraphina, her lips twisting in disgust as one would when viewing a rodent. "'Tis something about you. A stench"—she wrinkled her nose—"some power that interferes with my own."

"Aye, the sweet fragrance of Christ and the power of God." Seraphina lifted her chin.

"God, bah! He has no authority here." She poked Seraphina with a sharp fingernail. "We killed His Son and sent Him back home. What kind of power is that?"

Fear threatened to choke Seraphina, but she forced it down. "To sacrifice oneself for others is the greatest power of all—love."

Snorting, Panora dove for Seraphina, patting her hands over her chest, her waist, her legs, searching, groping, defiling her with her touch.

"What are you doing?" Seraphina shoved her away, striking the woman's arms, but she kept coming, kept touching places she ought not. "In the name of Jesus, stay away from me!"

Panora leapt back, terror twisting her features. "'Tis you who will stay away from the king. Offer him no more words of wisdom, no more reports of future events." She retreated several more steps as if Seraphina had the plague.

The vision of Panora swinging at the end of a rope flashed in her mind, softening her fear. Thus far, Seraphina's visions had always come true, and despite this woman's hatred for her, she did not wish that fate on anyone.

"Panora, I beg you to quit your association with the powers of darkness. They will lead to your demise in this life and eternal torture in the next. I have seen it."

The woman's eyes grew sharper and more hollow, if possible. "Liar! Traitor! Stay away from me, or I shall use all the powers of hell against you." Spit flew from her mouth ere she grabbed her tunic, spun about, and marched away, leaving an icy draft in her wake.

Hugging herself, Seraphina stared after her. One thing she had learned from Alexia, Cristiana, and the friar was that the powers of darkness were quite real and not things to be trifled with. She would need all the might of the Spear to combat this new threat.

Panora had no trouble finding Sir Adred Dowlinson. The caustic knight oft spent his evenings deep in his cups playing dice with servants in the main stables. 'Twas no easy task to pull him away from his winnings. Only the name Sir Damien coupled with the word *revenge* did the trick.

"What foolery is this, Panora?" His glazed eyes flitted over her face seeking a place to land. "I was winning! This better be worth my while, or you owe me, wench!"

Panora's blood raged. Did this man realize she could cast a spell on him? Make the rest of his miserable life even more miserable? How dare he speak to her thus? She was the king's mystic! Repressing a growl, she flattened her lips. "Do you or do you not want revenge on Sir Damien?"

He huffed, suffocating her in a cloud of sour wine and the veal he'd consumed for dinner. "Of course. But beware, if you send me on another fruitless mission—"

"How was I to know Sir Damien would appear?" She cut him off, furious that her plan at the lake hadn't worked. "I called Lady Rochford away and left the pompous harpy alone. If you had been quick about it…"

Sir Adred growled. "There was no time."

"Now there will be." She smiled.

He cocked his head, swayed slightly, and grabbed a nearby post for support. "Pray tell."

"She's alone now, wandering about the castle. Last I saw, she was heading toward the chapel."

Once she entered the holy place and closed the creaking door behind her, Seraphina leaned back against it and drew a deep breath of the musty, aged air. The scents of old parchment, tallow, wood, and holiness permeated the place as she moved toward the front, where a single candle provided the only light. Paintings colored the walls depicting scenes from the Bible, whilst before her stood an altar covered with white linen upon which rested gilded vessels, candles, books, and a censer.

Shoving back the hood of her cloak, she knelt before the altar and gazed up at the cross of Christ hanging on the wall. There was peace in this place. She could feel it. Such a contrast from the sensations swirling about Panora.

Hence, bowed there in worship, she lifted all her concerns before the Creator of all things, the lover of humanity despite their failings. She prayed for Panora to turn from the darkness, for Damien to see the light, for the protection of her friends at Luxley, for the magistrate to return with good news, for the king's health, for the queen's loveless marriage, for Lord Haleford to quit his philandering and love his wife. She prayed for herself, for strength and faith, to find her purpose in life, to find where she belonged, to find those who would be her family since her own had rejected her.

Those last prayers for herself brought forth tears she hadn't realized were stored up within her, brought forth feelings of loneliness, abandonment, and rejection that had haunted her for as long as she could remember. Feelings she had tried to lock behind doors she never wished to open. Yet here they were, pouring out of her in a small chapel at the royal palace. The last place someone like her should be.

Moments passed as she kept her head bowed, with only the wind whispering past the windows and the sputter of a candle for company. A vision appeared. 'Twas her friends, Alexia, Cristiana and their knights, imprisoned behind iron bars in a dark dungeon. Before she even had time to gasp in horror, the vision transformed into the figure of a man dressed in the finery of the king's court lying in a pool of blood on the ground.

Scuffing sounds jarred her from the vision and brought her to her feet. A man in a brown wool tunic entered from a doorway behind the altar, candle in hand, and a glimmering crucifix around his neck.

Wiping the moisture from her face and attempting to settle her heart, Seraphina took a step back.

The man did the same. "You startled me, my lady."

"Mistress Seraphina. I beg your forgiveness, Father."

"John, call me John, mistress. And 'tis I who should beg your forgiveness for the intrusion on your prayers."

"I was finished." Seraphina glanced behind her, wanting to leave. But something in the man's eyes kept her in place.

He stared at her for several seconds ere he said, "Something bothers you, child."

"Many things bother me, Father."

He gazed up at the crucifix. "In this world we will have trouble. Christ said it himself."

Seraphina gathered her cloak about her. "'Twould seem I have more than my share."

Smiling, he pointed at the cross yet again. "But He has overcome the world."

Candlelight reflected in the man's gentle eyes, bringing her comfort. "Mayhap in the next life, but I have friends in danger and 'twould seem their fate rests in me."

"Ah, you grant our Lord no credit, then?" His tone was playful.

"I have been assigned a task I am unworthy of doing."

He chuckled. "Then I know it hails from the Lord, for He rarely chooses those with the right skills for the job."

She hadn't thought of that before. Odd the Almighty would do such a thing.

"He is with you," the priest added, moving to light a group of candles on the altar.

Aye, she believed that, especially since the Spear was still warm on her thigh. Yet she wondered where God had been when her parents abandoned her. "All I've ever wanted is to belong, to have a family," she blurted out, unsure why she disclosed such a thing to a stranger.

Father John faced her, his expression one of unspeakable joy. "And you think you do not? Sweet Michael. You are

God's child, a member of the biggest family in all of eternity. There is none better, my child."

"Family of God?"

He went about lighting candles. "Aye, mistress. Once we belong to Jesus, we are all brothers and sisters." Stopping, he gave a slanted smile. "Though I admit 'tis ofttimes difficult to find your true siblings, for many false converts have gone out in the world."

She nodded. "I was just threatened by one. Panora."

"That witch!" He waved a hand through the air. "She has no power over a child of God. Ignore her. Use the Lord's name to defang her. Works every time."

Seraphina liked this man. "I am surprised the king listens to a witch."

"The king has been ill for quite some time. I fear he does not think clearly." Setting the first candle back in its holder, he faced her, folding hands over his prominent belly.

Seraphina suddenly felt uncomfortable disclosing so much to this man. "I should go. The hour grows late."

"Remember, child, you are a daughter of the King of Kings, a child of the living God. There is no servant, nor slave, nor nobility in God's kingdom. And he would not assign you a task you could not complete with his help."

What wonderful words. They eased over Seraphina like a sweet balm over a wound. "You remind me of someone." Friar Josef, to be exact.

"A happy resemblance, I hope."

"Indeed. Thank you." Turning, she started for the door.

"Come back any time, child."

Nodding, Seraphina exited the chapel to a blast of chilled air and a mist hovering over the dirt. Hurrying through it, she lifted her hood about her head. She had been overlong at the chapel and 'twas well past midnight. Yet despite the chill, hope returned, along with joy and a strength she'd not felt in quite some time. To believe she was part of a huge family encouraged her, made her believe God was with her, Spear or not, and that He would answer all her prayers. Why wouldn't He, if she were truly His daughter?

Passing through an open gate, she made her way across another large bailey, doused in shadows.

One of the shadows in the corner moved.

Seraphina's heart seized as she continued forward, hoping 'twas merely a horse or other animal.

"I thought you'd never come out of that chapel." The voice was male and unfamiliar. A frame nearly as large as Damien's blocked her path.

"If you please, sir, step aside."

"Adred Dowlinson at your service, mistress. And nay, I do not please. You see, Damien owes me something."

Seraphina dared lift her gaze to his but saw only the outline of a head in the darkness. "What has that to do with me?" She hated the tremble in her voice.

"Naught. You are a mere means to an end…to do him harm."

"Then pray, find him and do it. I have naught to do with him."

"But I disagree. He loves you. I see it in his eyes. And because of that, you are the only way to get my revenge."

Clutching her cloak about her neck, Seraphina backed away, trying to scream, but her voice had abandoned her. The Spear sat cold upon her thigh.

God, where are You?

CHAPTER TWENTY

Damien dropped the coins into the servant girl's hands, one after the other, each *ching* ringing guilt through every fiber of his being. Ten groats, the price of his betrayal.

"Thank you, Sir Damien." The young maid's eyes glittered in delight as she closed her hands over the precious coins and dipped a curtsey.

"Two days then." He glanced down the shadowy corridor, making sure no one was about. "I'll give you the signal."

She nodded, then hurried away. Damien watched her for a few minutes, feeling as low as he had in a long while. What kind of man betrayed the woman he loved? Even if the purpose was for good and not evil, even if it would save their lives, their friends' lives. Yet that wasn't the entire reason, and he knew it.

'Twas for his own selfish revenge.

A brisk wind whisked past one of many open windows lining the corridor, whistling a morbid tune, as moonlight shot silver spears over the stone floor. He'd spent the remainder of the day walking by the lake, alternating between anger at himself for upsetting Seraphina and anger at her for being so stubborn. He must have the Spear, and now she gave him no choice.

Plucking a flask from inside his doublet, he took a long draught, then started on his way. The wine warmed his throat and settled in his belly, where it joined several other gulps he'd imbibed during the day. In truth, he'd been drinking for hours. 'Twas the only way he could get the courage—or numb his heart enough—to betray Seraphina. Alas, now that the task had been initiated, the hard part was completed. The easy part he would do on the morrow.

If, in the meantime, he could somehow beg her forgiveness and return to her good graces.

For now, his bunk, as uncomfortable as it was, beckoned him ere he drank any more and ended up passing out and sleeping with the swine in the pigsty.

Speaking of swine, was that the bishop heading toward him? He could not mistake the flowing black robes and silvery hair, despite how the vision wavered across his wine-hazed eyes. Turning, Damien descended a flight of stairs to his left, hoping to avoid an encounter, especially in his current condition. He couldn't be sure he wouldn't stab the man in that black heart of his without the inhibitions of sobriety.

"Sir Damien."

Too late. Damien halted on the stairs, listening as the man padded down and stopped on the step above him. Of course the bishop would love to speak to Damien from an elevated position, just for effect.

Damien started to take a step up, but found he already towered over the man, even from the lower tread he stood upon. "If you don't mind, bishop, I am most weary and in need of a bed."

The bishop sniffed, then scowled. "Alack, you are in need of more than that. A day or two without drink should suffice, I'd say."

The bishop's face would not remain still, swinging here and there, up and down in Damien's vision. "What do you want, *Your Eminence*?" He gripped the railing ere he fell.

"Humph." The bishop retrieved a handkerchief from within his robes and drew it to his nose, then glanced around, no doubt to ensure they were alone. "Only to inform you that the king's magistrate is dead, along with the knights sent to accompany him."

Ignoring the palpable pain in his gut, Damien attempted to focus on the man's thin lips. "And how would you know such a thing?"

"I have my ways. 'Twould be in your interest not to cross me, Damien, for you see I have much power here at court."

"I see only that you have deceived the king and are an enemy of Enclasen." Damien reached for his long knife, but once again found his baldric empty.

"Be that as it may." The bishop smiled. "It remains that I have once again gained the king's favor, along with his ear, and, hence, enough power to destroy you, your lady, *and* your friends. Ergo, if you wish to know who murdered your parents *and* if you wish to live, you will get me the Spear!" The last phrase exploded in a huff of rage.

Knife or no knife, Damien pondered the ways he could rid himself of this nuisance. But he needed the bishop. Rather, he needed the information the man possessed.

The man must have sensed the immediate threat for his life, for he shrank back, ascending one tread of the stairs.

"You will have your Spear, bishop. Soon. But if you ever threaten me again, I will gut you and dump your body for the wolves to devour."

The man's lips tightened, and if Damien weren't so inebriated, he could swear he saw real terror cross his eyes. But in a swish of black robes, he disappeared.

Judas! If what the bishop said was true and the magistrate was dead, then the bishop was the only one who could save them now. What else could Damien do? What other plan could there be but the one he'd already put into motion? His mind grew cluttered with a myriad thoughts. Nay, he would think of it on the morrow.

Stumbling over the last step, Damien was barely able to right himself as he made his way out the door into the main courtyard.

A shriek, followed by a muffled scream, filtered to his ears. He shook his head. No doubt 'twas the wine which made him hear things, for no woman would be out at this hour.

He stumbled across the bailey, blinking to focus in the darkness, when another muffled scream echoed through the mist. Odd. Attempting to shake off the fog in his head, he hurried toward the sound through an open gate into the next courtyard.

Naught but dust and shadows met his gaze, along with the squawk of a chicken, the wisp of wind, and snort of a horse. He drew a deep breath and halted, waiting, beginning to believe he was hearing things after all.

Movement from a corner by the stables drew his gaze. A yelp sounded, the tiniest yelp, barely perceptible. Damien moved in that direction.

A man lay on top of a woman, his hand pressed tight over her mouth. *Wait.* Hair the color of the moon spilled across the ground.

Rage tore away the drunken veil clouding Damien's world. Grabbing the man by his shirt, he wrenched it *and* the man from Seraphina. Then plucking a knife from the man's belt, Damien hefted it in the air, ready to plunge it in the man's arm, leg, anywhere to inflict pain but not kill him when—

'Twas Adred, his friend, his once good friend, grinning as if he'd won a prize.

Damien stayed his knife and released him. "What devilment is this?"

Adred plucked his sword from the ground where he'd laid it, then swung it out before him. "This is revenge, Damien, sweet, sweet revenge."

Keeping the knife in one hand, Damien tried to focus, his mind reeling from both wine and confusion. "You would ravish my lady? All because you believe me responsible for your present status?"

"I want you to feel pain, deep pain, as I did, abiding pain that ne'er departs." He couldn't make out his friend's face, but his tone was enough to tell Damien the man was out of his mind with hatred.

Glancing over Adred's shoulder, Damien sought out Seraphina, fearing he would find the worst. But she moved, and it appeared she was still clothed. Thank God. "Are you all right, mistress?"

A whimper was his only reply.

"Once I finish with you"—Adred chortled—"I'll finish with her."

"Seraphina," Damien shouted. "Leave now. Run!"

The lady rose just as Adred thrust his blade toward Damien.

Seraphina's legs wobbled like a newborn foal's. Clinging to the side of the stables for support, she could barely believe she'd been rescued. Yet had she been? 'Twas obvious Damien was cupshotten, for he could barely stand without swaying. His words slurred slightly, though they emerged with as much force as usual.

Her assailant, on the other hand, seemed to have sobered up quickly. In addition, he was quite strong, evidenced by the bruises she now felt on her arms where he'd pinned her down. With his body atop hers, she'd been unable to move, unable to breathe, and unable to understand how God could allow this to happen. Especially after she'd started to believe He actually cared for her as a Father would a daughter.

She had prayed, of course, even amidst her terror. She commanded the beast to leave her alone in the name of Christ, but no answer came save his mocking laughter as he began to unlace her overgown and take liberties with his hands. In truth, she'd nearly lost all hope when her champion arrived.

Damien told her to leave, to run. But how could she leave him in his condition? What if he got injured and needed her help?

Hence, she remained in place, gathering her breath, her hope, and what remained of her prayers. Why hadn't the Spear protected her? Even now, it remained cold on her thigh.

Adred lunged his blade toward Damien. She'd watched these two battle before but 'twas when both were sober and she'd seen them from a distance. This time, she was but a few feet from them, in the dark, and Damien had neither a decent weapon nor the full use of his senses.

Dipping out of the path of Adred's blade, he glanced around, found a pile of split logs, grabbed one, and fended off the next attack. Adred's sword split the log, nearly cleaving through Damien as well.

Seraphina shrieked.

Before Adred recovered, Damien thrust his knife toward the man's gut. Adred jumped out of the way just in time and circled Damien, taunting him with jeers and sneers. Pure hatred deformed his face as he swept his blade down once again.

But Damien, anticipating the move, grabbed log after log from the pile, tossing each one at Adred. The man stumbled backward against the onslaught, hacking at the logs. One hit him in the thigh. He groaned.

Damien halted. He wavered on his feet and rubbed his eyes, giving Adred enough time to recover and advance yet again, sword raised high.

Heart near bursting through her chest, Seraphina searched the darkness, found an ax sitting atop a nearby table, and dashed for it. In his drunken state, Damien had not seen it, though it sat in plain sight by the pile of firewood.

She rushed behind him, skirts flailing. He turned to see her just as she grabbed the weapon and hurled it his way.

He caught it and raised it in time to meet Adred's blade. Metal on metal clanged through the courtyard. Moonlight glimmered silver over the blades as the two men thrusted and parried back and forth, sweeping aside the mist hovering over the ground. Horses whinnied, chickens squawked. And Seraphina's heart began to tighten once again.

An ax was no match for a sword. Neither was the knife Damien held in his other hand. Yet he seemed to be holding his own as he staved off Adred's blade with the ax whilst diving at the man with his knife.

Damien struck Adred's leg. The man howled and limped backward, his face mottled in pain and shock ere he rushed in a blind rage at his friend. Damien dipped and rolled over the ground, leaping up behind Adred. But the man was too swift on his feet. He spun around ere Damien could attack.

He swept his sword down on Damien's right. The knight forced it down with his ax, but 'twas not enough to jar it from

Adred's hands. He raised it again, breath heaving and wearing a wicked grin that said he knew he'd eventually win.

Damien would not relent. Growling, he charged his opponent, ax raised in one hand, knife leveled in the other. The battle continued, both knights exhibiting such skill, such bloodthirsty skill, that Seraphina could only stare, wondering if she were having a nightmare, hoping and praying she was.

They separated. Adred whirled his sword in the air. Damien shook his head as if attempting to shake off a fog, the ax drooping slightly in his hand. Adred brought his blade down against it, knocking it from Damien's hand with a mighty clank.

Breath halting in her throat, Seraphina lifted a prayer, longing to feel the Spear heat on her thigh. But it remained like ice.

"So, this will be the end of the great Sir Damien," Adred taunted, twirling his sword about him. "And then I will have your lady."

Damien flung his knife through the air. Seraphina gasped. If he missed, he'd be unarmed. He didn't. The blade thrust into Adred's arm. Shrieking, he dropped his sword. Before he could gather it again, Damien plucked it from the ground and held the tip to Adred's throat. "I should kill you right here."

Adred's breath came hard and fast as he stared at Damien and raised both hands at his sides. "Then do it, my old friend. Put me out of my misery."

Seraphina gripped her throat. Despite the man nearly stealing her maidenhead, she did not wish his death. She tried to tell Damien so, but no words emerged.

Damien's sword wavered in his hand. Wind swirled about them, stirring the mist into a circle on the ground. A cloud moved and silver moonlight showered over the two enemies, one on the brink of murder, the other one, death.

Revenge. To watch it twist the features of his friend's face, to witness the hatred and violence it spawned, Damien began to see it in a different light. Still, he held the blade tight. With one short movement, he could end his friend's life. Punish him for daring to defile Seraphina, keep him from hurting anyone again. The urge to do so overwhelmed Damien. He had killed many men before in the line of duty. 'Twould be of no consequence to do so again.

Alack, this man had been his companion. He waited to see a glimpse of his old friend in Adred's dark, broiling eyes, waited for some reason to spare his life. But the man's hatred had changed him, transformed him into a creature so surrounded by darkness, he had forgotten the light.

Pity swallowed up Damien's rage. He lowered his blade. "Come near her again, and I will kill you."

Adred stared at Damien for a moment, a strange look in his eyes, as if he were sad to be kept among the living. Then without saying a word, he turned and dashed into the night.

Drawing a deep breath, Damien stood there a moment, trying to make sense of it all. A whimper swung him about. He searched the shadows for Seraphina, his fear rising once again that she had been hurt.

She emerged from the shadows, an angel among mortal man. A waterfall of pearly hair tumbled over her shoulders, her eyes misty sapphires, her lips red and bruised from Adred's rough hand, and the front of her gown ripped. But a smile lit her face.

"Damien." She rushed for him and fell into his open arms, and he swallowed her up, drawing her close.

"Shh. 'Tis all right now, my love. You are safe." Yet even as he said the words, he remembered that, if not for her, he'd be dead. If not for her tossing him the ax, Adred would be having his way with her again. Judas! He'd been too besotted to fight, too deep in his cups to defend his ladylove.

She trembled, and he rubbed her back as guilt assailed him. Guilt for a multitude of things, for the pain he nearly caused her. And the pain he *would* cause this lady who held his heart in her tender hands.

He took her face in his palms and gazed at her. "Did he harm you?"

"Nay." She gripped the torn laces of her gown and held them together. "Merely frightened. If you had not…"

"But I did." Though surely 'twas God who directed his steps this way at this precise time. Even in his drunken state. The thought amazed him.

He kept his gentle grip on her face. "What were you doing out alone at this hour?"

"I went to the chapel to pray." Tears spilled down her cheeks, and he wiped them away with his thumbs.

He pressed her head against his chest again. "I'm so sorry, Seraphina. Adred's hatred is my fault."

"No one's hatred is the fault of another," she returned, and he couldn't help but smile at the woman's kindness and wisdom.

Nudging her back, he brushed a strand of hair from her face. "Come. Let me get you back to safety."

"I *am* safe now." Reaching up, she tenderly rubbed the stubble on his jaw. "When I am with you."

This lady, this wonderful lady, made him feel things he'd never felt before. Made him want to give up his quest for revenge, give up everything that mattered, just to protect and love her forever.

He took her hand and kissed it, still feeling the effects of the wine and knowing his self-control was not at its strongest. Wrapping an arm around her, he led her back to her chamber in silence, halting at her door.

"You've been drinking," she said, a smidgen of disapproval in her tone as she adjusted his baldric.

"Aye, to my disgrace." Sighing, he looked down. "Thank you for your help. It pains me that I put you in that position." What a fool he was! "I hated that we argued earlier."

"I as well, strong knight."

"Will you join me on the morrow for a ride upon the lake?"

"Happily." Though he couldn't see the expression in her eyes, her tone bore such joy, it sent a flood of warmth through him.

He swung open the door and arched a brow. "Promise me you'll stay in your chamber?"

"I will." She stood on tiptoes and kissed his cheek. The sentiment overwhelmed him, and he could take it no longer. Lowering his lips to hers, he drew her close.

The kiss was sweet at first, but as passion rose, he drank in more and more of her, encouraged by how she yielded to him, her moans of pleasure, the way she clung to him as if she couldn't live without his touch.

Ah, such joy, such love, such pleasure! Whilst Damien's willpower sat at the bottom of a flask of wine! He kissed her cheeks, her neck, relishing in her moans of ecstasy, the way she sensuously whispered his name.

Nay! He pushed her back, their breaths, heavy with desire, filling the air between them. "You have won my heart, sweet Seraphina."

"My heart has been yours for a long while now, strong knight." She stood to kiss him again, but he placed a finger on her lips.

"I am far too drunk, and you are far too enticing. Now off with you!"

Instead of arguing with him, she smiled, turned, and slipped into her chamber, closing the door behind her.

Damien leaned back on the wall and released a sigh. *I am the worst scoundrel who ever lived.*

CHAPTER TWENTY-ONE

Once again, Seraphina found herself hurrying beside Lady Rochford, summoned to the throne room by the king. With Damien's kiss on her lips and his declaration of love filling her heart, she'd slept the remaining hours of the night more soundly than she had a thousand nights before, despite Adred's terrifying attack and Panora's vile threat. She had God and Damien on her side! What could a witch and a bitter knight do to her?

At least that's what she told herself when Lady Rochford woke her that morning. After all, sunlight flowed in sparkling waves through the window as birds sang a joyful tune outside. A morning breeze stirred her hair and brought in the musty scent of autumn leaves. The happy morning made it almost seem as though the events of the night had never occurred, as though they were but a nightmare. Almost. For she could see—and feel—the bruises on her arms.

"You had a smile on your face," Lady Rochford said as she ordered the maids to lay out Seraphina's clothing and bring in a basin of water.

"When?" Seraphina slid her legs over the side of her bed.

"When you were sleeping. I hated to wake you." Lady Rochford's tone teased.

Seraphina touched her lips, unable to stop yet another smile from forming as she thought of Sir Damien.

She thought of him whilst she washed her face, got dressed, and allowed the maids to braid her hair, something which still took much growing accustomed to. She thought of him now as they traveled down the many hallways and through various chambers on their way to the throne room. She thought of his strength, how he'd protected her, fought for her, even in his wine-induced stupor. She thought of his kiss. And awe! What a kiss it was! It warmed her even now as they moved along, nodding greetings to other court guests and residents in passing.

"You are smiling again," Lady Rochford said with a grin.

"Am I?" Seraphina laughed, feeling heat rising on her cheeks.

"Dare I assume your thoughts are on the handsome Sir Damien?"

"Indeed, my lady. How did you know?"

"I have been around many a courtship, mistress. I am aware of the signs."

Courtship? The formality of the word stole all giddiness from Seraphina. How could she ponder such a thing in light of the danger they found themselves in, in light of the danger her friends endured at this very moment, in light of her mission here? And especially in light of her low station in life. She, a mere servant, declaring her love for a knight who, with the ear of the king, would be better served with a match that would elevate his station.

Lady Rochford must have noticed her change in demeanor, for she stared at her quizzically and seemed about to question her when they arrived at the entrance to the throne room. Easing past people crowding the doorway, Seraphina made her way to stand with the nobles.

Upon seeing the king's expression, she suddenly wished she could hide amongst them. His skin was not only sunken and a deathly gray, but his scowl and pinched eyebrows indicated a current mood that would benefit no one present. Especially Sir Damien, who now stood before him.

"Mistress Seraphina," one of the heralds announced, and all eyes shot to her. Including those of the queen sitting beside her husband, her ladies standing behind her, Lord Haleford, and the bishop, who stood by the king. And of course Damien, who smiled and gave her an encouraging nod.

Swallowing her fear, she moved to stand beside him, faced the king, and dipped her head in a bow.

"My magistrate is dead," the king wasted no time in announcing. "Murdered along with my knights."

Gasps and whimpers of shock and dismay bounded through the crowd. Seraphina clutched her throat in an effort to slow her heaving breath. *Murdered*? Just as she had seen in her vision. The heinous act had to be on Sir Walter's orders. There was no other explanation, though it shocked her he would stoop so low, take such risk as to kill the emissary of the king himself!

The king inched forward on his seat, the effort clearly tasking him. "'Tis not the first men I have sent to Luxley who have not returned. Several suitors I sent over the years for Lady Cristiana never arrived." He coughed for several seconds, then gathered himself. "Something evil lurks at Luxley, and I intend to discover what it is."

"'Tis the witch Alexia and her sister Cristiana!" the bishop shouted, pointing his finger at Seraphina. "You know what they did, what they *truly* are."

Oddly, Damien uttered a growl beside her, his fiery gaze searing the bishop.

Nevertheless, the Spear warmed on Seraphina's thigh, and she knew God was with her and would grant her favor with the king. Hence, she allowed her tongue to speak what her heart shouted. "I know nothing of the sort. Alexia and Cristiana are no more witch than the queen."

The queen's brows rose. The crowd was stunned into silence, a calm before a storm.

"Blasphemy!" the bishop spat and leaned to whisper in the king's ear.

Damien groaned and took a step forward. "Your Majesty, I am sorry to hear of your magistrate, but his murder has naught to do with us or our friends. I believe 'tis Sir Walter LeGode, current steward of Luxley, who has been behind these murders."

The king appeared to be having trouble breathing, hence Lord Haleford stepped forward. "Do you have proof of this?"

"Nay," Seraphina replied. "But we know this man. He is evil and would do anything to keep Luxley in his possession."

Her gaze returned to the king, and she wondered if he'd allow her to pray for him again, mayhap heal him for good this time.

King Peter faced Bishop Montruse. "What say you, bishop? You spent months with Sir Walter. What is your opinion of the man?"

The bishop lifted his chin slightly. "Honorable, Your Majesty. He is an honest, God-fearing man who begrudgingly took over the management of the Luxley estate when Lord and Lady D'Clere died."

Seraphina laughed. 'Twas the only way to avoid shouting.

The bishop's hard gaze snapped to her as he continued. "A man who has taken over the task of running an estate that is not his, merely because of his promise to Lady Grecia D'Clere on her death bed."

Damien squeezed the bridge of his nose. "He lies!"

"Watch your tongue, Sir Damien!" the king said. "He is a bishop in our Lord's church, and you will offer him his due respect."

Damien made no reply, but from the way his jaw tightened and his hands fisted, Seraphina sensed his temper would explode at any moment.

The king folded back into his throne like an old, used parchment. "My magistrate was a decent man. I suffer the loss of him and my knights."

Lord Haleford leaned to whisper in his ear.

The king raised a hand. "I will send thirty of my best soldiers. If such a force does not return, then I must believe witchcraft is at play and the bishop speaks the truth. If so, Sir Damien and Mistress Seraphina will hang. Ergo, if they return with a different tale"—the king narrowed his eyes at the bishop—"then we shall see what we do with you."

The bishop showed no fear. Only smiled and dipped his head.

Seraphina, however, could not control the fear that pinched every nerve. Thirty well-trained soldiers. 'Twas a formidable force, to be sure. Surely Sir Walter and his knights would not be able to kill *all* of them. Yet, 'twas the *warlock,* or whatever evil Sir Walter had aligned himself with, that she feared the most. Would thirty soldiers be enough to defeat such evil? *Wait.* She had the Spear! Alack, since she made no progress here, surely she must go back to help her friends fight.

"Your Majesty, may I travel with your army back to Luxley? There is evil there you cannot imagine, and it does not hail from my friends, but from within Luxley itself."

Sir Damien shot her a look of alarm.

The bishop huffed.

King Peter laughed. "You are a bold one, mistress, I grant you that." He cocked his head. "But since I have yet to determine your innocence or guilt in this matter, nay, you remain here. If you attempt to leave, you will hang. Do you understand me?"

"You have been most clear, Your Majesty." Seraphina bowed her head, longing to be dismissed, longing to leave this place where one word from the king would end her life. But a voice rang from behind her, followed by footsteps, and Panora swept past her in a bright red tunic and a cloud of darkness that chilled the air around them.

After firing a seething glance at her, the witch halted before the throne. "I have seen the future, my king. There is good news and bad news."

The king sighed and flicked fingers toward her. "I will hear the good first,"

"You are to have a child soon, an heir, a daughter." Panora gestured toward the queen with a sweep of her hand and then glanced over the audience with a smile.

For a moment, color returned to the king's face and his eyes brightened. "A daughter?"

"Aye, Your Majesty."

He glanced at the queen and took her hand in his. "There could be no bad news after this." He faced the witch again. "Continue."

"Forgive me, but I have seen your death, Your Majesty. And 'twill be soon, I fear."

The cheers of joy that had filled the room only moments ago transformed into moans of agony. The king released the queen's hand, and though she tried to regain it, he refused her. The bishop remained stoic.

Lord Haleford shouted, "Nay, we reject this prophecy!"

Seraphina closed her eyes. That could not be. Surely the Lord would have shown her such a tragic event. *Lord?* She sought for a word, a vision from God that would prove Panora wrong, that would prove that this good and just king would not die before his time.

And then it appeared, amongst the moans and sobs of the courtiers, amongst the crackle of torches, the whisper of wind, and the desperation, fear, and sorrow in the air. A flash, a scene—there in her mind one second and gone the next.

Clearing her throat, Seraphina dared to step forward beside the witch. "The king will not die but live and declare the works of God!"

Seraphina could feel the sharp stab of Panora's eyes.

The crowd exploded in mutters and mumbles. The king inched forward again, his eyes locked upon her. He raised his hand, and the room fell to silence.

"What have you seen, Mistress Seraphina?"

"I saw a daughter as Panora has said, a grown daughter. I saw you, the queen, and your daughter walking along the shore of the lake, laughing and rejoicing."

"And what did my daughter look like?"

"I do not know. Her face was turned from me. But I knew 'twas your daughter. And that means you will live to see a daughter grow into a lovely young lady."

"Liar!" Panora spat, her lips twisted into a snarl. "She tells the king what he longs to hear, not the truth."

Yet the witch's words were unable to steal the hope from the king's eyes. Even as he sank back in his chair, it remained, though his labored breathing clearly showed he was too taxed to continue.

Lord Haleford immediately dismissed the crowd, and Seraphina was only too happy to leave on the arm of Sir

Damien. Nothing was said as they pressed through the mob leaving the throne room. So much had happened—between them, with the king, Panora, the bishop—that Seraphina assumed Damien's mind was as befuddled as hers.

Hence, she barely noticed Lady Rochford appearing by her side, barely heard her words that sent a tiny spark of alarm through her heart.

"Mistress Seraphina, the queen demands your presence in her chambers at once."

After Lady Rochford escorted Seraphina away, Damien went in search of the bishop. He found him on his way to his elaborate quarters, a young servant girl by his side. "What devilment are you about, bishop?"

The bishop spun, eyed Damien with disdain, and instantly dismissed the girl. "How dare you speak to me in this way!" He moved into a small, circular alcove barely big enough for the two of them, but one that, aside from a narrow window facing the lake, offered them privacy.

Damien knew that one word from the man would have him tossed into the dungeon again—or worse. In return, the bishop knew Damien had something he wanted. "Our bargain did not include your condemning the D'Clere sisters as witches."

The beast stared at Damien, his eyes dull and empty, as if someone had leeched the very soul out of him. "I grow weary of waiting for the Spear," he seethed. "I have but given you a taste of what is to come should you not fulfill your end of the bargain." He waved a hand through the air and huffed. "'Tis too late for Lady Alexia and Cristiana, but I can still put in a word for your friends, Sir Jarin and Sir Ronar. You would like to see them, as well as yourself, reinstated as King's Guards, would you not? And your lady absolved of all charges and suspicions?"

Raising his hand, Damien fully intended to grip the man by the throat and toss him through the window to his death below. Instead, he lowered it, his jaw so tight he could barely speak.

"You will have your precious Spear in two days."

Seraphina knew the minute she entered the queen's private chambers that something was terribly amiss. Anger and frustration hung heavy in the air. Directed toward Seraphina? If so, she knew not why, for she'd seen naught but good things for the queen's future in her vision—the king healthy and hale years from now, and a child! What woman would not be pleased with such news?

Hence, she stood but a few feet from the door, watching the queen pace before the hearth, giving Seraphina a chance to examine the luxurious room. Gold-framed paintings of lords and ladies hung about the walls, along with elaborately woven tapestries of kings and knights. Covering the floor at the center of the room lay a jade silk rug, upon which sat stuffed chairs upholstered in cream-colored fabric. Red velvet draperies framed two narrow windows, whilst gold lattice covered the ceiling from which hung a chandelier. Next to the marble hearth stood shelves lined with books, vases, and gold and silver trinkets.

The opulence made Seraphina feel small and insignificant.

The queen finally halted and stared at Seraphina. "Come in. Sit." Her shimmering violet overgown, fitted with long, wide sleeves, and tightened at her waist with a silver belt, did naught to distract from the exquisite color of her eyes, fawn-brown with golden specs, as well as her auburn hair, a color more stunning than the most beautiful sunset.

No sooner had Seraphina lowered to a chair than the queen spoke in a tone that sent a shiver down her. "How dare you lie to the king and grant him false hope?"

Seraphina swallowed hard, confusion and fear battling for preeminence. "Alack, Your Majesty, I did not lie. 'Tis what I saw, a most glorious vision."

The queen frowned and moved to the hearth, stopping to stare at the coals. "Are you sure 'twas me in the vision?"

"Indeed. I would know your lustrous hair anywhere."

This brought the lady around, wearing a small smile, which did much to lessen Seraphina's fear.

A servant approached with a tray of cheese and a pitcher of drink, and after she set it on the table, the queen ordered her to leave.

Queen Eleanor released a sorrowful sigh. "Alas, the prophecy, or whatever it is you saw, cannot be true."

"I beg your pardon?"

"I am barren." She spun to face Seraphina, sorrow tugging at her eyes.

Seraphina rose, moved to stand beside her, and dared to take her hand in hers. "God can perform a miracle in your womb, Your Majesty."

"Nay!" She snatched her hand away. "You don't understand."

Seraphina's mind swirled in confusion as she searched the woman's face for any sign she was taunting her, but naught but sorrow and shame stained her lovely complexion.

"You had best sit, mistress." She gestured toward a chair. "As should I."

Seraphina complied, and the queen took a seat across from her. The moldy scent of cheese wafted over Seraphina, eliciting a rumble from her stomach. She pressed a hand against it as the queen finally lifted her gaze.

"I told you of the king's first wife and his love for her, and how she died in childbirth."

Seraphina nodded.

"I also told you how 'twas William, Lord Haleford, who arranged my marriage to the king, though not a speck of noble blood runs in my veins."

"Aye," Seraphina said. "In exchange for a position and title for your father."

The queen looked away. "My beauty was the only thing to recommend me, though it fades now with age."

"Nay." Seraphina shook her head, baffled. "You are the most beautiful woman I have ever met."

She smiled. "You are kind, but I am nothing. I should not be queen. I am baseborn and unworthy. And the king knows it as well." Her eyes moistened, and Seraphina moved to kneel before her.

"The circumstances of someone's birth are of no consequence, Your Majesty. 'Tis the measure of one's heart that makes one noble. A kind, loving, and generous heart is of more value than being born into royalty." She squeezed her hands, her own eyes pooling with tears as she realized she had much in common with this lady, for she had felt unworthy since the day she'd been born. "God cares not for pedigree and rank."

A tear slipped down the queen's cheek, and she withdrew her hand to wipe it. "Would that man felt the same way as the Almighty."

"Who cares what men think?" Seraphina stood, her anger rising. This lady before her was nobler and kinder than most highborn people she'd met. "You are queen of Enclasen now, Your Majesty. Leave the past where it belongs."

"You are most kind, Mistress Seraphina. I have liked you from the moment we first met." She swiped at her remaining tears, then gathered herself and gestured for Seraphina to sit once again. "Alack, I never told you how Lord Haleford benefited from my marriage."

Seraphina waited, her heart breaking for this sorrowful lady.

"He asked only one thing of me. Just one thing." She looked distant and sad. "It seemed a simple request at the time, and of course, my father demanded I comply."

Seraphina waited.

"I was to drink a potion William gave me that would make me barren."

The strange words hung in the air for several seconds, swirling in the wind coming in through the window and transforming the birdsong into a morbid tune. "I don't understand. Why would Lord Haleford not want an heir to the throne? Wasn't that the reason he arranged the marriage in the first place?"

The queen merely stared at Seraphina, as if she knew the answer would surface without a word.

And it did. If there was no heir to the throne when the king died, Lord Haleford would be king.

CHAPTER TWENTY-TWO

William Huntley, Lord Haleford, grew more and more anxious every moment Mistress Seraphina spent in the queen's quarters. What could they possibly be talking about? Surely the queen was not foolish enough to divulge the details of their arrangement. *Ignorant plebeian*!

He gripped the porch railing and gazed down upon the courtyard where the royal vegetable and herb gardens were being tended by servants. The scent of heather, yarrow, and honeysuckle wafted beneath his nose as he squinted into the sun, now a hand's breath above the horizon. Blast it all! He pounded the railing and took up a pace, the gold braid of his doublet shimmering in the sunlight.

There was something strange about Mistress Seraphina, something disturbing he could not put his finger on. Something dangerous. Gads! She was a mere servant, a peasant, a person to whom he normally would not grant a moment of his time. Yet she held herself with dignity, spoke with authority, and now appeared to have the ear of both king *and* queen.

Why they listened to her, sought audiences with her, he could not imagine. Surely 'twas only to determine her guilt.

Ridiculous prophecies! They could not come to pass. They *would* not. But what was her purpose in saying them? What was her true purpose here? Was it only to free her friends, as she said, or did she have a more nefarious goal? Was she a conniving charlatan or merely an innocent imbecile? By God's bones! He must find out!

He would question her again. Thus far, she had answered most of his inquiries, but he must continue, wear her out, frustrate her. Surely she would slip and divulge the truth eventually. Those of low birth always did.

But was she of low birth? William rubbed his temples where one of his headaches threatened to unleash hell upon him. Not now! Not now! He ground his teeth just as the sound of footsteps alerted him to someone coming.

Mistress Seraphina appeared in the corridor, coming his way, as he knew she would from the queen's quarters.

She spotted him, slowed, glanced about her as if seeking another route, but then, upon finding none, proceeded, head held high.

Held high! In *his* presence! First minister to the king! Growling inwardly, he smiled her way. He would put her in her place.

"Mistress Seraphina, how fares the queen?"

She barely glanced his way, stopped, and dipped her head before him. "She is well, my lord."

"What was it she wished to discuss with you?"

She lifted her gaze to his, her blue eyes stark and bright in the sunlight, the look in them one of purity and confidence. Yet, much to his delight, a hint of fear peeked from behind the dauntless veil. "I suggest you ask her yourself, my lord."

Impertinent wench! He gave a tight smile. "I will do that, mistress. However, if you will indulge my curiosity, how is it you claim to know the future?"

She gazed over the courtyard below. "God shows me things. He has since I was young."

Something had changed. Where she'd been kind and accommodating to him before, now her disdain for him was evident. He fisted his hands to keep from wringing the impudent woman's neck. "May I escort you to your chambers?"

"No need, my lord. If you'll excuse me." Turning she started on her way before he dismissed her.

William watched her, the way her ivory braid glistening in the sunlight as it wavered over her blue gown, the lift of her chin, the regal way she walked as if she were someone of import.

Bah! The woman was a threat to all his plans. A threat to the kingdom. He felt it deep within his bones. Though he knew not why. Not yet. Whether spy, traitor, or far worse, as he now began to suspect, he knew one thing for sure.

He must eliminate Seraphina de Mowbray.

Seraphina turned the corner, halted, and leaned against the wall to calm herself. Heart racing, she drew deep breaths and closed her eyes, listening to the sounds of the castle around her—distant chatter and laughter, servants bustling about, the thrum of a harp, the neighs of horses and clank of blades in the baileys below where knights practiced their arts of war. She did not hear the sound she feared, Lord Haleford's footsteps following her.

She had felt his gaze stab her back all the way down the long hallway, could feel the prick of his hateful stare deep into her soul. The man was pure evil. She could see that now. She'd seen the darkness around him before, had doubted it in light of Damien's admiration of the man, but now it had appeared in its full vile form, a cloud of black chains circling him, locking him in a prison of his own greed and hate. She had thought only Alexia saw such things, but now she realized the terror of possessing such vision, the burden of seeing a person's true nature.

She started on her way again. 'Twas his eyes she found the most disturbing—swirling pools of lust, greed, and an emptiness, a lack of life that frightened her. She must tell Damien. But would he believe her? Not unless she could divulge the queen's story, which she had promised she would never do.

Opening her chamber door, she found Lady Rochford standing by the wardrobe, smiling in her direction with a look on her face of a naughty child caught in some mischievous act.

"Lady Rochford, what brings you to my chamber?" For surely the lady had other duties to attend.

"I knew you'd return here after your audience with the queen, and I wanted to see if I might escort you anywhere today?"

Closing the door, Seraphina approached her, confused as always with the attention the lady gave her. "Why are you so kind to me, my lady? You treat me as though I am the noblewoman and you are the servant. 'Tis most unusual, and I must say I am not accustomed to it. I should be the one serving you, not the other way around." Yet, surely 'twas only the Spear that brought such favor.

The lady shrugged and walked to gaze out the window. "I do the queen's bidding. That is all."

"Yet I sense 'tis more than that." Still unnerved by both the queen's story and her meeting with Lord Haleford, Seraphina sank into one of the chairs before the brazier. "You are truly the humblest noblewoman I have met."

Lady Rochford whirled about, a smile on her face. "I have much to be grateful for. The Lord has blessed me. Why should I not be kind to others, no matter their station?"

"If I may be so bold, my lady, how did you come to be one of the queen's ladies? Where is your husband?"

Lady Rochford clasped her hands before her and glanced toward the window, a sudden sorrow draining all joy from her expression. "I have no husband now, though I was married once. Cassius Stewart, Lord Rochford, was an honorable, good man." She paused, and the hint of a smile graced her lips. It vanished as quickly as it had appeared. "He died just a few years into our marriage. 'Twas an accident, a fire that overtook our stables."

"I'm so sorry, my lady." Seraphina started to rise, hoping to offer comfort to the lady, but she waved her back down.

"'Twas many years ago." She faced Seraphina with a shrug. "After the king's first wife died, I and her other ladies were dismissed from court and I returned to my husband's estate."

"Then how did you end up serving the new queen?"

"She heard of my husband's death and the condition of our estate, small as it was. He was a good man, but a horrible lord." She smiled. "Our lands were in poor condition, our tenants starving, and I was left to manage things. Hence, when the queen offered to put one of her stewards in charge of my holdings and return me to court, I was thrilled." She drew a deep sigh and pressed down the folds of her lavender tunic. "She saved me, really. Gave me purpose, provided me with all the comforts of a courtly life. In addition, she has been my friend. I owe her much."

"Now I understand your devotion to her." What a lovely lady. Seraphina had known only two other noblewomen so humble and kind—Alexia and Cristiana. "You are my sole friend here at the castle, my lady. The only person I feel I can trust."

The lady cocked her head. "Not even Sir Damien?"

Seraphina smiled. "I suppose I *do* trust him."

Lady Rochford approached and took a seat beside her. "You are right not to trust many here. 'Tis surely a palace of intrigue. But you seem unusually unsettled." She reached for her hand. "Was it something the queen said?"

"Aye, but also"—Seraphina looked at the lady, wondering how much she should disclose— "I met Lord Haleford on my way here."

"Ahh, I see. He does have a way about him that is alarming."

At this, Seraphina laughed. "I am astonished you would admit such a thing."

"Are you now?" She smiled. "I have eyes to see and ears to hear. And I would not trust Lord Haleford if he were the king himself."

Odd that she would make such a reference. Seraphina stared at her quizzically. "But Damien does. He owes him much, considers him like a father."

Lady Rochford nodded. "Aye, he has done much for Damien, though I wonder his reasons."

"What do you mean?"

"Only that there are motives aside from kindness." She lowered her gaze. "But I have said too much."

"Ah, to know the secrets of this place as you do." Then mayhap Seraphina could make sense of it all.

"I fear you would ne'er sleep again, should I tell you." A playful sparkle lit Lady Rochford's eyes.

"I hardly sleep now." She studied the lady, still comely though lines appeared at the edges of her eyes when she smiled and curved around her lips. She must be nearing forty years of age. "You were in the castle when the king's first wife died?"

Rising, she walked to the window. "I was."

"What was she like?"

"Lady Ascilia, countess of Naville." She smiled fondly as she gazed outside. A breeze wafted in and stirred a tendril of her hair. "She was kind, wise, beautiful. The king loved her very much."

Seraphina drew her braid over her shoulder. "Her death was such a tragedy. And the death of the child."

Lady Rochford made no response.

"Were you there when she died?"

"I was…nearby." Her voice caught, as if the event still caused her pain. "As I said, I was one of her ladies-in-waiting. 'Twas the worst day of my life. I loved her very much. We all did. She was the kind of lady everyone adored."

"The king loved her as well, I hear."

Nodding, she faced Seraphina. "But enough of such sad talk. What do you wish to do today?"

"I am to meet Sir Damien for a boat ride on the lake, though in truth, I fear I won't be good company." She sighed. "As you heard, we are to be hanged if the next contingent of king's men do not return."

"That is far off." Lady Rochford approached. "Much can happen in the meantime. You must have faith. God has protected you thus far."

"You are right." Smiling, Seraphina rose.

Lady Rochford extended her hand. "Why not enjoy the day? When you are ready, I will escort you to your knight."

CHAPTER TWENTY-THREE

Luxley Village, Northland Goodryke

Jarin the Just hobbled up to the gate of Luxley village, heavy sack of fruits and nuts slung over his shoulder. If Alexia had done her job of disguising him as a disfigured old man, the guards should pay him no mind. That same disguise had worked well enough when he'd sneaked into the castle months ago right into Sir Walter's study, where he'd been able to glean vital information from Sir Walter and the bishop's conversation.

Now his only hope was to make it into the village where he'd hand over these meager supplies to the vicar. 'Twas barely enough to feed a family for a week, but it came with the friar's blessing and instructions that if the people prayed over it and gave thanks, God would multiply it, as he'd done so oft for others in the Holy Scriptures. A year ago, Jarin would have laughed at such a ludicrous notion, but his faith had grown, and he'd witnessed too many miracles to doubt now.

"State your business, old man!" One of the soldiers leveled a spear across his path.

Jarin adjusted his staff and bent lower beneath the hump Alexia had formed under his ragged robe. "Just hopin' to sell some trinkets, sir, to buy some food."

The soldier laughed and glanced at his friend, who joined in his mirth. "You won't find much food here." Taking his spear, he poked the sack flung over Jarin's shoulder and struck one of the pewter plates Alexia had surrounded the food with. Satisfied that Jarin posed no threat and was not one of the knights they sought, he waved him on.

Smiling, Jarin hobbled down the muddy street and made his way to the chapel. The vicar was most pleased to see him and receive the food, along with the instructions.

"We shall trust the Lord for our food, Sir Jarin. Thank you. Oh—"

Jarin had turned to leave but spun back to face the man.

"There is bad news, I fear." The vicar glanced toward the castle. "The servant, Anabelle. She is a friend of yours?"

Jarin nodded, his heart tightening at the man's next words.

"She has been arrested on charges of consorting with witches and is to be hanged on the morrow."

Jarin couldn't get back to their underground haven fast enough. He stopped only once at a creek within the woods to remove the hump and wash the clay from his face and hair. Now, as he entered the tunnels behind the waterfall, made his way to their home, and gave the secret knock, he wondered whether he should say anything at all.

Ronar answered the door with a smile. "Success?"

"Aye." Jarin marched in, and ere he could say anything, Thebe ran for him, arms outstretched. "Jarn! Jarn!" Kneeling, he swept the girl into his arms, kissed her cheeks, and relished in the feel of her tiny body against his.

Cristiana smiled his way from her seat on one of the couches, whilst Alexia looked up from the desk where she read a book.

"They have Anabelle." He carried Thebe and set her down on the floor beside her doll and a wooden horse Ronar had carved for her.

Alexia rose. Cristiana shook her head.

"What do you mean?" Ronar asked.

"They are to"—he glanced at Thebe to make sure she was occupied, then lowered his voice— "hang her in the morning."

"They know." Moaning, Alexia closed her book and walked toward him. "They know she helped us. We must rescue her." Her anxious eyes shifted between Jarin and Ronar.

"'Tis a trap." Jarin said the one thing he'd been thinking all the way home.

Ronar nodded. "I agree."

Cristiana stood and joined them. “Then what are we to do? How can we possibly save her?”

Friar Josef entered from the back room. “We are to pray and then trust God’s deliverance.”

Placing a hand over her chest, Cristiana glanced at Thebe and then at Jarin. “How can we rescue her when every inch of the village and the castle is guarded day and night?”

The friar took her other hand in his. “You must not doubt, child. With God all things are possible.”

“He’s right,” Alexia said. “Have we not seen greater things than this?” She faced Ronar. “Remember when you rescued me when I was about to be burned at the stake?”

Ronar frowned. “’Twas under much less dire circumstances.”

“For you, mayhap.” Alexia chuckled. “I was the one who could feel the flames licking my feet.”

“Circumstances, bah!” The friar gripped the cross that always hung around his neck. “God takes no note of circumstances.”

“I agree.” Jarin crossed arms over his chest. “Ronar, my friend, where is your faith?” Jarin had always envied Ronar’s belief in a good and powerful God. Why did the man falter now? More importantly, why did Jarin, who was but a babe in Christ, feel such confidence in the Almighty?

Ronar ran a hand through his hair. “My faith still lives, though I sense it has been bludgeoned a bit.”

“Mine as well.” Lowering back to the couch, Cristiana hugged herself. “’Twould seem God may have other plans, for we’ve had so little success of late. And now we have no idea whether Damien or Seraphina are even alive.”

“Dear sister.” Sitting beside her, Alexia swung an arm around her and drew her near. “’Tis always darkest before the dawn. Have you not been reading the Holy Scriptures? Many of those who came before us suffered great losses, endured many trials, but were victorious in the end.”

“’Tis that suffering I fear most.” She looked once again at Thebe. “Especially for those I love.”

Jarin could well understand the sentiment, for he must remember they had a precious child to look after. Yet did that mean they never took any risks? Never ran into danger for the sake of good? Especially when on a mission from God. He could not believe that.

"I am sorry to be so weak." Cristiana swiped a tear away, shifting her glance from Alexia to Ronar. "It brings me shame."

Ronar shook his head and huffed. "To me as well. I've seen too much to doubt now, even if the situation seems impossible."

Friar Josef smiled and gestured for all of them to stand and draw near. "Even the greatest saints falter sometimes. Remember Elijah, who thwarted four hundred and fifty prophets of Baal by calling down fire from heaven but then ran off to hide from Queen Jezebel? We who are strong will hold you up."

Nodding, Jarin helped Cristiana to her feet as Alexia and Ronar moved closer.

"We must pray," the friar said in his usual calm tone. "We pray, we plan, and then we fight!"

That night, with their prayers lifted up to heaven and their plan firmly in their minds, Alexia, led her friends and fellow Knights of the Eternal Realm through the forest she knew so well, around the right side of the castle to a tunnel entrance several yards from the walls. Disguised in their usual servant attire, they had a simple plan. Sneak into the castle and then hide until the guards came to get Anabelle from the dungeon to escort her outside to the noose.

Sir Walter would expect them to attack when Anabelle was outside about to be hanged. Hence 'twas there he would position most of his troops, in hiding, no doubt. But he would not expect them to be so bold as to rescue the woman *inside* the castle, where close quarters would prohibit there being more than a few soldiers by her side. At least that was what they hoped—the plan they believed came from God and the one upon which the friar had placed his approval.

"God will be with you," he said with his usual assurance, and Alexia had kissed his cheek as was her custom. The holy man had been the only father she'd known, and the bond between them would span into eternity.

"Watch after Thebe, dear friar," Cristiana had said as Jarin gave the little girl one last hug and promised her they would return anon.

"Never fear." The friar smiled. "There are warrior angels surrounding this place. Can you not see them?"

Cristiana had glanced around, but then shook her head with a frown. But Alexia could see them, and she nodded in affirmation.

Brushing aside a leafy branch, she plodded onward, her shoes crunching over a carpet of fall leaves. Above them, a half-moon sprinkled silver dust over branches made bare from brisk autumn winds. Those winds now whistled around her, squeezing a chill beneath her tunic. She drew her cloak tighter and glanced behind her where Ronar, Cristiana, and Jarin followed. Facing forward again, she lifted up a prayer and then sought the Spirit within. Instantly, beings of light appeared, each bearing a shield and sword—two columns of massive warriors, one on their right and one on their left. She smiled at the one who strode beside her, but his gaze remained steadfast before him.

She wanted to tell her friends what she saw, especially Ronar and Cristiana, both of whom had been plagued with doubts of late, but she knew it would do no good unless their eyes were opened. If only people could see into the spirit realm as she did. If only people could see the angels God placed around His people, there would be no need to fear anything. Or anyone. Yet, didn't the Scripture plainly say that God always provided angelic protection for His children? 'Twas then a matter of faith and not of sight. Surely those who believed without seeing would be rewarded far more than she.

With these thoughts in mind, she halted before the tunnel entrance and waited whilst Ronar and Jarin moved aside the leaves and branches and lifted the heavy iron grate.

Then one by one they all descended into the darkness.

"They are here! Wake up, you blithering oaf!"

Sir Walter must be having a nightmare, for he was hearing the warlock's voice, that scratchy buzz that always made Sir Walter squirm.

"Get up, you lazy dizzard!" Hands as cold as ice grabbed Sir Walter's arm and shook him.

He sat up with a jerk and glanced over his dark chamber.

Drago's slit-like eyes simmered like hot coals in his vision.

Shrieking, he leapt back. "What are you doing in my bedchamber?" The warlock never left his dungeon, a fact of which Sir Walter had always been exceedingly grateful.

"I had no way to summon you." One side of the vile man's lips lifted in a churlish sneer.

"What is it, then?" Shaking off his sleepy haze, Sir Walter flipped off his quilt and swung his legs over the side of the bed.

"The Knights of the Eternal Realm. They are here!"

"In the castle?" Sir Walter could hardly believe it.

"Of course, you incompetent ninny! Why else would I leave the protection of my lair?" Drago's eyes widened as he glanced toward the door. Was that fear shrieking within them? Nay. No doubt the darkness was playing tricks on Sir Walter's hazy vision.

"They are weak!" The warlock's maniacal chuckle bounced off the high ceiling. "They doubt our enemy. This is good, *very* good." He swung his gaze back to Sir Walter, his long braid of gray hair swinging over his chest like a pendulum. "Capture them. What are you waiting for? 'Tis the perfect time."

Then, with a flap of white robe and a puff of gray smoke, the fiend disappeared. Sir Walter flung a hand to his nose at the stench he left behind. Rising, he donned a tunic, belt, and shoes and charged out of his chamber to find the guards.

Cristiana knelt in the small alcove beside Jarin. Across the stone corridor, Alexia and Ronar hid behind a wall, swords at the ready. Rushlight flickered over Jarin's blade, tight in his hand. With his other, he gripped hers and squeezed it in an effort to settle her nerves. He must have noticed the tremble that coursed through her, the tremble she seemed unable to stop. What was wrong with her? She'd had such faith on her journey to Luxley. Many a time she and Jarin had faced far more formidable odds than these. Of course, she'd had the Spear then, but she knew now that the relic had no power on its own, that 'twas the Spirit of God inside her that gave her the power to heal and protect. Then why was she shaking like a squire going into his first battle?

Why was she even here? She was no warrior like the rest of them. The friar had said they needed her faith. He'd said that physical fighting was but a small part of a true warrior's skills. Faith and love and hope and the power of prayer were much more powerful. Yet she seemed to be failing on all four of those at the moment.

Nothing is going right. Seraphina and Damien are dead.

There was that horrifying whisper that constantly invaded her thoughts these past weeks.

God has abandoned you. The warlock's power is too great.

Nay! Releasing Jarin's hand, she rubbed her temples where her pulse pounded like a drumbeat in her head.

Muffled voices drifted from the main castle above. No doubt servants who rose at dawn to prepare the morning meal. 'Twas almost time then.

Thebe. What of Thebe? Oh, how she had grown to love that child! As if she were her very own. But what kind of mother plunged her child into such a dangerous situation? What kind of mother risked her own life, possibly making the girl an orphan again? Thebe had lost her mother and father once. 'Twould be too much pain for her to endure a second time.

At the thought of the precious girl, fear reached sharp claws around Cristiana's heart and squeezed until she could barely breathe.

Jarin placed a finger beneath her chin and turned her to face him, confusion in his eyes. "Are you ill?" he whispered.

Aye, in more ways than one. She smiled and shook her head. Pray. She must pray.

But there was no time. Footsteps and the clank of chains rang over the stone walls. Jarin had picked this spot—the perfect spot he had said—for he had once been brought forth from the dungeon at dawn to be hanged just as Anabelle was now, and he'd examined every inch of the path the soldiers had taken. This particular spot was not only the narrowest, but it had places to hide and was still deep enough within the castle so as to limit the number of guards assigned to escort the condemned.

Across the way, Ronar peeked around the corner, then lifted two fingers toward Jarin. Two soldiers, apparently. No match for them at all.

Cristiana's breathing began to settle. *Lord, help us to save Anabelle without loss of life and return home safely.*

The footsteps grew louder. Almost there. Ronar nodded at Jarin, and together they stepped into the passageway, blades hefted before them.

"Give us the girl and you will live," Jarin said.

Alexia, still positioned behind the wall, gave Cristiana a smile of comfort.

The soldiers chuckled. *Chuckled*? "By whose authority?"

"By the authority of God Almighty," Ronar answered.

Again they chuckled. Rising, Cristiana stepped out behind Jarin. In the dim rushlight she saw Anabelle, her feet and hands chained, her face a mask of terror, and her arms clutched by two armed knights who smirked as if they knew a grand secret, as if they bore no fear for their lives at all.

"Well, well, what do we have here?" Sir Walter's squeaky voice sent a shiver down Cristiana's spine. The chime of blades being drawn, along with the rumble of many footsteps, sounded behind them. "The infamous Knights of the Eternal Realm."

Cristiana couldn't move. Ronar's jaw flinched, but he remained looking forward. Jarin spun around, gave her a fearful look, then faced their nemesis. Cristiana did the same. Alexia attempted to slink back into the shadows.

"Ah, ah, ah, little falcon. You have nowhere to fly today." Sir Walter gestured to one of his soldiers, and the man was on Alexia within seconds, dragging her to join them. She kicked him and tugged from his grip, but the man drew a knife and pointed it at her neck.

Spinning, Ronar leveled his sword at the man. "Release her, or this ground will soak up your blood."

Anabelle began to sob.

Sir Walter stepped closer beneath the rushlight. The lines on his face appeared deeper than the last time she'd seen him, whilst pale skin hung about his jaw. Cristiana wondered at how quickly he had aged. Behind him, at least twenty knights crowded the pathway. "There's no need for violence, Sir Ronar. Drop your weapons, and your lady will live."

"Order your man to release her, or *you* will die." Ronar swept his blade to Sir Walter's chest.

Sir Walter chuckled and fingered the brooch at his neck. "I do admire your pluck, sir, but you are in no position to make demands. Kill her," he ordered the soldier holding Alexia.

Ronar and Jarin tossed down their blades.

"Knives as well." Sir Walter gestured to their belts ere he faced Cristiana. "Have you any weapons hidden among your skirts, my lady?"

Jarin and Ronar plucked knives and axes from their belts and dropped them to the floor, their clangs ringing through the hallway.

Cristiana said naught, merely stared at the monster who had killed her parents and ruined her life.

Sir Walter approached, a disgustingly sensual smile on his lips. "Would you like me to search for them? We were, after all, nearly wed."

"Leave her be!" Jarin stepped before her. "She has no weapons."

"How gallant." Sir Walter gestured for the knight to release Alexia. Pressing a hand to the trickle of blood at her throat, she cast him a scathing glance before moving beside Ronar.

"I have waited a long time to catch you Knights of the Eternal Realm. Seems the God of that realm has either abandoned you or finds you as worthless and miserable as I do." He grinned. "Take them to the dungeon."

"What should I do with this one?" one of the soldiers holding Anabelle said.

Sir Walter sauntered over to her and cocked his head, scanning her from head to toe. "'Twould be a shame to put such a beauty in the grave. Put her back in her cell. I will think of some use for her, to be sure."

"Why don't you just kill us all?" Cristiana stomped her foot, weary of this man's charade, weary of the battle, the fear, the endless hiding and running.

One crooked brow rose. "Patience, my dear. Patience." He glanced over them. "I have a bargain to offer you. The first one who admits to treason and witchcraft and implicates the others will live. The rest of you will burn at the stake." He snapped his fingers at the soldiers. "I'm not without mercy. You have a day to consider it. If no one comes forward, you will *all* burn."

And with that, the beast spun on his heels, shoved his way through his band of soldiers, and disappeared into the shadows.

Taking with him all of Cristiana's hopes and dreams.

CHAPTER TWENTY-FOUR

Damien spotted Seraphina the moment she stepped onto the sand from the stone stairway at the far end of the castle, Lady Rochford by her side. Sunlight transformed her hair into glittering diamonds as she walked toward him with a majestic grace to match any queen. She wore an emerald overgown, slit at the sides to reveal a lacy tunic beneath, and a gold-braided corset that revealed every curve. But 'twas the look in her sapphire eyes as she drew near that made him reconsider his plan, made him long to never betray this enchanting woman, but rather to swear his love to her forever and never leave her side.

She halted before him, staring at him with affection, longing…*trust.* Guilt, followed by self-loathing, threatened to force him to his knees to beg her forgiveness. Instead, he took her hands in his and kissed them.

Lady Rochford smiled and left.

"You came. I wasn't sure you—"

"Of course. Why wouldn't I?" She reached up to adjust the loose ties at the top of his shirt.

He stayed her hand. "I thought mayhap the queen upset you."

"She did. But I would never miss spending time with you." A breeze blew in from the lake, dancing through her hair.

Grabbing a silky strand, he fingered it. "I should like to hear what happened."

"It matters not." She glanced over the lake, sparkling in the sunlight. "Damien, what are we to do? Surely Sir Walter's warlock can defeat thirty soldiers."

He stifled a grimace yet grudgingly admitted, "I had the same thought." Which was precisely why he must go through with his plans today. Unless the king believed them about the evil at Luxley, unless the soldiers returned with a good report, this precious lady would hang. Alongside him. And he could not allow that to happen.

"Let us not think of it now. We have today, this beautiful lake, and"—he turned and pointed to a small rowboat—"this humble craft."

"And the Spear," she added. "Surely things will turn out well." She glanced at the boat and laughed. "'Tis rather small, indeed."

"I shall keep you safe."

"Of that, I have no doubt, strong knight."

After helping Seraphina settle in the thwarts of the craft, Damien pushed it from shore, grabbed the oars, and leapt inside. Within minutes, he'd rowed them out several yards, then halted to catch his breath. The lady's eyes were upon him, admiring eyes that made him feel all the more guilty.

Wind wisped over her, stirring loose strands of ivory hair and fluttering the lace at her neckline. Lips as pink as a virgin rose lured him to kiss her again, to take her in his arms and keep her safe forever. If only he could row to the other side of the lake and they could escape, put all this madness behind them. But that meant a life on the run, always looking over their shoulders, living in terror of getting caught and hanged. And what good would that do their friends?

Damien took a deep breath and gazed over the calm water, a mirror in the morning sun. At its far edge, the mountains of Gladdick rose like staunch guardians of Regalis, ready to defend her against all attacks, as had been Damien's task as King's Guard. He'd been so proud of the responsibility of his position. In a way, he still was. Yet lately, he'd felt a stronger draw to a more important purpose, not only to clear his friends' names and return Luxley to Alexia and Cristiana, not only to protect and love this precious lady sitting before him, not only to get his revenge. Instead, he felt an odd lure to an invisible God who appeared to be orchestrating events behind the scenes, a God of great power and love.

Damien shook his head. What was he thinking? A God who left evil men unpunished and good men to die made Him either unjust or impotent.

"Share your thoughts with me, Sir Damien," Seraphina said. "You seem perplexed."

He faced her. "Merely wishing I could keep rowing and we could escape."

She glanced over his shoulder at the mountains beyond, then back at him, "A wonderful dream."

"Someday we will be free, Seraphina." He lied, for, in truth, the odds were against such a miracle. But he'd do anything right now, say anything, to erase the fear from her face.

It worked, for she smiled, and in that smile, he saw a future of love and affection he had never dreamt possible.

Cocking her head, she looked at him coyly. "Why, Sir Damien, do I detect a hint of faith blossoming in your heart?"

"I would not admit to it, mistress," he teased as his eyes dropped to her lips again.

She touched them with her fingers as pink fanned over her cheeks. "I keep meaning to ask you, strong knight, just what are your intentions?"

Setting down the oars, Damien made his way to sit across from her, careful not to overturn the boat. Her fragrance of lilacs and innocence joined the fresh scents of the lake as he took her hands in his. *To wed you, make you mine, have children, and love you forever.* "Surely, you harbor little doubt as to my affections for you, Seraphina," was all he said, for how could he divulge his true intentions in light of what he was about to do?

A hint of disappointment flickered in her eyes. "I do not doubt you desire me, Sir Damien. Your kiss was evidence of that."

"'Tis much more than that."

"Do tell." She leaned closer, so close he could almost taste those lips again. Longed to taste those lips again. To tell her how he truly felt. *Nay*! Releasing her hands, he sighed and glanced over the water. “Alas, this talk is for another time. A time when we don’t find ourselves facing the noose.” He moved back to his seat, picked up the oars, and began rowing again.

Pain tugged upon her expression. She closed her eyes and dipped her fingers in the water as the boat moved along. Several moments passed with naught but the swish of water and squawk of birds for accompaniment.

And Damien knew he must do what he planned. If he waited much longer, spent any more time in the presence of this angel, he’d change his mind, declare his love, and hence, get them both hanged.

“What did the queen say?” he finally asked.

Without looking at him, she answered, “She argued with my prophecy that she would have a child.”

“And…”

“And I can tell you no more than that.”

Damien stopped rowing and rubbed his eyes. They were nigh thirty yards from shore, where he could see noblemen and courtiers strolling along the sandy beach.

Despite his cold treatment of her, Seraphina smiled his way. ’Twas a sad smile, nonetheless. “I thank you, Sir Damien, for this ride on the lake. ’Tis a beautiful morning and quite refreshing.” She glanced toward the palace, rising like a cold stone Leviathan from the water, threatening and full of secrets. “’Tis almost as if all our problems have been swept far away. At least for a time.”

“That pleases me greatly, mistress.” Damien started for her, longing to comfort her, to take her in his arms, but he held himself back.

Her lips drew in a serious line. “I must warn you about Lord Haleford, Damien. He is not who you think he is.”

“Pshaw! What do you have against the man?”

“I know things. I see things you don’t. Prithee, Damien, you must heed my warning.” Her eyes pleaded.

Anger burned deep in his gut. He grew weary of the lady’s accusations against the one man who had been kind to Damien, the man who was responsible for his success in life. He embraced the anger, for it gave him the final impetus to do what he must.

Standing, he carefully made his way toward her and extended his hand. She took it and he raised her up, drawing her into a gentle embrace, knowing she would happily do so, thinking he was considering her warning about William. Then feigning a loss of balance, he teetered this way and that, uttered yelps of distress as he shifted the boat with his weight. Alarmed, Seraphina clung to him, attempting to steady them both.

Finally, Damien grabbed her, and together they tumbled over the side of the boat and splashed into the lake.

"What are you doing in here?" Lady Rochford entered Seraphina's chambers to continue what she'd started earlier, searching the lady's satchel for some evidence of her past. Instead she found two women, both she recognized as servants of Lord Haleford, combing through the room, peeking in drawers, behind curtains, and under the mattress as if they, too, harbored the same suspicions. But that couldn't be. An armed guard stood just inside the entrance.

Both maids halted and dipped their heads toward her. One of them had Seraphina's opened satchel in her hand. The other an old cloth. "Lord Haleford ordered us to search Mistress Seraphina's chambers, my lady."

"How dare he? To what purpose?" She marched toward them, her gaze latched upon the old rag. "What are you searching for?"

The maids eyed each other, then lowered their gazes. "We do not know. Anything that doesn't belong, he said."

"I order you to leave at once." Lady Rochford extended her hand. "Give that to me. How dare you go through the woman's private things!"

The maid moved the rag behind her back. The other shook her head. "We cannot do that, my lady. We answer to Lord Haleford."

Behind her, Lady Rochford heard the guard clear his throat and take a step toward her.

The first maid smiled. "I believe this cloth is what his lordship is looking for."

"You will hand it to me this minute." Lady Rochford shoved her open hand toward the woman.

Though fear sparked in the maid's eyes, she did not comply.

The guard appeared beside Lady Rochford. "Let us all take it to Lord Haleford and allow him to settle it."

Lady Rochford knew 'twas not a request.

Hence, she now stood before Lord Haleford in his private chambers, guards on either side of her, as the maid handed him the cloth.

Dread soured the food in Lady Rochford's stomach. Why hadn't she searched Seraphina's bag before? She could have found the cloth, removed it, and hidden it ere anyone else discovered it. She'd been hesitant, doing her best to honor the woman's privacy. In truth, she doubted there'd be anything incriminating in her satchel at all. Hence, she'd stayed away. Until today. Things had grown worse for the woman and her knight. And Lady Rochford knew if she didn't find proof of her suspicions, the lady would hang. With the king increasingly ill, Lord Haleford issuing the orders, and Bishop Montruse desiring both their heads, 'twas only a matter of time.

"Have you seen this?" Lord Haleford's expression transformed from haughty tranquility when they'd first entered to insolent rage as he examined the cloth.

"Nay. Unlike you, I do not intrude upon a woman's private things."

A blade would have trouble slicing through the hatred fired her way from his lordship, and, gulping, she realized he held her life in his despicable hands.

"'Tis a swaddling cloth." He fingered the tattered rag as if he loathed the sight of it. "Here." He held it up to show her the emblem embroidered on the corner—a sword encircled by a wreath of flowers—Queen Ascilia's crest. Faded, dirty, but there none-the-less.

She didn't know whether to shout for glee or fear for her life. Mayhap both.

"What is that to me?" she answered as cavalierly as possible.

"You told me the babe died."

Lady Rochford tightened her lips but said naught.

"You lying wench!" He charged her, hands gripping the hilt of his sword as if he would draw it and run her through right there. He was certainly capable of such a deed.

"I am the queen's chief lady-in-waiting and good friend," she said with all the authority she could muster, hoping it would stay his hand.

He backed away with a huff. "Which is why I will allow you to live. Get out of my sight!" He spun around, his blue tunic weaving a trail of fury behind him.

Lady Rochford was happy to comply.

Dashing out of the room and down the long hall, she knew one thing for certain.

Seraphina de Mowbray was in mortal danger.

Thanking the servant who escorted her, Seraphina entered her chamber and shut the door. Water dripped from her saturated tunic onto the floor. In truth, she'd left a trail of it from the sand, up two flights of stairs and through three long hallways on her way here. She still could not believe what had happened. Sir Damien lost his balance?

The knight could fight off a dozen warriors blindfolded, but he could not keep his balance in a boat on a lake as calm as a bath?

In truth, she hadn't minded his strong arms around her. At least he hadn't become angry when she insulted his esteemed

Lord Haleford. But the slap of the cold water on her body still stung, the feel of it pushing her down into its dark depths still terrified—her desperate need for air, the ache of her lungs, the sudden panic that she'd be lost to this world and never see Damien again.

She should have known the knight could swim. Was there nothing he could not do? Once again, his strong arms surrounded her, his thick hands lifting her back into the boat with ease.

"Are you all right, Seraphina?" He climbed in after her and embraced her again. "Pray, forgive me. I am so clumsy."

Clumsy was one thing the man could ne'er be accused of.

She was well, of course. A bit scared and completely saturated. But their romantic outing was ruined, for a brisk wind rose and sent a shiver down her wet body.

Sir Damien rowed quickly back to shore, all the while apologizing profusely. Once there, he called a passing servant to escort her to her chambers and begged off with the excuse he would inform Lady Rochford to send maids to assist her in donning dry attire.

His behavior had been odd to say the least.

Yet here she was, a sodden mess, shivering beneath the breeze drifting in through the window.

By the time she had removed most of her outer clothing, two maids appeared with a basin of hot water and a dry gown. One glance at a small table by her bed showed her the Spear remained safely wrapped within its binding where she'd placed it when she'd first begun to undress.

It felt good to get out of her wet attire, even better to sponge warm water over her icy skin. The maids were most kind to assist her in donning her new clothing and run a comb through her tangled hair.

All the while Seraphina's thoughts were on Sir Damien. Not only his strange behavior, but on his cold reply to her coquettish interest in his intentions. She would have thought at the very least that he'd sweep her in his arms, kiss her, and ask if he could court her formally. What she didn't expect was some impassive statement about his affections and a request to discuss it at another time.

She had tried to hide the pain stabbing her heart, but she feared she'd failed. Was that why he'd pushed her in the water? Nay. That made no sense at all.

The maids inquired whether she was in need of anything else.

"Thank you, nay," she said, and it seemed they couldn't hurry out fast enough.

With a sigh, she sat by the brazier and combed her damp hair for several moments, relishing the warmth of the coals whilst pondering the odd events of the day.

Finally, she rose and moved to her bedside for the Spear, intending to strap it back onto her thigh.

The holy relic was gone.

CHAPTER TWENTY-FIVE

Taking the tiny spearhead from the maid, Damien held it up to the rushlight in the dark hallway. Though rusty and blood-stained, the relic seemed to shine from within as if it had its own source of light. Was it truly the Spear of Destiny? Yet how could he deny what he'd seen of its power? He slipped it in his pocket, then grabbed his money pouch and counted out ten more groats for the woman. "No word of this to anyone."

Taking the coins in her greedy hand, she nodded and disappeared into the darkness.

And thus Damien broke the heart of the woman he loved and ruined any chances for his own happiness.

But at least they would be alive, and he might still be able to save their friends back at Luxley. Not to mention discover the villain who had murdered his parents. Finally his quest for revenge would be over. Finally justice would be served. And with Seraphina and her friends free and living their lives in peace, he would be content, mayhap find some purpose and joy elsewhere.

Even if he could never be with the woman he loved.

Hence, he turned and made his way to request an audience with Bishop Montruse.

He hated to make a deal with the devil, but sometimes the devil had exactly what one needed most.

Seraphina had never seen Lady Rochford in such a state. The usual peaceful calm that radiated from the woman's eyes now fired in terror as she dashed into Seraphina's chambers.

"You must leave the palace at once!" Rushing toward the wardrobe, she flung open the doors, grabbed Seraphina's satchel and began stuffing it with underthings.

"What? I don't understand. The king said I would hang if I left."

"Much worse will happen to you should you stay." The woman moved to grab a brush, comb, and a fresh tunic from a hook.

Panic seized Seraphina's heart, and she stumbled to the bed and sat down. Had everyone in this palace gone mad? She glanced toward the table again. Regardless, she couldn't leave without the Spear! Lifting her hand, she examined the inside of her wrist. The mark was still there. She was still the Protector. She closed her eyes and rubbed her temples. All while the sounds of Lady Rochford dashing about the room blared in her ears.

This couldn't be happening. Some protector she was.

"Come." Lady Rochford tugged on her arm. "You must go."

Seraphina opened her eyes. "Even if I agreed, I've lost something of great value, and I cannot leave without it."

"What could be of more value than your life?" The lady halted before her, her breath coming in spurts.

Seraphina moaned. "A holy object entrusted to me by God. I cannot leave it behind, don't you see? Besides, the palace is guarded. I cannot flee without being caught, and I won't leave without Damien."

Lady Rochford took a deep breath and sat beside her. "I know a way. I can get you to safety. Now, where did you last see this holy object? I will help you search."

"On the table." Seraphina gestured to her right. "'Tis gone. I've already searched everywhere."

"Could someone have taken it? Was there anyone else here?"

"The maids you sent to help me dress."

"I never sent maids." Confusion lined the lady's brow. "I thought you were still on the lake with Sir Damien."

An icy chill enveloped Seraphina. "Damien did not…?" She stared at the woman as a horrid suspicion clamped around her heart.

"Who were they?" Lady Rochford asked. "I'll go question them."

"I had never seen them before." She looked up at her. "But why would they take it? 'Tis of no value to them."

"It must be of great value to someone."

Indeed. Too many to count here at court.

But there was only one who knew where it was.

Damien.

Nay. Surely he would not betray her. Unstoppable tears flooded her eyes as the truth swept away all doubt. Had he not asked her to give it to him more than once?

He pushed her in the water! They didn't lose balance and fall. He *pushed* her! To get her wet, to prompt her to return to her chambers to change her clothing.

The maids…he must have paid them.

A tear slipped down her cheek. A palpable pain etched across her heart, threatening to tear it asunder. How could he do such a thing? She loved him. She had trusted him.

Lady Rochford knelt before her. "I can tell from your tears that mayhap 'twas Damien who stole your object?"

Seraphina could only nod.

Lady Rochford handed her a handkerchief. "I'm so sorry. Betrayal cuts deep."

Seraphina dabbed her tears, but they kept flowing down her cheeks in abandon.

"Forgive me, dear one, but I beseech you, we must leave posthaste!" Lady Rochford stared up at her, terror and pleading in her eyes.

Dear one? "Who wishes me dead?"

Lady Rochford flattened her lips. "If I tell you, will you leave?"

Swallowing, Seraphina drew a shaky breath. "Aye."

"Lord Haleford."

Seraphina leapt to her feet, her broken heart pounding against her ribs. Had she not just seen how evil the man was? "I believe you, though I know not why."

"That is for another time." Lady Rochford stood and took Seraphina's hand in hers. "We must away. And quickly!"

Lady Rochford hurried through the halls, her nerves still wound tight, for she had one last task to complete this night. The most important one—getting Seraphina to safety—she had already accomplished, thank the good Lord. She'd even managed to procure her a soldier, a lady companion, and three horses. It helped to have the ear of the queen. Now that the precious lady was out of danger, Lady Rochford must speak to the king.

But first, the cloth. Somehow, she must retrieve the swaddling cloth. Hence, the reason she now quietly slipped into Lord Haleford's private quarters. From the clamor emanating from the great hall, she knew the evening repast was being served. The perfect time to retrieve the item in question, for Lord Haleford never missed an opportunity to eat, drink, and flaunt his powerful position for all to see.

As expected, his chambers were dark and quiet, save for a single lantern, which she took with her as she walked about, shuffling through trinkets and papers, searching over couches and chairs. She had just begun to fear that the man had burned the evidence, when she spotted the frayed edge peeking out from a drawer in his desk. Opening it, she pulled out the precious cloth and held it to her nose. It smelled of age and tears and much love, and she nearly crumpled to the floor with emotion.

Memories assailed her from so many years ago, of wrapping a newborn within the folds of this very cloth and whisking her away to safety, depositing her into the arms of a trusted wet nurse with orders to take the babe to the Lady of Our Peace convent at the other end of Enclasen, as far away from the palace as possible. 'Twas the only way to save the child from the same fate her mother had suffered.

With no time to reminisce, Lady Rochford rose and tucked the cloth beneath her skirts in a pocket she'd sewn into the fabric, then started on her way.

She must see the king, and she must see him now.

A few minutes later, she was nearly at the king's chambers when Lord Haleford emerged from within, flanked by two guards.

"Lady Rochford." He grinned at her as a snake would a mouse. "Where is Mistress Seraphina?" He slowly approached and with one gesture toward the guards, ordered them to stand on either side of her.

Trapped. Lifting her chin, she stood her ground. "How should I know? The queen has summoned me. Step aside."

"I heard no such summons, and I've been with the king and queen for the past hour."

"Nevertheless, I am the queen's lady, and she is in need of me." She attempted to circle him, but he gripped her arm so tightly, pain radiated down to her fingers.

"Where is Mistress Seraphina?" he seethed. "I won't ask again."

"Then I won't answer you again, for I do not know. Mayhap with Sir Damien. They are quite fond of each other." Fear tightened her chest until she could hardly breathe.

He shook his head. "Tsk, tsk, tsk. I had so hoped to avoid this. Arrest her at once." He flicked his bejeweled hand.

The guards grabbed her arms.

"On what charge? You can't do this!" She struggled, but their grips only tightened, causing more pain.

"Oh, but I *can* do this. Helping a prisoner escape against the king's orders, well, I'd say that's as close to treason as you get. Away with her!"

Turning, the soldiers began dragging her away.

"Your Majesty!" she yelled, hoping someone within the king's chambers would hear her. "Help! Your Majesty!"

But no one came to her aid.

Finally rid of that surly shrew, Lord Haleford made his way to the throne room. With the king indisposed and the queen by his side, 'twas the perfect opportunity to take his rightful place, to sample the seat of power that would soon be his. Ascending the steps, he stood atop the dais and whirled about, staring into the empty room lit only by two torches hooked in walls on either side. Nevertheless, he imagined a host of courtiers and nobles crowding the floor below, vying for his attention, for his favor, waiting breathlessly upon every word that proceeded from his mouth.

He slid onto the throne, chin held high, sensing the power of the seat rush through his veins, sparking every bit of royal blood within him to life. This was his purpose, his destiny. He'd been born to rule, and he would do so much better than his soft-hearted brother! Oh, how he had waited for this moment. And he hadn't much longer to wait.

Footsteps jarred him from his imaginings, and he turned to see Bishop Montruse emerge from the shadows on his left, his black robes shifting about him like the restless sea at night.

"A bit premature, aren't you?" The bishop halted at the bottom of the dais and sneered. "I have not heard of His Majesty's death."

Lord Haleford studied the man. The holy fiend had been a thorn in Haleford's side for decades, demanding he do his bidding, demanding he keep that witch Panora in the king's favor. Or else. 'Twas the else that worried Haleford, the else that could destroy all his plans. And as soon as his plans came to fruition, he'd pluck out this particular thorn and burn it in the fire.

"I am praying, if you must know, for the king," Lord Haleford responded.

"Bah!" Chuckling, the bishop ascended the remaining steps to stand beside the throne. "Where is the king? I saw neither you nor he at the evening repast."

"Ill again. Much worse this time."

The bishop huffed and fingered the jeweled crucifix hanging about his neck. "What good news for you, my lord."

Lord Haleford rose, his blood boiling. "How dare you say such a thing? He is my brother. I have great affection for him." 'Twas true enough. Peter had been good to him, had given him power and position at court though his birth was illegitimate, and Lord Haleford had grown to love him in a way. Which made it even harder to long for his demise, though it would benefit Haleford immensely. In truth, he took no pleasure in seeing his brother suffer, and he oft prayed the Almighty would take him home ere it became too much to bear.

The bishop gave a sickly-sweet smile. "Forgive me, my lord."

Lord Haleford flung out his tunic and took his rightful seat again. "'Twould do you well, Your Eminence, not to anger me. The king has made me regent whilst he is ill. Hence, I have all the power of the king to do as I please."

For the briefest of seconds, fear darted across the bishop's eyes. "I answer not to the king, my lord, but only to the Holy Prime. *And* to God, of course," he added as if it were of less significance.

Lord Haleford leaned on the golden arm of the throne. "Whilst you are in my palace, you answer to me."

"Your palace?" He smirked, but then dipped his head. "Then how may I assist you, my lord."

Lord Haleford sat back with a sigh. "The wench, Mistress Seraphina, has defied the orders of the king and fled the palace."

The bishop's face suddenly crumpled as if Lord Haleford had struck him. Fear and rage stormed across his cold eyes. Odd. "Are you sure?"

"I can find her nowhere, but I suspect Lady Rochford assisted her." Pain seared through his head, and Lord Haleford rubbed his temples.

"Then question her."

"I have. She denies it and is now in the dungeon."

"There are ways to get her to talk."

Lord Haleford looked at him curiously. Did the man know about the swaddling cloth? Did he know who Lord Haleford suspected the common maid was? “What is Mistress Seraphina to you?”

“Nothing,” The bishop blubbered, clearly frustrated. “Alack, I am quite familiar with her companions back at Luxley. She should not be allowed to return and assist them in their evildoings.”

“Pshaw! What can one maid do?”

The bishop frowned, alarm tightening the lines of his face. “You must send more soldiers after her.” He began to pace before the queen’s throne. “The thirty the king sent are not enough. Send an army if you have to. ’Tis the only way to completely destroy her and these Knights of the Eternal Realm!”

“Knights of the Eternal Realm?”

“’Tis what these devil worshipers call themselves. Blasphemy!”

The bishop had obviously gone mad. But no matter. His suggestion was a good one. Regardless of whether Mistress Seraphina knew who she was, he could not allow her to live. He would, indeed, send an army to kill her and defeat the treasonous band of knights along with the D’Clere witches. Surely if the king recovered, this success would only grant him favor in His Majesty’s eyes.

Haleford rose. “I agree. I will send an army first thing in the morning.”

The bishop smiled. “You are far wiser than the king, my lord. And now, I should be by his side.” He dipped his head and floated down the stairs and out the door.

Lord Haleford reluctantly left the throne and took the steps down to the bottom of the dais. Not only would he send an army, but he would go with them—to make sure the job was done right.

CHAPTER TWENTY-SIX

Something landed on Damien's belly. Small feet padded over his leather doublet, but he couldn't bring himself to care. His mind floated listlessly upon a sea of mulberry wine, devoid of oar or paddle or concern for where he went. *Sweet oblivion.* Could he not remain there a few more minutes?

But sunlight attempted to pry open his eyes whilst the lap of wavelets and the cry of an eagle shouted in his ears.

The creature on his belly pecked at his belt.

Judas! Damien lifted a hand that felt as heavy as a rock, and the creature took off, wings flapping. With great difficulty, he lifted himself up on his elbows and dared to open his eyes. The world spun for a moment ere settling in his vision, a beautiful vision of dawn's light transforming the lake into a golden mirror. 'Twould be beautiful if Damien's head didn't feel like it was at the bottom of said lake.

Judas! He sat up and spat sand from his mouth. His eyes landed on the empty jug lying beside him as memories of the night returned. He'd gone in search of the bishop, but could not find the man anywhere, neither at the evening repast, nor his quarters, nor with the king. Frustrated and feeling more guilty than he'd thought possible, he'd grabbed a flagon of wine and had gone down to the lake to think…to wait. But the more wine he drank, the worse he felt about betraying Seraphina, which led to drinking more wine, of course, until his mind grew numb, along with his heart.

That was the last thing he remembered.

He pressed a hand against his doublet and felt the Spear. Thank God. Now, he must find the bishop. Before Seraphina realized who had betrayed her. Before he had to face her, for he couldn't be sure he wouldn't bend his knee and return it to her forthwith.

He attempted to rise. Egad! Who let loose a herd of wild horses in his brain? Rubbing his temples, he groaned, and found even uttering that sound difficult, for his mouth was drier than the deserts of Elam.

Voices drifted down from the portico above him, and he knew he must rise ere he became a spectacle. He did so, but with great pain. Then drawing a deep breath, he went to kneel beside the water and splashed it over his face and hair. Finally feeling a tad bit better, he gathered his sword and headed back into the palace.

This time, the bishop was easy to find. The indolent man was still fast asleep in his chambers.

"You will wake him at once," Damien ordered the guard outside the door.

The man shook his head. "I am under strict orders not to disturb him."

Damien had no time to argue with the man. Shoving him aside, he opened the door and entered the dark room before the guard could draw a blade. Damien, however, *did* draw a blade and held it to the man's throat. "Away with you. I'll inform him 'twas not your fault."

He didn't wait to see if the man complied, but he heard no footsteps following him. What he *did* hear was a rumbling akin to a corpulent hibernating bear hailing from a room to his left. From what he could tell in the shadows, the bishop's receiving chamber was nearly as opulent as the king's. No wonder he had not enjoyed his time at Luxley.

Yet now as Damien entered the bishop's bed chambers, he found them equally resplendent. A woman sat up in the large bed, quickly covering herself with a blanket. Her shriek woke His Eminence, who stuttered, spat, and mumbled as he opened his eyes. Of course. Men of God so rarely abode by the same rules they enforced on others. Damien merely waited with amusement as the lady slipped from the bed, grabbed her clothes, and darted out the door.

"What is the meaning of this!!?" Bishop Montruse swung his legs over the side of the bed and rubbed his eyes. "How dare you! I'll have you hanged for this."

"Not if you wish your greatest dream to come true, Your Eminence."

The man lit a nearby candle and squinted at Damien, understanding registering in his eyes. He slipped from the bed wearing only his nightshirt and looking rather pale and impotent without his grand robes and jewelry.

"You'd best be in possession of the Spear of Destiny, for that is the only thing that would prevent me from having your head for such an affront."

Reaching into his pocket, Damien pulled out the Spear and held it up to the candlelight.

The bishop licked his lips and reached for it, but Damien backed away. "Our bargain?"

Frowning, the man grabbed a robe and flung it around himself ere leaving the room for the main chamber. He moved to the single window and opened the slats, admitting streams of golden light so at odds with the sense of evil weighing down the room. Stranger still was that Damien would sense such a thing. 'Twas something that Alexia or Seraphina would feel. *Seraphina.* He gazed down at the Spear, feeling a slice to his heart so painful, he nearly ran from the room.

If only the bishop hadn't turned toward him. "As promised, I will tell you who murdered your parents. Let me see the relic first."

"And you will tell the king that Mistress Seraphina and I and my fellow King's Guards are not traitors to the crown and ensure he absolves us of any charges."

"Aye, of course, of course." He waved him forward. "A bargain is a bargain."

"You will do so today. Or, Spear or no Spear, I swear I will hunt you down and gut you."

The bishop speared him with a pointed gaze. "You have my troth."

Damien handed it to him and watched as the bishop held it up to the sunlight. After a few moments, he grinned so wide, Damien thought his perpetual frown lines would crack. When he faced Damien, greed and power-lust flickered from his eyes.

"'Tis truly it! The Spear!" He cupped it in his hands and held it to his chest. "I doubted you, Sir Damien, but you have proved yourself valiant and wise."

Damien shifted his stance, feeling neither of those things. "And now?"

The bishop frowned and gestured toward a stuffed chair. "You may wish to sit for this tale."

"I'll stand." Damien folded arms over his chest.

The bishop stared at him a moment as if pondering how best to phrase the information. "'Tis the same man who both murdered your father and ravished your mother."

Damien's blood rushed madly through his veins, causing bile to rise in his throat.

"Who?"

"Lord William Haleford."

Damien rammed his shoulder against William's closed door, thrusting all of his weight against the thick oak. It wouldn't budge. He still could not believe that his mentor, his friend, the man who had been a father to him all these years had murdered his parents. He'd always suspected the bishop, but something in the holy man's eyes told Damien he spoke the truth. For once.

Still, he needed proof. He needed to hear it from the man's own lips.

Leaping back, he kicked the door with all his might. It crashed open and slammed against the wall. He charged inside, fury blinding him to all else but his determination to discover the truth.

Lady Marion, dressed in naught but a silk nightshirt and robe, stood by the hearth hugging herself, fear spiking across her eyes. "Oh, Damien, 'tis only you." She breathed out, flinging a hand to her chest. "I feared for my life."

He moved toward her. "Did you not hear me knock?"

"I did, but I'm here alone, and I dared not answer."

Alone? Casting all propriety aside, he rushed into the bedchamber where he searched the rumpled coverlet, the wardrobe, and in every corner ere he returned. "Where is your husband?"

"Not here."

"I can see that. Where did he go?"

"He left before dawn. With the king's army."

"Army?" Damien eyed her. He'd not heard of any uprising or attack. Nor one that would require the king's adviser to accompany the royal forces. "Where are they heading?"

"He did not say exactly. Mayhap to Luxley?" She moved toward him.

"Luxley?" Confusion clouded Damien's already wine-befuddled thoughts. Rubbing his eyes, he growled.

"You know, don't you?" She looked at him with sympathy.

He gripped her arm. *Tight*. "What do you know of it?"

She winced and attempted to tug from him. "I know he never meant to hurt you, Damien."

"*Hurt* me? He murdered my father and mother!" He released her with such force, she stumbled backward. Yet no shock appeared on her features. So, 'twas true, then. Damien didn't know whether to give into his rage or his agony. He decided on rage.

"He was young," Lady Marion blubbered, "so young. Just eighteen."

"You knew?" Damien could hardly believe the woman had not reported her husband to the king.

She hugged herself, eyes alight with fear and sorrow. "He told me he ravished a young married lady, aye. Told me he'd been drinking, and he regretted it very much."

"Regretted it?" Damien fisted his hands. "My mother was a pious, God-fearing woman. She was so ashamed, so devastated at being defiled, she took her own life. Did he tell you that?"

She nodded and swallowed. "He was truly mortified."

"So mortified that he had my father killed when he came close to figuring out who had done the vile deed?"

"There is no proof for that."

Damien huffed. "My father, the Constable of the King's Calvary, killed in a training accident? Do you take me for a fool?"

"Never." She moved slowly toward him. "I am truly sorry, Damien. He hated what he'd done. Tried to make it up to you by moving you to the palace, giving you a chance to become a King's Guard."

The words struck Damien in the gut. Alas, he had not earned his position at all. Everything he had, all his successes, were naught but blood payments. "Judas! All pretense. To assuage his guilt over what he'd done."

"Mayhap." She inched toward him and took his arm, leaning her head against it. "I told you he was a monster. Can you not now see why I sought you out for comfort?"

He thrust her away and shook his head, disgust swirling a vile brew in his belly. "Even now you play the temptress with me. You knew all this and did not tell me."

Frowning, she whirled about. "He threatened to kill me."

Damien wondered. Or had the woman kept her tongue for the same reasons she stayed with the man all these years, for the power, wealth, and position he offered. "You disgust me," he spat out before turning and marching from the room.

He would find William. He would find him and plant a sword in his heart, make him feel a smidgen of the pain Damien had felt all these years, force him to admit to his crimes, beg for his life. Sweet revenge! 'Twas so close Damien could taste it. Surely it wouldn't be too hard to track an army. But first he must speak with Seraphina, convince her to come with him. He did not want to leave her unprotected in this place. If she had figured out his betrayal, he'd take her by force. Besides, if the bishop could be trusted at all, then she and Damien would soon no longer be wanted for treason, and hence would have naught to fear in leaving.

He darted down hallways, past rooms, up stairs, passing sleepy courtiers heading to the great hall to break their fast. He knocked on Seraphina's door. No answer. He knocked again. Finally, impatient, he opened it and went inside. The lady's bed had not been slept in. In truth, none of her things were neatly placed about.

A maid entered and shrieked, halting in the doorway.

"Where is Mistress Seraphina?" he demanded.

She shook her head. "I know not, sir. She has not been here since yesterday."

Fear started to rise. "And what of Lady Rochford?"

The maid, a timid girl of no more than sixteen, dropped her gaze to the floor. "I have not seen her."

"You know something. Tell me." He took a step toward her, his boots thumping on the floor though he tried not to frighten this little bird.

"I have heard, Sir Knight, that Lady Rochford has been arrested and is in the dungeon."

Damien rushed past the maid and out of the room with one thought in mind. He must speak with Lady Rochford and find out what happened to Seraphina.

CHAPTER TWENTY-SEVEN

Once again Damien found himself in the palace dungeon. Thankfully, this time on the right side of the iron bars. Proceeding through the dank passages, he shifted his shoulders beneath the cloak of misery hanging heavy in the air. 'Twas a place that reeked of agony and death, if there were such odors, a place where the condemned lay in chains of hopelessness, awaiting execution.

He'd been forced to use the rest of his coin to bribe the head guard to allow him entrance. Good thing he'd been a friend of Damien's or no amount of money would have been enough to entice the man to defy Lord Haleford's strict orders that no one see Lady Rochford.

As he passed cells full of the condemned, hands reached for him through rusty bars. Holding his torch high, he kept his gaze forward, not wanting to look upon their agony, wishing he could close his ears to their cries for help, their moans of despair. He wondered how many of them were innocent. How many had merely been tossed here because they threatened someone in power—because they knew too many secrets.

Just like Lady Rochford.

Turning a corner, he swept his torch out before him, sending a cluster of roaches skittering across the moist stone wall. The sound of someone retching echoed through the dank air. He passed a man—or what remained of him—left to rot in chains hanging from a wall. Damien covered his nose.

Rounding another corner, he approached the cell the guard had directed him to, halted, and knelt before it, peering inside as far as his torchlight would allow.

"Lady Rochford," he whispered, praying this was the right cell.

Finally, a slippered foot appeared, then a blue cote, and then the lady herself, shadows beneath her eyes, dirt smudged on her face, her hair askew, but with a peaceful smile upon her lips.

"Sir Damien." She gripped the bars and reached for him as he stood and took her hand. "You are the last person I thought to see."

He had no time for idle talk. "Where is Seraphina?"

Soft brown eyes searched his. "Gone."

"Where?"

"To Luxley."

"Judas!" Damien slammed his fist against the bars. Dust rained down upon them as he shook his hand from the pain.

"What is it?" she asked, her tone suddenly anxious.

"Lord Haleford and an army are on their way to Luxley as well." He growled.

Lady Rochford hugged herself as terror streaked across her eyes.

"Is he after Seraphina?" Damien whispered in a harsh tone. But why would he be? Merely because she escaped the palace? Would that warrant an army?

The lady did not respond, merely lowered her gaze.

"When did she leave?"

"Last night." She gripped the bars. "Never fear. I sent a lady companion and a soldier with her."

"What is that against an army?" Anger and confusion tore through him.

She pursed her lips and swallowed.

"Why did she leave without telling me?"

Her eyes searched his, *accusing* eyes. "She was distraught over something that had been taken from her."

Now 'twas Damien's turn to grow silent, to lower his gaze beneath the weight of his guilt. "I should have been there for her." He mumbled, running a hand through his hair. But he'd been drinking. *Again*. Drinking himself into a stupor. When his lady needed him the most. And now she was out there all alone, defenseless against Lord Haleford and his army.

Without the Spear!

"Why would Lord Haleford wish her harm?" Damien rubbed his eyes and groaned.

"I cannot tell you, Sir Damien, but I will ask this one thing of you."

"What?"

Turning about, she lifted her skirts and pulled something from beneath them. Then facing him, she handed him what appeared to be a rag. "Give this to the king. Tell him I found it among Seraphina's things. Tell him Lord Haleford has gone after her. He will know what to do."

Angrier with himself than he'd ever been, Damien made his way to the king's chambers. What would the king want with an old rag? He should simply discard it and be on his way to rescue Seraphina. But something in Lady Rochford's eyes, a desperation he'd ne'er seen in her usually peaceful gaze, gave him pause. When he'd asked, she had said the cloth could save Seraphina's life, but Damien could not see how. Had her hours in the dungeon caused the poor woman to go mad? If so, he was on a vain quest that was wasting time and putting the woman he loved in more danger with each passing minute.

All of which was entirely his fault. He hung his head.

God, if you're listening, I'm sorry.

Pain radiated through his mind and thrust deep into his heart, the pain of betrayal, the heartache of loss, and the self-loathing of his own failure.

If he hadn't stolen the Spear, hadn't been drinking all night, Seraphina would not be on the run, would not have left without speaking to him, and Lord Haleford would not be in pursuit. Or was the blackguard even after Seraphina? Why would the king's top adviser and next in line to the throne go after a simple maid who escaped the palace? Nay, there was more to this tale, more that Damien must discover. So many questions. But they would have to wait as Damien approached the king's chambers and tapped lightly on the door.

A servant answered.

"I must see the king immediately."

"The king is ill." The door shut.

Damien knocked again.

"I am Sir Damien of the King's Guard, and I have information vital to the safety of the king and Enclasen."

The servant, a wiry fellow with a hook nose and eyes spread too far on his face, merely stared at him for a moment before he started to shut the door again.

"I will see him." The queen's voice hailed from behind the man, and he opened the door and gestured for Damien to step inside.

Queen Eleanor slowly rose from her seat before the hearth and turned to greet Damien. Sorrow hung deep beneath her eyes as she attempted a smile that faltered on her lips. "What is it, Sir Damien? The king sleeps now, but I can relay your message."

Damien pulled out the rag from within his doublet and handed it to the queen. "Your Majesty, prithee give this to the king immediately when he awakens."

"I don't understand." She examined it, her forehead wrinkling.

"Lady Rochford insisted the king see it right away. She says it belongs to Mistress Seraphina and is of the utmost importance and that the king would understand."

The queen nodded. "Very well. I will do so. But why didn't Lady Rochford deliver it herself?"

"You do not know?"

Her brows rose.

"The lady is in the dungeon. I assumed…" He glanced toward the king's bedchamber. "I assumed on the king's orders."

"The dungeon!" Shock widened her eyes. "Nay. He has given no such order. I knew naught of this, though the king granted regency powers to Lord Haleford." She snapped her fingers and a servant came running. "Summon Lord Haleford at once."

Damien reached out to halt the servant. "He is gone. With an army. Marching to Luxley, I hear."

"To Luxley?" Shock spiked the queen's tone.

"'Tis what Lady Rochford told me, Your Majesty."

"Why?" She flattened her lips. "I warned the king not to grant him such power." She turned to the servant. "Release Lady Rochford immediately from the dungeon and bring her here to me."

The servant sped out the door.

"This is most troublesome." The queen wobbled, and Damien led her to a chair.

Most troublesome, indeed. Damien rubbed his eyes. Lord Haleford must have put Lady Rochford in the dungeon, but for what crime? He could make no sense of it. "Your Majesty, something evil is afoot. Do I have your permission to go after Lord Haleford and discover his intentions?"

"But the king…you are commanded to remain here."

Damien's anger simmered. "The bishop has not spoken to you?"

"Nay. I have not seen him. I have summoned him to come pray for the king, but he is nowhere to be found."

Damien wanted to punch something. *Hard.* He wanted to find the unholy fiend himself, retrieve the Spear, and then strangle the life from him. Instead, he knelt before the queen.

"The bishop is not to be trusted, Your Majesty, nor is Lord Haleford. I beseech you, allow me to find and confront Lord Haleford and bring him back to stand trial. He has betrayed all our trusts."

Her eyes searched his. Her lips parted. Her breath grew heavy. "I don't know what to do. Whom to trust."

Damien dared to grip her hands. "You are stronger than you believe, Your Majesty. What does your heart tell you?"

Taking a deep breath, she raised her chin. "Go, Sir Damien, and I beseech you, do not make a fool of me."

King Peter II struggled to sit up in his bed, waving away the physicians who attempted to help him. Out of breath, he leaned back against his pillows and stared at the old rag the queen had given him.

'Twas well made, he could tell, woven from the finest wool. Long ago, it must have been a fine cloth, but age had stained it with dark smudges and frayed its edges. He glanced up at the queen and Lady Rochford standing by the bed, their expressions full of anticipation and hope. In truth, Lady Rochford seemed hardly able to stand still.

The room tilted, and Peter closed his eyes for a moment until it righted. He felt a bit better, at least better than yesterday, but he was still unable to leave his sickbed, unable to eat much at all, and hardly fit to run a kingdom.

"Your Majesty," Lady Rochford said, her voice cracking slightly. "Turn it over."

He did. An emblem, an embroidered emblem screamed up at him. He ran his thumb over it, attempting to focus, but his vision blurred. Squeezing his eyes shut for a moment, he opened them again and drew the cloth near for a closer look.

His heart picked up its pace. Blood raced through his veins.

It couldn't be.

But it was.

The Wynter family crest. *Ascilia's crest*. He'd know it anywhere. The queen had it embroidered onto her personal items.

Items such as a swaddling cloth.

Emotion clogged his throat. Could this be? Was this? He looked up at Lady Rochford.

"'Tis hers, Your Majesty. I would know it anywhere."

"I thought 'twas buried with her." His princess—the stillborn baby whom his precious Ascilia had borne him ere she died.

Lady Rochford knelt and leaned on the king's bed. Tears streamed down her cheeks. "She is not dead, Your Majesty. She lives!"

"What?" Peter's breath came too fast. His head lightened, and the room began to gyrate.

One of the physicians poured an elixir of medicaments into a cup and handed it to him.

He waved both the man and the cup away. "I don't understand. Explain, Lady Rochford."

She drew a shaky breath. "Nineteen years ago, I was with the queen when she died in childbirth. Something wasn't right." She folded her hands together on the coverlet as if in prayer. "I didn't believe she died of natural causes."

Peter's mouth dropped open, his mind struggling to accept her words.

"She had not lost too much blood. The pains had been difficult, but not overmuch. Then"—Lady Rochford squeezed her eyes, pushing tears down her cheeks—"she gasped and moaned and arched her back as if she were being stabbed. And then she was gone."

The pain of that moment—that moment when he'd learned of Ascilia's death—pricked him anew. "And the babe?"

"A maid took her away ere I could see her, declaring her stillborn." She wiped her tears, the sorrow on her face suddenly lifting. "But I heard her cry!"

Peter could only stare at her, a plethora of conflicting emotions battling in his chest.

The queen covered her mouth in shock.

"By God's grace," Lady Rochford continued, "I stole the babe away ere the servant could kill her or deliver her to whoever had ordered such a horrendous thing."

Peter studied her, suspicion rising to join his anger. "But I saw her tiny body. I buried her alongside my wife."

She swallowed and looked away. "I'm told the servant somehow found a dead newborn babe and declared it to be the princess. No doubt she feared whate'er punishment would come her way for her failure."

Peter closed his eyes. What madness was this? "What did you do with her?"

"I put her safely into the care of trustworthy wet nurse with instructions to take her to the furthermost part of the kingdom, to the Lady of Peace Convent, where she would be raised to womanhood in safety."

Could this possibly be true? He longed to believe it, but…Nay! He would not endure another heartache. "Forsooth, 'tis an incredible tale, my lady," he mumbled, unable to hide the mistrust in his tone.

Her bottom lip trembled. "You have my troth, my king, I speak the truth!"

"Then why did you not come forward before now?"

Lady Rochford rose and swiped the moisture from her face. "I had no proof, Your Majesty. No proof and no idea who would do such a thing. Who would have believed me? I was young and had barely been made a lady-in-waiting."

Peter glanced at Eleanor, and the lady seemed to know his question ere he asked it.

"Aye, my lord, you can trust her." The queen glanced at Lady Rochford. "I have never known her to be anything but honorable."

Peter fingered the cloth. His daughter alive! He drew it to his nose, longing for the scent of his wife, his child, one more time. But all he smelled was age, mildew, and lilacs.

"All this time…" He snapped harsh eyes to Lady Rochford. "I should have you lashed and tossed back in the dungeon!"

No fear appeared in her eyes. "I beg your forgiveness, Your Majesty. I feared for her life. I fear for it still. Whoever wanted her dead nineteen years ago remains at the castle even now."

"Can I not protect my own daughter?" He raged. "Why keep her from me all these years?" He wanted to scream. He wanted to cry. Instead, he coughed, all strength draining from him.

The physician made another attempt to give him medicine, but he waved him away.

"How came you by this cloth? Where is my daughter now?"

"The convent was attacked not shortly after she arrived, and all I could discover was that one of the nuns might have escaped with her." Tears glistened once again in Lady Rochford's eyes. "I had no way to discover her whereabouts or whether she was even alive. Until now."

A moment passed in which Peter began putting the pieces together. Visions of Mistress Seraphina with her alabaster hair and blue eyes, the regal tilt of her chin. And her courage! "Where did you find this?"

"'Twas among Seraphina de Mowbray's possessions, Your Majesty. She was taken to Luxley where Lord and Lady D'Clere raised her as companion to their daughters."

The queen sank to a nearby chair, her face a mask.

Elation battled shock within him. "Bring her to me at once!"

"She is gone. Prithee forgive me, but Lord Haleford discovered the truth and intended to kill her. I sent her away."

"Lord Haleford?"

"Aye, Your Majesty. He has betrayed you. I believe he's the one who murdered the queen and intended to kill your baby daughter. 'Tis why he put me in the dungeon. So I could not tell you."

"But he is…he is…" Peter's breath caught as he sank back yet again onto his pillow. "My half-brother, my friend."

Peter doubted his heart could take such a blow. First the elation of discovering his daughter lived and now to find out his brother, his friend, the man closest to him, had betrayed him in the worst possible way. He must discover the truth.

"Summon Lord Haleford at once!" he shouted to the servant standing at the door.

"He has fled with an army, Your Majesty," Lady Rochford said. "In pursuit of the princess. Sir Damien has gone after him."

Sir Damien? "So these Knights of the Eternal Realm are not traitors at all?"

"I do not believe so, Your Majesty."

"Bring me pen and paper at once. And call the captain of the King's Guard."

Servants fled and returned within minutes.

Peter drew up orders to arrest Lord Haleford immediately and for the army to return. He informed them that Seraphina de Mowbray was the princess of the kingdom and, should they encounter her, they were to treat her as such. He signed it then spilled wax upon it and sealed it with his signet ring.

Sir Tybalt LeReed entered the room and bowed before the king.

"You are to pursue my army, led by Lord Haleford and deliver this to the commander, who I assume is Commander Sadon. And bring my daughter back to me!"

"May I go as well?" Lady Rochford asked. "To ensure her safety."

"I should have you flogged for hiding the truth from me, my lady. But I see your reasons were pure and just. Aye, go. Just prithee, bring her back to me."

CHAPTER TWENTY-EIGHT

Luxley Castle Dungeon

Alexia D'Clere, true lady of Luxley, slid down the craggy stone wall and sat on the dirt floor in the dungeon of her own castle. Sighing, she dropped her head onto her knees, wondering how things had become so dire. Hadn't they been doing everything God asked of them? Hadn't they been praising Him, worshiping Him, obeying Him? Indeed, they'd been fighting evil where'er they found it, feeding the poor, helping the needy, and praying without ceasing.

Yet here they all were, locked behind bars with rats and roaches. And as far as she knew, Damien and Seraphina had suffered the same fate. To make matters worse, Sir Walter had separated them, locking them in separate cells so they were unable to console one another or pray together.

Smart man.

"Why is this happening, Lord?" She lifted her head and scanned her cell, a six-foot-square cage of stone with iron bars on the end. Beyond the bars, a torch perched on the wall in the passageway allowed but a few ribbons of light to flutter within. Enough to see the vermin that crawled all over the ground and walls.

The cold stone bit through her doublet, and she jerked from it and finally stood. Her poor sister. How she must be suffering. She hated bugs and filth and darkness. Moving to the bars, Alexia shouted. "Cristiana! Are you there?" But only the echo of her own voice responded.

Pushing away, she took up a pace. If none of them confessed the lie Sir Walter required—and none of them would—they would all be burned at the stake. Damien and Seraphina would likely also die, and Sir Walter would acquire Luxley estate.

Evil would triumph over good.

Halting, she took a deep breath and closed her eyes. That wasn't right. *That wasn't truth!* A dozen stories from the Holy Scriptures flooded her mind, stories of saints of old in similar situations, in prison, on the run, facing death, shipwrecked, stranded, outnumbered, beaten, flogged, abandoned, rejected, even swallowed by a great fish! And each time, they were victorious through God's mighty power and love.

Hadn't she learned the lesson of the Spear? She had once thought it to be her source of power. She had put all her faith in a mere relic. But God had shown her that once she submitted herself to His Son, all the power she would ever need came to reside within her. All she had to do was believe!

Dropping to her knees, Alexia D'Clere repented of her doubts and began to pray the prayer of deliverance, the prayer of faith.

Ronar LePeine leaned his head against the cold iron bars and cursed. Aye, cursed. Something he hadn't done in quite some time. Familiar doubts assailed him, mocking him, chipping away at the wall of faith he'd built up over the past year.

"Alexia!" he shouted into the dark passageway in front of his cell. "Alexia!"

No answer came, save the patter of little feet and a stench of something so foul, it made his stomach curdle.

How could this be? He banged his head against the hard iron. Pain radiated through his temples and down his neck. Good. It would keep him angry, awake, thinking of some way to get out of this mess.

He was a warrior. He'd been trained to use his skill, strength, and wit to escape situations like these. But in here, none of those things mattered. He thumped his head against the iron yet again, then backed away.

Why, God, why? Why have you allowed our defeat?

It made no sense. He'd once thought God was a brutal dictator, inflicting heavy punishment on those who defied His laws, on anyone who made the slightest mistake. He'd spent his life trying to pay penance for deeds he'd done in his youth, but it never seemed to be enough.

Then he'd met Alexia. And she had shown him the real God, a loving, merciful God who sacrificed His own Son so wretches like Ronar could be forgiven, their slates wiped clean. She'd shown him there was a world beyond this one—the real world—where they would live forever with God in a paradise beyond imagining. He'd even seen glimpses of it, delightful visions God had granted him.

A rat scampered across his cell, stood on its hind feet, and stared at Ronar as if he were a curious addition to his home. Or mayhap a tasty meal.

"Not yet, little one. Not yet."

Ronar squatted and ran his finger across the dirt. Why then, when he and his friends had done everything God asked, were they about to be burned alive? Could he have been wrong about God? Was He the tyrant who demanded penance of His children, after all?

Yes, you were right about him. The voice in his head was all too familiar, a voice that had haunted him most of his life. 'Twas a torturing voice, nagging, judging, and always bringing confusion and despair.

He's not worth following.

Ronar stood and glanced over his dark cell. A shadow darker than the others drifted in one of the corners. *Did not God say He would never leave you, that He would order his angels to lift you up, lest you strike your foot against a stone*?

Ronar well remembered that Scripture from the Psalms, for the friar oft quoted it. The past few days, Ronar had doubted those words and others in the Bible. How easily he had reverted back to his old way of thinking when things went wrong. Granted, *many* things had gone wrong. But he should have been stronger.

Nay! Nay! He slammed his eyes shut and ground his fists into his temples. Scriptures popped into his thoughts, holy words he had read and memorized.

"Jesus said in this world we would have tribulation," he began in a low tone. "But He said He has overcome the world. He also said that if the world hated Him, it would hate us and persecute us." He increased his tone until he was all but shouting. "Jesus is worth everything! And even if I should die, I will never stop following Him. He is the truth, the life, and the way. He is pure love, and you are death and misery and despair."

The shadow dissipated, and the faintest hint of light took its place, though no torches were near.

Ronar fell to his knees, begged forgiveness for his doubts, and worshiped the Savior who would never leave him.

Cristiana hated bugs. She'd always been fearful of them, though it made no sense. In truth, they couldn't hurt her, most of them anyway. 'Twas simply that they were so ugly and slimy and skittery. Just like the rats and other vermin infesting the dungeon. Hence, she stood in the middle of her cell, leaping from foot to foot to keep the pests away.

She wished it would keep the doubts and fears away as well, for those particular scourges threatened her peace more than the bugs.

God has abandoned you. You are not worthy of His love.

The words kept pounding through her mind, hammering away at her faith, chipping away at her newfound belief that God would never leave her, that He loved her unconditionally, that He thought her so precious and valuable that He died for her. Not only died but was brutally tortured and then went to suffer in the depths of the earth before rising from the dead. All so she could also rise from the dead and be with Him. 'Twas the ultimate love story, and one that had brought her to her knees in praise.

Yet now, all alone in the dark with the dirt, stench, and frightening vermin, Cristiana felt her strength falter, her belief fade that she was loved by God, that He would never leave her. In truth, the past few days of bad news had already been dissolving her faith. She'd listened to the voice of the enemy, taunting her, filling her with despair.

"Lord, where are you?" She glanced upward, but saw only darkness, heard only the scampering of tiny feet. Hugging herself, she approached the iron grate keeping her prisoner and leaned her head against it, listening for the sound of her friends, desperately longing to hear a kind word, to hear the strong faith in her sister's voice, to feel Jarin's arms around her. When she'd doubted in the past, 'twas her friends who had come around her, prayed, encouraged her. 'Twas the friar who always had the right Scripture to recite, the right words of life that flooded her and cast out all fear.

But here, alone. Frightened.

Unworthy.

The voice was so loud, she glanced around, sure she would find someone standing there.

Your sister was always the strong one.

Indeed. Alexia was most likely singing praises in her cell right now as the Apostle Paul had done in a similar situation. Her faith never seemed to founder, whilst Cristiana's barely staggered along.

And now they were all to burn at the stake on the morrow.

A shiver coursed through her. She could not imagine the pain. How long would it last ere she fainted? Would she have to watch her friends burn along with her?

"Jarin!" She screamed through the bars, tears running down her cheeks. "Jarin! Alexia!"

No answer came, save a taunting chuckle in the distance from one of the guards.

Alone. Unloved.

"Nay!" She'd come too far. She'd seen too much to give in to despair now. The Lord had healed many people through her and, most of all, He had healed her. In more ways than one. Would a God do that for someone He found unworthy?

"Nay!" she screamed again.

Precious daughter.

That voice. That loving voice that brought hope and joy and life! "I am here, Lord."

A light appeared. A speck on the ground by her feet. Wiping away her tears, she stared at it, bewildered. It grew, spreading like a pool of fresh water on the dry ground, flowing over her feet, up her legs, and all around her. Bugs scampered back toward the shadows.

Cristiana lifted her hands. The light shone on them. She glanced up. It extended to the ceiling. *She was encased in a cone of light!* Yet it wasn't like any light she'd seen. It had no source but glowed from within, faint and golden.

She began to laugh. She twirled and moved to the back of the cell. It followed her.

God had never left her. God was with her. Always.

Fear and doubt skittered away with the bugs as Cristiana fell to her knees and prayed. Whether God rescued them from this trial or not, she was loved. She was His. And should she die, she'd instantly be in His arms. Forever.

Once again, Jarin found himself in the dungeons of Luxley. Hadn't he been in this same cell not three months past? He'd laugh if the situation weren't so ominous. How was the Lord going to get him out of here this time, get them *all* out of here? With each of them locked up, there was no one to rescue them. And since none of them would betray the others with the lie Sir Walter demanded, they would each be burned at the stake.

He paced across the tiny circular cell, stopped at the door to peer through the bars out into the dark hallway, then took up his pace again, something he'd been doing for hours. He had no fear of death. He knew where he was going. God had graced him with a vision of heaven in a dream, and he would never forget it. 'Twas so real, so beautiful, so full of hope and love, he'd not wanted to wake up.

But God had told him his tasks in this place were not yet complete.

Were they complete now? What had he accomplished in the past few months other than feeding hungry villagers? And praying. He'd been doing a lot of praying and praising. Two things the friar said were weapons mightier than sword and ax.

Regardless, he found himself wishing for sword and ax at the moment.

He'd once believed that he couldn't trust God. That bad things happened to people who chose the right path, as they had his family. He'd believed God was distant and unworthy of Jarin's attention.

He couldn't have been more wrong.

Cristiana had shown him a different path. She had shown him love. *Real* love. The love that blossomed in her could only have come from the Almighty. *Cristiana.* He gripped his head and raked back his hair. His biggest fear right now was not for himself but for her. How frightened she must be in this place. She had entertained doubts of late, and it had pained him to watch. But he supposed everyone doubted now and then. Particularly since they had an enemy who loved to whisper lies in their ears.

As the fiend had been doing since the guard tossed Jarin inside this cell.

But he had come to recognize the beast's lies for what they were—impotent attempts to lead God's children astray. In truth, Satan had no power. The Lord had defanged him on the cross. All he had left were lies.

And Jarin wasn't buying them anymore.

Even the enemy's attempt to separate the Knights of the Eternal Realm was a pathetic lie, for they were not united by mere physical presence, but in Spirit, the Spirit of the Living God! Their prayers, joined together, bore the same power as if they linked arms.

He smiled and glanced over the familiar stone walls that rose high above him.

The enemy made a huge mistake in putting him in this cell, for 'twas here in this place devoid of hope and love that he had found both.

In full measure.

In the person of His Lord and Savior.

Dropping to his knees, he spread his arms out in worship. And once again, just as before, his Savior appeared in a swath of golden light. He smiled at Jarin.

"My God and my King." Jarin bowed before him and prayed for his friends, for Damien and Seraphina, and finally for God's will to be done.

How long he knelt there basking in God's love, he could not say. What he could say is that all his fears, all his despair had long since departed, and he never wanted the moment to end.

Keys jingling and a lock clanking snapped him from his worship. His door screeched open, and a torch made him blink. Rising, he glanced behind it to find…*Cedric LeGode*?

Nay, the man looked different than he remembered. He'd aged. His hair was no longer light but the color of dirt. His silly smile had been replaced by a somber expression. And though he wore a fine velvet tunic, he appeared ragged, as if he'd fought a thousand battles.

Jarin charged him. "You abducted Cristiana. You tried to kill her—us!"

"I did." Cedric backed away, flinging the torch before him.

Shoving aside the flame, Jarin clutched the man's throat and shoved him against the open door. One glance down the passageway revealed no guards had accompanied him.

Cedric dropped the torch and gripped Jarin's hands, coughing and sputtering. "If you kill me, I cannot help you," he managed to stammer out.

Pushing down his rage, Jarin released him. Raising hands to his neck, Cedric gasped for air, all the while keeping his eyes on Jarin. "I beg your forgiveness for what I've done, Sir Jarin."

Jarin could make no sense of the man's behavior. Nor did he care. He had a mind to grab the keys and go find his friends, but he still had no idea where they were.

"Show me where my friends are," he demanded.

"I intend to." Cedric retrieved the sputtering torch and started into the dark passageway. "Come. We haven't much time."

'Twas a trap. It had to be. But what other choice did Jarin have?

"Why are you helping us?" He hesitated to follow.

Cedric faced him, the torch light reflecting in eyes no longer lifeless and dull. In truth, there appeared to be a new sparkle within them.

"Cristiana showed me another path, a better path than the one I was on. Now, prithee make haste."

Smiling, Jarin hurried after him. That sounded just like Cristiana.

In fact, 'twas to her cell they went next. Though she gave a wary glance toward Cedric as he approached and opened her cell, she flew into Jarin's arms nonetheless.

Ah, sweet ecstasy. To feel her safely in his arms again. He kissed her cheek and stroked her hair and wished he could never let go. But she withdrew and smiled at Cedric.

"You sought God. You turned from the darkness," she said.

"I did, my lady. Now"—he turned—"come."

Slipping her hand in Jarin's, she followed Cedric. How easily she trusted. Still Jarin had no choice, though he kept himself wary and at the ready.

Nevertheless, despite Jarin's doubts, Cedric released both Ronar and Alexia as promised and then went up a level to Anabelle's cell. All were elated to see each other. All remained hushed as Cedric led them through the darkened passageways to a row of storage chambers in the back of the castle.

Jarin finally allowed himself to hope. If 'twas a ploy to capture and kill them, it made no sense, for Sir Walter already had them in his grip.

"We can find our way out from here." Alexia turned toward Cedric. "Come with us. It won't be safe for you here now."

"Nay." He glanced over his shoulder, up the stairs they had just descended. "I have work to do. There is great evil in the castle, and it must be stopped."

Ronar frowned. "Then we should stay and help."

Cedric shook his head. "I am trusted. You are not. Now go. My father and his warlock will no doubt send an army after you."

"Won't they know 'twas you who released us?" Cristiana asked. "Prithee, join us."

"You are kind." He shook his head as what appeared to be tears filled his eyes. "Far kinder than I deserve." He smiled. "I am safe in my Father's hands."

And Jarin knew he didn't mean Sir Walter.

"Aye, you are." Alexia gripped his arm, then turned to leave.

Jarin could still not believe that Sir Walter's son had forsaken his evil ways and turned to God, but Cristiana bore no doubt, for she gave the man a gentle hug. "God bless you, kind sir."

"And you, my lady. Go with God."

And as Jarin grabbed Cristiana's hand and followed Alexia and Ronar into the tunnels, he knew they needed God now more than ever.

CHAPTER TWENTY-NINE

Damien had not only been trained in the art of battle, but also in the art of tracking an enemy, a skill well-honed when he and his fellow King's Guards oft escorted His Majesty on journeys. Hence, he had no problem finding William and his army, a troop of at least three hundred soldiers, from what he could tell, well-trained and well-armed, led by a man who Damien now knew was evil incarnate.

'Twas but three days travel to Luxley, and they'd already gone two. Thank God they had not found Seraphina, or he'd have to affect her rescue as well. Now as they made camp in a wide meadow beside a creek, built their fires, hunted for game, and roasted their meat, Damien did the same, waiting for nightfall. He needed his strength for the impossible task before him.

Sneak into an enemy camp. And kill their leader.

But not until he confronted him with his lies, his betrayal, and the murder of Damien's parents. He wanted to see the man's face, to witness his terror when he realized he was about to die for his crimes, when he realized he was about to be thrust into hell.

Then, with his revenge complete, Damien would seek out Seraphina, and together they would find their friends and warn them of the coming army.

Damien lowered to sit on a log he'd dragged before the small fire. A rabbit hung on a skewer over the flames, filling the air with the scent of roasted meat. His mouth watered. Removing a water pouch from his belt, he uncorked it and took a long drink. Aye, water. He vowed to give up wine. Made a promise to the Almighty, if He was listening. Damien's overindulgence in drink had cost him too much over the years, disappointments, missed opportunities and last but not least, failing to protect the ones he loved. No more.

The fact that he was even talking to God yet again astounded him. After his parents died, he'd made up his mind that God didn't care about the affairs of men, that He didn't see the pain evil men caused. Or surely the man who had murdered his parents would have been brought to justice. In truth, Damien had ignored God for years, so bent on getting his revenge, on taking the place of God and judging the guilty.

Then he'd met Alexia and Cristiana, and he witnessed the power and love of God in ways he never imagined. He saw how God changed his friends, Ronar and Jarin. But 'twas Seraphina who had shown him what love really was, what forgiveness and humility looked like.

Though she'd been abandoned by her parents, left in the hands of strangers, she never sought revenge, never expressed anger or resentment. Though she was a mere servant in Luxley Castle, her devotion and love for Cristiana and Alexia put all other love to shame. Her thoughts were always on the happiness of others, in the service of others. She was majestic and pure, like an angel sent from heaven to grace this world for a short while. No wonder he'd fallen in love with her. No wonder he'd do anything for her.

Nay. He hung his head. He'd do anything *save* give up his need for revenge. And for that cause, he'd betrayed the woman he loved. In the worst possible way.

What kind of man did that?

Taking his knife, he stabbed the cooked rabbit, thrust it onto a cold rock by his feet, and began carving it up.

Revenge will destroy you.

Halting, he glanced upward at the dark treetops rustling in the wind and the expanse of stars popping out across the darkening sky.

Revenge is your idol.

The voice lingered on a breeze that swirled around Damien and caused leaves to dance over the ground. Nonsense. He was hearing things. Then why did the words ring true within him?

He stabbed a piece of meat and slid it in his mouth. The succulent morsel soured on his tongue. Judas! What was wrong with him? A vision of Adred, his one-time good friend, blazed in his mind, the hatred, the misery on his face. Adred's need for revenge had destroyed him, reduced him to an empty shell of a man.

Wasn't it doing the same to Damien? How much of himself, of his friends, of his soul was he willing to sacrifice to see justice?

Vengeance is mine. I will repay.

Nay, Lord! He was so close. Could he not simply get his retribution and then vow never to seek revenge again? How could he go on with his life when he knew the man who murdered his parents still lived? Not only lived, but could possibly become king? Nay. William must pay. And pay he would.

Several hours later, with his belly full, his fire doused, and blade in hand, Damien peered through the foliage toward the army camp. Lord Haleford, William, was easy to find. Though there were only two tents, one for the commander and one for him, his was the one with the royal crests and emblems all over it. Pompous snod.

All Damien had to do was take out two guards, make his way through the sleeping camp, and enter William's tent unawares. Not a problem. He'd been in far more perilous situations.

The first guard went down without a fight. He neither heard Damien creep up nor made a sound when Damien knocked him unconscious with the hilt of his sword. After tying him to a tree and gagging him, Damien moved on to the second man. Unfortunately, he was more alert than the first soldier, but in no time at all, the man was sleeping like a babe, also tied and gagged. He did, however, let out a shout in the process. Hence, Damien now waited at the edge of camp to see if anyone came.

No one did.

Rising to his full height, with sword at his side and wearing his King's Guard uniform, Damien LaRage marched into his enemy's camp as if he were one of the many soldiers who belonged there. And in the darkness, who would know the difference? In truth, he passed a few men sitting by a crackling fire, but they barely afforded him a glance. Hence, 'twas no trouble to slip into the shadows beside William's tent, glance around for anyone watching, and then open the flap and step inside.

Snoring filled the darkness.

Squinting, Damien searched for a candle, then lit it with flint and steel and approached his nemesis. He looked so peaceful lying there, so much like the friend Damien had always known. Setting the candle beside the man's cot, Damien drew his knife and held it to William's throat.

He jerked up with a squeal, eyes wide and hands reaching toward his unknown assailant.

"Shh." Damien forced him down and grinned. "One sound. One shout, one move, and I'll slice your throat."

"Damien. What are you doing?" William's voice emerged muddled with sleep.

"What I should have done years ago."

There it was. Terror finally sparked across William's eyes. "I don't know what—"

Damien pressed the blade. Skin broke and a trickle of blood spilled down William's nightshirt. "I will hear no more of your lies. You ravished my mother. You murdered my father. You left me an orphan."

William swallowed hard and glanced toward the tent door.

"By the time your guard arrives, you'll be drowning in a pool of your own blood." Damien longed to bring that about, but he needed the man to admit what he'd done. He wanted the fiend to beg for his life.

"And you'll be captured and hanged," William managed to say.

"You think that wouldn't be worth it? I've been waiting for this moment my entire life."

William's breath became labored, for he must have realized how serious Damien was.

"Admit what you've done." Damien held the blade so tightly, his knuckles began to ache. "Admit it."

"I never meant to—"

"Ravish my mother?"

"I was young, Damien." He shook his head. "I was foolish."

"Foolish is getting drunk and sleeping with the milkmaid. Ravishing a young married woman is naught but evil."

William had no response, yet Damien could see him plotting behind his eyes.

"And my father. He didn't die from an accident. He had figured you out. He was going to tell the king, wasn't he?" Gripping William with his free hand, Damien shook him. "Wasn't he?!"

"What are you going to do with me?" Terror stung in William's tone.

"I'm going to kill you. I'm going to gut you from head to toe for what you did to my parents *and* to me." Damien leaned forward, every nerve, every muscle wound tight and hot with more hatred than he'd ever felt. One quick press of his blade, and the world would have one less monster. "You pretended to be my friend, my mentor. How could you?"

The monster's eyes grew wild with fear. "I hated what I'd done. I wanted to make it up to you."

"You only wished to appease your guilt. You cared naught for me. Liar! Murderer! You will never be king!" Damien pressed the knife. More blood spilled.

"Prithee! I beg you," William stammered. "I'm sorry. I'm so sorry." He began to sob like the coward he was.

Revenge will destroy you.

Damien's hand shook. Hatred raged through him so fast, he could hardly contain it, feared he'd end William's life before Damien had his fill of listening to him grovel.

Revenge is mine. Trust me.

Trust you, God? Damien had seen too many evil people succeed and too many good people suffer.

I am the judge of the quick and the dead.

Damien pressed the blade. More blood streamed. William whimpered and shook like an infant on a cold night. The friar had said there would be a reckoning for each person at the end of time, a judgment that would render justice fairly.

Warmth swirled around Damien as if someone wrapped him in a blanket. Yet 'twas a warmth that was alive, a warmth filled with love, joy, and peace, the likes of which he'd never known. It soothed every nerve, loosened every muscle, and swept away all his hatred.

Withdrawing his knife, he stood back. If he murdered this man, would that not make him as much a monster as he? Would not God's justice suffice, whene'er it was meted out? Damien had no proof of this man's crimes, merely the word of a bitter wife and an absent bishop. Hence, he could not bring him back to court.

But did he trust God? He stood for a moment, staring at the pathetic excuse for a man, a nobleman cowering on his bed, eyes screaming with fear and lips trembling, and he found naught but disgust for him.

Breathing hard, William scrambled to sit and swung legs over his cot. "I knew you couldn't kill me, Damien."

"'Twas not you who stopped me. You owe your life to God."

"God, bah! We have a bond, you and I, an affection." The man dared to glance up at Damien, the smug look in his eyes making Damien long to return the knife to his throat.

"We have neither. Why do you pursue Seraphina de Mowbray?"

He pressed fingers over the blood trickling down his neck. "She defied the king's order to remain at the palace. As did you, I see."

Damien knew there was more to it than that, for William would not accompany an army for so small an infraction. Nay, the man was scheming something far more odious, but Damien found he no longer cared.

Sheathing his knife, he stared at the man he had once considered a father. "You will be judged for your crimes one day, William. And when you bow before the Almighty, there will be no mercy given. Ergo, I encourage you to repent long before that day."

William's thin lips curved to one side ere a pompous snort emerged from his mouth.

Damien shook his head, turned, and marched from the tent.

Crisp night air wafted over him, sweeping away all remaining anger and hatred. Only pity remained. Pity and sorrow for a man who, if he didn't change, would spend eternity in hell.

A shout of "Intruder" blared from William's tent, but Damien cared not. He proceeded through the camp as if he were king himself, as if he were escorted by a host of warrior angels. In truth, he sensed them all around him as he made his way to the forest. Soldiers rushed here and there, alerted by William's calls, but none stopped him. 'Twas like he was invisible as he marched through their ranks.

Once within the protection of the forest, Damien LaRage dropped to his knees, bowed his head before the King of Kings, and repented of his hatred and revenge, his lies and anger. A burden lifted off him, a burden he'd been struggling to carry for far too long.

He was free at last.

CHAPTER THIRTY

Seraphina adjusted her long skirts over the side of the horse as she led him deeper into Emerald Forest. To her left, Mistress Matilda of Andro rode on a fine palfrey, whilst to her right, fully armed and ever-vigilant Sir Gregory Manchow, knight of Enclasen, watched over them both.

As he had done for nearly three days.

Though she was grateful for the protection *and* the company, Seraphina could still make no sense of how Lady Rochford had procured both for a mere maid. Nor why Lord Haleford would bother sending an army after such a lowborn prisoner. The three of them had spoken little on their journey, merely ridden as fast as they could and stopped only to rest and eat. The silence had given Seraphina much time to think, to plan, and unfortunately much time to mourn Damien's betrayal.

What had she accomplished in Regalis in risking her life by going to the king? Nothing. The king had not granted clemency for her friends, nor had he restored Luxley to Alexia and Cristiana. To make matters worse, Seraphina had lost the Spear, or rather, it had been stolen by the one man she had trusted most in the world, the one man she loved.

Lifting her arm, she absently rubbed her wrist where the mark of the Spear no longer resided. She missed it. She missed being its protector, and she prayed it had ended up with someone more worthy than she.

Hence, she'd not been able to keep tears from streaming down her face through most of the journey. Thankfully, it appeared neither Matilda nor Sir Gregory took note. Or mayhap they were merely being kind.

Regardless, she could not deny the leap of her heart when they first entered Emerald Forest. *Home.* Even though she'd spent most of her childhood in Luxley Castle, this was the forest which surrounded it, the lush forest where she'd spent the last several months living in an underground home with her closest friends in the world, her fellow Knights of the Eternal Realm.

Matilda turned to her. “Are you sure this is the right way, mistress?”

Seraphina smiled. “Aye. We are nearly there. Your journey has come to an end, and you can return home anon.” She reached over to touch the woman’s arm and give it a squeeze. “I am so grateful for your company.”

Matilda smiled and gripped Seraphina’s hand. “’Tis been my pleasure.”

Seraphina turned to Sir Gregory. “I am grateful to you as well, sir.”

“’Tis my honor, my lady.” The knight dipped his head.

She thought to correct him regarding her title but remained silent. Instead, she eased her horse down a narrow path lined with oak and elm trees and drew a deep breath. The scent of pine and musk and the pungent odor of fall filled her nose, bringing back memories of happier times hunting and foraging with Alexia and Sir Ronar and Sir Dami—Nay! She would not think of him. She *would* not.

Fire and Ashes! Tears burned her eyes yet again. She slapped them away and proceeded. She must only think of the future now, not the past. Soon the forest would prevent the horses from going further, and she’d say goodbye to her new friends, for she couldn’t risk them discovering the friar’s secret hideout.

The task was more difficult than she imagined, for they both insisted they were under strict orders to see her to safety. But with much assurance, Seraphina finally convinced them that she had but a few yards to walk and all would be well.

Now, alone once again and on foot, she gripped her cloak about her neck against a sudden chill and brushed aside a leafy branch. Finally the sound she longed to hear danced about her ears, the soothing gurgle and splash of the waterfall that hid their secret home.

She heard something else. Leaves shifting, twigs snapping…and voices. Ducking behind a thick shrub, she waited, peering through leaves to see who was coming.

What if it was Lord Haleford's soldiers? She'd be hauled back to Regalis where she'd no doubt be executed for escaping. She'd never see her friends again. Never see Damien again. Heart pounding so hard, she feared others could hear it, she bowed her head and prayed. She no longer had the Spear. Would God protect her?

Believe, precious daughter. Only believe.

The words swirled within her, caressing her tight nerves and easing the thrashing of her heart. When she opened her eyes, a distant figure emerged from the greenery. 'Twas but a pair of legs, clad in breeches and leather armor. But she'd recognize them anywhere. Along with the sword that hung by his side.

Sir Ronar LePeine.

Slowly rising, she took a tentative step from behind the shrub and waited. 'Twould do no good to charge toward him if he was being escorted by soldiers.

But a shock of bright red hair appeared as laughter filled the air, and Seraphina grabbed her skirts and dashed through the forest, shoving aside branches and leaves as she went.

She was met with the sight of two swords pointed her way, an arrow drawn tight in a bow, a stiletto, and five faces filled with shock. That shock slowly transformed into wide smiles as they each lowered their weapons and ran toward her.

"Seraphina! Seraphina!" Cristiana reached her first and flung both arms around her.

"We thought you were dead." Alexia joined her sister in giving Seraphina a tight embrace.

Ronar's smile couldn't have been wider as he watched the ladies' reunion. He glanced at Jarin who offered him a wink.

Cristiana and Alexia nearly smothered Seraphina, but she didn't mind. 'Twas so good to be among friends again. Finally, Alexia pulled back. "Where have you been? What happened?"

"Where is Damien?" Jarin asked, glancing around.

Gripping Cristiana's hand, Seraphina took a deep breath and swept her gaze over them all. "I have so much to tell you. So much has happened." Her eyes landed on Anabelle. "Mistress Anabelle, why are you here?"

Jarin chuckled. "'Tis a long story as well. Suffice it to say we have just escaped the dungeons at Luxley."

Dungeons? Then her vision had been true. Seraphina's mind spun. "I'm so glad I found you, but we must—"

"Did you speak to the king? Are we pardoned?" Ronar interrupted.

"I reached the king, aye. But there has been no pardon." Seraphina bit her lip.

"Is Damien…?" Ronar stared at her, his blue eyes full of angst.

"Alive as far as I know," she said, ignoring the pang in her heart.

"Alive and well!" Damien's voice filtered on the breeze, making Seraphina question her sanity. Surely she was hearing things. Nay. The stomp of boots sounded, and she looked up to see the strong knight himself plunging through leaves and branches, a grin on his otherwise austere face and his eyes locked on her.

Heart racing, she averted her gaze, angry at the thrill she felt at the sight of him.

"Damien!" Ronar gripped his arm whilst Jarin slapped his back. "We heard you and Seraphina were imprisoned at the palace."

"For a time, aye." His eyes were still on Seraphina, which made her all the angrier. Good. 'Twould keep the tears away.

Without looking at him, she tugged on Cristiana and started toward the waterfall. "We must away at once. There is danger. Come." The quicker they entered the safety of their hideout, the better.

"Aye. The king's army is fast approaching." Damien nodded. "We have much to tell you, but let us away to safety first."

With nods of agreement, they all started for the waterfall.

Jarin held up one hand to stop them whilst placing the other over his lips. He and Ronar exchanged a glance—not a good glance from what Seraphina could see, but a wary glance, a warrior's glance.

Every muscle within her stiffened.

Jarin slowly drew his blade, and Ronar and Damien did the same. Alexia slipped the bow from her shoulder.

The tips of a dozen swords poked through the foliage.

Cristiana stiffened beside Seraphina. Anabelle gasped and moved closer to them.

A soldier Seraphina recognized as the commander of the king's army emerged from the greenery, a blade in his hand, and a victorious grin on his face.

His gaze landed on Jarin and Ronar in recognition, then over to Damien. "God's favor has surely shone down on me today. Not only have I caught the witches of Luxley, but the traitors to the king as well."

Stripped of his weapons and hands bound behind his back, Damien was once again led to the slaughter. Only this time, everyone he cared about in this world walked beside him.

And it was all his fault.

He'd been so confident, so joyful after his encounter with the living God, after he'd relinquished his hatred and revenge, that he had not noticed the soldiers who followed him.

The soldiers he had led straight to his friends, to the woman he loved—the woman who would not even look his way. Yet how could he blame her?

The tips of swords jabbing their sides had forbidden them conversation on the four-hour trek back to the army camp. Back to Lord William Haleford, regent of the crown, and the troops he commanded.

Now as the seven of them stood before the gloating knave, Damien ground his teeth so hard, he felt they'd loosen and pop out. He should have killed him when he had the chance. Yet deep within his spirit, he knew he'd done the right thing.

Trust me.

Trust. A skill Damien had not perfected as of yet.

"Erect poles and tie them to each one in the center of camp," William commanded two soldiers who stood at the front of a growing crowd around them. Sunlight glinted off the gold chain around his neck, nearly blinding Damien.

"What are you going to do with us?" Ronar asked.

Spinning to face them, William tapped a finger on his bearded chin. "Much less than you deserve, I assure you. I should burn you all at the stake for witchcraft and sorcery, but alas, the king will wish proof of your demise." He smiled. "Hence I will have you all run through with the sword and your bodies dumped before the throne."

Commander Sadon stepped forward. "Is that wise, my lord? Should the king not have a chance to question them?"

"I am regent!" William raged, his face reddening. "You will address me as Your Majesty."

Sadon lowered his gaze and backed away, but Damien could feel his fury from where he stood.

"Question my orders again, and you will join them!" Spinning around, William marched away, leaving the soldiers to make quick work of fashioning stakes from fallen trees, driving them into the ground, and tying each prisoner to them.

The soldiers, knights, and men Damien had once commanded gazed at them from a distance, horror and pity on their faces. Was this to be his end? *All* their ends? Damien glanced up at the sky where white clouds drifted past the bright sun as if all was well with the world, then down beside him where, as fate would have it, Seraphina was tied a few feet away. Sweat streaked down his back as the scents of the forest and the stench of unwashed bodies assailed him.

"I'm sorry, Seraphina. I never meant to hurt you."

Though clearly in pain from the tight bindings on her wrists, she held her head high. "You betrayed me. You lied to me. Why?"

"The bishop promised to tell me who murdered my parents and to convince the king to pardon all of us." He had once thought it a valid reason for his betrayal, but of a sudden, it sounded rather pathetic.

She finally glanced at him, her blue eyes sharp as ice. "Why did you not tell me? Did you trust me so little to think I would not willingly give it to you?"

"Would you have? I asked you many times."

She turned away. "Nay. I needed it. I need it still. 'Tis what kept us alive, what granted us favor."

"You no longer have the Spear?" Cristiana asked from Seraphina's other side.

Seraphina shook her head. "We are all doomed now."

"Nay, sweet Sera. The Spear bears no power. 'Tis the Spirit of God within us that grants not only favor but all we need."

Damien hung his head. "I wish I had not taken it. 'Twas a huge mistake. I have made my peace with God, and He has set me free from my hatred and revenge."

Sir Jarin's voice boomed from beyond Cristiana. "I am pleased to hear it, my friend."

"Took me long enough." Damien chuckled, then grew somber. "I hope you can forgive me, Seraphina."

Wind whipped her ivory hair about her. "I forgive you because I must, strong knight, because we are about to stand before God, but I doubt I shall ever trust you again."

Damien nodded. 'Twas a start and more than he deserved. A tear slipped down her cheek, a diamond sparkling in the sun, and he finally saw how deep was the wound he had inflicted.

"We must not give up," Alexia said.

Ronar added. "Aye, we have been in worse situations than this."

"And God has always seen us through," Jarin said.

Anabelle began to sob.

"Stay strong, dear friend." Cristiana leaned forward to look at her. "God is with us."

"Nonsense! We are about to die!" Seraphina shouted for all of them to hear. "Do you not understand? I don't have the Spear!"

A few of the nearby soldiers glanced up and laughed.

Silence reigned for a minute ere Alexia spoke. "We must all pray. Together. There is power in the combined prayers of the saints."

"Agreed," Ronar said, and Damien joined his friends in bowing his head and appealing to the only One who could save them now.

Minutes later, his prayer was interrupted by William's vile shout and the stomp of soldiers approaching with swords in hand.

The Knights of the Eternal Realm lifted their heads to meet their fate.

CHAPTER THIRTY-ONE

Seraphina did her best to pray with the others, but her heart was so heavy, her body so unsteady, and her mind so confused, no words came to her. She heard her fellow Knights of the Eternal Realm praying. Nay, not praying, not pleading for their lives, but *praising* God, glorifying His Holy name, worshiping the One who had rescued them in every way possible.

Rescued? Did she believe that? Tied to a stake about to be run through with a sword? When she'd failed at every attempt to help her friends, to do the will of God? And now without the Spear, who was she? What power did she hold?

Cristiana had said the Spear held no power in itself, yet Seraphina had witnessed otherwise so many times, she found that hard to believe. What simple maid would have been allowed to set one foot inside the grand palace at Regalis? What simple maid would have been granted an audience with the king himself, granted a chance to speak to the queen? And then to be given freedom to wander about the palace, a lavish chamber, and maids to serve her? 'Twas unheard of. Only the Spear could have done that. In truth, once it was no longer in her possession, she'd been asked to leave.

Indeed, she'd failed in more ways than one. And now, she, along with Damien's help, had led their enemies right to her only friends in the world. They would all die here, a bloody and painful death,

And it was all her fault.

You are my princess.

The voice was so clear and strong, she raised her gaze. But all she saw was Lord Haleford marching toward her with ten soldiers by his side, all with swords drawn.

You are priceless.

"Did you say something?" she asked Damien.

Hair hanging around his face, he looked at her curiously, shook his head, and then faced Lord Haleford, who had stopped before them, an imperious grin on his face. Oddly, the man's narrowed eyes were on her, not the others. Why the man wanted her dead, she could not say. What had she ever done to him? More important, why would he want Damien dead?

As if sensing her question, Damien peered at her through strands of his hair. "He's the one who ravished my mother and murdered my father."

Seraphina blinked and drew in a deep breath to calm the shock gyrating through her.

Lord Haleford shifted his gaze to Damien. "You should have killed me when you had the chance."

Damien smiled. "Why bother when you are already dead."

Jarin laughed. "Well said, Damien."

"Welcome to the kingdom, Damien." Alexia leaned forward to offer him a smile.

Anabelle continued her sobbing.

"Let the maid go," Cristiana said. "She is not with us."

Lord Haleford snapped his gaze to Anabelle, flattened his lips, then shrugged. "I am not without mercy. She means naught to me." He snapped his fingers. "Release her."

Seraphina whispered her thanks to God as they cut Anabelle's ropes and she stepped back, rubbing her wrists. "I can't leave you." Her frightened gaze traveled over them.

"Go," Ronar said. "Go with God, Anabelle. There's naught you can do here."

She nodded, her eyes filling with tears as she turned and rushed away.

"Now, any last words?" Lord Haleford adjusted the lace at his cuffs. A crowd of soldiers had formed around him, including Commander Sadon, who looked none too happy.

Still Seraphina knew he would not defy the regent or surely he would join them.

You are royalty.

That voice, that sweet, strong voice that filled every crevice of her being with hope and joy. *And* love.

The Spear has no power. 'Tis the Spirit of God. Cristiana's words blared through Seraphina, striking against the walls of her heart, chipping away at all untruth.

You are majestic in Me.

Breath hastening, heart pounding, and a tingle of power spreading over her, Seraphina lifted her head and locked her gaze upon Lord Haleford.

"You will not kill us," she said with the authority of a queen.

He stared at her, no doubt shocked at her audacity ere he slunk toward her, placed a finger beneath her chin, and cocked his head. "Oh, my dear, I assure you, I will."

She jerked her face away. "You can only kill our bodies. And only should God allow."

"Amen!" her friends said in unison.

"Bah!" Lord Haleford laughed and retreated, then gestured for the soldiers to step forward with their swords.

Her friends began singing praises to God.

A flood of light and peace swept over Seraphina so strong, she felt it would carry her away. She glanced up to heaven and smiled, basking in the love of God. When she lowered her gaze, 'twas to a very confused look on Lord Haleford's face.

"Our God will rescue us," Seraphina said. "And if He should not, then we shall be with Him soon in paradise."

Her friends smiled her way.

"Enough of this madness!" Lord Haleford grimaced and raised his hand. "Kill them! Kill them all!"

The soldiers approached, swords ready to thrust into Seraphina and her friends. She closed her eyes and prayed, preparing herself for the pain, knowing it would last but a moment before she'd see the face of her Savior.

Moments passed. The sun poured molten heat upon them. Perspiration formed on her neck and arms. Pounding sounded in her ears. The beating of her heart no doubt. Nay. 'Twas horses' hooves.

Fire and ashes! Get on with it! Pressing her lips together, she felt her body tighten, bracing for the thrust of a sword.

Other sounds reached her ears. Lord Haleford's groan, the crank and squeal of a carriage, then a shout.

"Cease at once!"

Seraphina opened her eyes. At least a dozen members of the elite King's Guard shoved through the soldiers and marched up to Lord Haleford, who turned and fisted both hands at his waist.

"What goes on here? You defy the order of your king!"

"Nay." Sir Tybalt LeReed, captain of the King's Guard, held up a sealed paper. "I come with orders from the *true* king."

A flash of crimson drew Seraphina's gaze to the crowd where Lady Rochford appeared, red skirts in hand, weaving through the soldiers in their direction. Her eyes met Seraphina's, and a huge smile lifted her lips as she approached and bowed to her knees before her. "Your Royal Highness."

Lord Haleford's brow rutted as huffing and blubbering streamed from his lips. "Get up, you fool!" He went to grab Lady Rochford's arm, but Sir Tybalt stepped between them.

Seraphina could make no sense of it. She exchanged glances with her friends, but they all appeared as confused as she.

"Lower your swords at once!" Sir Tybalt ordered as he gestured for the King's Guard to release Seraphina and her friends.

Rubbing her sore wrists, Seraphina stepped away from the stake. Alexia and Ronar praised God as Jarin drew Cristiana in a tight embrace. Damien took up a protective stance beside Seraphina, though there was no need. The King's Guard stood on either side of them, weapons drawn. A few of them turned to give an affirming nod at Ronar, Jarin, and Damien.

"Rise, my lady." Embarrassed, Seraphina gripped Lady Rochford's arm and assisted her up. "Have you gone mad?"

Lord Haleford snatched the paper from Sir Tybalt, broke the seal and read it. Whatever it contained, it caused his face to sink, his eyes to widen, and his breathing to halt.

"Lies! Naught but lies!" he blubbered.

Retrieving the paper, Sir Tybalt handed it to Commander Sadon. After perusing it, he glanced at Seraphina with an odd look and then shouted, "Restrain Lord Haleford on order of the king."

"With great pleasure." Sir Tybalt gestured to two soldiers standing nearby, and they immediately grabbed Lord Haleford.

"I am regent! I'll have your heads for this!" the man shouted, struggling against the soldier's grips.

"'Tis *your* head you should worry about, my lord," Tybalt responded.

"Tybalt," Ronar called to his former captain. "What is this about?"

"Not that we are complaining," Jarin added.

Sir Tybalt approached them, a slight grin on his face. "'Tis good to see you, Sir Ronar and Sir Jarin. We have missed you in the Guard." He held out his arm, and they both gripped it, one after the other, though tentatively at first.

"Have you come to arrest us, Sir Tybalt?" Jarin asked.

He laughed. "Nay." He glanced over them. "The king has issued pardons for all of you. Even the D'Clere sisters." He smiled toward Cristiana and Alexia.

Yet before they could celebrate, he grew somber and shifted his gaze to Seraphina. A most curious look overcame him, almost a look of awe, but that couldn't be. Dipping his head in her direction, he turned and faced the army which surrounded them.

"Bow before the princess of Enclasen!"

Seraphina glanced behind her. *Princess*?

Mumbling rumbled across the crowed. Lord Haleford growled. Sir Tybalt raised the paper. "She is the daughter of King Peter II!"

Shock froze Seraphina as he continued. "Taken away at birth to save her from this man!" He pointed to Lord Haleford.

"He murdered the queen and now attempts to take the throne for himself!"

Princess? Daughter of King Peter? A buzzing filled Seraphina's head, spinning her thoughts, ere it traveled down her neck, her spine, and caused her legs to buckle.

Damien took her arm and shored her up ere she toppled to the ground. She wouldn't look at him. She *couldn't* look at him, for surely he was laughing at the ludicrous notion.

Drawing a deep breath, she closed her eyes for a moment, hoping to clear her mind, her thoughts from this insanity. Shuffling sounded. When she looked up again, the King's Guard, the soldiers, Lady Rochford, and Sir Tybalt all knelt before her. She glanced at her friends, who stared at her aghast ere they, too, took a knee.

"She is but a maid, a common servant!" Lord Haleford shouted, even as the soldiers forced him to his knees. "I am the true king!"

I am the princess of Enclasen? Seraphina gazed over the crowd bowing before her. Her parents hadn't abandoned her, after all! Reaching down, she lifted Lady Rochford from the ground once again. "You knew? How? I don't understand."

Lady Rochford wiped a tear from her eyes. "The queen's babe was not stillborn, as all believed. I suspected Lord Haleford had murdered your mother. Alas, I knew he would kill you as well. I knew not what to do, so I whisked you away to a convent on the far edge of the kingdom where you would be safe." She frowned. "When I went back to get you, you were gone, and the convent was burned to the ground. Can you forgive me, Your Royal Highness?"

"Prithee, don't call me that. 'Tis far too strange to my ears." Seraphina shook her head. "But of course, I forgive you. You saved my life."

One glance around her revealed everyone remained on their knees. Bowing to her? "Prithee, rise!" She turned back to Lady Rochford. "How did you know 'twas me?"

"I didn't. I found your swaddling cloth. The emblem on it was unique to your mother." Her eyes lit up. "I gave it to the king. He knows, and he longs to see you."

"I have a father…" Seraphina breathed out, unable to stop the tears from filling her eyes.

Her friends surrounded her with smiles and looks of shock. "I cannot believe it. We had the princess in our home all along!' Alexia gripped Seraphina's hand.

"I am so pleased." Cristiana embraced her.

Ronar took her hand and dipped his head. "Your Royal Highness."

Jarin chuckled. "We have been in the presence of royalty."

Damien remained by her side but said naught.

"We are *all* royalty," Seraphina returned. "The Lord has shown me this. We are all children of the great King."

"Indeed," Jarin said.

Sir Tybalt approached. "What are your orders, Your Royal Highness?"

Seraphina stared at him in wonder then glanced over the crowd. All eyes were upon her, but she didn't care. God had granted her favor! More favor and power than she could ever have dreamt. And without the Spear! 'Twas true then. The relic held no power. All power and favor and glory came from God's Spirit within her. In the kingdom of God, all His children were royalty!

The crowd parted as Seraphina moved toward Lord Haleford. He stood, head held high, arrogance riding on his stiff shoulders. His arms wiggled from his attempt to free himself from the ropes behind him.

This man had caused so much pain, so much heartache. He had ravished Damien's mother and murdered his father, sending him on a journey of revenge that nearly killed him. He had taken her mother from her, the king's beloved wife from him, and nearly killed her and all her friends. And for what? The throne? Power? How empty.

"You are a vile and evil man who has caused much pain for many people. But I will not have you killed as you would have done to me. Nay. You will return to face your brother and admit your crimes."

No shame, no fear appeared in the man's eyes as he stared at Seraphina. A chill ran over her at the evil she saw within them. "Take him away," she ordered and turned to join her friends.

A mighty growl roared behind her.

Damien grabbed a sword from one of the King's Guards and rushed toward her.

"You will never be queen!" Lord Haleford shouted, and Seraphina turned just in time to see a blade slicing toward her heart.

Soldiers scrambled to react, their movements oddly slow and cumbersome as if they moved through syrup.

No time to pray. No time to even scream.

CHAPTER THIRTY-TWO

Damien had been watching William closely. He'd seen him struggle against the ropes binding his hands behind him. He'd seen the soldiers' grips on his arms loosen as time went on. He'd watched the other men around them distracted by the revelation of their new princess. Hence, it took him no time at all to reach the fiend, sword in hand, when he attempted to take Seraphina's life.

Shoving her aside, Damien plunged his blade into William's arm, nearly severing it. The man dropped his sword with a scream that would wake the dead. Soldiers swamped him, restraining any further attempts. But the man would cause them no more trouble, for he collapsed to the ground, holding his arm together, and dropped into unconsciousness.

Seraphina fell against Damien, breathing hard. "Thank you, Damien. I didn't… I didn't see him."

Flinging an arm around her, Damien drew her close. It felt so good to have her near again, but he knew 'twould be a long time ere he gained her trust. If ever. *Seraphina, princess of the kingdom*? The truth refused to sink into his reason. He'd fallen in love with the princess, but now she could never be his. A princess would not marry a simple knight. A more important and noble match would be made for her. She'd always thought she was too far beneath him. He'd laugh at the irony if his heart weren't breaking. Regardless, she was alive and in his arms, and he would cherish the moment.

She pushed from him. "Why did you not kill him?"

Damien glanced after the soldiers as they led William away. "And send him to hell? Nay. Who knows? He might still repent."

She smiled, that sweet, alluring smile of hers that made his insides warm. "You've changed, Strong Knight. I perceive a joy has replaced your hatred."

He ran a finger down her cheek. "You perceive correctly, for when God's love filled me, I found no room for revenge."

She stared at him with such admiration, he nearly forgot they weren't alone and almost kissed her. Instead he glanced up to see his friends smiling in their direction.

Sir Tybalt winked at him. "It appears, Sir Damien, that as King's Guard you are already protecting your princess."

Damien looked down at her. "As I pledge to do always."

Pink blossomed on her cheeks, and she tore her gaze from his.

"Your orders?" Sir Tybalt asked her.

Seraphina stepped away from Damien. "Ensure Lord Haleford's wound is properly tended. Then…" She glanced around at the soldiers who were starting to disperse.

Ronar cleared his throat. "Seraphina…I mean, Your Royal Highness. If I may."

Seraphina huffed and slanted her lips, obviously exasperated at the title, which only endeared her more to Damien. "Of course, Ronar. What is it?"

"Since we are all pardoned and Lady Alexia's and Cristiana's positions restored at Luxley, mayhap we should make use of this…*your* army and evict the usurpers." He grinned.

"Excellent idea!" Seraphina agreed, then turning to Sir Tybalt and Commander Sadon, she said. "Make ready the troops. We march on Luxley Castle at once."

"Devil's blood! How did they escape?" Sir Walter cursed at the guard standing before him. "They were locked in the dungeon!"

The man shook his head. "Someone released them, my lord. The locks were not broken."

"Who!?" Sir Walter let out a wall-rattling growl, then pushed past the guard and stormed across the great hall of Luxley Castle. Servants going about their tasks for the noon meal stopped to stare and then shrank away from the wrath of their lord.

Halting, Sir Walter spun to face the guard. "Summon Sir DeGay at once!"

The man nodded and sped off.

"Those infernal Knights of the Eternal Realm!" Fisting his hands, he growled. They had an ally within the castle. A traitor! And he would find him. But first...He flattened his lips and gripped the ruby brooch at his throat. First, he would send every soldier and knight after them. They couldn't have gone far.

Feeling slightly better after he did just that—with orders that Sir DeGay was to kill the knights on sight—Sir Walter made his way down the winding stairs to Drago's lair.

"Who let my prisoners go?" he demanded as he charged into the dungeon chamber and searched the room for Drago. He grew weary of being frightened of the warlock, if the monster even *was* a warlock, for surely a man of his powers should have seen the traitor in their midst.

Oddly, Drago sat in one of the few wooden chairs in the room, large book opened before him. Sir Walter could not recall when he'd seen the warlock sit, nor when he'd seen him look so…*frail*? Nay, not frail. But somehow smaller than usual.

The warlock glanced up. "How should I know?"

Sir Walter huffed. "You see things. At least 'tis what you claim."

Drago sat back in his chair, staring at Sir Walter with that dark look that pierced Sir Walter's soul.

"Never mind." Sir Walter gave an indignant huff. "I have sent my soldiers after them. Can you not do something as well? Mayhap, tell me where they are?"

With an annoyed groan, Drago struggled to rise and then moved behind the long table housing his elixirs and trinkets, animal parts, and books. Gathering a handful of hot coals from a fire pit, he tossed them onto the iron slab and stared at it, a puzzled look on his face.

Unbearably long moments ensued, and Sir Walter finally said, "What do you see?"

"Nothing." The warlock shrugged. "'Tis been that way for a while." He ran black fingernails through his white beard. "My powers are weakening."

"Weakening?" Sir Walter rubbed his eyes. This couldn't be happening. "What are you saying?"

"I will send what wolves and demons I can to join your army. That's all I can do." Then opening a pouch, he flung black powder in the air and uttered a string of Latin Sir Walter could not make out. Bats that hung around the ceiling took off in a frenzy up the long narrow tower whilst Drago grabbed a bottle of something from the shelf behind him and poured it into a pot simmering over the fire pit. More Latin rang through the room, the words slicing an icy chill down Sir Walter.

"Good," he said when Drago appeared to be done. "Now, who betrayed me?"

"I did, Father."

Sir Walter spun to find Cedric standing at the open door, a confident and peaceful look on his face. "What?"

"I did." Cedric moved forward. "They had done no wrong."

Sir Walter could only stare at him. "They were witches and traitors! Where is your head, boy? I ordered you to continue your apprenticeship here with Drago."

Drago hissed and backed away from him. "He's been infected by our enemy. He's been deceived!"

"Tell me this isn't true." Sir Walter approached his son.

Drago began huffing uncontrollably. "He's the one who has caused my power to weaken! He's been fasting, praying to our enemy. Praising him in this very castle!"

Cedric smiled. "Aye, I have turned toward the Light. I have bowed my knee to the Son of God."

Lifting hands to his ears, Drago screeched so loudly, the remainder of the bats took flight.

If Sir Walter still had a heart, it now sank into his boots. His son. His poor boy. Following Christ would only bring him misery, poverty, and persecution. He would never rule, never have wealth, never become a man of great import. Even worse, Sir Walter's bargain with Drago was now undone.

He faced the warlock, wondering what he would do, what curse he would inflict on him, but he found the man had turned his back to them, searching for something on his desk.

"Quit your evil ways, Father." Cedric's tone bore no anger, no bitterness, only a desperate pleading. "You can be forgiven and start anew."

Naught but love filled his son's eyes, a love Sir Walter had ne'er seen there before, a love he suddenly longed to possess.

"To the devil with you!" Drago's scream brought Sir Walter around to see the warlock rushing toward Cedric, hefting a large knife above his head.

"Nay!" Without thinking, Sir Walter stepped in front of his son. The thrust of cold steel sliced through his chest.

Cedric's arms were around him, holding him as he fell to the cold stone floor.

Oddly, Sir Walter felt no pain, only his body tumbling helplessly down and the lifeblood draining from his body with each diminishing beat of his heart.

Something wet struck his forehead. He glanced up to see his son, tears sliding down his cheeks. Crying for him? After all the evil he'd done to him?

With the last breath he could gather, Sir Walter mumbled, "Oh, Lord. What have I done?"

"No, no!" Cedric held the lifeless body of his father. He had seen his spirit leave, watched it depart from his eyes, leaving them glassy and empty, leaving his body limp and cold. Gathering himself, he pressed fingers to his father's eyelids and closed them, then made the sign of the cross on his forehead.

The man's fate was sealed now. Cedric could only hope he would see his father again someday. Sounds reminded him he was not alone. Drago, bloody knife in hand, backed away from him, eyes full of hate and fear.

"You cannot touch me," Cedric said. "You have no power here."

Dropping the knife, Drago spun an arm around himself and disappeared in a column of black smoke.

CHAPTER THIRTY-THREE

Seraphina sat upon a white steed, the fur-lined royal mantle Lady Rochford had given her draped over her shoulders and spilled down the horse's side. Lady Cristiana and Sir Jarin rode on her left, whilst Lady Alexia and Sir Ronar rode on her right. Sir Damien, Sir Tybalt, and Commander Sadon rode before them. Behind them, a row of elite King's Guards preceded the three hundred soldiers Lord Haleford had sent to kill her.

The sun began its descent in the west, sending golden rays weaving through treetops and branches lining the road and sprinkling the ground with light as they traveled. She drew a deep breath of fresh crisp air, laden with the scents of pine, oak, and horseflesh, and tried to settle her nerves *and* her thoughts. The events of the past few hours seemed like a dream. She went from plebeian to princess, from condemned to free, from failure to victory. And all in a moment's blink. How wonderful was God! How awesome His power. His love! His plan! 'Twas why His Word said never to worry, never to doubt, for if a person followed Him with all their heart, all things worked out well in the end. Aye, she was a princess in this life, but more importantly, everyone who followed Jesus was royalty in the next—sons and daughters of God who would rule and reign with Him. She'd never truly understood that until this moment, until she realized the favor granted her had not come from the Spear, but from God.

"A princess, eh?" Cristiana winked at her with a smile. "All this time I should have been serving you instead of you serving me."

Seraphina sighed, then glanced down the row of her friends. "If you all would do me one favor. I beseech you, don't treat me any differently, and prithee don't call me Your Royal Highness."

Her friends laughed and even Damien glanced back at her with a smile.

The growl of wolves put a stop to their amusement.

They exchanged glances, knowing full well what attack was upon them. Alexia nodded to Ronar, who glanced at Jarin and Cristiana, and they all bowed their heads. Unsure what to even pray for, Seraphina did the same.

Commander Sadon raised a hand to halt their progress, instantly drawing his blade. Black snouts thrust through leaves on either side of the road, malevolent yellow eyes followed as the beasts, at least two dozen of them, formed a wall of snarling jowls and sharp fangs before them.

Their slit-like eyes were not locked on the commander, nor Sir Tybalt, nor even the army behind them. But on the Knights of the Eternal Realm.

Seraphina swallowed. Her friends had told her of these demonic wolves, but she'd never seen them before. In truth, she'd not pictured them quite so large, so ferocious, nor their fangs so long.

"I've ne'er seen anything like this." Commander Sadon shook his head. "A pack of wolves attacking an army."

Sir Tybalt plucked a knife from his belt. "There are a mere twenty of them. My knights and I will dispatch them quickly."

Commander Sadon huffed. "Not before some of you will die."

"Nay." Alexia broke rank and nudged her horse forward beside Sir Tybalt and the commander. "Allow me to handle this."

Sir Tybalt laughed. "What can you d—"

"In the name of Jesus, the Christ, I command you to leave!" Alexia shouted with all the authority of a general.

The growling ceased. Yet the wolves remained. Suddenly, bright flashes of a dozen golden swords cleaved down upon the beasts—glimmering swords that appeared and disappeared faster than the eye could see.

The wolves vanished in a swirl of black mist that dissipated in the sunlight.

Smiling, and seemingly ignoring the shocked gasps around her, Alexia moved her horse back to join them. "Do you see the warrior angels, Seraphina?" She leaned toward her to say.

Seraphina shook her head. "Only their blades, but I sense them." Indeed, she did sense their presence, their power and strength, surrounding them. A good thing, that, for she also sensed more evil up ahead.

Soon they entered another wide meadow, the last one before Emerald Forest led them straight to Luxley. Seraphina found herself oddly nervous, though she knew God and His angels were with them. Still, there was a growing darkness ahead that could only mean danger for her and her dear friends. Alexia and Ronar must have sensed it too, for they shifted uncomfortably in their saddles and glanced around. As did Jarin. She wished she could see what they saw, but mayhap 'twas for the best. She was already frightened enough.

They'd not gone more than ten yards across the meadow when Sir DeGay emerged from the greenery on the other side followed by several knights on horseback. Behind him, line by line of soldiers in full battle gear stepped from the forest like a stormy wave upon the shore.

Commander Sadon raised his hands to halt them. Horses nickered behind them, and the chime of weapons being drawn filled the air.

"Sir Walter's army," Damien said.

Tybalt reined in his anxious steed. "He knows not whom he fights—the princess herself!"

Seraphina nudged her horse forward, barely glancing at Damien, and halted beside Sir Tybalt. "He only follows orders."

"Then I will tell him who you are."

"He will not believe you." Alexia came alongside them. "'Tis not an army of mere men. There are dark beings among them. Many of them, deceiving them."

Seraphina exchanged a knowing glance with her.

Commander Sadon laughed. For the second time that day, Sir Tybalt glanced at Alexia as if she were mad, but quickly his expression changed to one of consternation and then respect, for he must have remembered the wolves.

"I would listen to them if I were you," Damien added with a snort.

"Then we fight them!" Commander Sadon said. "They are outnumbered."

Alexia shook her head. "They are more than us. We must fight them by the power of God, or we will lose."

Seraphina glanced once again at the mighty knights and soldiers of Luxley. Though she could not see what Alexia did, she felt the dark warriors alongside them. Sir DeGay, who had halted his horse at the head of his troops, suddenly bent over as though in pain.

"We fight them with God's greatest weapon," Cristiana shouted so all could hear.

All eyes shifted toward her.

"Love." She smiled. "Allow me to speak to him."

"Nay." Jarin glanced at her and reached for her reins.

"Have you all gone mad?" Sir Tybalt shook his head. "What strange manner of warfare is this?"

"He's right," Commander Sadon added. "'Tis not safe, my lady. Besides, why would he listen to you?"

Cristiana leaned to place her hand on Seraphina, her brows raised, her eyes pleading. And Seraphina knew God had spoken to her.

"Allow her to go," she commanded with the authority of her station.

"I'll go with her." Jarin urged his horse forward.

"Nay, I should go," Alexia said. "We are the ladies of Luxley. Prithee, the rest of you stay here."

"I don't like this," Ronar said, and Damien agreed. Even his destrier stomped the grass in protest.

Commander Sadon faced Seraphina. "Your Royal Highness, this is madness. Sending two women to fight an army. They will be killed."

Seraphina raised her chin in the air. "They are not alone."

Alexia wasn't entirely sure she knew what she was doing, but she had become accustomed to that still voice within her, the one that brought peace, though it oft made no sense whatsoever. Cristiana, no doubt, had heard the same voice, for as they both nudged their horses forward, she cast a knowing smile at Alexia.

Creatures dark and tall, part bird, part reptile, with pointed snouts, fangs as long as a man's arm, and sharp talons, stood amongst the soldiers, growling, drooling, and hissing at the sight of Alexia and Cristiana approaching. But she paid them no mind, for circling them stood warriors of light, larger, better armed, and intent on victory.

Cristiana halted before Sir DeGay. "Step aside, knight. Lady Alexia and I are the rightful owners of Luxley."

"Bah! You are both wanted for witchcraft." The poor knight held his stomach, his face grimacing, though clearly he tried to hide his pain. "I take my orders from Sir Walter."

"You have been deceived by an evil man and forces beyond your control." Alexia stared into the man's eyes and spotted demons slithering behind their glazed exterior. "In the name of the King of Kings and Lord of Lords, Jesus the Christ, I command the forces of darkness to leave at once!"

Sir DeGay laughed, as did a few of the knights behind him.

Yet at the command, the warriors of light charged toward the army, crashing blade-to-blade with the demon reptiles. Unable to see the battle, the human army remained standing, awaiting orders from Sir DeGay, though they fidgeted uncomfortably, as though they felt the rage around them.

Alexia nodded toward Cristiana to reassure her that their battle was being fought and would soon end in victory.

Cristiana faced Sir DeGay. "You are in pain, sir. Do you wish to be well?"

The strangest look came over him, as if he'd just woken from a long nightmare to find sunlight streaming into his chamber.

"Who wouldn't want to be well, but what are you—"

She eased her mount beside his and reached to touch his arm.

Several knights behind him drew their blades, but he lifted his other arm to stop them.

Cristiana smiled. "Be well, then, in the name of Christ."

The lines on his face disappeared, along with the crease in his forehead. He sat up straight, removed his hand from his stomach, and stared down at it, then back at Cristiana. "What? How?"

"'Tis God's doing, Sir DeGay. He is on our side. Which puts you on the wrong side."

"You…you made me well." He stared at her bewildered. "I was going to kill you."

"God loves you, Sir DeGay."

He shook his head and glanced up to see Seraphina galloping toward him, Sir Tybalt and Damien on either side.

Sir Tybalt handed him the king's missive. "I am Sir Tybalt, captain of the elite King's Guard. Bow before your princess."

Sir DeGay skimmed the note, then stared at Seraphina in shock. Handing the paper back to Sir Tybalt, he swung his leg over his horse and slid to the ground, his expression still one of shock but tinted with shame. He faced his troops and shouted. "The princess of Enclasen. Seraphina De Mowbray is the daughter of the king!"

Then turning, he bent his knee before her.

With Sir DeGay and the Luxley knights riding behind them, Seraphina and her friends, along with Sir Tybalt and the King's Guard entered Luxley village around midnight.

They had left the king's army camped on the edge of Emerald Forest at the ready, should they have need of them.

Seraphina doubted they would. Though it wasn't their combined forces she trusted, nor the battle expertise and myriad weapons of the soldiers and knights accompanying them. For she had finally learned that the battles they fought were not of this world but were against principalities and powers in the spirit realm and forces of spiritual darkness. Hence the only weapons that worked were weapons of the Spirit—faith, love, power, favor, truth, the name of Jesus, and the Word of God.

With one word from Sir DeGay, the guards at the gate allowed them entrance. Now, as they walked their horses through the village, Seraphina could not help but notice how quiet it was. Save for the low of a cow, cluck of a chicken, and a baby's cry, silence settled as deep as the night. How oft had she ventured here on some errand for Cristiana to purchase fresh flowers, herbs, or a trinket from the vendors. On those occasions she'd been naught but a maid.

Now she rode through as a princess.

A few curtains moved from windows where those still awake peered outside with candles in hand, but otherwise no one dared emerge from their thatched homes.

Up the hill they rode and around a bend heading to the bridge that led to Luxley Castle's gate. She felt the evil ere she saw it, before a cloud abandoned the moon, allowing silver light to drift down upon them.

She'd heard the warlock had become strong. Still it did not stop her breath from catching at the sight of the dark shroud that hung over the castle, so thick, naught of the pinnacles and turrets could even be seen.

Indeed, their battle was not against flesh and blood, for there was no army in the empire that could defeat such evil.

Only the King of Kings.

Dismounting, Alexia gestured for her fellow Knights of the Eternal Realm to follow her. Ronar leapt off his horse and was by her side within seconds, whilst Jarin helped Cristiana from hers. Sir Damien appeared by Seraphina's mount, hand extended, and though she was still angry with the strong knight, she took it and allowed him to assist her down. Together, the six of them pushed past Sir Tybalt, his knights, and the commander, who had all stopped to stare at the oddity.

"What? Where are you…what is this darkness?" Sir Tybalt muttered behind her, but they paid him no mind as they marched to stand at the bridge leading to the castle gate.

Alexia stood at the center of them and held her arms out to either side, and together they all gripped hands and faced the castle. "We have come a long way, knights," she said. "We have fought and won many battles by the power of God."

"And by the power of His love," Cristiana added.

Seraphina smiled. "And the majesty of Christ and those who belong to Him."

"We have also each learned many things," Ronar said. "Salvation is by grace alone."

Jarin nodded. "That there is an eternal world beyond this one that is beyond our imagination."

Damien grunted. "Forgiveness."

"And now, together." Alexia glanced down her row of friends. "Using the gifts our Father has granted us, we defeat the darkness that has taken over our home. For there is great power in the prayer and agreement of the saints."

They all faced forward once again, and Seraphina glanced up at the darkness, which now swirled and churned like a cauldron full of black ink.

"In the name of Jesus," Alexia began, but they all joined in as if they knew the words she would say. "We bind, rebuke, and command this evil to depart Luxley and not return."

Seraphina knew the moment the darkness left, for she had kept her gaze above. A flash of bright light, almost like lightning, cut through the black shroud, and within seconds, it vanished.

Moonlight showered upon them, dripping silver over the castle walls, gates, and turrets.

"Praise be to God!" Cristiana shouted, and they all joined her in shouting their thanks to the Almighty.

Sir DeGay, the commander, and Sir Tybalt remained upon their horses, their wide eyes fixated above.

A shout, followed by the crank and grind of the gate, brought their attention forward as the person Seraphina least expected to see slipped through the opening and stepped into the moonlight on the bridge.

Cedric LeGode.

CHAPTER THIRTY-FOUR

Damien, along with Jarin and Ronar, swords at the ready, descended down the circular stairs of the main tower dungeon. 'Twas where Cedric informed them Drago, his father's warlock, resided.

"He's not there," Cedric had insisted after they entered the main hall of Luxley and Ronar had inquired after the warlock's whereabouts. "I felt him leave just minutes ere I opened the gate for you."

Damien was not taking any chances. This was the devilish fiend that had created walls out of thin air, hordes of spiders and snakes, and nearly drowned them in a flood. Not to mention a host of other vile acts that had threatened his life and the lives of his friends. This beast was the source of evil that had taken over Sir Walter and caused him to commit all kinds of atrocities.

Sir Walter LeGode. Dead. His body reverently laid out on a table in the great hall. Damien should feel anger toward the man or at least some measure of relief, but all he felt was pity.

"Do you trust Cedric?" Damien asked Ronar, who descended the stairs ahead of him.

"Cristiana does," Jarin said from behind him. He chuckled. "When he captured her, she told him to turn toward the light. Apparently he did, for she says he's not the man who tried to kill her."

"In addition," Ronar added. "Alexia sees no evil circling him."

"Nor does Seraphina sense anything."

Halting, Ronar stared up at his friends from the tread below them. "Incredible women we have managed to attract."

"Indeed," Jarin said. "Who knew a pack of unworthy knights like us would find such treasure?"

Damien nodded, still unsure what Seraphina's feelings were toward him—still unsure whether the princess of Enclasen would wish to wed a lowly knight.

They continued downward, even as a stench akin to a thousand rotten eggs swept over them. Damien held a hand to his nose. No matter. They were victorious! They had defeated the evil plots against them. They had defeated both William and Sir Walter, and now hopefully they would find the warlock gone.

Cedric had said he'd been praying fervently against Drago for days, but it wasn't until Damien and his friends came and joined his prayers that the warlock finally left.

Truly God was all-powerful, all-knowing, and all-loving! And the prayers of the saints in the name of Christ were the most powerful weapons He gave them.

Regardless of whether Seraphina still loved him, Damien had made up his mind to serve this great God the rest of his days, for he could not deny the joy bubbling within him. He lifted up a prayer of thanks as they took the last step down and shoved aside the door.

A foul odor struck them. They shrank back, coughing. Yet as they entered the lair and raised their candles, all they found was an empty, dusty old room with an iron cauldron hanging over coals that simmered with their last sparks. Not a book, not a trinket, not a bottle remained on the shelves lining the walls.

The warlock was gone.

Seraphina had not slept so soundly in months, mayhap years! Not only was she back inside the only home she'd ever known, but Alexia and Cristiana insisted she sleep in their mother and father's solar, the chamber of the lord and lady of the castle. 'Twas fitting they said for a princess to have the best room and the softest bed, though in truth she didn't yet feel like royalty.

After bathing and donning fresh attire, she spent an hour in prayer and praise, for she had much to thank God for, ere she went in search of Alexia and Cristiana. She also had much to tell them of her time at Regalis, whilst they were excited to inform her of what had occurred at Luxley. Hence, they spent most of the day together in Cristiana's chambers, sharing, laughing, and enjoying being together again.

When the topic of Sir Jarin and Ronar came up, Seraphina could see that both ladies were quite smitten and anxious to wed. But when they asked about Sir Damien and she told them of his betrayal, they understood her pain.

She forgave him as was her Christian duty, but now what to do with the man?

"He stole the Spear for good reasons," Cristiana said. "To affect our release from the charges of witchcraft and the men from being hanged as traitors to the crown."

"Mayhap." Seraphina nodded, glancing out the window where sunlight streamed inside in dusty glittering trails. "But he also stole it so the bishop would tell him who murdered his parents."

Alexia grimaced. "The same man who murdered your mother and tried to kill you. Hard to believe he was the king's chief adviser."

"And half-brother. He will pay for all the lives he has ruined." Seraphina would see to that when she returned to Regalis—as a princess this time instead of a pauper. To a father she'd never known. How would he receive her? She was both excited and frightened at the prospect.

Alexia laid a hand on Seraphina's arm. "The Spear had no power anyway."

"I know. But he betrayed me nonetheless."

Cristiana shrugged. "He seems quite repentant and is now following the Lord."

Seraphina pondered her friends' words as she dressed for the evening meal. Cedric insisted on having a feast, complete with the finest fare and minstrels to entertain. 'Twas to be their final meal here for a while since they all agreed to return to Regalis in the morning with the kings' army. Cedric had promised to manage Luxley until the D'Clere sisters returned to take their rightful place. Oddly, Alexia and Cristiana seemed to trust the man. Hence, who was Seraphina to doubt their judgment?

Once at Regalis, her friends, along with Sir Tybalt and Commander Sadon, would relay the happenings at Luxley to the king. Then—although the missive from the king had already stated thus—he would grant them all a formal pardon and allow Alexia and Cristiana to return to Luxley and assume their proper stations.

Where did that leave Seraphina? Where did it leave Damien? She had not seen him all day. Yet now as she descended the grand stairway to the great hall, she searched the crowd for the strong knight. She spotted him at the raised table sitting beside her friends. His eyes met hers as she crossed the room, and something unrecognizable flitted across them. He rose, along with everyone else as silence descended.

She would have to grow accustomed to this. Waving a hand to bid them continue in their revelry, she ascended the dais and lowered to sit beside Damien.

The feast consisted of chickens covered with egg yolks and sprinkled with spice, wild boar, sliced cheese, and strawberries and plums stewed in rose water. Truly 'twas one of the finest she'd had at Luxley. But the noisy chatter in the room, accompanied by the minstrels, forbade conversation. Instead, she enjoyed watching her friends happy and at peace, for they had suffered much these past years. Ronar and Alexia could barely keep their eyes—as well as their hands—off one another. Surely they needed to be wed soon! Cristiana and Jarin took turns holding little Thebe, who giggled profusely at all the festivities and who consumed more of her meal than anyone. Staring at them, at the looks of love they shared, Seraphina suddenly longed for a family of her own.

Even the friar joined them, sitting at a table below the dais in deep conversation with a group of townspeople who had also been invited. Seraphina smiled. No doubt he was telling them of the love of Jesus and convincing them to follow the Savior. Lady Rochford sat beside him, enjoying the conversation.

What a humble lady. She should be positioned with them at the main table, yet she preferred to sit among peasants.

Anabelle approached with flagon in hand and offered to pour more wine into Damien's cup, but the knight covered it with his hand and shook his head. Seraphina took the opportunity to thank the maid for all she'd done to help them and all the danger she had put herself into on their behalf.

She curtsied and seemed suddenly shy in Seraphina's presence. "'Twas my pleasure. To think you are a princess." Her beautiful eyes sparkled ere she moved to offer wine to others at the table.

When the meal was completed and the minstrels began packing up their instruments, Damien rose, took her hand, and lifted her from her seat. "I can stand it no longer, Seraphina. I mean, Your Highn—I mean…" He growled. "Prithee, I must speak to you."

Ignoring the jolt of her heart and excitement soaring through her, Seraphina gladly followed him through the staring crowd, out the door, and into the garden, still fragrant with the scent of fall herbs. She should be indignant at how he was ordering her around, but she found she much preferred it to everyone fawning over her.

He led her to a bench beneath a flaming torch and bade her sit. Clearing his throat, he began, though she heard pain in his voice. "I am a cad, a scoundrel of the worst kind. I betrayed you. I lied to you. I stole the Spear from you for reasons both selfish and unselfish. I have asked your forgiveness, and you have granted it to me. But now I must ask something else, though I have no right."

Seraphina stared at him, enjoying the way the torch light brought out the gold flecks in his eyes, his dark hair blowing in the breeze, the look on his face of…fear and…uncertainty? A rare emotion for this strong knight.

He raked back his hair and huffed. "I have made a commitment to God, one I did not have before. One that would have kept me from such betrayal." He grabbed her hands in his. "You have my troth I will never lie to you again."

At his touch and his words, warmth shot up her arms and across her shoulders, and she lowered her gaze to her lap. His fingers, so rough and calloused, were twice the size of hers, which for some odd reason, only warmed her further.

"You have told me this, Damien. It is enough. I forgive you."

"But it isn't enough. You see, I love you, Seraphina. I've loved you for a long time, and I care not whether you are a milkmaid or a princess. I cannot imagine my life without you."

A tremor ran through her at his words, and she raised her gaze to his to find moisture had covered his eyes, eyes full of love and desperation. And suddenly beneath that love, all her hesitancy, all her pain, dissipated as quickly as the black cloud had over Luxley.

She smiled. "What exactly are you saying, strong knight?"

Excitement lit his expression, and he brought her hands up for a kiss. Then rising from the bench, he knelt before her. "I'm asking you to be my wife. I care not that you're a princess. I want no position at court. I simply wish to protect you all your days and never leave your side."

For a moment, Seraphina could only sit there, stunned by such a proposal, a declaration of love that would warm the heart of any woman. And the words she had longed to hear from this man.

For so long she'd felt unworthy of the love of any man. But then God had shown her real love. Not only that, He'd shown her that she was valuable beyond measure. She was royalty in His kingdom.

"Rise, strong knight," she said as she stood as well.

He did. Yet after a few moments of silence, he dropped his hands by his side and frowned. "Forgive me. I have overstepped. No doubt 'tis the king's task to find you a worthy husband, and that man will not be a lowly knight such as I."

Seraphina reached up and adjusted the ties of his shirt, then unbuckled and rebuckled his baldric in the right holes. "Alack, then who is going to ensure you are dressed properly, if not I?" She smiled up at him.

His brows met in confusion as he searched her eyes. "Are you saying—"

She sighed. "I'm saying I suppose 'tis me to whom this duty falls. Though I must admit to loving you more than my heart can contain." She gave him a coy smile. "Hence, I say yes to your proposal, and—"

But his lips were on hers before she could finish. And ah, what a kiss! The depth of love within it made her nearly swoon. 'Twas as if he could not get enough of her, couldn't get close enough to her. And she, him. In minutes, he withdrew, leaving them both breathless and staring into each other's eyes. A world of hope and promise shone within his as he picked her up and spun her around, both of them laughing with more joy than she thought possible in this world.

CHAPTER THIRTY-FIVE

The last time Seraphina approached the king in his palace at Regalis, she was beyond terrified. She had felt so out of place, fearful for her life, unsure of what to say to the king of Enclasen.

This time was no different.

Regardless of her position as his daughter, she still felt as though she was meeting a stranger, a king who had the power of life and death in his hands. Was he pleased to discover she was alive? Would he welcome her with love or bring her into his family out of obligation? She had never had a family before, a father and mother, and certainly these circumstances were most extraordinary.

She and the Knights of the Eternal Realm, along with the Sir Tybalt, Commander Sadon, and the king's army, had returned in the wee hours of the morning. Seraphina had been escorted to a lavish chamber and told the king and queen were asleep and would see her on the morrow. Sleep, however did not come to her, nor to Lady Rochford, who remained in the chamber through the long hours of darkness, and who now helped her don a fine tunic and braid her hair in preparation for meeting her father.

He was not in his chamber, nor the throne room.

"He and the queen are walking by the lake," one of the guards told her as he escorted her and Lady Rochford down the stairs onto the sand.

Morning sun sent shimmering waves of gold over the water and lit the sand as if it were made of pearls. Biting her lip, Seraphina spotted the king and queen strolling along the shore about twenty yards from where she stood.

"Would you like me to accompany you?" Lady Rochford said.

"Nay, thank you." Seraphina touched her arm. "I must do this myself."

Raising her chin and saying a prayer for courage, come what may, she clutched her skirts and walked toward them.

The queen noticed her first, tapped her husband on his arm and nodded in Seraphina's direction. He turned and watched her approach, an unreadable expression on his face. When she was but a few yards from him, Seraphina considered bolting in the opposite direction, for His Majesty's face bore no love, no affection, only shock, and a bit of dismay.

"Courage, Lord, grant me thy courage," Seraphina whispered as she fell on her knees before him. "Your Majesty."

"What is this, child?" His voice was indignant, his tone jovial as he gently hoisted her up by her arm. "I'll not hear of this, *daughter*." His eyes met hers, and tears filled them as he ran a finger over her cheek and down her jaw. "My precious daughter!" He drew her close and folded his arms around her, laughing and crying at the same time.

Seraphina's heart nearly burst from the joy, the relief, the thrill at being in her father's arms after all these years. Tears slipped down her cheeks and onto the king's tunic as she, too, began to sob. The queen stood nearby, watching them with a smile on her face.

"All these years I thought you were dead. All these years…my beloved daughter." He hugged her all the tighter.

'Twas several minutes before the king released her. Much too soon for Seraphina, for she could stay in his arms forever. Gripping her shoulders, he held her back to study her once again. "You look just like your mother. Your hair, eyes, the way your nose upturns slightly." He shook his head. "I should have seen it the moment you walked into my throne room."

Seraphina found herself unable to utter a word. She could only stare at her father, tears streaming down her cheeks.

"Come, walk with us, my dear." He swung an arm around her and started forward, whilst the queen looped her arm through Seraphina's. "What you must have been through all these years. We have much to catch up on." He winked at her.

"Including this young fellow of yours, Sir Damien? I understand you are betrothed *without the king's permission*."

That last statement bore a hint of reprimand, tightening Seraphina's nerves once again. "I…yes…I mean…."

The king laughed, and the queen joined him. "He's a fine man and will make you a good husband, though I shall have to make him an earl or something."

Relief spread over Seraphina, and as they walked and talked, she couldn't recall a moment in which she'd been happier. They talked of Luxley and the happenings there, of Lord Haleford awaiting trial in the dungeon, of Lady Haleford being banished, and of poor Panora hanged for witchcraft. Exactly like Seraphina's vision.

"But you are well, Your Majesty?" Seraphina had noticed the color in his skin and the sparkle in his eyes the minute she saw him.

"If you don't call me Father, I shall be very hurt," he replied. "But aye, Lady Cristiana D'Clere found me at dawn ere I'd barely left my quarters and offered to pray for me. Turns out 'twas a curse put on me by Panora."

Of course. Seraphina smiled. "I am so pleased, Your…I mean, Father. But how did you discover Panora's treachery?"

"'Twas easy to figure out after I discovered who you were and Lord Haleford's deception. He had always encouraged me to listen to Panora, swearing she heard from God." He frowned and glanced over the lake, the pain of his brother's betrayal evident in his expression.

Seraphina longed to comfort him, but he shook off the dour mood as quickly as it had come. Then, drawing her close, he kissed her cheek. "Today is not the day for such morbid discussions." He winked at Queen Eleanor. "I have not only promised God to become a great father but also a better husband."

A blush blossomed on the queen's cheeks as she returned his smile, then wrapped her arm around Seraphina's waist. "And, though I could never replace your own, I shall strive to be a mother to you."

Seraphina leaned her head toward her, unable to speak for the happiness flooding her. In truth, wasn't this moment exactly like the glorious vision God had granted her? Of the king and his wife walking with their grown daughter? She couldn't help the giggle that rose in her throat. God truly was an amazing God.

The king suddenly halted, spun around, bringing her with him, and started back toward the castle. "Enough of this. We have years to learn about each other, but for now, we have a wedding to plan."

Queen Eleanor nodded. "Indeed, my husband, but I believe we have *three* weddings to plan!"

Damien had fought in many battles, had been outnumbered in most of them, been severely wounded twice, near death once, faced ten fierce warriors on his own, defeated three well-armed knights with a single blow, but here, standing outside on the front steps of the cathedral of Regalis, he was more nervous than he'd ever been.

On the tread below him stood Ronar and Jarin, who, from their expressions and fidgeting, seemed as nervous as he. Beyond them, filling up the main street from right to left, a crowd of Regalis citizens assembled, eager to see their princess wed. Laughter, song, and well-wishes bubbled in the crisp autumn air. The scent of a multitude of bodies filled Damien's nose, mixed with the sweet smell emanating from the myriad flowers that lined the stairs and spread across the front of the church.

A drop of sweat slid down Damien's back beneath the satin shirt he wore, molding the garment to his skin. Ridiculous attire! He shifted his shoulders, feeling more like a prancing princock in the silk hose and breeches and gold-embroidered doublet he wore. Yet he was to marry the princess of Enclasen, and he must dress to honor her.

Marry the princess? What was he thinking? He was a man devoid of both title and land, a mere warrior unworthy of such an honor. A touch on his arm turned him to see King Peter, who, along with the queen, stood to his left in their own dazzling attire.

Where once the king's cheeks had been pale and sunken, they now bloomed full and ruddy. Where once his shoulders had slumped, they now stretched tall and wide as befitting a king. His clear eyes, so full of wisdom and kindness, found Damien's. "'Tis normal to be nervous on your wedding day." He smiled. "Never fear, she will be here anon."

"Unless she has changed her mind about marrying a mere knight."

"Aha!" The king laughed. "You forget I have made you a duke and named you my personal adviser."

"How could I ever forget, Your Majesty? And I vow to spend my life honoring that privilege and serving you all my days."

"I have no doubt, my boy. No doubt, at all."

Damien forced back moisture from his eyes, still finding it hard to believe that the king had been so generous, had not only given him his daughter in marriage, but a title and William's position at court. He was also charged with being personal guard and protector of the king, the queen, and Seraphina. How wonderfully surprising was the work of God. Truly He did give His children the desires of their hearts!

Trumpets sounded, immediately silencing the crowd, and shifting all gazes to the right where a white carriage with golden trim, pulled by two white horses, parted the mob and halted before the church. A liveried footman leapt from the seat, opened the door, and let down the stairs.

Damien's heart pounded so hard, his head grew light.

The most beautiful angel this side of heaven, emerged from within. Seraphina, in a white silk gown, embroidered on the sleeves and hem with gold flowers, stepped down from the carriage. The crowd gasped in awe and bowed before her. Smiling at them, she waved her hands, gesturing for them to rise, as she started toward the cathedral. White fur trimmed her neckline and down the sides of her gown as wind tossed waves of sunlit alabaster hair down her back. But 'twas the look in her eyes as she ascended the stairs that nearly sent him to his knees—a look of such love, admiration, and joy. At marrying him?

Behind her, Cristiana and Alexia, both in luxurious satin gowns, one of blue and one of red, emerged from the carriage and mounted the stairs to stand beside their intendeds. Lastly, the friar stepped down, Thebe in his arms. The little girl wiggled to be free and dashed to Cristiana who hoisted her in her arms as she took her place beside Jarin. Ronar took Alexia's hand and whispered something in her ear that caused the brazen warrior to blush, something Damien had never seen before.

Shifting his gaze back to Seraphina, he extended his hand, and together they turned to face Father John, who offered them a smile. The king had preferred the cathedral's bishop to perform the ceremony, but Seraphina had requested the humble priest she'd met one night at the palace chapel.

'Twas just like her, this glorious meek lady with the heart of a servant and the majesty of a queen.

And he intended to spend the rest of his life loving her as she deserved.

Seraphina had never been so happy, so excited, and aye, so nervous! Alack, she barely heard herself repeat the wedding vows Father John pronounced so eloquently, the vows he also pronounced over her friends behind her. How fitting, and yet, how miraculous, that each lady should be married on the same day to the knights they loved, the knights who so long ago wandered into Luxley forest in search of the Spear.

She rubbed her wrist absently, wondering where the relic was, but suddenly not caring. The power and love of God resided within her and would only grow as she learned more of Him, as both she and Damien learned more of Him. She cast the strong knight a quick glance as Father John pronounced them man and wife. He looked so handsome in his regal attire, though she could tell he was uncomfortable.

Turning, he took her hands and bent to give her a kiss. A spark of fiery warmth shot through her at his touch and, along with the sensuous look in his eyes, made her long for the night to come when they could seal their loving union.

Father John pronounced her friends wed and the crowd cheered. Minstrels began playing a lively tune as flowers were tossed in the air and people began to dance. Truly she would never forget this day. Nor the many blessings God had bestowed on her.

Five hours later, after they had all enjoyed a lavish meal and celebration in the great hall of the palace, came the only sad moment of the day. Seraphina must bid her friends adieu. They were to leave for Luxley before dawn.

Unable to stop tears from slipping down her cheeks, she embraced first Alexia and then Cristiana. "I shall miss you terribly."

Cristiana withdrew, wiping the tears from her own face. Behind her, Jarin placed a hand on her shoulder, whilst Ronar wrapped arms around Alexia from behind.

Damien took Seraphina's hand and gave it a squeeze. "They are a mere three days' journey away, my love. I can imagine"—he winked at her—"that the king will oft require news from Luxley, now that he has deemed it to be one of his strategic military outposts. Hence, I have no doubt, he will need to send his daughter to assess the situation."

"And his new adviser." Jarin gripped Damien's arm. "Who would have guessed?" He laughed.

Ronar joined him. "Indeed. God is full of surprises."

Alexia nodded. "And we have much to do at Luxley to make it ready for the king's first visit."

"Finally, we shall be able to feed the villagers." Cristiana smiled and gazed up at Jarin with love.

"God speed to you on your journey, my dear friends," Seraphina said, wiping one last tear from her cheek.

Cristiana leaned forward to kiss her. "We shall see you again. Very soon."

Damien once again gripped his fellow knights' arms and nodded.

"I do wonder what happened to the Spear." Alexia rubbed her wrist where the mark had once been.

Seraphina did the same. "Only God knows."

"It may not have had any power in itself," Alexia said. "But in a way, it helped all of us to realize that God lives within those who put their trust in Jesus."

"And He will never leave us or forsake us," Ronar added.

"Amen," they all said in unison.

"Now off with you." Damien waved them away in jest. "My bride and I must away to our wedding chamber." His sultry glance flooded her with warmth as their friends laughed and soon headed for their own chambers for the night.

"Shall we?" Damien extended his arm.

Slipping her arm through his, she smiled. "We shall, Strong Knight. Now and forever."

Bishop Montruse tapped the side of the carriage and shouted out the window. "Halt there, you imbecile!"

The driver reined in the horses, and the conveyance slowed, wheels squealing, and finally stopping on the road that traveled through a wooded glen.

The guard sent to accompany him leapt off the back and opened the door. Huffing his displeasure, the bishop emerged from the vehicle and glanced around. No other carriages or horses were in sight. To be expected on this part of the highway. Thus far, he'd made it out of Enclasen undetected and was well on his way to the city of the Holy Prime.

"I told you I wished to stop and rest nigh an hour ago, you fluffheads!" he shouted to both the driver and the guard.

"I was waitin' to find a safe spot, Your Eminence," the driver shouted from his perch, though he dared not step down and face the bishop. "Highway robbers travel this road."

"Robbers. God's bones!" The bishop waved away the man's stupidity as he made his way down a small slope to a bubbling creek that ran beside the highway. "We are safe enough."

Safe enough, indeed. For he had the Spear of Destiny! Nothing could harm him now. Alack, 'twas truly unfortunate that wench Seraphina turned out being the king's daughter! Who would have considered such a thing? And that buffoon Haleford. If he'd only killed her while he had a chance, he'd still be in line for the throne! *If* Sir Damien didn't kill him first. But Montruse had no choice but to reveal who had murdered the knight's parents. The truth had granted him the Spear. A far better prize than merely having the ear of the king.

Flipping back his long black cassock, he knelt before the stream, glanced behind him to make sure the driver and guard weren't watching, and then withdrew the holy relic from a deep pocket in his robe.

Carefully holding it between two fingers, he lifted it up to a stream of sunlight drifting through the trees and nearly salivated at the sight. This spearhead was the key to his power and success. Giving it to the Holy Prime would put him next in line for his position—head of all Christendom!

He smiled. Or mayhap he'd just use it against His Holiness and take the power he so deserved.

Rising, he glanced around for a private spot to relieve himself, and upon finding one, headed in that direction. His foot hit a rock. Pain shot up his ankle as a curse fired from his lips. Arms flailing, he lost his balance. His legs gave way, and he toppled downward. The forest spun around him. His head struck something hard. The last two things he saw ere his spirit left this world for eternity were the Spear dropping into the creek with an ominous splash and a red-eyed, grimacing demon come to escort him home.

About the Author

AWARD WINNING AND BEST-SELLING AUTHOR, MARYLU TYNDALL dreamt of pirates and sea-faring adventures during her childhood days on Florida's Coast. With more than twenty-nine books published, she makes no excuses for the deep spiritual themes embedded within her romantic adventures. Her hope is that readers will not only be entertained but will be brought closer to the Creator who loves them beyond measure. In a culture that accepts the occult, wizards, zombies, and vampires without batting an eye, MaryLu hopes to show the awesome present and powerful acts of God in a dying world. A Christy award nominee, MaryLu makes her home with her husband, six children, four grandchildren, and several stray cats on the California coast.

If you enjoyed this book, you might enjoy the other books in the series, ***She Walks in Power,*** and ***She Walks in Love***.

One of the nicest ways to say "thank you" to an author and help them be able to continue writing is to leave a favorable review on Amazon! Goodreads, Barnes and Noble, Kobo, Itunes (And elsewhere, too!) I would appreciate it if you would take a moment to do so. Thanks so much!
Comments? Questions? I love hearing from my readers, so feel free to contact me via my website:

http://www.marylutyndall.com

Or email me at: marylu_tyndall@yahoo.com

Follow me on:

FACEBOOK: https://www.facebook.com/marylu.tyndall.author
TWITTER: https://twitter.com/MaryLuTyndall

BLOG: http://crossandcutlass.blogspot.com/
PINTEREST: http://www.pinterest.com/mltyndall/
BookBub: https://www.bookbub.com/authors/marylu-tyndall

To hear news about special prices and new releases sign up for my newsletter on my website Or follow me on Bookbub or Amazon!

https:///www.marylutyndall.com
https://www.bookbub.com/authors/marylu-tyndall
Amazon

Other Books by MaryLu Tyndall

THE REDEMPTION
THE RELIANCE
THE RESTITUTION
THE RANSOM
THE RECKONING
THE RECKLESS
THE FALCON AND THE SPARROW
THE RED SIREN
THE BLUE ENCHANTRESS
THE RAVEN SAINT
SURRENDER THE SEA
SURRENDER THE NIGHT
SURRENDER THE DAWN
FORSAKEN DREAMS
ELUSIVE HOPE
ABANDONED MEMORIES
VEIL OF PEARLS
PEARLS FROM THE SEA DEVOTIONAL
TEARS OF THE SEA
WESTWARD CHRISTMAS BRIDES
WHEN ANGELS CRY
LIBERTY BRIDE
WRITING FROM THE TRENCHES
SHE WALKS IN POWER
SHE WALKS IN LOVE

Made in the USA
Columbia, SC
04 February 2020

87501422R00166